F FRANKLIN LgPrt
Franklin, Ariana.
Grave goods

GRAVE GOODS

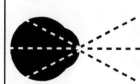

This Large Print Book carries the
Seal of Approval of N.A.V.H.

GRAVE GOODS

ARIANA FRANKLIN

THORNDIKE PRESS
A part of Gale, Cengage Learning

GALE
CENGAGE Learning·

Detroit • New York • San Francisco • New Haven, Conn • Waterville, Maine • London

GALE
CENGAGE Learning

Thorndike Press ® Large Print Historical Fiction.
The text of this Large Print edition is unabridged.
Other aspects of the book may vary from the original edition.
Set in 16 pt. Plantin.
Printed on permanent paper.

LIBRARY OF CONGRESS CATALOGING-IN-PUBLICATION DATA

Franklin, Ariana.
    Grave goods / by Ariana Franklin.
        p. cm. — (Thorndike Press large print historical fiction)
    ISBN-13: 978-1-4104-1501-1 (alk. paper)
    ISBN-10: 1-4104-1501-5 (alk. paper)
    1. Women forensic pathologists—Fiction. 2. Henry II, King of England, 1133-1189—Fiction. 3. Glastonbury Abbey—Fiction. 4. Large type books. I. Title.
PR6064.O73G73 2009b
823'.914—dc22   2008055780

Published in 2009 in arrangement with G. P. Putnam's Sons, a member of Penguin Group (USA) Inc.

Printed in the United States of America
1 2 3 4 5 6 7 13 12 11 10 09

To Datchworth

ONE

"And God was angry with His people of Somerset so that, in the year of Our Lord 1154, on the day after the feast of Saint Stephen, He caused an earthquake that it might punish them for their sins. . . ."

Thus wrote Brother Caradoc in Saint Michael's chapel on top of Glastonbury Tor, to which he'd scrambled, gasping and sobbing, so as to escape the devastation that God with His earthquake had wrought on everything below it. For two days he and his fellow monks had been up there, not daring to descend because they could still hear aftershocks making their abbey tremble and look down, appalled, at more giant waves submerging the little island villages in the Avalon marshes beyond it.

Two days, and Caradoc was still wet and had a pain in his poor old chest. When the earthquake struck and his fellow monks had scampered from the shivering abbey, making for the Tor that was always their refuge in times of danger, he'd run with them, hearing Saint Dunstan, strictest of saints though dead these one hundred sixty-six years, telling him to rescue the Book of Glastonbury first. "Caradoc, Caradoc, do your duty though the sky falls."

But it was bits of masonry that had been falling, and Caradoc had not dared to run into the abbey library and fetch the great jewel-studded book — it would have been too heavy for him to carry up the hill anyway.

The slate book that was always attached to the rope girdle round his waist had been weighty enough, almost too much for an old man laboring up a five-hundred-foot steeply conical hill. His nephew Rhys had helped him, pushing, dragging, shouting at him to go faster, but it had been a terrible climb, terrible.

And now, in the cold, dry but unshaken shelter of the chapel that Joseph of Arimathea had built when he'd brought the cruets containing Christ's sacred blood and sweat from the Holy Land, Brother Caradoc did his duty as the abbey's annalist. In feeble taper light and apologetically using Saint Michael's altar as a table, he chalked

8

this latest event in Glastonbury's history onto slate pages so that, later, he could transcribe them onto the vellum of the Great Book.

"And the Lord's voice was heard in the screams of people and the squealing of animals as the ground undulated and opened beneath them, in the fall of great trees, in the toppling of candles and the roar of resultant flames as houses burned."

The pain in his chest increased, and the shade of Saint Dunstan went on nagging him. "The Book must be saved, Caradoc. The history of all our saints cannot be lost."

"I haven't got to the wave yet, my lord. At least let there be some record of it." He went on writing.

"Loudest of all, our Lord spoke in the noise of an approaching wave that raised itself higher than a cathedral in the bay and ran up the tidal rivers of the Somerset Levels, sweeping away bridges as it came and drowning all in its path. Through His mercy, it only reached the lower reaches of our Abbey so that it still stands, but . . ."

"The Book, Caradoc. Tell that idle nephew of yours to fetch it."

Brother Caradoc looked to his fellow monks, immobile and huddled for warmth on the choir floor, some of them snoring. "He sleeps, lord."

"When doesn't he?" Saint Dunstan asked with some justice. "Either sleeping or singing unsuitable songs, that boy. He'll never make a monk. Kick him awake."

Gently, Brother Caradoc prodded a pair of skinny young ankles with his foot. "Rhys, Rhys. Wake up, bach."

He was a good boy in his way, Rhys the novitiate, a lovely tenor, but Saint Dunstan was right, the lad cared more for singing profane songs than psalms, and the other monks constantly berated him for it, keeping him busy to cure his idleness. Tired out now, he merely grunted and slept on.

Well, well, let him rest. Caradoc began writing again. He hadn't yet recorded the fissure in the graveyard. Yes, he must put that in. For as he'd run from the quaking buildings, he had seen a deep hole opening up in the abbey's burial ground between the two pyramids that had stood in it as long as time had gone. *As if,* he wrote, *the end of the world had come and the Almighty had sounded the Last Trump so that the dead might rise from their graves.*

"The Book," Saint Dunstan shouted.

10

"Caradoc, would you leave the record of our days to looters?"

No, he couldn't do that. So Brother Caradoc put down his chalk and, though his shivers were becoming uncontrollable and the pain across his chest an iron bar, he made for the door of the chapel and began stumbling down the winding terrace of the Tor. He knew now that the last trump had sounded for him and that even if he couldn't save the Book, he must die trying, or at least take his last breath in the beloved abbey that had been his home.

A lot of precious breath it cost him as he wavered downward, falling over hummocks, his gasps sending sheep galloping, but gravity was on his side, and it propelled him down to the gate, which swung open at his touch under the chevroned Norman arch and into the grounds. He staggered onward as far as the vegetable garden, where he collapsed among Brother Peter's lettuces, unable to go farther.

Now he could peer down the incline toward the towering church. There had been damage; the old bell tower had collapsed, and gapes showed where some corners were sheared away. The waters that circled the grounds had not reached so far; therefore, the Great Book and all the relics of the saints would still be untouched. Beyond them, though, the village outside the walls was still and smokeless, its pasture littered with dirty white lumps that were the corpses of sheep.

Caradoc experienced anguish for the drowned people and animals, for the ruined hayricks, cornfields — it would be a hard summer for the survivors, and an even harder winter.

Yet holy Glastonbury still stood. Beautiful, beautiful it was, crystalline under the bright new moon reflected in its skirt of floodwater, an island of glass. *The* Island of Glass.

Sucking in breath that couldn't fill his lungs, he turned his eyes to the graveyard awaiting him.

A flicker of movement caught his eye. Three cowled figures were pulling on ropes that dragged something up the slope from the abbey's great gate. Too far away for him to hear any sound they made, they seemed like ghosts. *And perhaps,* Caradoc thought, *that is what they are* — for what human could be abroad and busy in this devastation when even the owls and nightingales were silent?

He couldn't make out what it was they were hauling — it had the shape of a great log, or a canoe. Then, as the figures came to the fissure in the ground that the earthquake had opened, he saw what it was. A coffin.

They were lowering it into the fissure. Now they were kneeling, and from the throat of one of them came a great shriek. "Arthur, Arthur. May God have mercy on your soul and mine."

There was a moan from the dying monk. "Is King Arthur dead, then?"

For Caradoc, though a Glastonbury monk these thirty years, had believed that King Arthur was merely resting, waiting, until he was called to rise and fight the devil's hordes once more. And he rested here.

Avalon was Glastonbury, Glastonbury was Avalon, the Isle of Glass indeed, and Arthur slept somewhere among these hills, with their hidden caves and crystal springs. Arthur the brave, Arthur of the Welsh, who'd resisted the seaborne invaders and kept the flame of Christianity flickering in Britain during its Dark Ages.

It had been Caradoc's joy that he could serve God in the place where Arthur had been brought to be mended from his wounds after the last great battle.

Was he dead, then? Was great Arthur dead?

The earth trembled again, lightly, like a dog settling itself to sleep. Caradoc heard other voices, this time calling his name. An arm went under his head, and he looked up into the frightened eyes of his nephew.

"Look, bach," Caradoc said, trying to point. "They are burying King Arthur. Three of his lords in hooded cloaks, see."

"Lie still now, Uncle," Rhys said, and shouted up the hill to the other searching monks, "I've found him. Here, he's by here."

"There, boy," Caradoc said. "Between the pyramids, in the fissure. I saw them lower his coffin; I heard them mourning him."

"A vision, was it?" Rhys asked, peering toward the graveyard and seeing nothing.

"A vision, clear as clear," Caradoc said. "There's sad it is that Arthur is dead."

"Whisht now, Uncle," Rhys said. "There's help on the way." To calm and comfort the old man, he began singing, not a hymn but a song that Welsh mothers sang to their children — a song of Arthur Pendragon.

". . . when the land rang with minstrels'
    song
the sharpening of weapons,
the splash of oars coming into harbor,
a ripple of water in the sea-cave . . ."

Caradoc's eyes closed, and he smiled. "Good, good," he whispered. "At least I shall lie where King Arthur lies. There's company."

When the other monks came upon him, they found Rhys still singing as he cradled a dead man.

They buried Brother Caradoc the next morning. If there had ever been a fissure in the graveyard, the earthquake's last tremor had filled it in, for there was no sign of it.

Nor did Rhys ap Griffudd tell anybody of what his uncle had seen. Rhys, who was not suited to be a monk and knew now that he never would be, was a Welshman through and through, and it would not do for these English to know that Arthur was dead.

So for twenty-four years the two pyramids guarded the place where an old monk had seen Arthur buried, and nobody knew the importance of what lay between them.

Until . . .

March, A.D. 1176, and a wind hurtling down a ravine in Wales, blowing the haulms of reeds and the flare of torches in the same streaming angle as the hair on the severed heads that topped the line of poles leading up to the Plantagenet tents. It sent grass, leaves, and branches nodding in vehement agreement.

With a spike through their Welsh brains,

15

the heads couldn't nod, though they revolved slightly so that their blank eyes shifted, as if dividing their attention between the bottom of the ravine, where English soldiers were digging burial pits, and a limping mailed figure who was dragging a woman up the steep slope toward the tents.

As she was pulled level with the poles, the woman broke into a wail of Welsh lamentation, peering at each head and calling out what, presumably, were their names.

The mailed man paused, puffing — she was a big lady to haul. "Look," he said, "they were killed in battle. *Battle.* Understand? My lads got a bit carried away with their bodies, that's all. The king doesn't behead prisoners, at least not often — he's a good king. *Good.*"

But the woman was ignorant of English, no matter how loudly it was emphasized. *"Duw, Duw,"* she cried, lifting her arms to the sky. The man had to get behind her and push before she'd go farther.

The opening of the bigger tent was lit from inside, outlining the figure of Henry II, who stood at its entrance, also mailed, also shouting — this time at a line of bound men being made to kneel in front of him — while a man-at-arms undid the king's hauberk at the back and carefully peeled it off.

"There was no *point* to this, you stupid bastards. No *point*." To the interpreter at his side, the king said, "Tell 'em that. Tell them I've made peace with their lord Deheubarth, or however the bugger pronounces it. They won't have to pay any more taxes with me as their king than they pay him already." He paused. "Well, not much more." He pressed a cloth against his left arm to stop the bleeding. "Now look what they've done. Tell them I've had to mount an expensive campaign to put down their bloody rebellion, I've lost good men, *they've* lost good men, I won't be able to use my shield arm for bloody days, and they'll be taxed for it until their brains squeak — that's if they've got any and if I don't gouge them out. Tell 'em that. Tell them Arthur is *dead.*"

At the sound of the name, the kneeling prisoners raised their heads as one man and a shout of "Bywyd hir Arthur" rippled along the line.

"Arthur live forever," translated the interpreter, helpfully.

Henry Plantagenet exhaled with violence. "I know what it means." He extended his wounded arm. "The bastard who did this was shouting it. They all shout it. Tell them Arthur is dead. I'm as proud of him as the next man, but he lived about seven hundred years ago and . . . There you are, Bishop, and who in hell is *this?*"

The lady from the hill had arrived in the tent with her companion.

Rowley, bishop of Saint Albans, lifted off his helmet, then the coif beneath, and rubbed his nose where the nasal had chafed it. "I believe she's from the village down the valley, my lord. She was wandering among the dead — looking for her son, I think."

"It seems she's found him," Henry said — the woman had cried out and thrown herself at one of the prisoners, toppling him over in her joy. "Yes, that's his mother, all right. . . ." For now the woman had taken to slapping the prisoner around his head with some force. "You usually like 'em slimmer and younger."

Saint Albans ignored the slur. "My lord, one of our men down there, he speaks a bit of Welsh, he seems to think she's got something valid to tell us and wants to ransom her son with it."

"What in hell can she possibly . . . oh, all *right.* Fulk, take the others away, all except that one and the lady. And send up that pill-pissing butcher who calls himself a doctor."

Fulk signaled to two of his men, who began kicking the prisoners to their feet. "Do you want me to hang them, my lord?"

"No, Fulk, I don't," Henry told him wearily. "I want to enlist them. I want them to teach my bloody archers a thing or two, and they can't do that with their necks stretched."

As the prisoners were taken away, the king turned to Rowley and gestured to an unusually long bow propped in a corner. "How do they do it? I tried and I could hardly bend that damn thing, but those wizened little bastards pull it back as easily as a pump handle."

"It's a skill we've got to learn, no doubt about that," Rowley said. He set about taking off his chausses.

"And the penetration . . . one flight just missed me and hit a tree. I pulled it out later. Nine inches in, it was. I swear, nine inches into solid oak. If it hadn't been for the wind . . ."

"That's what saved me; the wind swerved mine and took off most of its force." The bishop looked morosely at the calf of his leg. "Still went in, though, and, *damnation,* it's taken a couple of links in with it."

"That'll need cauterizing, then," the king said, cheering up. "And now, Owain, my boy, what are those two yammering about?"

The interpreter, an elderly border Welshman with the gift of making himself near invisible, had been attending to the conversation of mother and son in the tent entrance, most of it pursued by the woman. "Interesting, my lord. Urging him to tell you about Arthur, so she is. Something about Glastonbury and a vision . . ."

"Arthur?" The king, who'd collapsed onto a stool, sat up.

"What I can make of it, my lord — the son's not a soldier by rights — he was with the holy men at Glastonbury a time ago, and she wants him to tell you something that happened, a vision, a burial, I can't make it out at all. . . ."

"Glastonbury? He can speak English?"

"So it would seem, my lord, but he's reluctant. . . ."

Henry turned to a crouching page. "Fetch a block. And fetch Fulk back. Tell him to bring an ax."

Apart from the sobbing pleas of the mother to her son, the tent fell quiet. Every now and then the wind from outside sent the burning logs of the brazier into a flare so that the shadows of the men who sat round it sharpened and then faded again.

The entry of the doctor and his assistant added the smell of drying blood — their hands and apron were covered in it — to that of bruised grass, sweat, and steel.

20

"How's De Boeuf?" the king asked.

"I have hopes of him, my lord. Thirty stitches but, yes, I have hopes."

"And Sir Gerard?"

The doctor shook his head. "I'm afraid not, my lord."

"Shit," the king said. When the doctor took his arm to examine it, he jerked it away. "Attend to my lord bishop first. His leg'll need cauterizing."

"So will that arm, my lord. The cut's gone deep." The doctor picked up the brazier's poker and stuck it into the glowing ash.

Accompanied by the page, who was weighed down with an ax, Fulk came in, cradling three feet of tree trunk like a baby. He set it down, relieved the page of the ax, and, at a nod from his king, dragged the prisoner to the block, shook him so that he folded to his knees in front of it, and showed him the ax. The blade gleamed in the firelight.

"Take the woman out," Henry said. "No, first get this fellow's name."

"Rhys," the interpreter said.

"Now then, Rhys . . ." He had to wait until the page, with some difficulty, hauled the screaming Welshwoman out of the tent. "Tell me about Arthur."

The prisoner's eyes kept blinking in terror. He was a tall, lanky man, probably in his thirties, with unfortunate teeth and straggling fair hair. His voice, however, was captivating, and, isolated from his comrades, with the yells of his mother audible outside the tent and the ax's blade practically touching his nose, he used it to answer questions.

No, no, he hadn't fought with the rebels, not actually fought. They'd taken him along to put their prowess to song. Very content he was, personally, with King Henry Plantagenet to reign, and there was a fine name for a eulogy that he'd be happy to provide anytime.

Yes, yes, he'd spent a year as an oblate in England, in Glastonbury. His uncle Caradoc ap Griffudd had been a monk there, see, but he, Rhys ap Griffudd ap Owein ap Gwilym . . .

Fulk hit him.

. . . had decided his vocation lay in the bardic world, and he'd wandered away back to Wales to learn the harp. A fine bard he'd become as it turned out, oh, yes, his "Marwnat Pwyll" — well, "Death Song for Pwyll" it was in English — was considered the finest composition since Taliesin had . . .

Fulk hit him again.

"Oh, well then, the vision. It was of Arthur in his coffin being buried and lamented. My uncle Caradoc saw it. Just after the earthquake it was, see, and terrible that was, the ground heaving like a ship . . ."

Slapping him was useless; the man wasn't being obstructive, he was physically incapable of keeping to the point. It was a matter of waiting it out.

Eventually, wearily, the king said, "So your uncle saw a vision of Arthur's burial. In the monks' graveyard at Glastonbury, between the two pyramids."

"Yes, yes, very old those pyramids, very exotic . . ."

"Take him away, Fulk. Better keep him separate from the rest; they're not going to be happy with him." Henry turned to his bishop. "What's your opinion, Rowley?"

The bishop of Saint Albans's attention was being dominated by the tweezers that were picking shreds of chain mail from his leg.

He tried to consider the matter. "There are true visions, I don't say there aren't, but a dying old man . . ."

"Worth telling Glastonbury about it, though?" While his friend havered, the king said, "I need Arthur dead, my son. If there's something down in that fissure, I want it dug up and shown to every bloody Celt from here to Brittany. No more revolts

23

because a warrior from the Dark Ages is going to lead them to freedom. I want Arthur's bones, and I want them on display."

"If they're there, Henry. *If* they're there, they'd require some sort of verification."

The poker end in the brazier had become a molten white, and the doctor was lifting it out.

Henry II showed his vicious little teeth in a grin as he held out his arm; he was going to get some reward from the situation. "And you know who can provide that verification — *saints' bollocks.*" The smell of scorched flesh pervaded the tent.

"Not her, my lord," the bishop pleaded, watching the poker approach his leg. "She's — *goddamn* — she's — *oof* — earned the right to be left in peace. So have I."

"She's my investigator of the dead, Rowley. That's what I pay her for."

"You don't pay her, my lord."

"Are you sure?" The king puzzled over it, then: "If she gives me a dead Arthur, my son, she can name her price."

TWO

"My dear child, you must leave *now*," Prior Geoffrey said. "*Please* understand. If you and Mansur are summoned to the consistory court, I cannot save you. I doubt if even the bishop could. The summoner will be here today. He'll have men to take you both by force."

"This baby was drowned alive," Adelia said. "Dear God, somebody threw her into the river alive — there's weed in the bronchus. Look." She held out a tiny tube that had been slit by her dissecting knife. "Three infants in three years found floating, and Lord knows how many others that haven't been discovered."

The prior of Cambridge's great canonry looked around for help, avoiding the poor little mess lying on the tarpaulined table. At one time, he'd have been outraged by it and used his power to have this woman put away as an offense against heaven — even now he

25

shook to think how he would explain his connivance when he came to stand before God's throne. But he'd learned many things since Vesuvia Adelia Rachel Ortese Aguilar, qualified doctor from the School of Medicine in Salerno — the only place in Christendom that suffered, and trained, women students — had come into his life. And saved it.

The fiction they had all maintained — that Mansur, her Arab attendant, was actually the doctor, and she merely his assistant and translator — would not save her; for one thing, it was wearing thin, and for another, her association with a Saracen, and therefore a heretic, would hoist her on the same gallows.

The prior wondered what his own association with this extraordinary and dangerous woman was doing to his own reputation, particularly in God's eyes. In the Almighty's presence he would have to seek forgiveness and give explanation for himself, and for her. He would ask the Lord why it was so wrong that a female should heal rather than a man. *Are women not natural nurturers? Did not Your holy servant Paul command in his letter to the Corinthians, "Thou shall not muzzle the ox that treadeth out the corn"? Lord, if we have the corn, does it matter if the ox should be feminine?*

Well, of course he'd have to admit that she cut up the dead. But, he would say, she has uncovered murder through it and brought the perpetrators to justice. *Surely You must approve of that.*

The prior sighed. God would send him to hell for his impertinence.

Yes, he was risking his soul for her, but he loved her like a daughter.

Also, Lord, she is humble in her way. You can't find a much humbler dwelling than this one in Waterbeach.

It was a typical Cambridgeshire fenland cottage, slightly larger than most: walls of lathe and plaster, a reed-thatched roof, a mud floor, a ladder to the sleeping loft, stools made of tussocked rushes. Nothing of stone — there was none in the fens. No animals except the disgusting dog she called Ward. The only steel in the place was in her dissecting knives.

Prior Geoffrey could hear the prattle of Adelia's daughter, her illegitimate daughter, from the cottage next door, where Gyltha, the child's nurse, lived in sin with the Arab eunuch, Adelia's childhood guardian, whom she'd brought with her from Salerno.

Prior Geoffrey tried to draw a veil over his memory of Adelia's explanation that though a castrated man was unable to have children, he could still sustain an erection.

Forgive her plain speaking, Lord; it is all she knows how to do.

Outside was a view that kings might envy: a soft, sinuous panorama of alder and willow exactly reflected in the waters of the Cam. Far off were the castle turrets of Cambridge itself and, nearer, a tiny landing stage where, at this moment, his barge was moored, with a path leading from it to her ever-open door.

The path, of course, was the trouble. It had been beaten flat and deep by the feet of Cambridge's sick and broken coming to be made better.

The town's doctors — Prior Geoffrey drew another veil across Adelia's plain speaking as far as *those* charlatans were concerned — had lost too many patients to "Dr. Mansur" and had complained to the archdeacon of that abomination — no matter that those same patients fared better.

At any moment, the summoner would be coming up that same path and, finding a partially dismembered baby, would have Mansur and Adelia put on trial, where she'd be at once condemned and handed over to the civil authorities to be hanged. Nobody could save her.

Yet Prior Geoffrey knew the woman; she was championing this dead infant that somebody had found and brought to her. Most likely its father had thrown it into the river as unwanted, which, to a poor man with too many children to feed already, it was, but its death, to Adelia, constituted an atrocity that must be brought home.

"A great evil, I grant you," he said to her, "but we can do nothing about it now."

Adelia was sewing up the incision. She paused to consider. "We could," she said. "I've often wondered if I could start teaching women how to prevent conception when they need to. There are some sure methods."

"I don't want to hear them," Prior Geoffrey said hurriedly.

That would finish it. The idea that the marital embrace could be for sinful pleasure rather than for the transmission of life would cause the judges to strike this woman down where she stood. Even he, Geoffrey, loving her as he did, was confounded by her temerity. What *did* they teach them in Salerno?

Picking up the embroidered hem of his gown, he left her and ran next door, the dog cantering interestedly after him.

Young Allie was sitting on the grass, weaving a birdcage under the tutelary eye of

Gyltha, both of them wearing rush hats to protect their eyes from the sun.

Mansur was kneeling on his prayer mat, facing east, his torso rising and lowering. Dear Lord, it was noon, of course, time for what the prior had learned to be the Muslim hour for Dhur. How many heresies was he to encounter this day?

Well, Gyltha would do, dear, sensible woman that she was.

He gabbled his explanation. "So the two of them must leave, Gyltha. Now."

"Where we going to go?"

The immediate reaction of the down-to-earth Gyltha — that she too would go with them — was a comfort. More calmly, the prior said, "Lady Wolvercote is at the priory. . . ."

"Emma? Young Emma's in Cambridge?"

"By God's mercy, she happened to arrive last night asking where to find you all. She is touring her estates and desires Adelia's company. It is at least a temporary expedient until I can arrange . . . something."

The prior removed his cap to wipe his forehead and think what the "something" could be, which he couldn't. "Gyltha, they're coming for her and Mansur, and she won't attend to me."

Gyltha's mouth set. "She'll bloody well

attend to *me*."

By the time the prior had signaled to his boatman to help transfer possessions to the barge, Gyltha had kicked Mansur to his feet, run with Allie to Adelia's cottage, wrapped the dead baby in a rug, and was now handing it to the Arab. "Here, hide this poor thing and be quick about it."

Adelia snatched it back. "Not like that. She deserves better."

So a funeral was held. Mansur dug a small grave in the orchard, under a budding pear tree. While the last of its blossoms fell on him, Prior Geoffrey rushed through the obsequies, again imperiling his soul, for certainly this baby had not been baptized and, according to Saint Augustine, would share in the common misery of the damned in hell for its inheritance of original sin.

Though, he thought, lately there had been a softening of this precept in the teachings of Abelard and others. Yet Abelard . . . The prior shook his head at his own propensity for fondness for the world's sinners.

"*Requiem aeternam dona eis, Domine, et lux perpetua luceat eis. Requiescant in pace. Amen.* And now let's *go*."

About to step aboard the barge, Adelia turned to look at what had been her English home for four years, as dear to her as that of her youth in the Kingdom of Sicily. "I can't say good-bye," she said, "I love this place, I love its people."

"I know," the prior said, grabbing her hand. "Come along."

"And I love you," she said.

As the boatman poled the barge into a tributary that led to the back of Saint Augustine's canonry, they saw a skiff flying the pennant of the consistory court being rowed swiftly up the Cam toward Water-beach, on its way to fetch two heretics to justice.

By the mercy of God, its occupants didn't see them.

THREE

As the cavalcade left Cambridgeshire and passed the old Roman milestone indicating that they were in the county of Hertford-shire, Emma, Lady Wolvercote, relaxed. "Being in the company of a wanted criminal was, well, somewhat exciting," she said.

They smiled at each other. "You still are," Adelia told her. "I imagine the authority of a bishop's court doesn't halt at boundaries."

"I hope it may when one knows the bishop." Emma said it tentatively. Adelia had once known the man who was now bishop of Saint Albans too well, having borne him a child.

"He's a man of God now," Adelia said. "I doubt he could break the rules for me. Or would."

Her tone suggested that the subject be dropped. Which Emma did, though dying to know more; she was, after all, in debt to this woman, who had made King Henry promise not to sell her, Emma, into a second marriage — her first having been forced on her by abduction and rape. The Baron of Wolvercote was dead now, God rot him, and his death had left her with estates and with a son who, somewhat to her surprise, considering the circumstances of his conception, she adored.

Ordinarily, the widow of one of his nobles was in the gift of the king to be conferred on, or sold to, whomever he wished. Also, because her husband had joined a rebellion against Henry Plantagenet, the land he'd left Emma could well have been forfeited to the royal treasury.

That neither eventuality had come about was due to Adelia. Wolvercote had been hanged not because he was a rebel — Henry II found it better to bring such men to heel by making peace with them once they'd surrendered — but because he'd secretly murdered the young man Emma had preferred to him. It was Adelia who'd uncovered the crime and brought it to the king's attention. For that, bless her, she'd demanded payment, not for herself but for Emma's peace of mind. Henry — usually the least generous of monarchs where money was concerned — had granted the boon to the one he called his "mistress of the art of death" because she'd asked for it.

Looking at her as they rode side by side, Emma marveled at this woman who hobnobbed with kings and had, once, more than hobnobbed with a future bishop. She looked so . . . dowdy. Emma, who delighted in fine clothes, longed to drag off the unattractive cap covering Adelia's dark blond hair and dress her in a style to show off the slim figure that at the moment was hidden under a brown and shapeless garment better suited to the lesser clergy.

Adelia, as she knew, preferred not to stand out in a crowd, but garbed like that, Emma thought, she wouldn't stand out in a clump of trees. It was like being accompanied by a servant — in fact, the Wolvercote servants in their bright livery were better dressed than this extraordinary female.

"Aren't you hot in that?" Emma asked, for the sun was exceptional, even for late May.

"Yes," Adelia said, and left it there.

But perhaps it was as well that the eyes of everybody they passed turned to Emma on her pretty white palfrey and not toward the small, brown-clad woman on the small brown pony. When he'd seen them off, Prior Geoffrey had insisted Adelia be hidden inside Emma's traveling cart until they were over the county border — and Mansur, too; that exotic and fearsome figure in Arab robes and headdress was too well known not to give the game away, for he was never far away from Adelia's side.

Now, however, and justified or not, tension evaporated in the Hertfordshire sunlight, and both Mansur and Adelia had emerged into it to take their places on horseback.

It was still a small group considering the danger on the roads from robbers, though that was better under Plantagenet rule than it had been. Emma traveled with her child's nurse, a serving woman, two grooms, a confessor, and a knight with his squire — such a knight, an enormous man, taller even than Mansur, with an air that left no doubt he could use the sword in the scabbard at his waist to effect, his nasaled helmet giving ferocity to a face that was otherwise gentle.

"Master Roetger," Emma had said, introducing him. "He's German. My champion." She meant it literally, for Emma was touring the estates her husband had left, ensuring that their tenants acknowledged her two-year-old son as heir to the property — not always successfully. Her forced marriage to Wolvercote had been abrupt and had so few witnesses that in the complicated system of feudal landholding, more than one lord was disputing the claim of Baby Philip, the new Baron Wolvercote, to the income from the land they'd held from his father. An elderly cousin, for instance, had refused to give up the rents from a thousand Yorkshire acres to a child he'd called a bastard and a usurper.

"The God of Battles told *him* whose land it was," Emma said with vengeful satisfaction. "Master Roetger had *his* champion disabled in twenty minutes."

It was the way things were done in England, Adelia the foreigner had learned. Trial by combat. A *judicium Dei.* Since Almighty God knew to whom disputed land truly belonged, the disputants — or more often, their champions — fought a judicial battle under His invisible but all-seeing eye, leaving it to Him to show which party had the right of it according to which contestant He let win.

"God is on our side," Emma said, "and will be again in Aylesbury."

"*Another* combat?"

"There was a married sister," Emma said — she never named her late husband if she could help it. "A widow whose children died before she did, so she inherited a nice property near Tring, which, by rights, is my boy's. Her brother-in-law is contesting our claim, but he's a miserable, cheeseparing creature, Sir Gerald. I doubt he will spend much in acquiring *their* champion."

"Master Roetger being expensive?" Adelia asked.

"Indeed. I had to send to Germany for him. We needed the best."

"That's hardly leaving the decision to God, is it?"

"Oh, God would have decided in our favor in any case." Emma looked down at the velvet-lined pannier in which Baron Wolvercote was traveling, sucking his thumb as he went. "Wouldn't he, Pippy? Wouldn't he, my darling? God always protects the innocent."

He didn't protect you, Adelia thought. Nobody could have been more innocent than the joyous young girl who was being brought up in the convent where Adelia had first met her, the same convent Wolvercote and his men had broken into to carry her off.

But Adelia didn't point out the illogic in Emma's argument — it would have done no good. Inevitably, the girl had been changed. Wolvercote hadn't even wanted her for herself, only for the money chests she was inheriting from a father in the wine trade.

The Emma of today still had the poise that her father's gold had given her, but she'd become obsessed with this sudden unforeseen ownership of land in various parts of the country, with manors, mills, rivers, pannages, meadows filled with cattle that her rapist had owned and that now, in her view, his son should have though the skies fell. There was a ferocity to her, a set to her young mouth, a carelessness for other people's lives that almost mirrored those of the man who'd abused her.

Worse, her singing voice had fallen silent. It had been Adelia's first introduction to her at Godstow Abbey, where Emma had been brought up — a pure soprano leading the responses of the choir nuns so gloriously that even Adelia, who had no musical ear, had been enchanted into thinking herself nearer to heaven for having heard it.

But now when she asked for a song, Emma refused to perform. "I have none left in me."

Friends though they were, Adelia suspected that Emma hadn't asked her to be a traveling companion solely out of affection. Young Pippy had been born prematurely and was still underweight for his age; his mother needed the company of the only doctor she trusted.

At the next wide verge on the road, they stopped to refresh themselves and let the horses rest. "Does he look pale to you?" Emma asked anxiously, watching the nurse lift Pippy out of his pannier so that he could run around with young Allie on the grass.

The child certainly looked less robust than Allie, even when the two-year difference in their ages was taken into account, but Adelia said, "It's the healthiest thing you can do for him in this weather." She set great store by fresh air and variety for children. Emma, after all, could afford the finest inns to stay at and, therefore, that other requisite for children — good food.

The travelers found both at Saint Albans.

Adelia had become increasingly nervous as they'd approached the town, but a private word with the landlord of its Pilgrims' Rest reassured her that the bishop was abroad.

"Gone to help the king put down the damned Welsh, so they say," the landlord told her. "He's a fine fighter as well as a good shepherd is Bishop Rowley."

Damn him, Adelia thought. *I worry in case I might have to see him again and I worry when I don't. A fine fighter; blast him. What's he doing fighting?*

Saint Albans was full of pilgrims come to worship at the tomb of England's first Christian martyr. The wealthiest of them, a party of twelve, were also staying at the Pilgrims' Rest, intending to ensure the good of their souls by finishing off their pilgrimage at Glastonbury, oldest and holiest of England's abbeys and, even more compelling, reputedly the site of Avalon.

They welcomed Emma's request that she and her people join them on their way into the South West. "The more, the merrier," their leader, a large burgher from Yorkshire, told her.

"And safer," said a Cheshire abbess. She looked with appreciation at Master Roetger. "I trust your knight shall be coming with us?"

"As far as Wells," Emma said, "but we shall be turning off to Aylesbury on the way for a day or two — Master Roetger is to uphold my son's claim to an estate in a trial by combat."

"A trial by combat?"

"Trial by combat?"

The inn's dining table was enlivened; visiting the saints might ensure one's place in heaven, but earth didn't have much more to offer in the way of entertainment than seeing two champions trying to kill each other.

41

It was decided. The pilgrims would loyally accompany their new friend, Lady Wolvercote, on her diversion to the judicial battleground at the Buckinghamshire county town of Aylesbury.

As her party was to be accompanied by too many people for robbers to attack them as they went, Emma felt safe to employ one of her grooms to ride on ahead and take a letter to Wells, where her mother-in-law, Lady Wolvercote, now the dowager Lady Wolvercote, occupied another of the estates that young Pippy had inherited from his father. "It announces my coming," she told Adelia. "It's supposed to be the best of the properties, and if I like it, I shall settle there. Somerset is the nicest of all counties. There is a dower house attached to it, I'm told, so the old woman will have accommodation that she's entitled to move into — that's supposing that she and I get on together. If we don't, she can have one of the other estates somewhere else — a smaller one, of course."

"Have you never met her?"

"No," Emma said bitterly. "Mine was not a wedding to which relatives, or anybody else, was invited."

It would be a strange situation — a bride and mother-in-law who were strangers.

Adelia experienced sympathy for the unknown woman; with Emma in this mood, the slightest infraction would see the poor lady uprooted from her home and sent to another. She said, "I am sure she will be too delighted at acquiring a grandson to be anything but pleasant."

There had been no children from Wolvercote's previous marriage; his first wife had died only weeks after the wedding, leaving him her considerable dowry — circumstances that, knowing the man, Adelia had always thought to be suspicious.

"She'd better be," Emma said ominously.

The Aylesbury judges sat on benches under an awning decked by flags. Another covered stand held the nonlegal rich and important. Lesser mortals, large numbers of them, braved the sun to line the spears that had been set in the middle of the field to mark off a sanded area, sixty feet square.

It was a day out. There were little tents selling ale and sweetmeats. Jongleurs entertained the crowds with songs, legerdemain, and tumbling. Market women sold clothespegs and herbs. In the fields beyond, swallows flipped back and forth over the corn strips.

The judges' herald blew a fanfare before

introducing the two combatants in a voice that traveled. "Under the eye of Almighty God, Master Peter of Nottingham representing Sir Gerald L'Havre, and Master Roetger of Essen representing Lord Philip, Baron Wolvercote, shall this day prove which holds the Manor of Tring, with all its appurtenances, by true right."

The trumpet brayed again. "Let the combatants come forth armed with *scutis* and *bacculis,* and swear to the justices that they have abjured all magic in this matter of trial, then let them fight until the God of Battles shall decide, or until the sun shall go down."

The two champions emerged from a small pavilion near the judicial stand, knelt before the judges' bench, and spoke in unison.

"Hear this, ye justices, that we have this day neither eaten, drunk, nor have upon our persons neither bone, stone, nor grass, nor any enchantment, sorcery, or witchcraft, whereby the law of God may be abused or the law of the devil exalted. So help us, God and His saints."

Adelia was in the stands only because Emma had begged her to be; she'd rather have stayed behind at the inn with the children. She had no liking for fighting of any kind — it took too long to put people together again afterward, always supposing

44

they were still alive to let her do it.

The two men strode into the arena. Both carried a shield and a stave. Each wore sleeveless hauberks, leaving the head and legs bare, and each was shod with red sandals — a tradition, apparently — that made them look vaguely ridiculous, like children who'd dressed up as knights without the proper footwear.

Adelia was relieved; staves were surely not as harmful as swords; less bloody, anyway. She said so to Emma.

"In Germany it is the sword," she was told, "but Roetger is a master with both — and the proper name is 'quarterstaff,' my dear, not 'stave.' "

Emma had become edgy; it didn't seem as if the cheeseparing Sir Gerald had economized this time. His champion was an inch or two shorter and probably a little older than Roetger, but the muscles in his neck, arms, and legs were formidable. So was the sneer that showed confidence and dark yellow teeth.

By contrast the German looked the slighter of the two, and his face was expressionless. Not a man of words, but on the journey Adelia had come to like him, mainly because both children did, always pestering him: "Master Roger, Master Roger." He had endless patience with them, making whistles from hazel twigs, showing them how to hoot like an owl by puffing into their clasped hands, tearing little pieces out of a folded leaf so that, unfolded, it had a face.

"Does he have children back in Germany?"

"I haven't asked," Emma said, with more energy than the question demanded. "He is here to fight; that's all I'm interested in."

There was another fanfare. Master Peter, representing the defendant, threw a mailed glove to the ground. Master Roetger, the prosecuting champion, picked it up.

"Let battle commence and God defend the right."

The quarterstaffs were six feet long and made of oak. Each man grasped his in fighting mode, one hand clasping it in the middle, the other hand gripping it a quarter of the way down so that half the staff was free to do the belaboring.

Except that there wasn't any belaboring — not at first. There was a lot of jumping as one man tried to take the legs out from under the other, skipping, grunting, loud cracks as stave met stave, but no smites on flesh.

Sitting next to Adelia, Father Septimus, Emma's confessor, rubbed his hands.

"Good, good, proper champions on both sides. We're in for a fine contest; it will take hours before they tire."

Hours? And what happened when they *did* tire and lost the agility to avoid the blows? Those were heavy staves.

The fight had hardly begun and she was sickened by it, by everything, the pavilions, the fanfares, the bunting, the judges, all the banal formality; everything here was tainted, including herself. She thought of Jesus and his plain, provincial humanity and how they were belittling His Father, as in all trials in which God was brought in to decide, diminishing Him to the status of a Caesar presiding over a bloodstained Colosseum, asked to stick up his thumb or turn it down.

She told Emma that she was going to answer a call of nature. Emma, twisting a kerchief in her hands and without taking her eyes off the arena, said, "Come back soon. Master Roetger may need you."

People who drew in their knees as she passed along the row to the steps merely peered round her, tutting at her momentary obstruction of their view.

A latrine had been dug behind the stands for the occasion; its cloud of flies could be seen even above its wattle fencing. Adelia avoided it and climbed a stile leading to a path through trees, following its way to a stream, the noise of the crowd fading behind her. She seated herself on the grass under a willow tree, took off her boots, and let the water cool her feet.

What am I doing here?

In deserting the fens she'd cut herself off from everything that anchored her. It had been a grief to leave her patients, to say good-bye to Prior Geoffrey, and an even greater unhappiness to make that brief, loving farewell at Saint Augustine's to Ulf, Gyltha's grandson, no longer the urchin who'd been her companion but now, under the prior's tuition, a young man intent on law. And, oh, she would miss Ward. The dog wasn't welcomed by Emma, and Adelia had been persuaded to leave him in the prior's care.

Without them all she was rootless, adrift, especially with her occupation gone. If she wasn't a doctor, she was nothing; even Allie couldn't fill the space. Where to go? What to do?

The dark trout in the stream were as aimless as she was, and she became weary of watching them. She leaned her head back against the tree.

Damn it, she'd go back to Salerno. Introduce Allie and Gyltha to her beloved foster parents — they'd written to say they longed to see their grandchild. That's what she'd do. She could earn her living again. Her old tutor, Gordinus, might take her back as his assistant, or she'd become a lecturer in dissection.

Yes, when she'd completed her obligation to Emma, she'd go home. Allie would receive a better education in Salerno than her mother could give her here — though, Adelia thought with pride, the child was already reading some Latin.

"And this time, Henry," she said out loud, "I'll *make* you let me go."

So far the king had always refused her a passport. "The dead talk to you, mistress," he'd told her, "and I need to know what some of the poor buggers are saying."

If the king remained obdurate? Well, there were other ways of getting out of the country — fenland boatmen who were both friends and smugglers would sail her to Flanders.

With her eyes on the thin willow leaves above her, Adelia began to consider how she could pay her family's way through France and across the Alps to the kingdom of Sicily . . . in a traveling medicine cart . . . attach herself to a pilgrimage as its herbalist . . .

She woke up, having dreamed that she was

sitting in the Colosseum with the crowd around her delighting in gladiator blood and yelling for more. The scene before her was still peaceful, but the stream reflected the color of amber.

Dear God, the sun was beginning to go down, she'd been asleep for hours, and the howls of the crowd in the distance had become loud and shrill, indicating that somebody was hurt. She didn't want to see it.

But she was a doctor.

Adelia got up, shaking off butterflies that had settled on her skirts. She put on her boots and hurried back up the path.

Nobody in the stand attended her return any more than they'd noticed her going. The kerchief in Emma's hands was in shreds, her face white.

The two champions had faded from what they were; the sand had stuck to sweating skin and hair and darkened them so that in the failing light, the silvery hauberks almost seemed to move by themselves — slowly, very slowly, as if through treacle. Both men were limping; Roetger held his staff in his right hand only; his left arm hung, useless, by his side. His opponent seemed to have trouble seeing, occasionally flailing his staff in front of him, like a blind man feeling for an obstruction.

The crowd's cry of satisfaction that Adelia had heard was fracturing into impatience. It would be dark soon, and neither champion had battered the other to death. Most unsatisfactory. The judges could be seen consulting among themselves. The God of Battles was letting everybody down.

And then the scene in the arena flickered. There were two cracks, almost instantaneous but not quite; one of them was caused by Master Roetger's quarterstaff connecting at speed with his opponent's head, knocking it sideways, and the other by Master Peter's staff slashing at Master Roetger's legs.

With Sir Gerald's champion toppled, Roetger hopped forward and pressed the end of his staff into the other's neck, pushing him flat to the ground.

There was a silence. A voice croaked, "Say it." It was Roetger's.

A murmur, sobbing.

"Say it. Loud, you say it."

"Craven." A curious shriek, a submission, the end of everything for the creature that made it.

The crowd exhaled in a howl that was not so much a cheer for the winner as contempt for the loser.

Somewhere the trumpet brayed again. The judges were standing. Emma was on her knees, her head in her hands. Perhaps she was thanking her god.

Adelia took no notice of any of it, not even of the wounded Roetger, who was using his staff as a crutch to hop off the field. She was watching a creature crawl through the sand into the shadows. "What will happen to him?" she asked Father Septimus.

"Who? Oh, that one. He will be infamous, of course. He's been publicly shamed; he has declared himself a coward."

That, then, was what "craven" meant, personal annihilation. Master Peter would not die, yet the essence of him had. And the man had fought for five hours.

They had all been shamed.

Master Roetger lay on a table in the champion's pavilion, his squire standing helplessly beside him. A doctor poked tentatively at limbs and raised his head as the women came in. "Fractures to the arm and ankle. I can apply a salve, a marvelous mixture of my own from toads' blood gathered at the full moon and . . ."

Adelia nudged Emma, who said, "Thank you, Doctor, that will not be necessary. We have salves of our own."

"Not as efficacious as mine, I assure you, dear lady. And cheap, very cheap — only sixpence for the first application, three for any thereafter."

"No, thank you, Doctor."

While Emma ushered the man out, Adelia set about her own examination of the patient. Roetger bit into his lip but made no sound.

The humerus of the left arm was undoubtedly broken, but the other injury was not to the ankle. What she'd heard when Master Peter's quarterstaff connected with Master Roetger's foot hadn't been the crack of a bone, more a "pop," like something being pulled apart — not a noise she'd heard before but one she'd been told about at the School of Medicine. And the blow had been to the back of the leg

Sure enough, when she took his right foot in her hand, it flopped to the touch; she was able to bend it until the toes touched the lower shin.

"This is not a broken ankle," she said. She looked at Roetger and then at Emma. "I'm afraid it's the heel, the Achilles tendon."

"What is that?"

"It's . . . well, it's like a piece of string attached to the muscles of the calf." She was seeing it as displayed in a dissected leg on the great marble table where her foster father had carried out autopsies.

She would have liked to tell them about it, how marvelous it was, the thickest and strongest tendon in the body, which seemed to enable the foot to push downward in a run or jump. And why it was named after Achilles, whose only weak point it had been because his mother had held him by the heel when she made every other part of the hero invulnerable to injury by dipping him into the River Styx. But neither Emma nor poor Roetger would be interested in a dissertation at this moment.

"It's ruptured, you see," she said. "That last blow must have been tremendous."

The champion made an effort: "How long?"

"Do we just strap it up?" Emma asked.

"We do, yes." Adelia turned to Roetger. "We must ensure you don't move it at all. As for how long it will take to heal . . ." She searched her memory for what the school's lecturer on limbs had said — she herself had never treated this particular injury. "It may be a very long time, longer than the break in your arm . . . perhaps six months . . ."

Roetger's eyes went wide with shock.

Aghast, Emma said, *"Six months?"*

Adelia grabbed her by the arm and took her outside the tent. "You can't abandon him. What would he do? How could he return to Germany on one foot?"

Emma was indignant. "I don't *intend* to abandon him. He was injured in my service. Of *course* I'll care for him."

Adelia sighed with relief. The gentle Emma of old still survived under the harsher surface of the new.

"But he'll have to travel with us," the newer Emma said sharply. "I may have a use for him after we get to Wells."

"Not for six months, you won't." Adelia began making a list. "The whole lower leg will have to be splinted. A decoction of willow bark for the pain. And comfrey, we'll need comfrey, but that grows everywhere, and we must hope it works on tendons as well as broken bones." She started off toward where the traders were dismantling their pavilions to beg some struts for a splint.

Emma called after her: "Is he in much pain?"

"Agony."

At last in bed at the Aylesbury inn at which they were all staying, Adelia worried about the heel most of the night. She had put on a rough splint for the time being, but that wouldn't be good enough, not if it was to endure the rigors of travel over rutted roads and prevent its owner from being tempted to put his foot to the ground, something that had to be avoided at all costs.

At dawn she was in the inn's stable yard, making inquiries to a sleepy ostler as to where she might gather comfrey. Since every county had its own name for the plant, he and she were at cross-purposes for a while until, finally enlightened, the man said, "Oh, you're a-meaning knit-bone," and directed her to an untidy patch of ground beyond a vegetable garden where clusters of young lance-shaped leaves and new yellow flowers were becoming visible in the dark green crowns of the old plants.

It was mostly comfrey roots that Adelia wanted, and she dug for them with her trowel, wishing she'd worn gloves — the hairy leaves were an irritant to the skin.

Carrying her spoils back to the inn, she found the pilgrims at breakfast and in shock. They'd received appalling news.

"Glastonbury is burned down," the York-shireman told her. "Aye, we had it from two separate peddlers last night. Burned down. Glastonbury. *Glastonbury.* Reckon the heart's gone out of England."

It was a heart that had been beating for more centuries than anybody could remember, empowered by the holiest of the holy — Saint Joseph of Arimathea, Saint Patrick of Ireland, Saint Bride, Saint Columba, Saint David of Wales, Saint Gildas. . . . And now it had stopped.

There was puzzlement in the room, as well as shock. A glove maker from Chester expressed it: "You'd have thought with all those saints, at least one of 'em would've put the damned fire out."

"King Arthur should have," said somebody else. "How could he sleep through that?"

There was a feeling that the blessed dead of Glastonbury had not pulled their weight.

Emma entered the room to be told of the calamity and was aghast. *"Glastonbury?"*

"Aye. Never have thought it, would thee?" the Yorkshire burgher said. "And a right conflagration it were, so it's said; noothing left, not noothing, sooch a pity. And I were looking forward to a blessing from Joseph of Arimathea." He shook his head. "Should've set out earlier."

The Cheshire abbess was less upset. "I said all along we ought to be making for Canterbury. With Saint Thomas we are assured of even stronger sanctity, his being the latest martyrdom. Ah, who would have thought such a blessed saint would be killed by his king. . . ."

The Yorkshireman cut her off in mid-flow; her companions had heard the abbess's strictures on Henry Plantagenet's perfidy in crying for the death of his obstructive archbishop many times before. He said, "Aye, well, that's where we're a-going now — to Canterbury." There was no virtue to be had from Glastonbury's bones and relics now that they had been reduced to ashes, whereas there was much to be gained from the vials of Saint Thomas à Becket's blood that were on sale in the cathedral where he'd died.

Bills paid, packing done, the pilgrims congratulated Emma on her triumph in the trial by combat, which, they said, they had much enjoyed, and bade her farewell. The man from Yorkshire kissed her hand. "Right sorry we are to be leaving your coompany, my lady."

"I'm sorry, too." Emma meant it. Without the pilgrims, and with Master Roetger disabled, the journey to Wells would be considerably less safe.

Adelia didn't stay to wave good-bye; she was already at work to ensure the immobilization of a heel.

Gyltha was ordered to the kitchen to begin pounding the pile of comfrey roots to a mash in the largest mortar the inn could provide, while Mansur, armed with an ax, a whittling knife, and instructions, was sent off to find an ash tree and a willow. Adelia herself impounded the services of Emma's most experienced groom, Alan, and both were to be seen in the stable yard drawing diagrams in its dust.

To facilitate matters, Master Roetger was carried to the cart and put on its cushions with his legs dangling over the tailboard until the bad one, which was bare, could be placed with care across a sawing horse. It was a maneuver causing excitement among the inn servants, who forgathered under the impression that they were to watch a Saracen doctor — Mansur's assumed role — perform an amputation.

Instead, they saw Gyltha hold some of the comfrey leaves to the heel while Adelia gently plastered them into place with the unpleasant-smelling green-black paste from the mortar, eventually encasing the entire foot, including the sole, and lower shin with it.

Under the lash of the innkeeper's tongue, his staff returned to work — it was, after all, only the usual home remedy of comfrey being applied to a breakage by a couple of women.

When the foot was done, the broken arm was treated to the same procedure. Pain compressed the patient's mouth into a straight line and sweat glistened in the furrows of his forehead, but he tried to show interest.

"In my country this plant we also eat," he said. "*Schwarzwurz,* we call it. Fried in batter, it is good."

Adelia was interested. England's peasantry ate boiled comfrey, as they did nettles, as a vegetable. To put the leaves in egg, flour, and milk argued a higher standard of living.

"And now we're batterin' *you,*" Gyltha told him, making him smile.

Finished, Adelia stood back. "There. How does that feel?"

"Six months, truly?"

"I'm afraid so."

"But I walk again?"

"Yes," she told him, hoping to God she was right, "you will."

Leaving the patient as he was while the plaster dried in the sun, she and Gyltha repaired to the horse trough to wash the stuff off their hands. Emma, who'd been watching, came up to them. "How long is this going to take?"

Adelia began explaining that there was more to do, but Emma, exclaiming, walked away.

"Temper, temper," Gyltha said. "What's up with her?"

"I don't know."

There was a *lot* more to be done. Adelia, the groom, and Mansur worked all morning weaving a cage of withies they'd devised for the leg. It had a base of wood that Mansur had whittled into a bowl that should, if Roetger accidentally put his foot to the ground, keep most of the pressure off his heel.

Occasionally, Emma came to the window of her room to watch them and huff with impatience, but Adelia took no notice — this was an injury new to her, and she was determined to mend it.

It was after noon by the time the comfrey plaster had dried rock-hard and the cage could be strung around it. Even then, Adelia delayed the start of the journey until she had attached the front of the cage by string to a hook in the edge of the cart's roof so that the champion's foot was gimballed and any jolt in traveling would merely sway it in the air.

"He looks ridiculous," Emma said.

For the first time, Roetger complained. "I am like trussed chicken."

But Adelia was adamant. "You stay trussed," she said. After Aylesbury, they would be turning southwest onto minor roads that were unlikely to have been kept in good repair.

Nor were they. During the early spring rains, the wheels of farm vehicles had scored ruts as deep as ditches into surfaces that nobody had subsequently filled in, leaving them to dry as hard as cement.

Time and again, the company had to pause while the grooms saw to a wheel in danger of coming off the cart, though Adelia preened herself on the fact that Roetger's leg had merely been swung from side to side in its cage and taken no harm. At each overnight stop, Emma summoned the local reeve and berated him for his village's lack of duty in repairing the section of road for which it was responsible, though whether her lecture did any good was doubtful — highway upkeep was expensive and time-consuming.

Apart from rough traveling, it was a lovely journey. The air was filled with the call of the cuckoo and the scent of the bluebells that paved every wood as far as the eye could see into the trees.

The risk of robbery was lessened by the amount of innocent traffic on the roads or crisscrossing them, brought out by the good weather: falconers, market people, bird nesters, families paying visits, groups of vengeful gamekeepers after foxes and pine martens. The cavalcade exchanged greetings and news with all of them. True, Master Roetger suffered as they passed through villages where rude boys mistook his chained and recumbent position for that of a felon being taken to prison and threw stones at him, but the going through increasingly lush countryside was good, and Adelia would have enjoyed it if it hadn't been for Emma's behavior and, surprisingly, that of her own daughter.

A strong character, Allie, despite her lack of years. At first her mother had thought the child was following her own footsteps in being fascinated by anatomy. Which, in a sense, she was — but only in that of animals. If it didn't have scales, four legs, fur, or fins, Allie wasn't interested in it. All living fauna delighted her, and should the subject be dead, she wanted to know why it had delighted her, why it flew, crawled, swam, or galloped. By the age of three, she had wept over the death of the jackdaw trained to perch on her shoulder — and then dissected it. By four, thanks to a local hunter, she was familiar with the muscles that made a deer run, the bones in the shoveling arms of a mole — a creature trapped mercilessly in the fens because its runs weakened the dikes that held back floods.

At the beginning of the journey Allie had been charmed by her two-year-old playmate. Yet, loving the train's horses and mules as she did, she wanted to be the center of attention to their grooms — a breed she'd always got on well with. But the grooms were employed by Emma and, by extension, young Pippy, who, if there was a ride to be had at the head of the cavalcade, came first. Little Lord Wolvercote was fussed over not only by his mother and servants but by Gyltha and Adelia as well, and the green-eyed monster of jealousy began to show in Allie's eyes and in the hits and pushes that sent the little boy to the ground. It came to the point at which the adults couldn't turn their backs without a wail from Pip as Allie attacked him again.

Mortified, Gyltha lectured, without effect.

"Don't like him," Allie said, explaining why she'd pulled a switch from a tree and beaten Lord Wolvercote's bottom with it.

"She's a spoiled little madam," Gyltha said to Adelia, having taken the switch from Allie's hand and whacked the child's behind in turn. "She won't say sorry. You got to do something."

Secretly, Adelia admired her daughter's defiance in the face of condemnation and whipping, but Gyltha was right — something had to be done to correct her. She tried an indirect approach and made a doll out of sticks and bandages on which she drew a hideous face, calling it Puncho. She gave it to her daughter. "You are not winning friends with behavior like this, Allie, so when you feel like hitting Pippy, hit Puncho instead."

Allie regarded the monstrosity with favor and tucked it under her arm. "I like Puncho," she said. "Don't like Pippy." And she continued the assaults until it was impossible, during rests on the road, to allow both children to run around on the verge together.

Incurring Adelia's gratitude, Emma was tolerant about the situation, though she made sure her son was kept out of Allie's way. "I know how the child feels. At the convent, I used to pinch little Sister Priscilla when I thought Mother Edyve was favoring her over me."

Yet she, too, was behaving badly. Adelia failed to realize why Emma, so understanding of Allie, showed resentment at the care lavished on Master Roetger, for whom she seemed to lack all sympathy. "Does he really need to be cooed over?" she would ask, as Gyltha and Adelia attended to their patient. She clucked with irritation when the grooms had to carry Roetger into the trees to help him with his calls of nature, and at the lengthy arrangements that had to be made for him on the ground floor of every inn at which they passed the night — Adelia refused to allow him to be carried upstairs in case his foot should encounter an obstruction in the process.

It was as if Emma's champion's needs embarrassed her as much as they did him.

Enlightenment eventually dawned during a rare moment of intimacy when, having reached Marlborough and seen the children to bed, Emma and Adelia were drawn by a lovely evening into the rose garden of their inn — one of the richest they had stayed at so far.

As they walked, Emma's voice came to her companion out of a scented dusk. "Should you like more children, 'Delia?"

"Yes. Very much, but I'm unlikely to have them now."

"You might marry."

"No." Having kept her independence by refusing marriage to Rowley, she wasn't going to surrender it now. She said, lightly,

"For one thing, any respectable man would regard me as spoiled goods."

Emma didn't disagree. They walked on. After a while, Emma said, "I don't want more children. Another son, for instance, might complicate Pippy's inheritance."

Adelia didn't see how it could; the laws of succession were strict, though she merely asked, "So you won't marry again?"

"No." Emma was sharp about it. "And thanks to you, I don't have to. But . . ."

It was a lingering conjunction. Adelia waited to hear what it led to.

Suddenly, there was an outburst of anguish. "They talk about the joys of the marriage bed, but I never knew them — not with him, he did things to me. . . . I was forced . . . I fought . . . I never consented, never. . . ."

"I know." Adelia took her friend's arm. "I know."

"Yet there must *be* joys," Emma said desperately. "You knew them with Rowley. There must be gentler men, loving men."

"Yes," Adelia told her with authority, "there are. You may meet one, Emmy. You *could* marry again, this time by your own choosing."

"No." It was almost a scream. "I don't trust . . . I shall not be subject again . . . You

of all people should understand that."

Nearby, a nightingale began to sing, its cadences refreshing the garden like silvery drops of water. The two women stopped to listen.

More quietly, Emma went on. "I am seventeen years old, 'Delia. If I live to be ancient, I shall never have known pleasure with a man."

Adelia waited. This outpouring was heading somewhere; she didn't know where. Emma was expecting something from her, but she didn't know what that was, either.

"But suppose," Emma said desperately, "suppose, for the sake of argument, one set one's heart on a man, an unsuitable man, someone . . . oh, I don't know, of a status below one's own."

She became irritated, as if she expected Adelia to answer a question she had not put. Going briskly ahead, she said over her shoulder, "Somebody one couldn't marry, even if one wanted to, because his occupation and birth would bring social obloquy on one . . . and one's child. Suppose that."

Adelia tried to. Ahead of her, Emma's figure was that of an elegant ghost in the moonlight, a pale shade that flicked petals from the roses it passed as if it disdained them.

Walking behind, Adelia attempted to follow the circumlocution that Emma had used to pose her question. What was it her poor friend wanted from her? No marriage, never marriage. No children, never more children. A life without physical love, yet a heart, such a sad heart, longing for the tenderness of a man . . . an unsuitable man . . .

Then understanding came. Adelia castigated herself. *What a fool I am. Of course. I should have known. That's it.*

She quickened her pace, caught Emma by the arm, and led her to a seat in an alcove of roses, made her sit down, and sat down herself.

"Did I ever tell you my theory on how it is possible to avoid conception?" she asked, as if she was raising a different subject.

"No," Emma said, as if she, too, found the matter a new one. "No, I don't believe you did."

"It's my foster parents' theory, in fact," Adelia said. "They are an extraordinary couple, I think I've told you. They refuse to be bound by their differing religions — he's a Jew, she's a Christian, but their minds are free, *so* free, of laws, prejudices, superstition, imprisoned thinking . . ." She paused, overwhelmed by longing to see them again and by gratitude for the upbringing they had given her.

"Really?" Emma said politely.

"Yes. And they traveled, you see. To gain medical knowledge. They asked questions of different races, tribes, other histories, customs, and my foster mother, bless her, went to the women, especially the women."

"Yes?" Emma said, and again it seemed of little interest to her.

"Yes. And by the time she returned to Salerno, she had gathered, first, that women through the ages have tried to have control over their own bodies — and the methods they've used."

"Goodness gracious," Emma said lightly.

"Yes," Adelia said. And because she was Adelia, to whom the dissemination of knowledge was essential and must be as fascinating to the listener as it was to her, she went into detailed account of the different ways, in different ages, in which men and women had attempted to achieve the dignity of choosing for themselves how many children they could cope with. First she spoke of "receptacles," sheaths for the penis that various peoples made from sheepskin, or snakeskin, sometimes soaked in vinegar or lemon juice. "Effective, my mother said, but many men do not like to

70

wear them."

Then came the subject of coitus interruptus, the biblical sin of Onan, who, forced by Jewish law to marry his brother's wife, had "spilled his seed upon the ground" rather than let it impregnate her. "But again, most men do not wish to do that."

The nightingale continued its ethereal song while Adelia labored on through earthy, human truths. "There are plant remedies, of course, pennyroyal, asafetida, et cetera," she said, "but Mother was wary of those; so many are poisonous and in any case do not work."

She paused for a moment, hoping for a response. There was none. Whether Emma, sitting so silently, was listening to her or to the blasted nightingale it was difficult to know.

"And then there are the pessaries," Adelia said. She enlarged on their history, speaking of Outremer women who placed sponges soaked in crocodile dung and lemon juice in the vulva, of an Arab tribe that used the same method, this time favoring a mixture of honey and camel droppings beaten into a paste with wine vinegar. She spoke of similar advice found in ancient writings, Egyptian hieroglyphics, Greek and Latin . . .

Emma shifted, and Adelia realized she was

71

losing her audience. She took in a breath. "What Mother found was that among all these recipes, when they worked, was what she called 'acidus,' a constant theme of the sour — lemon juice, vinegar. She was sure that it was that which killed sperm."

At the word "killed," Emma stiffened. "And what has God had to say of these ways to murder?"

"Not murder," Adelia said. "Prevention. According to the priests, God condemns them, but priests are men who overlook the death of too many women through the imposition of too much childbearing." Adelia thought of the murdered baby and its grave in the fens. "Or families struggling in poverty because they have too many mouths to feed."

Emma stood up. "Well, I think it is disgusting. Worse, it's *vulgar*." She walked away.

"And in the case of pessaries," Adelia shouted after her, "Mother recommends the attachment of a silk thread so they can be pulled down afterward."

She heard the inn door slam closed and sighed. "Well, you did ask," she said. "At least, I think you did."

She sat on for a while, listening to the nightingale.

"You been a time," Gyltha said when

Adelia returned to their and Allie's bedroom.

"I was talking to Emma. Gyltha, I think, I *think,* she's in love with Master Roetger but doesn't feel she can marry him."

"Could've told you that," Gyltha said. "Too high and mighty to look after him herself but jealous as a cat of them as do."

"Yes, I suppose that's it. Poor girl, poor girl."

"And she thinks as how you fancy him yourself."

"Oh, Gyltha, she *can't.*" To Adelia, the German was a patient. She saw him only as a broken arm, a ruptured Achilles heel, and a long-suffering nature.

"Maybe she can't, but she do."

The next morning, Emma tongue-lashed her people — the grooms for being tardy in saddling up, the nurse for dressing Pippy in the wrong clothes, even Father Septimus for an overlong grace at breakfast. Adelia and Master Roetger were ignored as if they did not exist.

"An oh-be-joyful journey this is going to be," Gyltha muttered as they set out.

Adelia agreed with her. If the situation continued all the way to Wells, it would be intolerable.

As it turned out, Adelia, Gyltha, Allie, and

Mansur did not have to endure it long. The company had been on the road only an hour when the sound of galloping hooves alerted it to riders coming up fast from the rear.

Master Roetger felt for the sword that he kept always by his side, though what, pinioned as he was, he could have done with it was uncertain.

There were three of them, all with the Plantagenet blazon on their tunics, each one leading a remount. Like their horses, they were lathered with sweat from hard traveling. Their officer addressed Emma. "Are you Mistress Adelia, lady?"

Adelia said, "I am."

"An' is he the lord Mansur?"

"He is."

The officer said, "We've been chasing you all the way from Cambridge, mistress. You're to come along of us."

"Where? What for?"

"To Wales, mistress. By order of Henry the King."

FOUR

"Look," Allie said, pointing upward as they approached the castle. "Poppies. Lots of poppies. Big ones."

Against the setting sun, the severed heads decorating Caerleon's crenellations bore a resemblance to wildly petaled flowers.

"That damned savage," Adelia said under her breath, and urged her horse forward up the incline so that they would reach the barbican more quickly and her daughter could be sheltered by its walls from the knowledge of what the "poppies" on the battlements were. "Barbarian. Pig. Just wait til I see the brute."

She was so tired that anger with Henry Plantagenet was the only thing keeping her in the saddle. All of them except Allie, who could sleep in the pannier attached to a horse, were exhausted — and by a journey Adelia had been loath to make.

She'd refused to accompany the soldiers

at first. "I am not going." Twice now she had served the Plantagenet in her capacity of investigator into unexplained deaths, and each time had nearly lost her own life doing it.

Emma, bless her, their contretemps forgotten, had joined the protest.

"I cannot spare this lady, she is —" Emma remembered in time that the title of doctor should not be applied to her friend. "She is attendant to my physician, the lord Mansur here."

"He comes, too." The officer's hand moved to his sword hilt as he said it, and Adelia knew he'd enforce his king's order if he had to.

Adelia had panicked. "Not without my child. I am not leaving my child." They'd have to drag her to Wales, she'd throw herself off her horse, she'd fight and scream at every step, she'd . . .

On that matter, however, the officer had been prepared to give way. "The king said as how you wouldn't."

"And I'm coming, too," Gyltha said.

The officer had nodded wearily. "King said that an' all."

They'd barely been given time to say good-bye. Concerned, Emma said, "If you can get away, I shall be at our manor with my mother-in-law. Ask for the dowager Wolvercote."

Adelia waved as one of the soldiers led her horse into a trot.

"Halfway between Wells and Glaston-bury," Emma shouted.

Adelia would have waved again, but she was now at a gallop and had to hold on with both hands.

The galloping proceeded, it seemed, for days. There was no planning for overnight stops such as Emma had made. When it was too dark to go on, they put up at whatever hostelry was available.

Their first night had been spent at a miserable tavern on the way to the Severn Estuary. It was little more than a shack where everyone slept together on one raised platform covered in straw. The next morning they were infested with fleas and Adelia found that, in their haste, the pack with her clean clothes in it had been left behind with Emma. The officer — his name was Bolt, which, Gyltha pointed out, "suits the bastard" — refused to divert to the local market where she could have purchased some sort of raiment. "Sorry, mistress. You'll have to grin and bear it."

"King's orders, I suppose," she said viciously. It was a phrase she was already sick of, and she knew she'd hear it a great deal more.

" 'S right." It wasn't that the man was unkind, but his lord king had insisted on speed, a requirement that literally overrode all others.

On reaching the Severn they'd transferred to a boat and disembarked at Cardiff Castle on the Welsh coast, their destination, only to discover that Henry had moved on with his troops.

"Been another rebellion," Bolt told them after making inquiries. "Young Geoffrey's holding out at Caerleon 'gainst another Welsh attack. The king's gone to relieve him."

"We'll have to wait here, then," Adelia had said, relieved by the thought of a rest.

"No, mistress. We'd better get on."

"Into a battle? You can't take us into danger."

Bolt was astonished by her lack of faith in Henry Plantagenet. "There won't be no battle by the time we gets there. The king'll have mopped up that load of bloody Taffies quicker'n sixpence."

And so he had, if the heads on the battlements and the quiet, darkened countryside all around were anything to go by.

Having quelled the revolt, Henry was

establishing the peace — not that there was any sign of it in barbican or bailey, both in a commotion as soldiers tried to pack up weaponry against a counterflow of clerks unpacking chests of documents, all this among braying mules, frightened, scattering hens and pigs, and a cracked voice from a high window shouting orders to those below. "Where are those bloody maps? I need more ink up here. For the love of God, will you bastards *hurry.*"

The place stank of urine and manure, nor did the smell improve as Adelia and the others were rushed up staircases and past arrow slits where archers had stood day and night repelling an encircling enemy.

The king was striding up and down a slightly less noisome though just as turbulent chamber, dictating the terms of two different treaties with two different and defeated rebel Welsh lords to two different scribes, occasionally shouting instructions out the window, while a fusty little man ran alongside him, trying to apply leeches to a bare and inflamed-looking royal arm. In a corner, a young man whom Adelia recognized as the king's illegitimate son and general-in-chief, Geoffrey, was talking to several tired-looking insigniaed men in heavy fur mantles, presumably Welsh chieftains. Pages were laying out food on a table, kicking away sniffing hounds as they did it. A line of hawks on perches were screeching and flapping their wings. Incongruously, a limp-looking man in another corner was playing a small harp and singing to it, though what it was was impossible to hear.

Captain Bolt announced the newcomers in a shout that only just penetrated the noise: "The lord Mansur, Mistress Adelia, and . . ." He looked despairingly at Gyltha, who was holding Allie. "And company."

Henry glanced up. "You took your damn time. Sit down somewhere until I've finished. . . ."

"No," Adelia said clearly.

Everybody stopped what they were doing, except the harpist, who went on quietly singing to himself.

Past caring, itching with fleas and fury, Adelia told him, "The Lord Mansur and company require a bath and a rest. And they need them now."

All eyes looked in her direction and then, in one slow movement, were turned on the king. Henry's temper when he was flouted was renowned — Thomas à Becket had died from it.

He blew out a breath. "Geoffrey."

"Yes, my lord?"

"Is there a bath in the castle?"

"I don't know, my lord." The young man's mouth twitched. "A bath wasn't, er, part of our armory."

"Better find one. And some beds."

"And clean clothes," Adelia said. "Women's."

The king sighed again. "Samite? Lace? Any particular size?"

Adelia ignored the sarcasm. "Clean will do," she said.

At the door she turned and addressed the little doctor: "And if you're supposed to be treating that wound, get those leeches off it and put on some bog moss — there's plenty of the bloody stuff in the valleys; we've been squelching through it for two days."

The bath turned out to be a washtub of enormous proportions, and the soldiers who hauled it up to the two rooms allocated to their guests at the top of a tower, along with great ewers of hot water, were out of breath and resentful when they got it there.

An inexorable Adelia sent them back down for soap and towels.

The beds, when they arrived, were rickety, but the straw and blankets that came with them were clean.

After a long night's sleep, Adelia woke up

feeling better, if chastened by the memory of her behavior toward a king whose empire stretched from the borders of Scotland to the Pyrenees. Apparently, though, it was even yet having its effect, for a polite knock on the door heralded the entrance of the emperor's bastard son, Geoffrey, still amused.

He was carrying an armful of women's clothing. "We, er, liberated these from one of the Welsh chieftain's wives," he said. "Don't worry, she has others, though I'm afraid the lady favors rather more avoirdupois than you do, but it was that or a mail shirt."

Adelia clutched her blanket more closely about her — last night she'd thrown everything she'd been wearing out the window. Luckily, Allie's extra clothes had been included in Gyltha's pack, along with Mansur's, and were fit for them to wear. "I'm grateful, my lord."

"Was the breakfast to your satisfaction? The cook's Welsh as well."

"Congratulate him for me," she said. Skewered lamb, the tastiest she'd ever eaten, along with buttermilk and a form of cake called *bara brith* so rich that even Mansur hadn't been able to finish all of it.

"Then when you're dressed, my lord king

would be happy to receive you and my lord Mansur. Only when you are ready, of course." The young man went to the door and then turned back. "Oh, and one of our lads carved this for the little one." He knelt to put his face on a level with Allie's and handed her a wooden doll.

Allie curtsied nicely. "I'll call him Poppy, like the ones on the roof."

"Poppies?"

"She's referring to the flowers decorating the battlements," Adelia said, getting angry again. "The ones separated from their stalks."

"Ah, yes." The young man's eyes were on Allie, but he spoke to Adelia. "You see, little one, they were already picked. The king doesn't take the heads off poppies unless they're dead." As he turned to leave, and Allie began playing with her doll, he added, "Hangs a few, of course, to encourage the others, but on the whole he's magnanimous to his flowers."

"Nice lad that," Gyltha said, when Geoffrey had gone. She began unfolding the clothes he'd brought. "Gawd help us."

With Mansur behind her, Adelia waded down the stairs in a skirt and bodice that had been pinned up and belted to enable her to keep them on. Since, at her age, it wasn't respectable to go bareheaded, she also wore the Welshwoman's headdress, an elaborate affair with something like curtaining on either side, which rested heavily on her ears.

Casually, to the page who was leading the way, she asked, "Is the bishop of Saint Albans in the castle?"

"He was, mistress, but he's gone to Saint David's to treat with the Welsh bishop."

The king's chamber had been cleared of chieftains and servants but retained the king, a scribe writing at the table, dogs, hawks, and the softly singing harpist. The page ushered them in, announced them, and then stood at attention with his back to the door.

Still dictating, Henry Plantagenet stumped up and down on legs that were becoming bandy from days of traveling his empire on horseback. As usual, he was dressed hardly better than one of his grooms, but, again as usual, he generated a power that sent out an almost palpable energy.

Mansur salaamed, and Henry nodded at him, then walked round Adelia, studying her swamping attire. "Can you hear me in there?"

"Yes, my lord. Thank you, my lord."

"You're a rude and graceless woman,

you know."

"Yes, my lord, I'm sorry, my lord." She looked at the king's arm on which the soft, vividly pale-green flower heads of sphagnum moss were held in place by a bandage. "How's your wound?"

"Better. Ready for some employment now?"

"I suppose so, my lord."

"See that fellow there?" The king jerked a thumb at the harpist. "Name's Rhys something-or-other. He's a bard. Comes from an unpronounceable bloody hole on the coast." He might have been introducing an interesting breed of hound. "Stand up, Rhys, and greet the lord Mansur and Mistress Aguilar." To Adelia, he said, "He started this business, so he's going to accompany you to Glastonbury."

Rhys rose and bowed vaguely in Adelia and Mansur's direction.

"Glastonbury?" Adelia was shrill. "My lord, I was already *going* to Glastonbury, or at least nearby. Lady Emma of Wolvercote and I were on our way to Wells. You could have sent a messenger and saved yourself trouble."

And me God knows how many bone-shaking miles, she thought. *What business?*

"Master Rhys is going to tell you a story,

aren't you, Rhys?" Henry said, his attention still on the bard as if about to make him do a trick for the visitors. "And in the name of God, don't *sing* it." To Adelia and Mansur, he said, "The bugger keeps *singing*."

"About Uncle Caradoc, is it?" Rhys asked.

"Of course it is, you clown. What else are you here for? Tell them."

The bard stepped forward. A thin, droop-shouldered man with protruding teeth, he put Adelia in mind of an elongated rabbit. Despite the king's injunction, his hand kept straying to his harp before he remembered and took it away again. Even so, his speaking voice, which belied his looks by being a pleasing tenor, had a lilt that was very nearly song, though the scribe at the table was unmoved by it and the bard's tale was told against the scratching of a quill, as well as the sound of soldierly activity coming through the open window from the bailey below.

So, in semi-song, Adelia and Mansur were taken back twenty years ago to when Rhys had been an adolescent at Glastonbury Abbey. "Never suited to the monastic life, me," he said. "No opportunity for true poetry."

He told them of the earthquake that had struck the Somerset Levels in which Glas-

86

tonbury stood. "Terrible, terrible it was, like the last trump trembling the heavens. . . ." A hiss from the king moved him on. "And my good uncle Caradoc, dying he was, had a waking dream . . ."

"A vision," the king said.

"Three hooded lords, see, bearing a coffin to the graveyard and burying it."

"Between the two pyramids," the king prompted.

"Two pyramids there are in the Glastonbury graveyard, very ancient, and Uncle Caradoc, he says to me, 'Look, bach, look down there in the fissure. They are showing me where Arthur takes his long rest, and by God's grace I have been witness to it. Now lettest thou thy servant depart in peace.' And He did, for beautiful, beautiful was my uncle Caradoc's ending. . . ."

"God rest him," Henry said, "and get on with it."

"And the next morning we buried that good old uncle of mine, but no sign of another coffin, only disturbed earth all over the graveyard — result of the earthquake, see. Terrible, terrible, that earthquake, like the last days. . . ."

Tapping his foot, the king said, "But you didn't pass on what Uncle Caradoc had seen, did you?"

"No, oh, no."

"We had to beat it out of him," Henry said, looking at Adelia. "He's been keeping it secret for twenty years. Only person he told was his mother." He turned back to Rhys. "And *why* did you keep it a secret?"

"Well, there." Rhys's large, vague eyes became sly. "There's some would believe . . ."

"And you're one of them, you little bastard," the king interrupted.

". . . believe as it couldn't have been the burial of King Arthur that my uncle Caradoc saw."

"And why couldn't it?"

"Well," Rhys said, still sly, "there's some credit that Arthur's only sleeping, see. In a crystal cave at Ynis-Witrin, the Isle of Glass. Avalon."

"Which is Glastonbury," Henry said briskly. He gestured to the page at the door. "Take him down to the kitchen and feed him again." To Adelia he said, "The bugger's always hungry." As the page ushered Rhys out, he shouted after him, "And don't *sing*."

When the door closed, the king said, "Well?"

"Yes, my lord," said Adelia. "But well what?"

"I'll tell you well what. He informed us of all this when we were at Cardiff — we've been dragging him round with us ever since — and right away I sent to Glastonbury's abbot and told him to set his monks digging between the two pyramids in the graveyard and find that coffin."

Adelia frowned. "So you think it was a real vision, my lord?"

"Of course it was real. The monks have found the thing." Henry waved a parchment at her, setting its large seal swinging. "This is a letter from Abbot Sigward, informing me they've dug up a coffin sixteen foot down, exactly between the pyramids. Two skeletons in it, one big, one small, Arthur *and* Guinevere, God bless her. Two for the price of one."

Adelia nodded carefully. "They dug it up *after* the fire, did they?"

"Well, of course they did — just after, otherwise the coffin would have been burned like everything else, wouldn't it?"

"I see."

Henry squinted at her. "Are you suggesting it's a fraud?"

"No, no." Nevertheless, she thought, it was a remarkably happy find for an abbey that had just lost everything else that would attract revenue.

"I'm glad to hear it. Abbot Sigward is an honorable man. He doesn't actually claim it's Arthur in that bloody coffin, but who else can it be? Haven't you read Geoffrey of Monmouth?"

She had not, hadn't needed to; she'd heard most of his book. In the forty years since Geoffrey's *History of the Kings of Britain* had been written, it had gained unstoppable popularity. Apparently recording the descent of Britain's kings over two thousand years and giving them an ancestry from the Trojans, those literate enough to read its Latin had passed on its stories to those who could not, wonderful stories of adventure and love and war and magic and religion — and most wonderful of all was the tale of King Arthur, who had stood against the pagan Saxon invaders and created a Golden Age of chivalry somewhere in the mist of Britain's Dark Ages.

Arthur had caught the country's imagination and still did. Tales of his prowess, his knights and battles, his marriage to Guinevere, her sexual treachery, were told by professional and amateur storytellers in palaces, on manors, in marketplaces, and around cottage fires.

At each inn Adelia had stayed in on her journey with Emma, somebody had been prepared to entertain the guests with one Arthurian legend or another, sometimes with embroidery that even Geoffrey of Monmouth wouldn't have recognized. More than that, nearly every town and village they'd passed through laid claim to a shred of the legend, boasting of a local Arthur's well, Arthur's chair, Arthur's table, Arthur's mount, Arthur's hill, Arthur's quoit, Arthur's hunting seat, Arthur's kitchen. . . .

His fame had even spread to the continent — Adelia could remember her foster mother in Salerno telling her about Arthur's exploits on Vesuvius. The stories appealed to women like no others; Emma adored them. "Don't you just *love* the bit where Uther Pendragon steps out of the darkness at Tintagel and seduces Ygraine?" she'd said.

"Well, yes, but isn't the account that he's taken on the appearance of her husband somewhat implausible?" Adelia had asked.

She'd been charged with lacking romance in her soul. "I suppose *you* prefer reading about boring things, like people's innards," Emma had said with some truth.

Prior Geoffrey, on the other hand, loathed the book and departed from his usual respect for the dead by heaping opprobrium on the late Geoffrey of Monmouth. "Called himself a historian?" he would say. "The man had no more idea of history than a carrot. He made it up."

It infuriated the good prior that some, especially the females, among his flock paid more attention to Geoffrey's *History* than to the Bible.

"Oh, yes, they remember the story of Arthur killing some giant who'd been slaking his lust on a fainting maiden, but quiz them on what the Parable of the Sower is about and they can't answer. Giants, I *ask* you. Geoffrey of Monmouth a great historian? Great liar, more like."

Yet here, Adelia thought, was Henry Plantagenet, most rational of men, giving credence to fairy stories and visions.

He had to have an ulterior motive.

Waiting to discover what it was, she was taken by the arm and led to the window so that she could look across the pleasant, though sadly churned up, valley of the River Usk.

"Looks quiet, doesn't it?" the king said. "But two days ago I had to carve my way through besieging Welsh lines a hundred thick to relieve young Geoffrey. And do you know whose name the bastards were shouting as we struck them down?"

"King Arthur's?"

Henry nodded. "Arthur's. The Welsh are

supposed to be a Christian race, but their pagan little minds hold Arthur as a more immediate Messiah than Jesus, God rot them. They claim him as their own. He's the one who will rescue them from what they see as the Norman yoke. And I'm not a Norman yoke, Adelia. For one thing, I'm an Angevin, and for another, I'm a bloody good peace-bringing, justice-giving king, if they'd only realize it."

She nodded. For all Henry's sins, that was what he was.

He turned away from her in order to look over his scribe's writing and point out a correction. "Four l's in Llewellyn, Robert."

Then, as if in disgust with himself for doing it, he shook his fists in the direction of the ceiling. "Why do I have to bother with spelling their damn names, eh? I've more important things to do. I've got trouble in Aquitaine, Louis of France is being his usual pain in the arse, the sodding Scots need driving back over the border . . . and where am *I?* Stuck in a bloody bog, trying to stop rebellion spreading through the entire Welsh nation." He struck the table, making the scribe's inkwell jump and spill. "I haven't got *time* to put out every little fire the belief in a living Arthur lights among the Celts. *Which it does.*" He glared at

93

Adelia as if she'd refute it. "The bloody Bretons are already threatening revolt. It'll be the sodding Cornish next. Damn all Celts."

"Ah," Adelia said. Light had dawned, hence the coffin at Glastonbury. "You need Arthur to be dead."

"Exactly." Henry's anger left him and he became persuasive. "And that's where you come in. You're my clever little mistress in the art of death. Prove those bones are King Arthur's beyond resurrection and I'll double what I pay you."

"You don't pay me," Adelia said wearily.

"Don't I? Are you sure? Well, this time you'll have a warrant enabling you and your company to receive every assistance and sustenance for as long as you require — expenses to be sent to the Exchequer."

As Adelia opened her mouth, the king's forefinger wagged it shut. "Yes, I know," he said. "Nobody's going to accept the findings of a woman, but I've seen to it. Glastonbury's been told that I'm sending them an expert in skeletons, my own Lord Mansur" — Henry bowed to the tall Arab, who salaamed back — "to authenticate the bones of King Arthur and Queen Guinevere, if indeed those are what they are. The monks won't like having a Saracen and a female on their sacred ground, but they can damn well put up with it. *And* I've sent ahead to the best inn in Glastonbury to accommodate Lord Mansur, his female assistant and interpreter, her child, and a nurse, *in luxury,* for as long as the investigation lasts. At my expense." The king was pleased with himself. "What do you say to that?"

Adelia summoned up her courage. "I don't think it can be done, my lord."

"Why not?"

"Skeletons are merely . . . skeletons. I doubt it's possible to say how old they are." She steeled herself. "Unless there's some other identification in that coffin, I cannot name those bones as Arthur's and Guinevere's. I'm sorry."

The room seemed to hunch in anticipation of the king's fury — in the past, when crossed, he'd been known to roll on the floor, biting its rushes.

But he was older now, and the anger that had caused the death of Thomas à Becket was contained — for today, at least. He nodded quietly. "I was afraid of that," he said. "Then we'll try another tactic. You'll go to Glastonbury and make sure no living person can say that those bones are *not* Arthur's."

She was puzzled. "I don't understand you, my lord."

"Yes, you do. If Glastonbury broadcasts

news of this wondrous discovery, I don't want some bugger popping up to say it's their Uncle Cedric and Aunt Priscilla in that bloody coffin. You're to find out whether anybody can refute the abbey's claim."

"How can I possibly do that?"

"I don't know, do I?" The king was exasperated. "That's why I'm employing you, for God's sake. You've got a nose for it; you can detect a puzzle like a hound sniffing the scent of boar — and solve it. I've seen you do it. You're a tracker. What I want you to do is ensure there *isn't* any scent, that there's no boar hiding in the undergrowth."

Now she understood. "You mean that as long as nobody can say those skeletons are *not* Arthur's and Guinevere's, they will be *declared* as Arthur's and Guinevere's, whether they are or aren't?"

Henry took her arm again and returned her to the window. Outside, soldiers were filling the trenches dug by the castle's besiegers; one of them was whistling as he worked. A thrush in a rowan tree was whistling back. From a fast-running stream came the jeweled flash of a diving kingfisher.

The king's voice was gentle. "You haven't ever visited Glastonbury, have you, Adelia?"

"No."

"Then wait until you do. Of all abbeys,

here or abroad, it is the holiest and most sacred; its very air is hallowed by a worship that goes back to the beginnings of Christianity and possibly beyond — it tingles with mystery. If Avalon is anywhere, it is there. If Arthur is anywhere, he is there. It has a vibration that sends you to your knees." The king paused, his eyes on the river. "And it's been kind to me. Abbot Sigward was one of the few churchmen not calling for my head after . . . the business at Canterbury."

He never spoke the name of the man who'd been his friend but who, having been appointed Archbishop of Canterbury, had turned against him, opposing every reasonable reform he'd tried to make, and whose murder had brought Christendom's vilification on his head and been the excuse for his jealous wife and his even more jealous eldest son to rise against him.

It had sullied his name forever, and he knew it; history would remember him as the king who'd martyred Saint Thomas à Becket.

Not for the first time, Adelia was aware of the depth of suffering that underlay this Plantagenet's energetic exterior — it was like being reminded that beyond a briskly choppy inlet was a turbulent ocean. His remorse at calling for Becket's death, that it was his knights who, with their own reasons for hating the archbishop, had ridden off to Canterbury and spilled the man's brains onto the floor of the cathedral, had been terrible — and the Church had made sure he displayed every ounce of it in public. His penance had been to walk barefoot to Canterbury and present his naked back to its monks to be whipped.

"And whip him they did," Prior Geoffrey, who'd been present, had told Adelia. "With enjoyment. Their scourges bit deep into his flesh, so that those of us who witnessed it were amazed he did not cry out. He stayed silent, though he will bear the stripes on his back forever."

By humiliating himself, the king had saved England from a worse punishment, appeasing an angry Pope Gregory, who had otherwise threatened to lay the country under interdict: a closure of its churches, a refusal to bless marriages, christen babies, hear confessions, anoint the sick and dying — in effect, the excommunication of an entire nation.

Yes, Adelia thought with pity, Henry Plantagenet had paid for his temper so that his people didn't have to.

He became brisk. "In turn, I must be kind to Glastonbury — it's got to be rebuilt.

When I can spare him, I'll send Ralph Fitz-Stephen — he's my chamberlain — to see what needs a-doing. It'll be costly, you can swear to that; God knows how much I'll have to spend. Unless . . ."

"Unless the pilgrims go flooding back in their thousands to visit Arthur's tomb," Adelia said, and smiled. Oh, he was a canny king.

"Exactly."

She thought about it. Almost Henry was asking the impossible — but not quite. While she would not be able to date the skeletons, the coffin was another matter. "When was Arthur supposed to have lived?" she asked.

The king turned to the table. "When was it, Robert?"

The scribe laid down his pen and pursed his lips. "The Welsh cleric Nennius tells us in *Historia Brittonum* that Arthur's last battle was at Mons Badonicus, where he single-handedly slew nine hundred and sixty men. Saint Gildas, who, as we know, lies in Glastonbury Abbey, informs us that this battle took place in the year of his birth, which, we believe, was either in the Year of Our Lord 494 or 506, though the *Annales Cambriae* places it somewhat later, while the . . ."

"All right, *all right.*" The king turned back

to Adelia. "Somewhere early in the sixth century — do you want the day of the month?"

"Hmm." A coffin found sixteen feet deep in the earth would likely be very ancient. "Does Glastonbury earth consist of peat?"

"How in hell would I know?"

The scribe intervened. "I believe it may, my lord. It is surrounded by marshland, which would indicate . . ."

"It's peat," the king said. "What's that got to do with the price of fish?"

Nothing, but it did have to do with the preservation of wood. In the Cambridgeshire fens, which were all of peat, a piece of bog oak would occasionally surface in an area where no oaks grew. According to fenland belief, the number of rings apparent in the wood of the trunk when it was cut indicated the years during which the tree had stood when it was growing. By that system of accounting, some pieces had proved so old as to have flourished in the long distant past.

"Is the coffin of oak, do you know?"

"No, I *don't*." The king was becoming impatient.

If it was, and if her fenlanders were right, she might be able to gain a rough, *very* rough, idea of when the coffin had been interred, perhaps as long ago as Arthur's time — and therefore beyond anybody's knowledge as to whom it contained.

She considered. The king was assigning her a task that, for once, had no risk to it and would enable her, Mansur, Allie, and Gyltha to be sustained until she could decide what to do with the rest of her life.

Actually, Adelia was intrigued, not so much by the search for an ancient and mystical king — though that, too — but as to why a woman had been put to rest in a monastic graveyard.

"Very well," she said. "I will try and ensure that the skeletons are old enough to be beyond identification, but further than that I cannot go. I will not say they are Arthur's and Guinevere's, because I doubt if anybody can. I won't lie for you, Henry."

"Or *to* me?"

She smiled at him. "Never that."

"I know," he said. "One of the few." If Henry Plantagenet hadn't been who he was, Adelia might have suspected that the sudden blur in the royal blue eyes came from tears.

He rallied. She was given a royal kiss on the cheek and a royal slap on the back. Robert the scribe was set to writing a warrant investing "my best beloved Lord Mansur and his interpreter, Mistress Adelia Aguilar" with almost enough power to raise an army and invade France.

But as always when he thought he was being overgenerous to her, the king made her pay for it.

"By the way," he said, dangerously casual. "Glastonbury and the bishopric of Wells have always been at daggers drawn — and now Glastonbury is saying that Wells bribed some poacher to set the fire. If I don't intervene, the Pope will — and I'm not putting up with an interfering Vatican. Bloody prelates, more trouble than they're worth. I'm sending a peacemaker down to get both of the buggers to kneel to me and promise to be good." The blue eyes became wicked. "Guess who the peacemaker's going to be. Go on, guess."

"The bishop of Saint Albans," she said dully.

"The very same." Henry, who had no more chastity than a tomcat, reveled in his favorite bishop's sexual dilemma.

Don't, she thought. *Leave us alone; we have come to terms. Rowley must serve God, I must serve medicine, and the two are incompatible.*

Not getting a rise out of her, Henry persisted. "I expect you'll meet."

"No, my lord," she said, "we won't."

"Still keeping to his oath of chastity, is he?"

She didn't answer, and he had to let her go.

On the way back up the staircase, she realized that neither she nor the king had consulted Mansur on an investigation in which, to all intents and purposes, he was to play the leading part. Not that there had been any choice in the matter — the king was the king.

"What is your opinion, my dear friend?"

"You answered wisely," he said. "Truth is the salt of mankind; we cannot proffer sand."

"I don't intend to. But about the vision . . . ?"

"There *are* true visions," Mansur said. "Did not Khadija, the Pure One, may the peace and blessings of Allah be upon her, see an angel guarding the Prophet with its wings?"

"Did she?"

Then who was Adelia to doubt the testimony of a monk from Glastonbury and Mohammed's first wife?

FIVE

They reined in their horses at a bridge outside the gates that led to Wolvercote Manor and stayed there for some minutes, looking beyond its lodge to the house.

Somerset had displayed richness of countryside and property from the moment they'd crossed its border but nothing, so far, quite as pleasing to the eye as this place in which Emma had said she intended to make her home. It was like coming upon Arcadia.

A rectangular house of yellow stone tucked among stables and barns and trees with the tower of a domestic church rising beyond jumbled roofs of tiny slates, its wide-mouthed, chevroned doorway and mullioned windows smiled out across a moat in which it was exactly reflected. Against the setting sun, pigeons exited and landed in the little arched entrances of a cote built in the shape of a pepper pot.

Whichever ancestral Norman built this, Adelia thought, had been a nicer person than its late owner — the unlamented Lord Wolvercote's taste would have run to a spiky grandeur.

"Don't know as I'd mind having that ol' cottage if as they'd give it me," Gyltha said.

Adelia agreed; usually, she didn't care where she lived as long as it was clean and functional and safe, but the charm of Wolvercote inspired in her a sudden and unwonted envy of Emma for possessing it.

They had come here instead of going straight to Glastonbury, partly because the road from Wells, to which their route from Wales had led them first, practically passed the manor's approach, but mostly because Adelia was impatient to see Emma and tell her of the happy coincidence that would make them neighbors for a while. Also, she wanted to check on Roetger's heel. It was June now, and they'd said good-bye in May.

The sky remained cloudless, and in such fields as could be seen over fruiting hedges, brown-faced, sweating men and women were cutting hay, causing an itchy, sweet-smelling dust to join that sent up by horses' hooves meeting the dried surface of the roads.

Anyway, it would be getting dark by the

time the cavalcade could reach the Pilgrim Inn at Glastonbury, which, for all the luxury Henry Plantagenet claimed for it, could hardly provide the comfort to hot, dusty, hungry, and thirsty travelers that Emma would extend to them.

King Arthur, Adelia thought, could wait; he'd waited some six hundred years — another day here or there wouldn't hurt him.

She nodded at Captain Bolt to lead the way over the bridge. So that she'd be safe on the journey, the king had given her a military escort of half a dozen men, which included a trumpeter to blow a fanfare announcing her coming wherever she went. She'd be arriving in style.

The gatekeeper of Wolvercote's lodge was suitably impressed and, when Bolt ordered him to tell the lady of the house that the Lord Mansur, Mistress Adelia, and their train wished to be received, went scampering across the moat's pretty little bridge with his instructions.

His manner on his return was constrained. Awkwardly, he announced, "My lady will be pleased to admit my lord Mansur and Mistress Adelia, but their escort must remain here."

Odd, Adelia thought. Perhaps Emma was

being careful and wanted to be sure that the soldiers were friendly.

The gatekeeper winced slightly as Adelia gestured to Gyltha, who had Allie bouncing in her horse's pannier, to follow them; she wasn't going to leave those two behind.

A steward with a wand of office bowed the four of them into a hall as pleasantly proportioned as the house's exterior.

Here, sun came only in shafts through the high windows. The thick stone of the walls, which was so warm outside, cooled the air, giving the room the greenish tint of a rock pool. A lovely oak staircase and fireplace, the furniture, and the setts of a rush-free floor gleamed with the deep patina of a century's careful polishing. Perhaps too many scarlet and silver Wolvercote battle flags, some of them tattered, hanging from the timber-and-plastered ceiling took away from the room's peace, but, presumably, Emma hadn't yet had time to get rid of them.

"My lady begs you to wait," the steward said. "She is employed in the solar going over the accounts with her cellarer but will attend you shortly."

Again, odd, *very* odd. The Emma of old would have come rushing downstairs to meet them. Surely she wasn't still jealous?

Adelia gave Gyltha an interrogative look. Gyltha shrugged.

They were left alone. After about a quarter of an hour, the steward appeared with cups and a jug of cooled ale on a tray, begged them to refresh themselves, and left.

More minutes went by without Emma's appearance, or anybody else's. Allie employed her time by climbing on an oak settle and jumping off it. There was no sign that another child was in the house; the only sound was the swish of a blade as somebody outside was cutting the grass.

Adelia became cross; this was deliberate rudeness. She went to the stairs to go up them, but at that moment a door at the top opened. A man with an apron came hurrying down, a ledger under his arm, doffed his cap to Adelia, and went out.

Another figure emerged onto the landing above. "Yes?" asked a female voice.

Adelia gave a brief bow and introduced herself and her companions. "Since the lord Mansur speaks little English, I am his interpreter, mistress," she said. "We are here to see Lady Wolvercote."

"I am Lady Wolvercote."

"Ah." This was the mother-in-law, then — a somewhat younger, well-dressed, and very much more formidable figure than the doting grandmother who'd taken shape in Adelia's optimistic mind. Emma herself must be out somewhere.

That the woman coming down the stairs was mother to the rebellious murderer Henry had hanged, there was no doubt. She was nearly as tall, with the same imperious, handsome features. Dark eyes exactly like those of the man who had once dubbed Adelia a witch looked down at her now, and with something of the same distaste.

Adelia remembered that though Emma had never met her husband's mother, she'd been impressed by her Norman ancestry, which went back to long before the Conquest. "She's descended from Rollo the Ganger," Emma had said admiringly.

Adelia hadn't seen what was wonderful about descent from a Viking who had harried and pillaged Normandy until it was surrendered to him, but Emma, being the child of a tradesman, though a rich one, set store by noble heredity and seemed to think it added value to young Pippy's descent, especially as it came down to him via the female line and not by way of his hated father's.

This woman set store by it, too. Her look made Adelia conscious of the clothing she herself had managed to acquire on the journey — certainly better than that of the Welsh chieftain's wife but still of very ordinary quality. However, she said politely, "I address the dowager Lady Wolvercote, do I?"

"You do not. I am *the* Lady Wolvercote. There is no other."

"I mean your daughter-in-law, lady."

"My daughter-in-law died five years ago."

That was partly true, of course; Wolvercote *had* been previously married before forcibly wedding Emma, though the wife had died without bearing him any children.

Oh, dear, was this woman, too, going to oppose Emma's claim to the manor? God prevent there having to be *another* trial by combat.

"I mean Emma, Lady Wolvercote," Adelia persisted.

"I know of no such person."

Adelia tried to be patient; the woman still wore mourning for her son, though her black silk bliaut allowed a scarlet underdress to peep through at the neck and skirt, echoing the colors of the Wolvercote battle flags.

"She sent you a letter . . . a sweet letter, I saw it . . . from Aylesbury. To say she would be coming."

Lady Wolvercote inclined her head. "A letter arrived a while ago from a creature claiming to be my son's wife — some whore, no doubt, trying to extract money."

"No," Adelia said, quietly, "she was not. She was bringing your grandson to meet you."

"Then she would have wasted her breath. I receive no bastards in this house."

The woman used the words "whore" and "bastard" without anger, as if she was merely stating facts. At no point did her expression change to wrinkle the excellent skin of her pale face, nor did her bejeweled folded hands make any gesture; her voice was as level as if she was giving everyday instructions to a servant. It was like exchanging remarks with a speaking statue. When she turned her head to look at Allie, who was making another attempt on the settle, Gyltha hurried forward in rescue, as if afraid the gaze would petrify the child into stone.

"Are you telling me that you didn't receive her?" Adelia asked. "When was this?"

"Am I not making myself clear?" Lady Wolvercote said. "There has been no encounter between me and the female you mention."

"She didn't come? Didn't arrive at all?"

"I have said so."

"Then where is she?"

"I do not know," Lady Wolvercote said. "Nor do I care." She went to a table and rang the small brass bell that stood on it.

Immediately, the steward was in the room. "My lady?"

"Take these people to the kitchen, John. See they receive the usual sustenance before they go. Also, you may carry food and ale to the creatures at the gate, but do not allow them inside — I will have none of the Plantagenet's rabble in this house."

She turned to go.

This was frightening. "But . . . but she *must* have turned up," Adelia said in desperation. "She was on her way here. Where is she?"

The only answer was the brisk tap of Lady Wolvercote's shoes on the risers of the staircase as she went up them.

As the door of the solar shut quietly behind its mistress, the steward stepped forward. "If you would come this way . . ."

"To the kitchen?" Gyltha shouted at him, as if she was above such places. "We ain't coming to no bloody kitchen. You can stuff —"

Adelia put out a hand to stop the inevitable invective; though deeply disturbed, she was trying to keep her head. "We would

112

be grateful for a supper before we go," she told the steward meekly, "and so would our men."

As they followed the steward, Gyltha gave her a look worthy of the gorgon who'd just left them. "You toleratin' this?"

"Yes. We may learn something." The servants were likely to know what had happened. Refused entry, Emma would not have gone quietly; people must have heard the argument — that encounter between mother-in-law and daughter-in-law would have been a case of Greek meeting Greek, the only trouble being that the marble-faced Greek upstairs had the advantage of possession.

As they were led through the hall's serving door and across a courtyard, Adelia asked Mansur quietly in Arabic, "What do you think happened?"

"A coldhearted bint that one, but why should she lie?"

That was what was so worrying: If Lady Wolvercote *had* thrown Emma out of her house, she would not, Adelia felt, have had any compunction in saying so. In which case, Emma had not reached Wolvercote Manor at all. It might be that she had delayed her visit for some reason — but for a *month?* Or, and this was the worst possible explanation, she and the others had been attacked somewhere on the road to Wells.

However shaming it was to be fed in the kitchen like a beggar, it would be an opportunity to ask questions, and Adelia was prepared to suffer humiliation if she could find out what had happened to her friends.

They crossed a courtyard to a square, pretty building in the same stone as the house and with an octagonal roof. The heat coming out of its open door was nearly enough to send its visitors teetering backward.

"Perhaps you would prefer to sit on the lawn and eat," the steward suggested.

Gyltha said with energy that she would prefer to eat with the soldiers at the gate and marched off, pulling Allie along with her.

Adelia and Mansur braved the kitchen. A single aperture near the roof allowed more smoke out than light in, leaving two fires set into the walls to illuminate a scene like Vulcan's forge. A man stripped to the waist, his skin gleaming with sweat, retrieved rounded loaves from an oven with the aid of an enormous spatula. Other figures were setting a table in the center of the room with a surprisingly dainty collation of carved chicken and ham, flaked trout, preserves, scones, butter, and honey.

A pewter jug held wine, another ale, but when Mansur shook his head at both and Adelia explained that alcohol was unacceptable to his religion, one of the servants was dispatched to fetch cooled barley water from a cellar.

Obviously, the immutable law of hospitality to travelers, however base, was one the descendant of Rollo the Ganger had trained her staff not to break. Which in itself was concerning because if Emma and her party had arrived on the Wolvercote threshold, the people in this kitchen would have known about it — and they didn't.

Or they said they didn't.

Adelia questioned them as a group and then individually. "Have you heard of or seen a lady traveling with attendants in the area? She is young and fair and has a two-year-old child with her. Did she come here?"

She was competing for their attention with Mansur, whose robe and kaffiyeh with its golden-roped agal around his head seemed to engross and almost frighten them, as if an angel or demon had sprung through the door. The brilliant whiteness of his clothes — how he kept them so clean while traveling, Adelia had never fathomed — was always noticeable, but in ports like Cambridge where the occasional Arab trader came and went, his appearance did not excite quite so much curiosity. Here in the depths of the country, they had never seen anything like him.

"A lady," Adelia reiterated, "with a child. In a traveling cart. Horses, maids, grooms, a priest."

For a moment, the man shoveling the loaves swiveled around to look at her and she went expectantly toward him, but he shook his head and turned back to his bread.

No, no, they had seen nobody like that. The boy turning a spit crossed his fingers while making his denial, and a maid was taken with hysterical giggles, but these responses Adelia, again, had to attribute to Mansur's presence. She gave up.

She tried questioning the steward when he led the two of them to the gates. He shook his head. "No, mistress, we have received no one of that description."

"I didn't ask if she was received, I want to know if she came here."

"No, mistress, I'm sorry."

Yet there was *something. . . .*

Captain Bolt and his men were sitting on the grass under the trees by the side of the lane, their horses casting long shadows against the setting sun. They had eaten and drunk well, but the captain was displeased; his mounts had barely been able to get enough water from the nearby stream, which the summer had reduced to a trickle. "Wouldn't let us in through the gates to get to a trough. Somerset hospitality? I spit on it."

He was unmoved by the fact that Emma and her party were missing.

"Couldn't you send one of your lads into Wells?" Adelia pleaded. "They may be putting up at one of the inns there."

"I reckon as that bitch has eaten 'em," Gyltha said, and met Adelia's glare with "Well, I wouldn't put it past her."

"No, I couldn't, mistress," Bolt said. "You seen how many inns that town's got? Going down High Street alone we must've passed dozens. I can't spare a man or the time."

As usual, he was in a rush; his orders were to deliver Adelia and company intact to Glastonbury, see them safely installed, and then return to the king as fast as possible. Looking for lost ladies was not in his brief.

"You could send *him*," he said, jerking a thumb to where Rhys the bard was sprawled in the shade of an oak, a flask of ale by his side, a chicken leg in one hand, the other rippling the strings of the harp held between his knees. "I can spare *him*."

They all could. At first the Welshman's playing and singing had sweetened the journey, but as Captain Bolt said of him with complaint, "He don't do anything *else*."

And it was true — as an aid in the tasks of traveling Rhys was useless. Asked to fetch or carry something, he invariably dropped it. Since most of his life had been spent on foot or bareback Welsh ponies, horses alarmed him to an extent that he wouldn't or couldn't tighten their girths or put a bit in their mouths, thus necessitating one of the soldiers to do it for him.

What he *could* do, amazingly, was attract women. Having eaten prodigiously of the supper provided by whatever inn they'd put up at, he managed to vanish and, before they could proceed in the morning, there had to be a search for him, which invariably ended in some female's bedroom. It sent Captain Bolt mad. "How does he *do* it?"

Adelia didn't know, either, but there was no denying that bucktoothed, vague, and none too clean though Rhys was, his music sent a maiden's knees wobbling, along with her virginity.

Mansur despised him, perhaps because

Gyltha, usually irritated by inefficiency, showed a sentimental forbearance of the man. "He's worth it for that lovely voice," she'd say, tenderly making sure his plate was fuller than anybody else's.

Allie was his slave, as he was hers. The only night on which he hadn't pursued his amours had been when the child, having eaten some unripe crab apples lying in an orchard, was taken with a nasty stomach-ache. He'd stayed by her bed, soothing her with a song celebrating the Arab star Almeisan, after which she was named.

Adelia was prepared to forgive him a great deal after that, though occasionally, when he'd once more reduced Captain Bolt to apoplexy, she wondered why on earth Henry had sent the bard with her.

"Because he wanted to get rid of him, that's why," was Bolt's response. "Couldn't give him back to the damned Welsh, could he?"

No, presumably, he couldn't. Rhys's fellow countrymen wouldn't look kindly on a man who presented the English king with a dead Arthur.

However it was, there was no use sending him to look for Emma. Even if Wells locked up all its daughters, it was doubtful he could find his way back.

There was nothing for it at the moment but to go on to Glastonbury and hope to locate Emma through more inquiries.

It was a winding road leading them there, and as darkness fell, it was empty of traffic.

The law ordering that verges be cleared of trees by the length of a bow shot so that travelers were not vulnerable to a surprise attack had been ignored here. And ignored for some years — the cavalcade rode through avenues that branched overhead, hiding the moon.

Torches and lanterns were lit, swords were drawn, silence demanded, the mounts slowed to walking pace — it had been known for robbers to bring down cantering horses by putting a wire across the road. Gyltha and Adelia, with a sleeping, pan-niered Allie, found themselves hemmed in by their escorts as they rode — and were glad of it. Rhys nudged his horse between theirs; the only weapon he had was his harp.

Michael, the trumpeter, muttered, "Most dangerous bit o' road in England this, so I heard."

"Why?" Adelia whispered back.

"Wolf. Outlaw. They call him Wolf acause he's a animal though he runs on two legs, and a pack with him. They say . . ."

But Captain Bolt hushed them. He was

listening to the hundred rustles that came from among trunks turned ghastly by the glare of the torches, his sword twitching toward the reflected green of animals' eyes that peered out at them from the undergrowth.

At one point, Adelia heard the sound of a cough from somewhere among the trees, but whether it came from a human throat or not she couldn't tell.

Wolf.

Because she was tired and scared, she became angry. Bolt should have taken them back to sleep over at Wells so that they could have made this ride in the daytime. Damn the man for refusing another delay. Always wanting to gallop back to his damn king, damn him.

And damn that female back there. Had she sent Emma and little Pippy out into another such dangerous night? She'd said she hadn't. Mansur didn't think she had. But there'd been a sense of suffocation in that pretty house *and* in its kitchen, a truth being choked.

Oh, God, suppose the hag was keeping them imprisoned? *Worse* than imprisoned?

No, this was the thinking of fatigue.

But there'd been something. . . . She kept remembering the eyes of the man at the bread oven when he'd turned to look at her. *Something . . .*

Damn it, how long before they reached Glastonbury? It was supposed to be only a few miles from Wells, but there was no sign of habitation ahead.

The only indication that they'd reached it was the sudden clatter of their horses' hooves on stone. No signpost, but there was a gap in the forest to their right. The men's torches showed a steep, cobbled hill that leveled out at the bottom, where moonlight shone on water.

"That's it," Bolt said. "Must be. That'll be the River Brue down there — comes right up to the abbey, I was told — but where *is* the abbey?"

Where, indeed? As one of the biggest, busiest, richest foundations in England, owning a good deal of Somerset and beyond, it should have shown some sign of activity even at this time of night, however much the fire had damaged it.

It wasn't until they began to go down the hill that Adelia fully realized the extent of the catastrophe that had overwhelmed the place. On the left, they were following what had been the monastery's great boundary wall, now a blackened, tumbled collection of stones with silence beyond it.

As pitiable — and nobody had mentioned this — flames had also leaped the wall to consume the little town that lay outside it. For on the right as they rode, torchlight fell on naked spars that had been the thatched shops and cottages belonging to laypeople serving both the abbey and the pilgrims who had come to worship at its shrines.

Here had once been a busy high street; now the smitch of ash hung acrid on its air; apart from the moon, there was no light anywhere, no activity, only silence. Adelia heard Captain Bolt say incredulously, making a sign of the cross, "God have mercy, it's dead. Glastonbury's dead."

Toward the bottom of the hill, where it met the river to flatten into a wide, paved market square and quay, the abbey wall remained intact and so, opposite, did a three-story building — proximity to water and the fact that it was built of stone had preserved it to be all that was left of a thriving town. Again, there was no sign of occupation; the frontage, with its stout door leading out onto the street, was dark, but Captain Bolt's lamp shone on a wide, high entrance arch to the right and, above it, carved into the lintel, was the unmistakable figure of a man in a brimmed hat carrying a scrip.

They had found the Pilgrim Inn.

Wheeling to go under the arch, the cavalcade entered a large, deserted courtyard formed by outbuildings and, on the left, the inn itself — from which the light of a single candle shone through the boards of one of the windows' shutters.

"God be thanked," Captain Bolt said. He dismounted and began hammering on the Pilgrim's side door.

Inside, a dog began barking. The candle above was snuffed out. There was a creak, as if somebody had opened the shutter the tiniest crack — other than that, nothing happened.

Adelia and Gyltha were lifted from the saddles, and their horses were led to drink along with the others at a trough standing by the head of a well. Two soldiers began investigating the stables and a barn.

"Open up there. Open in the name of the king." Captain Bolt was losing his temper.

A quavering voice came from the window, just audible over the barking. "I'll set the dogs on you. I warn ye, we'm armed in here."

"So are we out here," the captain yelled. "Open this door before I take a bloody ram to it."

Somewhat late in the day, Michael the

124

trumpeter remembered his office and blew a call that sent stately notes echoing around the walls, though their only effect was to set the dog barking again and startle a barn owl into clattering flight from its perch in the stables.

"All right, then," Captain Bolt said, looking around. "Find something to break this bloody door down."

At that the door opened an inch and the same voice asked, "Who are you?"

"Who are *you?*"

"Godwyn, sir. Landlord of this inn."

"We're king's men," the captain told him. He snapped his fingers at Adelia, who began searching through her saddlebag for the royal warrant. "You've received an order from King Henry saying as he was billeting guests on you, and don't say as you didn't, acause the messenger came back to say he'd delivered it."

The door opened wider, allowing Bolt's lamp to illuminate a short, rotund, barefoot man in his nightshirt, holding back a single slavering dog by its collar. "That was a month ago," he said. "No guests has come. No guests." He was trembling.

"They have now." The captain took the warrant from Adelia's hand and waved it under the man's nose. "The lord Mansur

— he's that Saracen gentleman over there, like it says on this scroll. Come to" — Bolt shifted his lantern so that he could read the writing on the warrant — " 'make inquiry into the recent findings at Glastonbury Abbey by permission of Henry, King of England, and his right beloved Abbot Sigward.' This lady here's Mistress Adelia, as is also mentioned, and likewise her companion, Mistress Gyltha, and there's . . . Hello, what's wrong with him, then?"

Godwyn the landlord had fainted.

Six

How it was done, Adelia never knew, because *while* it was being done, she and Gyltha and Allie dozed on a pile of hay in an empty stable, but by the morning, with the help of Mansur and the soldiers, Landlord Godwyn and his wife had brought their dead inn to life.

Everybody had been allocated rooms with comfortable beds, clean blankets, and warm water for washing. There was even breakfast for all set out on the vast table in the guest's parlor, a cavern of a room off the passage that led to the front door.

Hilda, the landlady, apologized for it. "Just porridge, cheese, and pickled eel, and a couple of coddled eggs each, for which I'm sorry, sirs and ladies, there being no suppliers in town anymore and six of our hens gone to the fox, God rot it, but later on, Godwyn'll row over to Godney and fetch proper provisions."

Since there was fresh, crusty bread to go with the meal, Godwyn, who did the cooking, had already managed to heat ovens, make dough, and let it rise before baking. Both he and his wife, Adelia thought, must have spent the early hours laboring like Trojans.

"I am sorry we alarmed Master Godwyn," she said to Hilda.

"Very impressible in his humors, our Godwyn," his wife said. " 'Twas a shock, what with thinking you was robbers and us not expecting guests, there not having been any since the fire, and no one arriving after the king's letter, the which we thought he'd forgotten and there was none to come. . . ."

She was a thin, jolly, freckled woman of middle age, taller than her husband, talking all the time while she served the table, never still, regretting that the Pilgrim wasn't up to its old standard, promising better.

The fire had emptied Glastonbury, she said. Most of the monks had already departed on missions around the country to raise money for the abbey's rebuilding. As for the townspeople, some had left forever, others had scattered to find work locally until they could return to restore the homes and shops they'd lost.

"The which is a waste of time," Hilda said

128

briskly, "seeing as how there won't be no trade until the pilgrims start a-coming again. The *which*" — and here she turned eager eyes on Mansur — "they will when they hear as King Arthur and his lady lies in our graveyard."

Adelia sighed. Obviously, it had been impossible to keep the matter quiet in such a small, depleted community, but to have its only expectation resting on her shoulders would be a burden. She hoped she would not be forced to disappoint it; the courage Hilda was showing in adversity was admirable.

"Course, you know who done it, don't you?" the landlady asked.

"Done what?" Bolt asked.

"Brought this calamity on us deliberate, lost us our living, killed our abbey, killed *us*." For a moment, Hilda's briskness went and her face withered as if all the juice had been sucked out of it, leaving it old and malignant. "Bishop of Wells," she said.

"A bishop?" Captain Bolt choked over his porridge. "A bishop set the fire?"

"Not him personal, but at his orders," Hilda told him. "What we want to know is, where's that useless falconer? Oh, yes, the bishop may say as he was dismissed from Wells for being that he turned to drink, but they'd been close — nobody closer than a hunting bishop and his falconer, lessen it's his huntsman. And where did that rascal come to, begging to be taken on after the bishop turned him out? To my dear abbot, that's who. And what happened but three weeks after that? The fire. That's what happened." Hilda's eyes compressed to stop tears from coming. "Glastonbury's murdered and Wells flourishes, and no sign of Useless Eustace since. For why? Because the bishop's spirited him away so's he can't be made to confess."

Inevitably there would be a scapegoat, Adelia thought. When whole towns became a furnace, as they sometimes did, as this one had, it was either put down to God's punishment of wickedness — and Glastonbury was regarded as too holy for that — or to arson. There had to be blame; it was too banal that such suffering was caused by the accidental fall of a lighted candle.

To divert a complaint that could carry on for a long time, and because anxiety for Emma gnawed at her, Adelia asked, "By any chance have you heard of a lady with a child and a wounded knight traveling in the vicinity? She was making for Wolvercote Manor but doesn't seem to have arrived there."

Hilda sat herself down at the table to think

about it. "Lady and a wounded knight, you say?"

"He's a foreigner, a German."

"No-o-o, can't say as I have. I do hope as nothing has happened to your lady, for the roads ain't safe anymore, what with men have lost their living and turned to robbery — and worse nor robbery, the which there's travelers having their throats cut over there by Wells, like it wasn't enough to lose their purses but their lives as well, poor things."

"That road from Wells is a right disgrace," Captain Bolt said through a mouthful of porridge. "Trees up to its edges, there's bound to be robbers. Who's to catch them in that forest? I wonder as the abbot don't make it safer."

Hilda turned on him. "Don't you blame my dear abbot, don't you dare. He'd make all safe for everybody, God bless him, but that's Wells forest — well, the king's really — but the bishop does his hunting in it and won't have a twig touched in case it upsets the deer. Oh, if I was a swearing woman, I'd tell you things about the bishop of Wells. . . ."

She proceeded to do so — at length.

The enmity of Glastonbury for Wells, and Wells for Glastonbury, was not just between their churchmen but, according to Hilda, had existed for years among the people of the two towns. Wells had always been jealous of its famous neighbor. "Them Wellsians ain't Christians, and I'd be sorrier for them when they come to the Seat of Judgment if they didn't deserve every flame in hell."

The bishop of Saint Albans, Adelia thought, was going to have his work cut out when he came to make peace between the two.

Captain Bolt cut the diatribe short. Despite only a couple of hours' sleep, he was taking his soldiers back to Wales immediately.

Adelia was amused to hear him quibbling over the bill for accommodating his men. "I'll expect you to charge the king only half a night's tariff, Mistress Hilda, that being all as we spent in our beds, seeing as how we had to set 'em up. *And* we saw to our own stabling — you can't expect the Exchequer to pay for comforts not provided."

Like king, like captain, Adelia thought.

And then she thought, *Damn Henry, he's done it* again.

There'd been a sharp exchange between her and the Plantagenet before she left him. "*My lord, I am* not *going to Glastonbury penniless and with only a paper warrant. Sup-*

pose there's an emergency necessitating cash?"

"Emergency? It's a holiday I'm giving you, woman."

In the end she'd managed to inveigle two silver pounds out of him, which — because he didn't carry money — he'd had to borrow from a reluctant chamberlain. Now at least one of those pounds would have to go to a landlord who'd otherwise be forced to accommodate her on credit that his devastated inn could ill afford to extend — it took a long time before anybody received payment from tightfisted Henry's equally tightfisted Exchequer.

Nevertheless, she was sorry to see Bolt go; she'd come to like him, impatient as he was, as well as his men.

She was touched to find that he'd already reconnoitered the abbey on her behalf and told its abbot to look out for her.

They all went out into the courtyard to wave the men off, leaving only Rhys still eating at the table.

"And when it's time for you to go," Bolt told Adelia, "the king says as you're to send to Bishop Rowley in Wells for an escort to wherever you're heading."

When hell grows icicles, she thought.

But she nodded.

"And make sure as you don't go wandering alone, not even in daylight."

"Oh, we shall be safe enough here, Captain."

He swung himself into the saddle. Then, for such a down-to-earth man, he said a surprising thing: "I ain't so sure. That fire did more damage than we know, I reckon. Something's gone out of this place and something else has come in."

Rhys accompanied them when they set off for the abbey. "Better pay my respects to Uncle Caradoc's grave," he said. Apparently, he was going to sing to it; he was bringing his harp.

Hilda came, too, carrying a heavy covered basket; so did Godwyn, though only as far as the short walk to the quayside, where a little way away from the quay a boathouse stood. The inn's rowing boat was tied to a pier. He was going to fetch supplies.

"Don't forget, now," Hilda shouted after him, "venison if they've got it and a good ham. And bring back the girl." To Adelia she said, "We'll be needing some help now, and Millie's a hard worker, even if she be half-witted. . . ."

She went on talking, describing the staff they'd had in the days when pilgrims flooded in, and the grandeur of some of their visitors. "Yes, Queen Eleanor's own ladies-in-waiting, there not being any room for them in the abbey's guesthouse; oh, yes, the Pilgrim's known its share of the nobility. . . ."

Adelia barely listened. She was entranced by the view from the quayside of what lay beyond it. Here at her feet was the River Brue, wending its way like a shining blue piece of marquetry set into a watery, untidy, reed-filled expanse stretching to the horizon. Seagulls wheeled in air that had a touch of salt in it — somewhere in that immense distance was the Severn Estuary and, beyond that, the Celtic Sea, only just being kept at bay by this flat, indeterminate meeting of earth and sky.

Allie was bouncing with joy. "It's like home, Mama." She switched to Arabic: "Can we go fishing, Mansur? Can we?" Back at Waterbeach, the two of them had provided the household's fish meals. She returned to English: "And, look, there's a man walking on stilts, like they do at home. Can I have some stilts, Mama? Can I?"

"No, you can't, missie." Hilda was suddenly severe. "Less'n you know the trackways, there's bog out there as'll suck you down and fill that little nose of yours with mud so's you won't ever breathe again."

"No need to frighten the child," Gyltha snapped, and Allie added, defiantly, "I'm not frightened. I'm a fenlander, I am."

"Don't care what you are," Hilda told her. "Them's the Avalon marshes and there's bugaboos out there."

They weren't as beautiful as the fens, Adelia thought, being almost treeless, but she knew how her daughter felt; that solitary stilt walker, like an awkward heron against the skyline, was a reminder of home, where men and women used stilts to stride ancient paths hidden under peat and shallow water. Out there was not only an enormous cornucopia of fish and fowl and fuel but also endless entertainment — a pelican rising with a flapping trout in its beak, as one was doing at this moment, otters sliding down banks for the fun of it, darting dragonflies, beavers building a dam, time-wasting marvels that had kept her and Allie entranced for hours.

Hilda, probably rightly, for marshland *was* a dangerous place to the uninitiated, was still trying to scare Allie away from it. "There's will-o'-the-wisps with lights to lure you into the mire at night. . . ." She flapped her arms. "Whoo-oo."

"We call them jack-o'-lanterns," Allie said,

not being a child who frightened easily, "and Mama says they're a national phenomenon."

"Natural," Adelia told her, "a natural phenomenon." There were islands out there, little humps among the flatness like the curve of dolphins petrified in the act of diving. Godwyn's boat was heading for the nearest. She would have liked to inquire about them, but this was the king's time she was wasting, after all. Any more of it and Gyltha's growing irritation with Hilda would result in a quarrel.

She nudged Mansur. "Lead on, my lord."

They turned left along the marketplace with its abandoned stalls and followed the abbey wall to the remains of a lichened gatehouse, now just another breach in the perimeter. Up a slope, past what might once have been a tithe barn . . .

And there it was.

"Mary, mother of God, look down on us," Gyltha said quietly.

Adelia's first thought was of how unmercifully the sun shone on a blackened and withered thing that shrank from the glare because it had once been beautiful.

It was still possible to see the former grace of an arch where only a half of it now stood; to mentally rebuild from those stumps of charred stone a long, elegant nave, a transept, a pillared cloister; to recognize the artistry of a master mason's carving under the soot of a tumbled, broken capital; to replace the ground's terrible scorch marks, like patches of disease, with the vast, upward sweep of a green hill that had once provided the backdrop to magnificence.

It would take years, decades, perhaps a century, to rebuild. Those who had tended this great church would live among its ruins and die without seeing the completion of what would replace them. Even to begin such a venture required a courage Adelia could not imagine — nor the faith.

"I am *so* sorry," she said, and wondered at the inadequacy of saying it, and to whom she had said it.

The fire had spread downhill from the church, leaving the upper slopes of the hill untouched. Up there, two men — one in Benedictine black and the other in the undyed woolen habit of a lay brother — were scything hay, watched over a paddock fence by a solitary mule, all of them forming a pleasing, bucolic miniature, like one on an illuminated manuscript, but throwing into relief the scene from hell that it was edging.

The monk straightened his back, saw

them, threw down his scythe, and began running downhill, shouting and waving his arms. "Go back," he was yelling, "we don't need you. In the name of the Father, go away."

Nearer, another monk strode energetically toward them from somewhere on their right in order to intercept the first. "James, Brother James," he was calling out, "No. No, no, no. Let us remember our manners. If these are the king's emissaries, they are our saviors."

He reached them first, smiling. To Mansur, he said, "I give thanks to the king and to Almighty God for your coming. All the world knows of Arab skill in the sciences. I am Abbot Sigward." He bent his head to each of the women as Adelia introduced herself, then Gyltha, then Allie — who got a special bow — and to Rhys. "Ladies, gentlemen, God's blessings on you."

Brother James came cantering up and went to his knees in the cinders. "Don't let them in, my lord." Long, nervous hands clutched at the skirt of the abbot's scapular. "I beg you, send them away."

"Why?" Abbot Sigward said. "For one thing, I am ready for whatever our good Hilda has in that basket."

With one hand on Brother James's trembling shoulder, he led them to the building he'd come out of. It was the only one left standing in the enormous acreage of the abbey's grounds — a lovely sculpted square of ashlar stone turned a warm yellow by the sun, with a tiled, conical roof rising to an elaborate chimney.

"Once the Abbot's kitchen," he said, ushering them in, "now our residence."

Three quarters of England's population would have been glad of it as a residence, Adelia thought. She wouldn't have minded it herself. It was spacious and cool and functional, though the mason who'd built it hadn't been able to resist lavishly sculpting stone leaves and fruit into the ceiling's eight ribs, which curved to meet in a central airhole.

Steps in a corner, where a bucket stood, led down to a dark glint of water. Another corner accommodated vats. A cat was curled up in a pen that also contained a goat. The fireplace beneath the airhole was empty.

Two monks, each with a pestle cupped in one arm, stood by a plain deal table, pounding herbs. One was fat, the other thin.

They glanced up at the visitors, their eyes guarded as they looked from Mansur to Adelia and Gyltha, to Allie, and finally to Rhys.

"Oh, dear God," said the thin one. "He's back."

Rhys bobbed. " 'Allo, Brother Aelwyn. You remember me, then?"

"Oh, yes," Brother Aelwyn said.

There were introductions all round. The fat monk was Brother Titus, and his attention, once he'd nodded to them, was on the contents of Hilda's basket as she began laying them on the table, especially the leather bottle of ale.

"You see," Abbot Sigward said to Mansur, "we laid a penance on ourselves by sending Brother Patrick, who was our kitchener, to the abbeys in Normandy so that he might beg them for rebuilding money — he has the gift of charm, has Patrick, and an interest in cuisine that will match theirs. Consequently, we are left barely able to cook our own meals. All but one of our lay brothers have departed to find employment elsewhere. . . ."

"Deserted, you mean," Brother Aelwyn said viciously. "The rats ran away. They think God's curse is on us."

"I'm afraid they do," the abbot said, "and perhaps it is, but at least we are blessed by our sister Hilda's sustenance." He smiled at the Pilgrim's landlady and then at Mansur. "And by your presence, my lord."

He looked more closely up at the Arab, who remained staring stolidly down at him, unspeaking. To Adelia he said, "Do I gather that the sage does not speak English?"

"I am afraid I must be the doctor's interpreter and assistant," Adelia said, using the ploy that had served the two of them well. It was a relief to find Abbot Sigward happy to accept the pronouncements of a Saracen, but she knew that such tolerance would not be extended to her. Prior Geoffrey, bless him, was the one churchman prepared to recognize her skill, but even he only because it had saved his life.

She asked if they had any knowledge of a lady missing with her companions.

They had not. None of them had left the abbey since the fire. "We are the guardians of the few holy relics we managed to save from its burning, you see," the abbot said, adding, "I am sorry for your anxiety; these are concerning times."

"Don't worry about that now, Father," Hilda told him. "See, I've brought ham cured just as you like it, and my quince preserve." She was noticeably proprietorial toward the abbot, brushing dust off his shoulder, filling a plate for him, producing a napkin that she tried to push into his hand. Nobody else had existed for her since he'd appeared on the scene.

"Any sign of that useless devil as Wells set on us, Father?" she asked.

Indulgently, the abbot fended off the napkin. "We mustn't assume that Eustace is our arsonist, my dear, nor that the bishop of Wells intended him to be so, though our belief lies in that direction and we have had to tell the sheriff so. But no, so far we have not discovered him."

"Course he did it," Hilda argued. "Brother Aloysius said so afore he died, didn't he? Saw him a-coming from the crypt as it flamed, didn't he?"

"He said something."

"He shall burn in hell if he did not in life," Brother Aelwyn said, "and who else but that satanic bishop would rejoice to see Glastonbury a bonfire? Of course it was Eustace."

To the still-fussing Hilda, the abbot said, "My dear, it would be discourteous to eat while our guests do not, and I can see that they are eager to be about the king's business."

He led the way out of the kitchen. Everybody followed — Brother Titus reluctantly, and covering up the food on the table to keep it from the flies until he should return.

As they headed toward the ruined church, tension rose. The animosity toward Mansur was palpable. Brothers Titus and Aelwyn became even more sullen. Hysterically, Brother James begged his superior not to submit sacred Christian bones to the touch of a Saracen.

Hilda, especially, was on edge. "Them's Arthur's and Guinevere's bones, everybody knows it," she said over and over, as if by reiteration she could make them so.

Only Abbot Sigward kept his poise. They hadn't known what to do with the skeletons, he said. "They deserve better housing than our kitchen, so we have built a temporary hut of withies for them on the site of the Lady Chapel, where we trust Saint Mary will watch over them."

"Should have been *two* huts for decency," Brother Aelwyn said.

"My dear, we've had this out," his abbot told him wearily. "This couple have been lying side-by-side all this time; I won't separate them now." Suddenly, he winked. "After all, if legend is right, Arthur and Guinevere were respectably married."

He stopped short of the site, gave Rhys permission to visit the graveyard, then bent down to talk to Allie. "It is time for you to go and play, little one," he told her. "Old bones are not for the young."

Allie opened her mouth to explain her

experience with bones, but Gyltha, giving her a sharp nudge, said, "We'll explore, shall us? See what we can find?" And to the abbot, "The child likes animals."

"There's a nice horsey up in the paddock," Sigward said kindly.

"It's a mule," Allie said, but allowed herself to be led away.

"Explain, my lord," Brother James was urging the abbot. "Tell this Saracen of Arthur's abnormality not granted to ordinary men." He turned to Adelia for the first time. "Tell your master, woman. Tell him that Arthur has six ribs, a grace given by Our Lord only to heroes."

Oh, dear, Adelia thought, *that old fable.* She said, "I think, sir, my Lord Mansur would instruct you that women and men have exactly the same number of ribs — six pairs, always six. The only way of telling a female skeleton from the male is by the pelvic bones."

"Instruct me?" Brother James's voice was high and became higher. "Instruct *me?* I take my instruction from the Word in Genesis: *'So the Lord God caused the man to fall into a deep sleep; and while he was sleeping, he took one of the man's ribs and closed up the place with flesh. Then the Lord God made a woman from the rib he had taken out of the man, and brought her to the man.'* Adam had but five ribs, and so have all men, except those given a special dispensation by God, as Arthur has been."

Don't they ever feel their own chests? Adelia wondered. *Why don't they count the damn things?*

It was something she'd met over and over. Whoever had written Genesis was no anatomist.

Damn it, she thought, *how can we make our investigation with an audience that's not only on tenterhooks but ignorant as well?*

Abbot Sigward solved that for her. "Come along, my sons," he said, "it is time for sext. And Hilda, dear soul, if you would finish grinding the wood bryony, for Brother James's stiffness of the joints causes him suffering. . . ."

Within a minute, everybody had gone — Hilda eager to fulfill a request by the abbot.

Adelia and Mansur stood alone outside the hut of withies, a large, fresh, sweet-smelling hump in the charred rectangle that had once been a soaring monument to the Virgin.

Mansur bowed his head. Adelia knelt, as she always did, asking the dead beyond the door to forgive her for handling their remains. "Permit your flesh and bone to tell me what your voices cannot."

When she stood up, Mansur said, "Can you sense it?"

"Sense what?"

They spoke in Arabic; it was safer for them, should they be overheard.

"We are on holy ground. This place is an omphalos."

She couldn't have been more surprised if he'd said it was Mecca. Mansur was not a man to show fervor; she had never known him to be awestruck before, and certainly not by anything Christian. His face was as impassive as ever, but that he should say he was finding in Glastonbury the same mystery that the ancient Greeks had attributed to the navel of their world in Delphi's dark cave was extraordinary.

She sniffed the air and looked around her. Was she missing something? Henry Plantagenet, another man difficult to impress, had mentioned much the same thing.

If he and Mansur were right, she should be receiving a vibration from the air, a tingling in her body from standing on one of the world's sacred centers, a place where the division between man and God was thinner than anywhere else.

Geographically, it was striking, she'd give it that — extraordinary sudden hills rearing up out of the plain as if to protect the abbey's back, the flats of salt marsh in front giving it a tang of the sea. Undoubtedly, there was a natural magnetism that had pulled people to worship a presence here long before Christ had set foot on his native heath.

She couldn't feel it. The sun shone hot on her head; birds twittered as they colonized the poor ruins. The scents of June were overcoming the stink of ash. Wildflowers were beginning to push through devastated ground. She was grateful to God for such blessings. But mystery? Not for her, to whom all mystery must have an explanation.

And she was sorry for it; perhaps the lack was in her, an inability to succumb to the divine. *I just don't feel it.*

She smiled up at Mansur, envious of an exhilaration that left her untouched. "Are you ready?" she asked him.

"I am ready."

They went in together.

Light dappled through the loose weave of the hut's roof onto two catafalques formed by piers of blackened tiles built to hold up two long pieces of stone like altars. Between them was a long coffin shaped like a canoe, its lid on the ground by its side.

Heavy cloths covered both sets of remains, and somebody had put pots of buttercups at the head of each, a shining yellow donation from the living to the dead that brought tears to Adelia's eyes. Here was a shrine; she was reluctant to disturb its peace.

They stood for a moment. From the hole that had once been a church's nave, the monks were chanting, their disciplined voices chopping up the sweet, linear sound of Rhys's song coming from farther away.

After a long moment, Mansur carefully lifted the cloth from the bigger of the two shapes. Adelia heard him take in a breath, and she took one herself.

Whoever these bones had belonged to, he'd been magnificent in life, nearly six and a half feet tall — a commanding height at any time, and one that during the Dark Ages would have inspired legend.

If he'd died in battle, it had been at the hand of a ferocious enemy; the skull was staved in, cracks radiating out from the hole like an egg tapped with a heavy spoon. Instant death. The ribs, the *six* ribs, had become flailed so that they had been broken and detached from the chest wall.

"Allah grant that he maimed his opponent before he went down," Mansur said.

"We mustn't, we must *not,* assume he was

a warrior," Adelia told him; she'd never known her friend to get carried away like this.

"What else could he have been?"

"Perhaps it was an accident." It sounded inglorious, even unlikely, but she was determined not to jump to conclusions.

It seemed appropriate that a woman should uncover the smaller skeleton. Adelia lifted the cloth and then let it fall from her hands onto the floor, unheeded. "Oh, *God,* who did this?"

There was a hole in the skull similar to the man's, but that was not all of it — this skeleton had been cut into two pieces, chopped twice, once just below the ischium and then at the hips, so that where the pelvis and sacrum should have been there was a gap. The entire pelvic structure, from the lower vertebrae to the top of the femur, was absent, as if whoever had done it had wanted to take revenge on femininity.

And they'd laid her out as if this was normal, as if it was natural that the tops of her legs should emerge directly from her spine.

Adelia's voice rose into a screech. "Who did this? *Who did this?*"

"Things are done in a battle," Mansur said sadly, "even to women."

Perhaps they were. "But they didn't mention it," Adelia shouted. "Plenty of fuss about Arthur's bloody ribs, but no word about this . . . this mutilation of Guinevere. Oh, she's a mere woman, it doesn't matter."

And then she realized that she had named the skeletons, which she should not have done. If she was to do the job the king had set her, they had to remain unclassified until she had more to go on.

"Maybe the bones fell away before she was put into the coffin," Mansur said.

"They were hacked off," Adelia told him. "Look here." She pointed to the splintered top of the femurs. "And *here.*" The lowest remaining vertebra had been cleaved in half.

Mansur tried to soothe her. "It would have been done after she was dead," he said.

"How do you know? How can you possibly know that?"

And if it *had* been done postmortem, she thought, was it by some woman-hating monk? Were female reproductive organs too unclean to lie in ground reserved for holy men?

She felt a ferocious protection for the woman this had been; the skeleton was so . . . so dainty. Perfect little teeth grinned up at her, slender hand and finger bones lay quietly on the catafalque, as if the appalling infliction on the lower body no longer mattered.

Which it probably didn't — not to her.

It mattered to Adelia.

At the sound of footsteps outside, she shot through the door, swearing in Arabic, ready to berate any damned monk in her path. But it was Gyltha and Allie waiting for her.

"Come and see this . . ." Adelia began, and then stopped. There was a look on Gyltha's face.

"We been up there." Gyltha jerked her head toward the upper pasture without taking her eyes off Adelia's. "We went to see the mule."

"Oh, yes?"

"An' she started to cry." Another jerk of the head, this time down at Allie. "Said she was sorry as how she'd been nasty to little Pippy, and why wouldn't he come and see her."

"Yes?"

"An' I said, 'We'll find him, pigsy. Him and his mama've been held up on the road.' And she said, 'No, he's here. That's his pet mule.' An' I said, 'Can't be.' And she said . . ."

Adelia crouched down to put herself on a level with her daughter. "Why do you think it's Pippy's mule, darling?"

" 'Cos it is," Allie said. Tears were still on her cheeks. "It's Polycarp. Pippy used to like him best of all because he could feed him and he didn't bite like the others."

"How do you know it's Polycarp?"

" 'Cos it *is*," Allie said again. "He's got a nick in his ear and a bit of rain rot on his rump — like a strawberry patch. Wilfred said they would put seaweed on it." She cheered up. "Just near his arse."

"You're sure?"

"It's Polycarp." Allie was getting irritated with the interrogation.

Adelia looked up to meet Gyltha's eyes.

"She ain't never wrong when it comes to animals," Gyltha said.

"No," said Adelia slowly. "No, she isn't. Oh, dear God."

SEVEN

"I think Brother Peter bought the animal for us at Street's market," Abbot Sigward said cautiously. "We shall ask him." He called to the man who was still scything the top pasture, beckoning for him to come down.

"Our stables went up in the fire, you see," he told Adelia. "All our horses burned to death." He put a hand to his eyes as if shielding them from a sight too awful to remember. There was a general shudder from the other monks. "After that a mule was all we could afford."

"Useless," Hilda muttered. "He's to blame. Them was Brother Aloysius's last words. 'Eustace, Eustace.' Heard him myself as I was putting the salve on his poor burns."

"They were not as distinct as that," the abbot told her patiently. "May God bless him, but we cannot rely on the incoherence of a dying man."

Nor, it seemed, on the word of an agitated woman and her four-year-old child. The monks thought Adelia was deluded. The abbot was trying to placate her; the others were impatient to hear the lord Mansur's verdict on the bones.

But for her, Arthur and Guinevere could stay dead; it was the living she was concerned with now — God only grant that Emma and the others *were* living.

"A mule's a mule," Brother Aelwyn said waspishly. "Who can distinguish between the brutes?"

Not me, thought Adelia, who had difficulty telling a charger from a palfrey. *But Allie can.*

She'd taken her daughter up to the pasture with Mansur and Gyltha and listened as the child pointed out the marks that, to her, set a grumpy-looking quadruped apart from all other horseflesh — and had been convinced Emma and the others had been attacked, their goods taken and sold.

"We've got to find them," Adelia said. "We've *got* to find them."

She couldn't rid herself of the feeling that they were somewhere near and in terrible need. The call of a blackbird was the voice of Emma pleading for her life; the faraway *eeyah, eeyah* shriek of a hen harrier quartering the marsh was the scream of young Pippy.

Coming back down, she'd challenged the monks emerging from holy offices, demanding to know where they'd acquired the beast.

It was possible, of course — as the abbot pointed out — that Emma had sold her mule train before settling down somewhere in the vicinity.

Adelia didn't believe it. Her friend had certainly not settled down at Wolvercote Manor if the dowager Lady Wolvercote was to be believed. Also, the arrival of a grand lady like Emma in the neighborhood would surely have caused a stir among the locals, yet none of them — here in Glastonbury, at least — seemed to have heard of it.

"Brother Peter will know," Abbot Sigward said, relieved to see the man approaching. "He'll clear the matter up."

Brother Peter was another shock. He wore the habit of a lay brother that showed him to be basically a monastic laborer, but his height, coloring, and features were those of the man Adelia had seen baking bread in the kitchen of Wolvercote Manor only yesterday.

After a moment, she knew he couldn't be — the baker hadn't had this one's tonsure, though the hair was otherwise the same —

but he was his twin, she was sure of that.

Interrogated, he became defensive. "What I done wrong now, then? I says to you, Abbot, as we needed summat to pull a plough and harrow. Get it, says you, but get it cheap."

"So I did, so I did," Abbot Sigward said. "Nobody is blaming you, my son. But *where* did you get it?"

"Street. Where else? There ain't a market here no more. Bought him at Street. Picked that un acause he's strong for all he's got rain rot."

"Seaweed," Allie piped up. "That's the thing for rain rot."

"Oh, yes," Brother Peter said sarcastically, regarding the child with the same truculence he was according everybody else. "I got a lot o' time to poultice a mule's rump with blasted seaweed, o'course I have."

"But who sold it to you?" Adelia asked.

It was no good. A mule seller, a man who went from market to market and turned up at Street's every couple of months. Brother Peter had bargained with him, bringing the animal's price down to what the abbey could afford. "Didn't know I had to ask its blasted ancestors, did I?"

"When was this?"

"Near a month ago," Brother Peter said.

157

"Saint Boniface Day. And now, *if* there ain't no more questions, I got hay to cut."

Abbot Sigward looked inquiringly at Adelia, who shook her head, and Brother Peter stumped off.

"A rough diamond, I'm afraid," the abbot said, "but a good Christian and a hard worker."

She was going to have to speak to the man alone. She was going to have to do a lot of things — and do them quietly. Innocence had departed from this sunny day. The abbey's people, the gibbering Brother James, Aelwyn with his antagonism, the obese Titus, even Hilda, *even* the lovely abbot, had suddenly become sinister. She remembered Captain Bolt: *"Something's gone out of this place and something else has come in."*

Gathering herself, she said, "The lord Mansur requires more time before he can make any decision about the bones." Then she bowed to the abbot and walked away.

At first she couldn't eat her dinner, though Godwyn had stewed venison with wine and mushrooms until it fell off the bone.

Where to go for help? To the county sheriff? But would he give her concern for Emma any more credence than the monks had? Unlikely. Not until she had more evidence. He would take the line that Emma had a perfect right to have changed her mind about their rendezvous and sell her mules.

Rowley?

No. Please, God, don't force me to that. We are severed, and it nearly killed me. Days can go by now — well, hours anyway — when I'm not thinking about him. He probably doesn't think of me at all.

Blast the man, would it have hurt him at least to see Allie while we were in Wales?

She felt a familiar rush of fury and, with it, the accompanying, equally infuriating, recognition that it was unfounded. On several occasions he'd broken their agreement that they have nothing to do with each other by sending her money and a present for Allie on her saint's day, but those had been so reminiscent of condescension to a kept woman and her bastard that — though she knew they were not — she'd sent them back.

Damn him anyway.

It was almost a relief to remember that there were still some days before he was due to arrive in Somerset so that, even if she needed his help, she couldn't ask for it.

How to get evidence? How to get evidence?

There was no reason to suspect the monks — the mule had obviously been bought in good faith — yet an instinct she couldn't account for was telling her to learn more about all of them.

Well, while she and Mansur were studying the skeletons, she was in a good position to do it. And she could set Gyltha on to Brother Peter. . . . Yes, that's what she'd do; Gyltha could get stones to talk.

Most imperative, though, was to scour the neighborhood for information. She discounted herself; despite all she could do to get rid of it, she still spoke with a trace of a foreign accent — and the English distrusted foreigners.

Gyltha again? No, if people were disappearing in the vicinity, they weren't going to include Gyltha or Allie.

The sound of slurping intruded itself on her attention. It was coming from the bottom of the table, where Rhys the bard was spooning venison stew into his mouth with an energy that spattered it onto his clothes.

Rhys.

Adelia picked up her own spoon and began to eat.

■ ■ ■ ■

"A vanished lady, is it?" Rhys said, his protuberant eyes becoming misty. "There's a subject, now. O lost dove, you are a cause for tears, lifeless we are without you . . ."

"Stop him," hissed Adelia.

Mansur grabbed the harp from the man's hand just in time.

Adelia closed her eyes and then opened them. "We don't want you to lament her, Rhys," she said. "We want you to find her."

For privacy, they had taken him to Allie's and her bedroom, a large, elm-floored chamber with a little window overlooking the road.

Rhys rubbed his head where Mansur had slapped it. "A quest, is it?"

"Exactly."

"How do I do that, then?"

"We told you, boy," Gyltha said patiently, wiping stew off his shirt. "All you got to do is go round the local markets, singing your songs like a . . . what is it?"

"A jongleur," Adelia said.

"Like one of them. Listen to the talk, let people talk to you. See, Lady Emma and her people disappeared round here some-wheres. Dirty work, we reckon, but a party

161

that large must've left a trace behind it —
stands to reason as somebody knows something."

"A bard, I am, the finest of the Beirdd yr
Uchelwyr, not a bawling street musician,"
Rhys said with dignity. "Haven't I sung in
the greatest halls in Christendom?"

Mansur expired with force. "Let me kill
him."

But Adelia was interested. "You get invited
into houses?"

"I have sung the prowess of lords in
Dinefwr, in Brycheiniog. . . ."

"Could you get invited into Wolvercote
Hall?"

"Inhospitable lady, that one. Said we
wasn't to go back, didn't she?"

"She did. But she didn't see *you* with us.
You'd just be an innocent traveling jongleur,
as far as she's concerned."

"Maybe I could, then."

"You must. It was where Lady Emma was
heading. The dowager said she didn't arrive, but I think the woman knows more
than she's telling; her servants are sure to
have been a party to whatever it was."

They began to describe the appearance of
the missing. Rhys listened without comment
to a description of the servants, the child,
Master Roetger, but when he learned of

Emma's fair hair, her youth and beauty, and, especially, the wonderful voice that she had let fall silent, he was fired with a sudden passion.

"The lady has made a leap into my heart, like sun through glass," he said, throwing his arms wide. "I am Fair Emma's champion and defender from this day forth. I shall find her, and I shall feed the ravens with the corpses of her enemies."

"Get on with it, then," Gyltha said. "There's a good lad."

Suddenly she barged across the room, flinging open its door and peering around the narrow passage that served it and the adjacent chambers. "Nosy bloody woman," she shouted into it.

"Was it Hilda listening?" Adelia asked, startled.

"Didn't see her," Gyltha admitted, closing the door. "Nobody there now, but some bugger set the floorboards a-creaking. Who else would it be? Wants to know too much of our business, she does." Gyltha's relationship with the landlady of the Pilgrim had not improved.

"Ghost, p'raps," Rhys said. "Haunted, this place is. I feel it."

"Nonsense," Adelia said. She hated talk like that.

But there was no doubt that it was an inn of inexplicable noises: footfalls on dark, twisting staircases that nobody was climbing, a moan in a windless chimney, whispers from empty rooms. Had it been busy, as in the days before the fire, these things would not have been noticeable, but with only five guests, there was no doubt the Pilgrim could be eerie, especially at night.

The maidservant, Millie, a wraith of a girl, did not improve matters. She'd been born stone-deaf and went about her work so silently that in the shadows, one tumbled over her.

Her eyes radiated misery, and a pitying Adelia wondered what it was like to see incomprehensible mouths moving without hearing what came out of them. There must, she thought, be some method of communicating with the girl — and she had put finding out what it could be on her list of things to do.

That night Rhys, sitting late in the inn's courtyard, began composing a new song. "I would walk the dew or a bitter desert to find you, O white phantom of my dreams. . . ."

"Emma's not a phantom," Adelia interrupted, pausing to listen before going upstairs.

"Like Guinevere, she is," Rhys said. "Nobody don't know what happened to Arthur's queen, either. There's those say she was torn in pieces by wild horses for her adultery. Some think she disappeared into the mists of Avalon. White phantom, white owl, that's what the name Guinevere do mean, see. Night spirit lost in the darkness."

"Well, Emma definitely didn't commit adultery," said Adelia, and then thought how stupid she sounded. "Don't be late back now. Promise."

Whether it was Rhys, the worry about Emma, or the skeletons, this was the night that the dreams began.

Adelia was not a dreamer usually, keeping herself so busy by day that in bed she slept the sleep of the just. But this night she found herself standing halfway up the Tor above Glastonbury Abbey, outside a cave.

It was misty. A bell hung on the branches of a hawthorn tree just beside the entrance. Unbidden, her hand reached out to the bell and touched it so that it rang.

She heard its toll echoing through the mist. A male voice came from deep inside the cave: "Is it day?"

Even in her dream, she knew from Rhys's Arthurian songs that she must reply, "No, sleep on," or she would awaken whatever or whoever was inside. But though she opened her mouth to give the answer, no sound came out. The mist swirled and darkened; someone was coming up the cave's tunnel toward her.

She managed, "Emma? Is that you, Emma?"

But the same voice said, "I am Guinevere. Help me. I am hurt."

There was a scraping sound, and Adelia knew that only the top half of the thing calling itself Guinevere was dragging itself along the tunnel toward her and knew, too, that she couldn't bear to see it. She began backing into the mist, away from it, still hearing its moans as it slithered.

She woke up sweating.

"A true dream, was it?" Gyltha asked with interest the next morning. "Like Jacob and the Ladder?"

"No, it wasn't like that. I just felt terror . . . and guilt. It was begging for help, whatever it was, and I ran away."

Adelia gave no credit to dreams, but she was still immersed in the awful reproach that this one had wrapped around her. She wasn't seeing something she should be seeing; she wasn't acting on something that had been shown to her.

"The cheese, then," Gyltha said firmly. "Shouldn't eat cheese close to bedtime — gives you nightmares."

"I didn't eat any cheese. Oh, God, Gyltha, we've got to find Emma."

"Doin' our best, girl."

It was a relief to go out into the sunshine and trudge across to the abbey so that she could begin work on the bones. Godwyn was taking Gyltha and Allie onto the Brue in his boat to find them bog moss with which to plaster Polycarp's rump.

Rhys had been roused from his bed and pointed in the direction of Wells and Wolvercote Hall. He'd become suddenly fearful. "Dangerous road, that. Suppose brigands set on me and rob me?"

"Rob him of what?" Mansur had wanted to know; the bard had been wearing the same clothes since Wales, despite Gyltha's pleas to let her launder them. Apart from his harp, which he kept in a dirty satchel, there was nothing about him to tempt the most optimistic thief.

Eventually, he was persuaded to go by the couple of pennies Adelia gave him to spend at Wells market.

Hilda insisted on accompanying the two investigators to the abbey, seeming intent on monitoring any conversation they might have with Abbot Sigward — "my dear abbot," as she constantly referred to him.

Adelia wondered if Godwyn was jealous; Hilda glowed for the monk as she didn't for anyone else, certainly not for her husband, to whom she was dictatorial — her raised voice in the kitchen could often be heard upstairs. Not that Godwyn seemed to mind; he appeared to be as devoted to his wife as she was to the abbot, perhaps because Hilda's adoration, Adelia thought, wasn't so much sexual as that of a worshipper at a holy shrine, feeding and protecting its frail flame.

The woman admitted as much. "He's a saint, my dear abbot," she said as, carrying another basket with food for him, she accompanied Adelia and Mansur across the empty market. "I was his housekeeper in the old days, young as I was, and nobody don't know how deep that man's goodness goes. God'd snatch him from us if so be as I didn't look after him."

"Was this before he became a monk?" Adelia asked.

Hilda was suddenly aggressive. "What you want to know for?"

Adelia shrugged; it had been a polite enough inquiry.

After a pause, as if unable to let another

opportunity for praise go by, the landlady said abruptly, "He was rich in them days. A nobleman, rich as a king. And I kept house for him — oh, yes, I did. See that island out there . . ." She pointed toward a large hump in the distant marshes. "Owned that, he did, and thousands of acres all over England. Gave the lot away, so he did, bless him. Gave it to God and took his vow of poverty like the holy man he is."

A Road to Damascus conversion? The abbot's gentle face was that of a man whose soul had been purified by fire.

"Did he have family?"

Again, Hilda hesitated. Then she said shortly, "One son. Died on crusade."

That would account for it, then. Adelia could imagine no worse thing than losing a child, a loss that would turn you either to God for help or away from Him.

"One of his islands is a leper colony now," Hilda said, still pointing seaward. "That's how good he is. Bought the Pilgrim for Godwyn and me, and gave an estate over to lepers. Lazarus Island, we call it. Godwyn do row him over so's he can give them communion and take supplies."

Mansur shuddered. "Allah commend the good man," he said in Arabic. "I could not do that."

Adelia commended him, too. She did not share Mansur's horror for sufferers of a disease that her foster father had taught her was not as infectious as popular revulsion accorded it, though it was terrible enough in its slow and creeping death from the tips of the limbs to the whole body, but she could understand why the law was strict in segregating them in order to protect the healthy. For once, it was the Christian Church — an institution with which she was usually at odds — that she admired for its provision of leprosaria, refuges where patients received medical and spiritual help, even respect, since they were suffering for their sins while living and would, therefore, find quick redemption in heaven.

So Abbot Sigward was one of those who treated lepers generously, was he? Adelia found herself liking the man more and more.

For one thing, he was prepared to give Mansur and herself facility in their investigation that his fellow monks would have denied them.

"Against some opposition from my brothers, I have kept open the grave where we found the skeletons," he said, greeting them. "Do you wish to examine it? And the coffin?"

"Let the dead rest, Father," Hilda pleaded, interrupting. "Them's Arthur's and Guinevere's bones, you know it. Let 'em rest in peace."

The abbot patted her on the shoulder but kept his eyes on Adelia, who, after pretending to consult the Arab, said, "Dr. Mansur is grateful to you, my lord, and will be glad to look at those things in the goodness of time, but first he will concentrate on the skeletons."

"And what can they tell him?"

Again, Adelia spoke to Mansur in Arabic, and again received a reply. "Not much, he fears," she told Sigward honestly. "Putting a date to bones may be difficult."

"Even to eliminating the possibility that they are *not* Arthur's and Guinevere's?" The abbot winked. "That is the doctor's purpose, is it not? And the king's?"

Adelia smiled back at him. "It's a gamble, my lord."

"Ah, gambling." The abbot's face creased into that of a tortured man. "Gambling was one of my sins when I was in the world, and still is, though pride was a greater — and one I pray that a merciful God will forgive me. By the way, there is no need to address me as 'my lord'; I am a servant now."

"He shines, that one," Mansur said, watching Sigward walk away, gently propelling Hilda with him.

"He does," Adelia agreed.

They went into the hut and stared at the two skeletons. The damage to that of the female reminded Adelia horribly of her nightmare.

"What do we do?" asked Mansur.

"I don't know. If we could find out how old they are . . . perhaps comparing them to bones we *know* to be old would help."

"The graveyard?"

"The graveyard."

After peering to see if anyone was about, they crossed the ruined nave of the great church and scrambled over the tumbled stones of its southern wall, a part of which was tall enough to hide what lay on the other side.

Neither the fire nor, yet, Brother Peter's scythe had touched the abbey's burial place. The gravestones had the pleasant higgledy-piggledy untidiness of a country churchyard. Being in the full path of the early sun, butterflies were adding to the color of its wildflowers, and bees were at work among some bluebells growing in the shade of a young oak leaning over the small wall that marked the graveyard's southern boundary.

What made the place different, what

skewed its bucolic restfulness into something alien, were the pyramids. Adelia had thought that the word must refer to conical gravestones, but these *were* pyramids — much smaller versions of the ones her foster father had drawn during his visit to Egypt and shown to her, but still too large and belonging to a more savage environment and a hotter sun than this; they were un-English, disturbing.

They didn't match, either — another attack on the eye. The tallest was more than twenty-five feet high, and stepped to its peak in five courses of stone; the other stood about eighteen feet, consisting of four stories. Each was covered in writing that Adelia couldn't decipher — more like runes than script, messages from a darker age.

Between them stood another pyramid, this time a teetering mountain of earth that had been displaced from the yawning hole beside it.

Adelia went to the edge.

The pit was a rectangle, at least sixteen feet deep and wide enough to accommodate the steps cut into one of its sides. The monks had gone down a long way to find Arthur's coffin.

"They must have dug like badgers," Adelia

said, peering into it. She stepped back quickly; the pit smelled of contaminated earth.

Mansur was already on his way down, examining the sides as he went. Bits of bone stuck out where the diggers had cut through the earth, showing that for one thousand years succeeding generations of dead monks had been buried on top of one another.

"Also, there is wood," he called up. "Some were in coffins, some were wrapped in just a winding sheet, I think. What do you want?"

Suddenly, she didn't want anything. "Mansur, we're grave robbing."

Her foster father, she knew, had bought dubiously acquired skeletons from dubious men in order to teach his students anatomy, but what was *she* advancing by desecrating these dead? Not science, not medical knowledge, merely a chance for an abbey to acquire riches and a king to get his dead Arthur.

"We shouldn't do this," she called down, and she heard Mansur spit in disgust at her vacillation.

He began climbing up again, but as he reached the top of the steps he held out his hand. On its palm was a small knobble of bone.

"It must be old because it was at the bottom," he said. "A bit of a foot, I think. Use it."

It was actually the distal phalanx of a second toe, and Adelia stared at it for some time, tapping her teeth in indecision before finally snatching it. "We can always stick it back on," she said.

After all, if she could find a method for dating bones, it *would* be a contribution to the world's knowledge.

Nevertheless, guilt followed her back to the hut, and when, two hours later, Brother James surprised the two of them at work and stared at the mess they'd made as if they had committed an obscene act, Adelia blustered an innocence she didn't feel. "We've said prayers. . . . Abbot Sigward gave the doctor license . . . The king requires . . ."

But apparently Brother James underwent periods of calm, and this was one of them. He merely looked sad. "May God forgive you for what you do," he said.

"I hope He will."

In fact, the bone had been useless. Adelia had shaved a sliver off it and an exactly similar slice off Arthur's toe — neither had displayed an interior any different to the other.

She and Mansur had pounded each sliver to dust and put it in the bowl of the tiny scales she'd brought with her — proving only that they weighed the same. They'd poured parts of the two sets of dust into water, then vinegar, with no reaction from either. Both were the same age or, as she'd feared, there was no way of gaining a comparison.

"You see," Brother James said, still lingering, still sad, "people need King Arthur, they need the dream of him. *I* need him."

"Why?" Adelia asked. "*Why* do you need him?"

"He flew his banner in the battle against savagery," Brother James said, "but he must come back to win the war. There is still savagery in this world. Nobody knows that better than I do."

He wandered off.

"It is as good a reason as any," said Mansur, watching him go. "All should battle against evil. Islam still fights under the Prophet's flag, Allah cherish it."

"It isn't good enough," Adelia said. "A dream isn't enough. Hard truth is the only flag to fight under."

"Brother James?" Hilda said when they returned, dispirited, to dinner at the inn. "Pursued by demons he is, poor fellow, but my dear abbot has managed to cast most of 'em out of him."

"What demons?"

Hilda didn't know. "Come to the abbey afore the abbot and me had anything to do with it. Screaming, he was, so they say."

Gyltha was more informative once Hilda had left the room. She and Allie had spent a productive morning being rowed around the marshes by Godwyn, and an even more productive afternoon talking to the lay brother Peter in the pasture where Polycarp the mule now sported a poultice of sphagnum moss on his rump.

Brother Peter's Christianity, she reported, didn't stretch to speaking kindly of his superior brethren.

"He don't like any of 'em much," Gyltha reported. "Says they don't treat him right — all except the abbot. Says the abbot do give him respect."

Brother James, according to the gospel of Brother Peter, was as mad as a ferret. "Story goes he came running to the abbey for sanctuary for cutting his cousin's arm off in a quarrel."

"Dear God."

"So Peter says. And Brother Aelwyn is sour as crab apples, wicked tongue, nothing ever right for him. Got something in his past an' all, but Peter don't know what it is. And

Brother Titus is a fat and lazy pig."

Oh, dear. Even allowing that these were the strictures of a resentful, overworked fellow, such a comparatively small collection of men confined together under a severe discipline with its demand of chastity were bound to get on one another's nerves.

Why did they do it? What drove them to accept it?

Everybody assumed that most nuns and monks submitted themselves to the holy rule because they'd heard a call from God, and perhaps some of them had, but, obviously, for others it was an escape from unendurable troubles in the outside world. Perhaps for Brother Titus its rigors were still easier than earning a living.

So Brother James had attacked his cousin, had he? Had he also taken an ax to Guinevere?

Rhys had not returned by nightfall, an absence making Mansur angry. "He is in some woman's bed, useless philanderer."

That reminded Adelia of something. "Did Brother Peter tell you anything about Useless Eustace that Hilda complains of?" she asked Gyltha. "Did he start the fire? Who is he?"

"Ah, I forgot him. Peter don't think he done it, but the rest all blame Eustace for the fire. Even the abbot blames him, though he thinks it was an accident — but he would, wouldn't he? Ain't got a bad word for anybody, that man."

"Is there any evidence this fellow started the fire? Didn't the monks bring in the county sheriff?"

"They did, but they reckon the sheriff's in the bishop of Wells's pocket and that the bishop was mighty pleased Glastonbury burnt down — the two of them have always quarreled over land, hate each other — might even have paid Eustace to set the blaze."

This was what Hilda had said. It was difficult for Adelia to believe.

"Well, see, Eustace *was* the bishop's falconer," Gyltha told her. "Lost his job on account of he drank, and came to Glastonbury begging his bread. The which he got, though even the abbot had to let him go after a bit — he kept raiding the crypt where they keep the communion wine. Went and lived wild in the hills after that, but they reckon he still got into the grounds o' nights because the wine vat kept going down. An' it was in the crypt where the fire started. *An'* Brother Titus saw Eustace running from the crypt that night."

Gyltha shook her head in wonder. "Ter-

179

rible thing, in't it? Deliberate or not, one man do bring down a great abbey and a good little town. And one of the monks died, you know. Trying to put out the flames in the crypt, he was, along of Brother Titus — but died of burns, poor soul."

It was sad; it was horrifying. Adelia shook her head over it. "But what's done is done. Emma is our priority now, and all this has nothing to do with her."

"Dunno so much," Gyltha said. "There's summat shifty about that Brother Peter. He ain't telling me all of it."

This time Adelia stood in a gleaming golden hall. Silver-clad knights held the fingertips of beautiful ladies and moved with grace to the tune of an unseen harpist. King Arthur saw her and approached, bending his crowned head in a greeting. He offered his hand. "Dance with me, mistress." His voice was as big and handsome as his figure.

"I can't dance in a dream," Adelia told him.

"There's stupid you are," Arthur said.

He turned away from her and walked to the throne at the end of the hall where his queen was sitting. He bowed and Guinevere got up, put her hand into the king's, and joined him on the floor. Her dress was of pure white feathers that fluttered as she moved. Whichever way she and Arthur turned, her face was hidden from Adelia, who saw only that a red stain was beginning to sully the feathers at the back of the queen's waist. Soon blood was dripping in pools onto the floor, but she danced on. . . .

"Stop it, stop it," Adelia shouted, and was grateful to be woken up.

There'd been a noise.

Still shaking, Adelia lit a candle, wrapped herself in a shawl, checked that Allie was safely asleep, and went out onto the landing.

It was a hot night, and a grilled window above the stairs had been left unshuttered to provide a draft.

Her toe stubbed against something soft. Looking down, she saw the maid Millie curled up on a mat on the floor, her big eyes staring up in terror.

Adelia had been frightened as well, and her "What are you doing here?" was sharper than she meant it to be, until she realized the poor child couldn't hear it anyway, and realized, too, that she'd disturbed the girl's sleep.

"Don't they give you a bed?" she asked uselessly. Servants as low-graded as Millie had to bed down wherever they could, mostly in the kitchen, but on a night like this the Pilgrim's kitchen would still be intolerably hot from the cooking fires over which Godwyn sweated, its windows closed against robbers. Millie had sought out the only coolness she could find — and even that was forbidden by the injunction that, unless she was cleaning them, she should not be seen near the guests' rooms.

"We'll have to do better than this, won't we?" Adelia gestured for the girl to come into her own room, where there was an extra truckle bed and another open window. She put her two hands against her cheek, indicating sleep, but Millie refused to move, her eyes more frightened than ever. It wasn't allowed.

"Lord's sake," Adelia said crossly. She went to her bed, snatched up a pillow and a discarded quilt, took them to the landing, and arranged them on the floor. Even then, the girl had to be persuaded and, eventually, pulled onto them.

There were still sounds from the courtyard as if some animal was barging blindly around it, but when Adelia started to descend the staircase, Millie put out a hand to stop her, violently shaking her head.

"You don't want me to go?" Adelia asked

her. What awful thing went on in the Pilgrim at night that this sad creature didn't want her to see?

Whatever it was, it would be better than returning to the haunting of a dream. Adelia gave a nod of what she hoped was reassurance and continued down the stairs. After all, robbers wouldn't be calling attention to themselves this loudly.

Godwyn was crouching, listening, by the inn's side door when Adelia reached it. "Who's out there?" she asked him.

"Don't know, mistress, and I don't want to."

They both heard a bleat as something bumped against the other side of the door.

"Sheep?" Godwyn said. "Where's bloody sheep come from?"

Then she knew. "Open the door," she said. "It's Rhys."

Godwyn was unpersuaded, so she had to pull back the bolts herself and was sent backward as the door flew inward with the pressure of the bard's body falling against it.

"Oh, Lord, he's hurt." He'd been set on by the robbers on that dangerous road, pummeled, knifed, and it was her fault — she shouldn't have sent him out on it.

Godwyn sniffed at the squirming bundle

at his feet. "He ain't hurt, mistress, he's drunk."

And so he was. That he'd managed to stumble his way home directionless and unnoticed by predators was witness to a God who smiled on the inebriated.

Godwyn was sent back to bed, and for the next hour Adelia supported the bard as she made him walk on tottering legs round and round the courtyard's wellhead, twice pushing him toward a pile of straw onto which he could vomit, filling a beaker from water in the well's bucket and making him drink it every time he opened his mouth to try and sing.

Eventually, both of them exhausted, she guided him into the barn and sat him on a hay bale to get out of him what information she could.

He seemed most proud of having returned at all. "Not to be late back, you said," he told her, "I remembered. So back, back I came and yere I am. Robbers, yach, I spit on them; they don't frighten Rhys ap Griffudd ap Owein ap Gwilym. I flew, like Hermes the messenger, patron of poets." He'd also crawled. The knees of his robe had been worn through and, like his hands, were stuck with horse manure — the least unpleasant smell about him.

Actually, he'd done very well when, finally, Adelia managed to piece together an incoherent story. He'd inveigled himself into not only the servants' hall of Wolvercote Manor but also the affections of its gatekeeper's daughter, who had succumbed to his mysterious charm and with whom he had later passed a pleasing and energetic hour in a field haystack — "Lovely girl, Maggie, oh, lovely she was, very loving."

"But did she *tell* you anything?"

"She did, oh, yes."

What the gatekeeper's daughter had told him in the haystack was that a month or more ago, a lady with an entourage had appeared at Wolvercote Manor's lodge gates late at night, expecting to be let in and claiming that she was Lady Wolvercote come to visit.

"But the gatekeeper, he didn't know her, so he called *his* Lady Wolvercote to the gates and there was a quarrel, though Maggie didn't hear all of it, see, because *her* Lady Wolvercote sent her dada up to the house to get men-at-arms to bar entrance to *that* Lady Wolvercote."

"Emma *did* go there, I knew it, I *knew* it. But what happened then?"

"Ah, well, there's a mystery. See, Maggie said her dada seemed shamed for days after

185

because of something that happened when our poor Emma was sent away."

"Ashamed? Oh, dear God, the men-at-arms didn't kill her?"

"No, no, don't think so. What would they have done with the corpses? No corpses at Wolvercote, see. Maggie would've known."

"But *something* happened. What was it?"

Rhys shifted; he was beginning to wilt. "Well, see, Maggie and me, we were interrupted then."

In fact, at that point, Wolvercote's hayward had been seen crossing the field in which the haystack stood and, since the hayward was affianced to young Maggie, the girl had advised Rhys to make a swift withdrawal — in more senses than one. Which he had, going back, fortunately unseen, to the hall's kitchen, where he'd again entertained the dowager Lady Wolvercote's servants, this time with some of his bawdier songs, his appreciative audience lubricating his voice with pints of the dowager's ale until he'd been turfed out into the night by the dowager's steward, a man lacking any appreciation of music, especially when it reached his bedroom window and woke him up.

How Rhys had managed the six miles back, he couldn't remember, partly because the loving and redoubtable Maggie had given him another blackjack of ale to help him on his way.

"And you learned nothing more?"

Rhys shook his head.

"I see." Then she said, "What about the baker? The man I saw in the kitchen? Did you manage to talk to him?"

"Wasn't there. Itinerant, he is. Only got called in last time because the kitchen baker was sick, see. Goes round the markets with his bread usually. Due at Wells market tomorrow, Maggie said."

"Today," Adelia said, firmly. "He'll be there today. It's gone midnight."

The bard's large eyes fixed on her and then begged for mercy. "Oh, take pity, mistress, you wouldn't . . . ?"

"Yes, I would. You'll be singing at Wells market nice and early this morning and talking to itinerant bakers." She patted his shoulder. "I'm truly grateful to you, Master Rhys. The king shall hear of your efforts."

If the praise was meant to invigorate the Welshman, it failed.

When Mansur and Adelia set off for the abbey the next day with Gyltha and Allie in tow — Polycarp's poultice needed changing — they found themselves perspiring before

187

they'd walked a yard.

From being pleasantly warm, the sun was sending out an aggressive heat that, with no cloud in the sky, threatened to become prolonged, wakening the fear of parched crops and thirsty, dying cattle, and sending Adelia back to the inn to fetch the wide-brimmed rush hats she'd bought for herself, Gyltha, and Allie on the journey from Wales.

It was obvious that the only way left now to give an age to the skeletons was by attempting to date the coffin they'd been buried in, and, somewhat late, she'd remembered that she should have asked Rhys a question. It had come to her in the otherwise blessedly dreamless sleep into which she'd relapsed on regaining her bed and which, thinking of other matters, she had forgotten on waking.

The bard had already left for Wells market, moaning and protesting, but it might be that either Godwyn or Hilda could give her an answer.

Adelia poked her head round the Pilgrim's kitchen door, apologizing for her intrusion. "I think Master Rhys once mentioned that there was an earthquake here many years ago and it opened up a fissure in the abbey graveyard. Would either of you remember that?"

It was not a good time. The kitchen had retained the previous day's heat and, though its shutters were closed against the sun, flies had found their way in to settle on the surfaces of boards and hanging meat.

Godwyn didn't bother to turn round. Even in the gloom, Hilda's face could be seen to be red as she put down her flyswatter to glare at Adelia. "How'd we know? We wasn't here then."

"Of course you weren't, of course you weren't. Silly of me. Er, don't bother to light a fire. It's too hot. We'll be happy to have cold cuts tonight."

"That's what you was going to get," Hilda said. And considering the temperature, she couldn't be blamed for saying it nastily.

Rejoining the others and handing out hats, Adelia suggested to Gyltha that her question about the fissure was one that could be put to Brother Peter if he was still around.

"Who'd be fishing in a graveyard?" Gyltha wanted to know.

"It's a hole, Gyltha. The earthquake moves the ground so that it slits open. I'm sure Rhys mentioned a fissure when he was telling us and King Henry about his uncle Caradoc's vision, at least I *think* I'm sure."

When they reached the abbey grounds, they found the monks, their hands folded under their scapulars, emerging from the Abbot's kitchen on their way to sing terce.

Mansur and Adelia joined them, and Adelia put her question to the abbot.

"In the name of God," Brother Aelwyn said furiously, appealing to his superior, "are we to be pestered even on our way to holy offices?"

"Answer her, Aelwyn," his abbot told him.

The monk turned to Adelia. "Yes, a fissure was opened by the earthquake, what of it?"

"Twenty years ago?"

"That was when the earthquake occurred, the day after Saint Stephen's Day, to be exact, if it's any business of yours, mistress."

"Between the pyramids, was it?"

"Yes."

"And how deep was it?"

"Deep, deep, woman. We didn't bother to measure it, we had other things on our mind. *Deep.* It closed itself the next day, in any case."

"Were you here, then?" Adelia persisted.

She had exhausted Brother Aelwyn's small store of patience, and it was Brother James who answered excitedly, "We were all here then, were we not, my brothers? Oh, no, Abbot, you weren't, were you? You came to us later. I thought the Last Hour was on us,

190

God have mercy." Tears came to his eyes as he looked round the blackened hill. "And now it has."

Abbot Sigward put his arm round James's shoulders. "With the Lord's grace, Glastonbury will rise again, my son. Let us go to our prayers." He nodded at Adelia, and led his flock toward the ruined church.

Gyltha and Allie headed up the hill.

"What is this about a fissure?" Mansur asked.

"We'll have to see," Adelia said.

She ushered him into the hut and pointed at the coffin lying between the two covered catafalques. "Look at that. It's in fairly good condition still, but they had to dig sixteen feet down to find it, in which case it must be very old, as old as anything in the pit. Yet it hasn't crumbled. You said there were other coffins down there, and I want to compare this one with those. I think we might be able to get a rough, very rough, dating from the state of the wood."

"And if this one turns out to be newer than the others?"

Adelia grinned at him. "Then it could only have been put sixteen feet down when the fissure opened, twenty years ago."

"And is therefore not Arthur's."

"No."

Mansur sucked his teeth. "That will not please the monks — nor the king."

And all at once, Adelia didn't *want* to find out how old this coffin was, nor to deny the title of Arthur and Guinevere to those poor bones.

This was not merely a matter of forensics; it had become *massive;* it crushed her. A great abbey's future, those faithful men singing out there, the rebuilding of an entire town, the welfare of an inn, the dream of so many — these expectations rested with her decision.

Oh, God, don't put this on me. I don't want to be hope's executioner.

But she was Vesuvia Adelia Rachel Ortese Aguilar, medica of the Salerno School, and if she was not a seeker after truth, she was nothing.

She gritted her teeth and said, "Let's get to it."

There was no point in sawing a piece off the coffin until she had wood to compare it with. The two of them left the hut and dodged between the tumbled stone of the church as they crossed the once-great nave where, in what had been the choir, the monks were chanting Psalm 119.

"My soul melteth for heaviness; strengthen

thou me according to thy word. Remove from me the way of lying and grant me thy law in graciousness."

Adelia couldn't look at them.

The huge section of wall that still stood between the church and its graveyard lessened the sound of the monks' voices, replacing it with the hum of bees. Perhaps because she was expecting them now, the two pyramids and the mountain of earth between them looked less monstrous than they had.

Mansur began unwinding a rope that had been round his waist, concealed by his robe. "I asked the man Godwyn for it," he said. "I suspect those steps into the pit, they are beginning to crumble."

Adelia smiled at him. He'd brought it because he knew that this time she would insist on going down the hole with him.

Gyltha and Allie were returning from the hill. "Too hot, bor," Gyltha said. "I'm taking madam home afore she frizzles."

"How's Polycarp?" Adelia asked Allie.

Her daughter was red-cheeked with heat and pleasure. "Better. Even Brother Peter said he thought he was better, though he didn't like saying it, did he, Gyltha? Rude man, but he likes Polycarp."

"And I asked the miserable bugg . . ."

Gyltha said, then, remembering Allie's presence, started again; "I asked un about the fissure. He were only a lad then, but he reckons the hole was sixteen, seventeen foot deep afore it closed up."

She looked suspiciously at Mansur, who was tying his rope around one of the pyramids, and then at the mound of earth that was casting a shadow over the pit beside it. "You two ain't thinking of going down that damn great hole, I hope. Nasty places, holes. Them's where demons come from."

"Oh, get on home. Mansur's made sure we'll be safe." Lovingly, Adelia watched them go, one tall, one short, like two ill-assorted walking mushrooms in their wide hats.

Mansur threw the free end of the rope down the pit, but even now he wanted her to stay at the top. "It is not enjoyable down there."

"You managed, so I can." She wanted to see for herself and, once he had climbed down, she followed him.

The steps down the side of the pit *were* beginning to crumble, but they had been well cut and, as long as she went down backward, holding on to the rope, feeling for the next with first one foot and then the other, they bore her weight well enough.

The great mound of displaced earth above took away most of the light. The smell of soil was overlaid by a less pleasurable reek. Bits of bone showed white-gray against the pit's sides; wood was smudges of brown.

She was descending into the past, through centuries, passing the level in which lay the remains of Glastonbury's great abbots. Down, down, past the bones of men who'd served the formidable Saint Dunstan. Another stratum and she had reached the resting place of monks who'd defied invasions by the Vikings and saved the literacy of Christianity from their raids.

"There, God leading them, they found an old church built, as 'twas said, by the hands of Christ's disciples, and prepared by God Himself for the salvation of souls, which church the Heavenly Builder Himself showed to be consecrated by many miraculous deeds, and many mysteries of healing."

So William of Malmesbury, the historian, had written.

And now, as Adelia's feet touched the bottom of the pit, who knew whether she was now standing in the entombment of those early disciples themselves, one of them Joseph of Arimathea, whose hands had lifted the body of Jesus from the Cross.

She was shivering.

Mansur's voice came through the gloom. "Can you see anything of a coffin?"

They were facing away from each other, far enough not to be touching, but the smell of the herbs that the Arab kept his robes in offset the reek in which the two of them stood, and she was glad he was there.

"I think I can," she said. There was just enough light to see a slight difference in the blackness of earth in front of her. She put out her hand and felt a protrusion that was harder than the soil around it, though, as she pulled it out, only a small section came away from whatever it had been attached to. "Can you see any more? It would be as well to have more than one piece."

Lord, this was a terrible place to be.

To comfort herself that there was still fresh air and life above them, she looked upward — and saw the light of day blotted out as earth came sweeping down the pit to bury them.

EIGHT

It came and it came, a landslide of soil pouring down onto her head, into her eyes, rising to fill the space she stood in.

There was a constriction round her waist; Mansur was holding her up, shouting, "Where's the rope? Find the rope."

Desperately, she groped for it. "It's not here."

And then it was — all of it, loose, brushing her face as it slithered downward amid the falling earth. It had come away. It draped itself over her.

The avalanche stopped. Adelia blinked the muck out of her eyes. "Phew. Oh, dear God, that was close. The mound up on top tipped over."

She looked down and saw that Mansur had been engulfed almost up to his shoulders; his elbows were at ear level as he continued to hold her above the debris. He was panting from the strain on his arms.

"The steps, I can't see." Her body was obstructing his view.

She looked for the steps; they were behind her.

Then a shadow blocked out the light above and black earth engulfed her again, coming down in rhythmic, vicious plunges. They were being buried alive.

"Help us." Screaming, she scrabbled at the side of the pit like a spider trying for a hold against a sudden rush of rain. *"Help us, God help us."*

The coffin lid was closing on them.

She heard Mansur start to shout and then choke as earth entered his mouth. But still he held her up.

She shouted for him. *"No."* And tried kicking out a space round his head so that he could breathe, but her legs could move only a few inches against the constraining earth. His grip weakened and she fell sideways, her lower body pinioned against his shoulders.

Wrenching her back, she squirmed so that she could get to him. One of his hands was still visible, its fingers outstretched. There was a patch of white, the top of his headdress, and she began digging round it, frantic, yelling, not knowing she was yelling, scooping earth, baling it away from that beloved face. *"No, no, no!"*

He was sinking, dear Christ, he was sinking, they were both sinking, and she couldn't dig fast enough against the soil that trickled through her hands.

She felt her body arch as something tugged at the waist of her gown and began dragging her up. She thrashed against it; Mansur was choking; he must breathe — O God in Heaven, let her help him to breathe.

A voice shouted, "Keep still, damn you. I'll pull you up."

"*No.* Mansur. Mansur's dying."

"I can't get to him until you're out of the way, you stupid bitch. Keep still."

She was too terrified to put a name to it, but it was a voice she'd once known, a loved voice she'd trusted. Even so, letting herself dangle as she was pulled upward was the most unwilling thing she'd ever done. Tears poured out of her eyes, and she kept screaming for Mansur.

The hand attached to her was in turn attached to a man with his feet planted on one of the steps. His other hand was holding that of a second man lying down on the pit edge, his arm extended as far as it would go.

She was hauled in like a fish that flapped in the sunlight trying to return to water.

"Mansur, Mansur. It's Mansur down there."

"I'm getting him, aren't I?" The snapping voice, unacknowledged but still familiar, addressed itself elsewhere. "Jesus, she's got a rope round her. Get it off her quick."

It took time, it took *time.* She was disentangled from the rope, knots were tied, things were done, but she was blind to everything except the thought of nostrils and throat blocked with soil; he'd be unconscious by now, beyond recovery in . . . how long, how long to suffocate?

She crawled to the edge and saw his fingers, a little picket fence sticking out of the blackness. Saw a hand grasp them. Heard the voice: "Pull. *Again.* Christ, I can't get purchase."

More time. A scrabbling as the rescuer heaved earth from round Mansur's head and shoulders. One arm was free. A rope was looped round it. "Now *pull,* Walt, pull as you've never fucking pulled."

The man at the top pulled, the man in the middle pulled, and slowly, like Lazarus from the dead, Mansur rose from the pit.

They laid him on the sweetgrass. He wasn't breathing. Adelia fell on him, picking soil from his nostrils. She cleared his mouth and then puffed her own breath into it.

And felt his chest rise and fall. And

crouched back on her knees to give thanks in three languages, to God, to Allah, to her foster father's Jehovah, for the grace they had accorded her in letting this man live.

Somebody had fetched a ewer of water, and she used it to wash the rest of the earth from the Arab's face and head. His kaffiyeh had come off in the struggle to leave the pit, and she, who had never seen him bareheaded, saw that he was becoming bald.

"His headdress," she said. "Find his head-dress." He would be shamed without it; she couldn't have him shamed.

Somehow it was produced. Shaking the earth from it and tenderly raising his head, she put it on him, arranging its folds as he would want.

He opened his eyes and she looked into them. "Do you know who I am, dear friend?"

"My sun and my moon," he said.

She sat back and rested against the man who knelt behind her.

Time resumed. There was warmth and the smell of wildflowers and, above, a sky as blue as sailors' trousers, the hum of bees, and — oh, God, how strange — the sound of plainsong coming from the ruins of a church where, unknowing, impervious holy men still celebrated the third hour of daylight, allowing the six-note hexagons of their song to bring order back to a universe in which, for her, there had been chaos.

Her eyes cleared. A little way away, a young man held the reins of three horses — he had a fluttering peregrine on his arm and was trying to soothe it. Looming over her with concern was a face she recognized. She smiled at Walt, an old friend, groom to the diocese of Saint Albans.

He smiled back. "A near thing, mistress."

She rubbed the back of her head against the chest of the man holding her. "Hello, Rowley," she said.

There was a huff of angry breath against her hair. "Don't you hello me. In the name of Christ, how many more times have I got to rescue you from a pit? What in hell were you doing down there?"

"Just looking," she said. "What are *you* doing here?"

"Paying an unofficial visit to the abbot of Glastonbury, ready to arrange a peace between him and the bishop of Wells, flying my hawk over his grounds while I waited for him to finish terce, hearing screams from a hole in the graveyard and finding a woman squirming round in it like a bloody worm. Usual sort of morning."

How I love him. Let him cradle me forever.

Abruptly, he let her go and she fell back on the grass as he stood up. He was the bishop of Saint Albans now, a man of God; that he had touched her at all was merely because she'd been in extremis. He said, "We shall give thanks to our Savior, who directed our steps to the rescue of these two souls in peril," he said.

While he prayed, she put her hand over Mansur's heart and felt a strong beat. She looked round her. Rowley wore hunting clothes and was still furious. A curly-coated water dog sat at his feet. Latin floated over the wall that hid the church. *"Pater noster, qui es in caelis, sanctificetur nomen tuum . . ."* The service was nearly over.

When the monks emerged there was much exclaiming and concern over the accident. They wanted to take Mansur to the Abbot's kitchen to wash and restore him, but he asked to be allowed to rest for a while, so they carried him into the shade of the church wall.

Adelia said she would stay with him.

Rowley frowned but had the sense to see that both of them needed a time of quiet. "There is much I need to discuss with Abbot Sigward," he said, as if she'd said he should not.

"Then go and do it," she told him.

"And I am engaged at Wells Cathedral this afternoon."

She felt a flare of jealousy; God's business must always supersede any care for her. With anger came recovery, and with recovery came the recall of another matter of importance. She said, coldly, "And while you're about it, I should be obliged if you would make inquiries about Lady Emma Wolvercote." Briefly, she told him the mystery of her friend's disappearance, Allie's recognition of the mule, her suspicion that there had been foul play. "It must have been somewhere round about."

She could see he was not impressed.

"I doubt if a child of four can identify one mule from another," he said. "Emma changed her mind about the meeting place. You should not take it amiss; she will be in touch when she's ready."

"Ask, will you?" Adelia spat at him. Her head ached.

"I shall."

Yes, he will, she thought. She could trust him for that. She remembered that she owed him her life and Mansur's, and changed her tone. "I am grateful, my lord bishop."

He was so beautiful to her still, that was the trouble: the way he strode and talked, his nice hands, the eyes that could be easily amused — not bishop-like at all but lust-worthy, blast him.

As he went, she heard him lecturing the abbot on the danger of keeping open pits in his ground, especially those with towers of earth beside them.

Mansur's eyes were closed, and she shut her own, listening to him breathe. She had lost her hat somewhere in the pit and, vainly, she tried clawing some of the earth out of her dark blond hair. Her fingers encountered something substantial that had got entangled in it. With difficulty she retrieved it — a piece of wood that crumbled, as had the spar she had touched in the pit. It was proof, if she'd needed it, that her theory about Arthur and Guinevere's coffin had been right.

It hadn't been buried in the Dark Ages; wood from that time rotted in this earth. But the wood of Arthur and Guinevere's coffin was much, much newer, which meant that the only time it could have reached sixteen feet down was during those few, so few, hours twenty years ago when the earthquake's fissure had made such a depth available.

Rhys's Uncle Caradoc hadn't been vouch-safed a vision; he had seen an actual event.

Misery overtook her. For all her hard-headed search for the truth, something in Adelia had been touched by the golden rays of Arthur. Not so much by the legend itself as the fact that so *strong* a legend must mean that in the swirling mists of Britain's darkest time, one man had ensured that the essence of what it was to be British, its very matter, stayed alive through his courage — and that she had been privileged to look on what remained of him.

A greater misery was for the disenchantment and blighted hope of those to whom Arthur's magic was their life's blood.

She gritted her teeth. Magic was ephemeral — you couldn't and shouldn't depend on it.

So now that she had dispelled it, what was she left with? Something uncomfortable . . .

From beside her, Mansur said, "They tried to kill us, Adelia."

She looked at him. His eyes were still closed in exhaustion. "*Kill* us?"

"The earth did not come down on its own. The mound has stood for many weeks; why should it tip now?"

Dear Father Almighty.

In the relief of being rescued, her joy that Mansur had survived, and seeing Rowley again, she had not questioned that it had been an accident. Now, mentally, she went back into the pit, looking up, experiencing again the terror of that cascading earth.

It had stopped at one point; there had been a pause in the fall. And then *it had started again* — yes, as if somebody had been dissatisfied with the original push that tumbled the mound on top of them. Whoever it was had then begun shoveling or kicking the residue into the hole to fill it up completely.

Who could hate us that much?

Only Rowley's appearance on the scene had stopped a murder that, if it had been successful, would have remained undiscovered. She and Mansur could have been blotted out. People would have seen merely that the mound had overtipped.

There was no time to absorb the shock. She was on her feet and running to the abbot's kitchen.

The bishop of Saint Albans and Abbot Sigward were in conclave at the table; she didn't notice anybody else.

"Who was there?" she demanded of Rowley. "Somebody tried to bury us. Who was it?"

"Eh?"

"When you rode up. Somebody was at the top of the pit." She danced from foot to foot in agitation. "They pushed the mound over so that it would bury Mansur and me."

"I didn't see anybody."

"You must have. Somebody was *there,* Rowley. They kept on. . . . The earth came and came. . . ."

"I swear to you, mistress." He looked around. "Walt? Did you see anybody by the pit when we came up?"

"I didn't, my lord."

"Gervase?"

The young man with the hawk shook his head. "Nobody, my lord."

Rowley got up from his stool, suddenly full of compassion for her. "It was dreadful for you, my child. . . . For God's sake, one of you, give this lady some brandy, a restorative. I should not have left her alone. . . ."

"I'm not mad, Rowley," she said.

"Of course you're not, but it was too much for you. It was an accident, mistress, a fearful accident."

They tried to get her to sit down, to drink something, to rest — and their faces all had the same look, not just concern but pity for a woman so unnerved that she had lost her wits.

"Damn you," she shouted at them. "There was a pause, and then it started again."

For heaven's sake, why couldn't she put into words what she had so clearly seen, tell them what it meant? There must have been somebody. . . .

She stopped short. But there had been another pause. While she'd been struggling to free Mansur's face, there had been no descent of earth — because whoever it was had seen or heard the approach of Rowley and had run away.

Eventually it was decided that Mansur must be questioned, men being less hysterical than women in the face of adversity.

With irritating gentleness, still offering her various remedies, they escorted her across to the church and rounded its far wall.

Mansur wasn't there.

Adelia stared at the empty patch of grass on which he'd been lying.

Shouting, they wandered in search of him.

"He's gone back to the inn," Rowley said.

They took her to the Pilgrim. He wasn't there. There were long explanations to the landlord and his wife, and to Gyltha, during which time Adelia watched Gyltha's face go gray.

Out again. Some to go calling up the empty village street, others to search the abbey grounds more diligently.

Walt forestalled Adelia from going down into the pit again by using the rope to go down himself, but it was obvious — even to

Adelia, frantically peering down from the edge — that its earth had swallowed no one since she and Mansur had been lifted out of it.

The bishop of Saint Albans missed whatever appointment it was that he had in Wells in order to ride up into the hills with his men, calling, always calling, so that the sky resounded with the Arab's name. Until it got too dark to see anything — except the fact that Mansur had disappeared.

Like Emma.

"I'll be back in the morning," Rowley said. "As soon as it's light."

She nodded. She was holding Gyltha close to her.

"Confusion," Rowley said. "He was confused after the accident, and who could blame him? He's just wandered off, but he can't have gone far. And it's a warm night, he'll take no harm. Not Mansur."

She nodded again.

Desperately, he said, "I *have* to go back, you do see that?"

She saw that. The diocese of Wells expected it; he was one of the most important men in England, and a busy one, God's representative for thousands of square miles. What the diocese of Wells did not expect was that he should spend the night at an inn with a woman.

"I promise you, mistress," Rowley said, trying to smile. "This time the earth has not swallowed him up."

Hadn't she told him about Emma, whom the earth *had* swallowed up? She couldn't remember whether she had or not; fear seemed to be rendering her dumb. "Emma," she mumbled.

"I'll attend to it. God bless you, then, mistress. I shall see you in the morning."

Hilda's concern for her guests, though no doubt meant kindly, was bothersome. Adelia and Gyltha were offered everything that the landlady thought might raise their spirits, from Godwyn's calf's-foot jelly to her own specific against melancholy, a thick herbal concoction that they drank to satisfy her before escaping to Adelia's bedroom. Gyltha, to keep herself busy, insisted on washing Adelia's hair and finding fresh clothes for her. Then she sat down and, holding on to Adelia's hand, rocked back and forth in anxiety.

"Silly old bugger, where's he got to? Can't hardly find his own arse in the dark, so why's he go wandering off? What's happening to us, 'Delia? First Emma, now him. Where's he gone? Who's got him? Why didn't he stay close, silly old bugger?"

The lament went on and on until Hilda's specific took hold and Gyltha was persuaded to lie down on the bed where she fell into a whimpering doze.

Watching her, Adelia thought how ironic it was that Gyltha was the one person who would have believed that somebody had sent the mound of earth crashing into the grave deliberately, and yet was the one person who must not be told. That a murderer was abroad . . . no, she mustn't be made aware of that, not until Mansur was found. If he ever was.

It was stiflingly hot. Disengaging her hand from the sleeping woman's, Adelia went to the window to breathe.

Twenty years ago, she thought. Twenty years ago a crime had been committed. Twenty years ago it had been necessary to bury the bodies of a man and a woman so that they should never be found. And now, when they *had* been found, it was vital to whoever had buried them that the skeletons should not be identified and the crime brought home.

The Year of Our Lord 1154. The day after Saint Stephen's Day, when, by tradition, servants were allowed to leave their employer and return to their family for a while.

Was that significant? Possibly. People not usually free to travel would have been on the loose. Also, heads of households, for once, had been left to look after themselves — without servants to watch them.

But the greatest suspicion must fall on the abbey itself, the only place where it was known that a convenient hole had opened up and was ready to receive bodies.

Who had been in situ on that day? Nearly a hundred monks, all but four of them now scattered around England and France, broadcasting the plight that had befallen Glastonbury.

No, Abbot Sigward must be excluded — he'd still been holding sway as a great landlord on his island, perhaps mourning the son who'd fallen on crusade.

For a moment, Adelia thought of the shining goodness that had propelled Sigward from the position of a novitiate to that of abbot over the heads of monks who had served their abbey much longer.

Of the three who remained, all had shown hostility toward her and Mansur in their investigation. Had it been caused by more than just a desire to claim the bodies as Arthur's and Guinevere's?

Was one of them a murderer? All three?

No, wrong again. If one of them had crept

out of terce to the graveyard, the abbot
would have noticed it and said so. Wouldn't
he?

But somewhere out there was a killer
who'd known what she and Mansur were
about, and tried to put an end to it. He'd
failed that time, but had Mansur succumbed to him now?

And Emma? Had Emma disappeared into
the same web, to be eaten by the same
spider?

Tired, tortured by worry, her head re-
sounding with unanswered questions, her
back aching from her efforts in the pit,
Adelia laid herself down next to the twitching, muttering Gyltha. And dozed. And
dreamed . . .

Inevitably, she was belowground, in a
warren where stoats dressed in golden
regalia were shouting huzzahs at King Arthur as he and his troops rode on horses up
the tunnel toward its exit. In passing, he
looked kindly down at her, as he always did.
"Another dragon to fight," he said. "Will
you come with me?"

"I must search for Mansur and Emma,"
she told him.

"Stupid, stupid you are," he said.

Guinevere, still dressed in white feathers,
her back to Adelia, stood at the mouth of

the tunnel to wish farewell and good fortune to her lord.

As the cavalcade passed her, one of Arthur's knights drew his sword and cut her in half. The blood from the severed waist filled the tunnel, catching Adelia in its torrent and carrying her, struggling, deeper into the earth.

When she woke up, it took a moment before she found out that the dampness making her clothes stick to her was not Guinevere's blood but her own sweat.

The light of a big moon coming through the window like pale roadway was the only cold thing in the room. She got up to look out again. The street below was deserted; she leaned forward so that she could see the marketplace. It was as empty as ever.

Where is he? Almighty Father, keep him safe.

Somebody coughed. It was a human cough.

He's come back.

Adelia ran out of the room, jumped over the sleeping Millie, skipped down the stairs, and drew back the bolts on the courtyard door. There was nobody outside. Hurrying, she went into the street. "Mansur?"

Her arms were grabbed. Somebody put a hand over her mouth; somebody else whipped a rag over her eyes, tying it tightly and catching her hair in the knot so that it pulled against her scalp.

"Nice of her to come an' meet us," a man said. "Save us goin' in to get her." There was a general snigger.

NINE

She tried biting into the hand, but its owner kept it in place as he lifted her onto the bare back of a horse and climbed up behind her.

"Leave wrigglin', blast you," he said. Uselessly, she was kicking out with her bare feet. "You ain't going to get hurt."

She was not reassured — it wasn't a reassuring voice, and its owner was clasping her too tightly — but after a while she stopped struggling. For one thing, it hurt her strained back; for another, it was useless. She sensed that there were several of them, whoever they were. The unshod hooves of their mounts made little noise, but their thudding suggested a cavalcade.

Rape? It was the great and immediate terror. Had she been earmarked for it? Or would they have rampaged into the inn taking any woman they found?

Wherever they were going, it was uphill; the incline was forcing her back against the strong-smelling coat of her captor. And it was quiet except for the song of nightingales and the occasional shriek of an owl.

They can do anything. God save me. How will Allie manage without me?

Was this what had happened to Emma and the others? To Mansur? It was even more frightening when the man removed his hand from her mouth — he knew there'd be no help forthcoming even if she yelled.

She tried to stay calm. "Why are you doing this?"

"You speak the darky's jabber, don't you? Can't understand a bloody word he says."

Mansur. They were taking her to Mansur, who was pretending he didn't speak English, so he was in desperate straits or he would have tried to stop them from fetching her. At least it meant they were demanding her services and not her body.

Adelia's heart rate slowed down a little. "What do you want?"

"You'll see."

"Not with this damned blindfold on, I won't. Take it off."

"Feisty, ain't she?" There was more sniggering, but with another tug on her hair, the rag's knot was undone.

Moonlight shone on trees and undergrowth and, as she looked round, a steep slope that fell away to a valley and the marshes. Which of the hills that reared up around Glastonbury they were on she couldn't tell. "Where are we?"

"Never you mind."

Wherever it was, it was their destination. She was lifted down from what she now saw was a donkey — they were all on donkeys, five men as shaggy-looking and as evil-smelling as the mounts they were tying to a stake.

Somebody lit a lantern. She was pushed, stumbling, over rough ground until, by the lantern's light, she saw that they stood outside an outcrop, almost like an oriel window set into the hill, curtained from above by the trailing fronds of an alder fed by a spring that trickled down one side — a sylvan scene, its loveliness spoiled by a smell that Adelia knew too well.

The branches were pushed aside. Sitting in the entrance to a cave were three men, Mansur, a guard holding a knife on him — and Rhys the bard.

Adelia had forgotten that Rhys hadn't come back to the inn; in all the upheaval, she'd even forgotten he existed. Her eyes were only for the Arab, and she fell on him, jabbering in Arabic. "Are you all right? Have they hurt you? We've been desperate. . . ."

He was angry, though not with their captors. He gestured toward Rhys. "That son of a whore and a he-camel. I did not show that I understood them. I did not know he would tell them where to find you. May shaitan use his skull as a pisspot. . . ."

Adelia had never heard Mansur swear like this, though she was relieved that he had the energy to do it. Of the two of them, Rhys, the betrayer, was the worse for wear, battered, on the edge of tears. "Taken my harp, they have," he said. "You tell them they got to give me back my harp."

It was a plea for a lost limb, and automatically Adelia said, "I will," though her attention was for Mansur. "Have they hurt you?"

"I am well. They are ignorant fellahin, yet I think they mean no harm."

"What do they want of us?"

One of the men had stepped between the two of them. "Stop your jabber." A dirty finger was directed toward Mansur. "He's a Merlin, ain't he? A wizard? Talks to the dead, don't he? An' they talk back?"

"Er, up to a point," Adelia told him cautiously.

"Tell him to chat with this un, then." The man pushed past them to go farther into the cave, and with a tug removed a screen of withies that had been blocking its interior.

The stink of mortification intensified. The lamp was held higher so that she could see what lay inside. It was a skeleton.

"Chat to it?"

" 'At's right. Ask him where he's been, what he was a-doing of afore he got dead."

Great God, was that why Mansur had been kidnapped? A misinterpretation of his reputation? Did these men truly think that he, that *anybody,* could converse with a corpse?

In wonderment at the infinite credulity of the ignorant, Adelia raised her head to stare at the man. The beginning of dawn fell on a face that lamplight had merely disguised with shadows. She recognized it.

"You're the baker," she said. "You were at Wolvercote Manor." She got to her feet in excitement. "Emma. The lady who went there. My friend. You know what happened to her. *I saw* you know it."

Happenings were beginning to relate to each other. Rhys had found the man, talked to him, and, it seemed, given more information than he'd received.

"Never you mind who I am. Get that bloody wizard to work."

"Tell me about Lady Emma. What happened to her?"

"Him first." The baker nodded toward the

object in the cave. "Then maybe I will."

It was at least admission that the man had information. She asked, "What do you want to know?"

"What happened to him. What killed the poor bugger. 'Cos we don't think as he did what they say he did."

"What was he supposed to have done?"

The baker brandished a knife at her. "Ask him, I'm telling you, aren't I? Afore I cut all three of you into pig meat."

"Ask him what?"

But Mansur had not been wasting his time; supposedly unable to understand English, he had accrued a great deal of information by listening as his captors talked among themselves. In Arabic, he said, "The dead man is the Eustace who is supposed to have set the abbey fire."

"And what is he to them?" Adelia asked in the same language.

"They have to answer for his crime. Already four of their number are in gaol awaiting the coming assize in Wells. These others expect that they may be arrested at any moment and brought to book for arson. They are Eustace's" — Mansur paused because he had to say the next word in English, there being no Arabic equivalent for it — "frankpledge."

222

The baker was startled at hearing the word. "Here, how'd that black bugger know about our frankpledge?"

"Oh, be quiet," Adelia said crossly. The man was getting on her nerves. "I expect Eustace told him."

There was a new respect in the eyes of the men standing around her. "He's good, ain't he?" one of them said.

Frankpledge. An English legal system to keep order — an alien concept to Adelia when she'd arrived in the country. It was a way of enforcing the law and policing the common people — upper classes were exempt — by grouping every male the age of twelve into a unit of ten, known as a *tithing,* that was responsible for a misdemeanor or felony committed by any of the others.

Periodically and with rigid efficiency, the courts held a "view of frankpledge" all over the country, during which each member of a tithing had to reaffirm his oath that he would bring to the bar of justice any of his nine fellows who had committed an offense, that he was answerable for their behavior as well as his own, that he would pursue them if they fled their crime. The penalty was a fine in accordance with the severity of the offense.

It was an old law, rooted in Anglo-Saxon

custom, and Adelia, who had seen innocent men lose their homes through the wrong-doing of one of their tithing, thought it unfair. She'd questioned Prior Geoffrey about it, but he had shrugged his shoulders. "Mostly it works," he'd said.

Obviously, it was working here. These five men — nine if you counted the four who'd been remanded — were responsible in law for the corpse in the cave. If they couldn't prove it innocent of destroying the biggest abbey in England, their punishment didn't bear thinking about.

That they had committed the crime of kidnapping in pursuit of that laudable aim didn't seem to have occurred to them.

"Why do you believe your friend *didn't* start the fire?" she asked.

The baker apparently thought that this was another matter the late Master Eustace could settle. But a younger man who'd been employing his time with his hand up the skirt of his tunic, nervously scratching his testicles, answered for him. "See, Useless never took a light into the abbey when he needed a drink. Like a fox, Useless was; he could see in the dark."

" 'S right," said another, even younger. "Maybe he'd filch a bit here or there, swig of wine, p'raps . . ."

The baker hit him. "Don't tell her that, Alf, you fucking booby."

"But he wouldn't never start a fire," Alf insisted.

"These are *not* honest fellows," Mansur told Adelia. "I have listened to their talk. Petty criminals, poachers, all of them, so far undiscovered. This cave is their haven in time of trouble. They seem to have had a fondness for this Eustace, bringing food to him here, winking at his thieving as long as it did not reach the ears of the sheriff. Now that he has been accused of arson, they are frightened of what will happen to them."

"Not desperados, then," Adelia said. "Just desperate."

"Yes, but desperate men are dangerous men. We must be careful."

"How? How can we prove anything one way or the other?"

"I do not know."

"Neither do I. From the look of him, he's been dead some time."

"Over a month. They found him lying here dead a day or two after the fire. They did not know what to do. Then they heard that a wizard who listened to bones would be arriving."

"You."

"Me. They waited for me. The body has

decomposed."

"Well, it would, wouldn't it?" In the heat of this summer, decomposition would have set in quickly. The withy screen that had held off hungry animals hadn't been proof against flies.

"You two goin' to jabber all day?" In his impatience, the baker was brandishing a knife. "I'll cut you, I swear I'll have your tripes out. Get in and *talk* to the poor sod, will you? And you" — he turned on Rhys, whose ceaseless lament had provided a counterpoint all through the discussion — "shut up about your fucking harp."

Stooping, Mansur and Adelia went into the cave. Which, if it hadn't been for its contents and the odor rising from the earth beneath them where putrefying juices had soaked into it, would have been beautiful. The rising sun shone straight into it — *so, Adelia thought, wherever we are, we are facing directly east* — lighting the elfin green of delicate ferns growing from the rock, giving a sparkle to a drip of water from the roof that ran in a channel to join the bigger flow outside.

Caverns like this one were a feature of Glastonbury's peculiar countryside; indeed, the abbey made money from sick pilgrims who paid to be healed from drinking the waters of what were claimed to be sacred springs. Adelia had hoped to visit one of them when she had time, to test the properties of its holy water. However, this secret place was not one of the sanctified springs — and now was most definitely not the moment.

She and Mansur knelt on either side of their patient, meeting each other's eyes for a moment, then bending their heads to say their prayers. Whatever this man had done, he had paid for it in a lonely death.

"Get out of the doorway," Adelia demanded of the men clustering around the entrance. "The doctor needs more light. Bring it."

The lantern was handed in, and the cave entrance became decorated with peering heads, the bodies staying obediently outside.

The skeleton was still clothed, if bloodied rags qualified as clothes. Its one decent possession was a short, empty scabbard attached to the string that served it as a belt. The knife belonging to it lay a little way away from the left hand; the right hand had been wrapped in leaves and moss that were now in a disgusting condition.

There was a protest from the cave entrance as Mansur started to undress the bones.

Sharply, Adelia quelled it. "Be quiet. Do you want the doctor to do his job, or don't you?" She'd lost interest in anything except the cadaver before her, and woe betide anybody who tried to divert her concentration.

The bones had become disarticulated, and Mansur was able to pick up the skull so that they could examine its back and front. It bore no injury, unlike the heads in what Adelia still thought of as the Arthur-and-Guinevere coffin.

They left the site of the most obvious injury — the right hand — until they had checked to see if there were others.

Mandible, neck, scapulas, rib cage, spine, pelvis — all correct.

Femur . . . *"Hmm."* Adelia raised her head. "Did he limp?" The left patella had an old fracture.

There was delight from the doorway. "Fell off a roof when he were a nipper, never could walk proper after. He's telling you things already, ain't he?"

This had to stop. "Listen to me," Adelia said, "Master Eustace is not *talking* to my lord Mansur; his soul has passed on to wherever it is going. The doctor can only read what the bones are showing him."

"Oh, *reading*. Ain't magic, then?"

"No."

The testicle scratcher said admiringly, "Still, *reading* . . ." It was a skill none of them possessed and, though a disappointment, was yet an activity rated as marvelous.

Fibula, tibia.

Now they looked to the arms: humerus, radius, ulna. Finally, they unwrapped the hand.

"How did he lose these fingers?" Adelia asked.

She was answered by a surprised chorus from the entrance.

"Didn't know as he had."

"What fingers?"

"Had all his bloody fingers last time I saw him."

There was a move to enter and look for the lost digits, as if Eustace had mislaid them somewhere and they might find them tucked away at the rear of a shelf.

"Get back," Adelia snarled. "Which of you saw him last?"

"That'd be me," Alf said. "Brought him up a collop of venison for his supper. . . ."

The baker smacked him again. "You want us up afore the fucking verderers?"

Adelia became worried. She was learning altogether too much about these men, and it was unlikely they would leave Mansur and her alive to be in possession of the knowledge. If they'd brought venison to Eustace, the deer they'd cut it from had most definitely not been theirs to kill. In the eyes of hunt-loving kings and nobles, deer poaching was the most heinous crime in the legal calendar, and the verderers, guardians of their chases, held courts from which a poacher could be sent to have his limbs cut off and hung among the trees of the forest in which he had offended.

". . . an' he had all his fingers then," Alf finished defiantly. "Night before the fire, that was. What's he done with 'em?"

"Mmm."

Mansur said quietly to Adelia in Arabic, "Have you noticed what is at the rear of this cave?" He angled the lantern so that its light reached deep into the interior and fell on not a rock face but a slightly convex wall built of tightly packed stones.

Adelia experienced a moment of sickness, remembering another such wall in Cambridge that had shut in a living, erring woman whom the Church had seen fit to punish with entombment.

Sharply, she called out, "What's behind the stones at the back here . . . the lord Mansur wants to know."

"Never you mind," the baker shouted back. "None of your business."

But the voice of Alf, bless him, said, "Eustace's dad went and rebuilt that wall after the earthquake, didn't he, Will? Keeps the demon in."

"Demon?"

"Nasty demon back there. Came screamin' out at Eustace's dad when the wall fell down in the earthquake and Eustace's dad had to shut it in again. Never the same after that, Eustace's dad wasn't."

"Weren't much before it," came the voice of the testicle scratcher, gloomily.

Mansur and Adelia exchanged looks. The earthquake again. There had been a good deal more than just seismic activity around Glastonbury on that day twenty years ago.

Will was yelling at them to get on with it, so nothing could be done to find out what lay beyond the wall at the moment, but Adelia promised herself that she'd come and look when there was an opportunity. It might have nothing to do with anything. On the other hand, it might.

At the moment, though, she had other business. At a nod from her, Mansur gathered the remains of Eustace's right hand and took them out into the open air for them both to examine in the light of a dawn that was promising another hot day.

"Hmm."

This was peculiar. The proximal phalanges of the middle fingers had been cut through so that the upper joints were missing, leaving the thumb and little finger intact, like two sentinel trees guarding the stumps of three that had been felled.

Had every skeleton in Glastonbury been hacked about?

"A sword fight?" Mansur asked.

"*Mmm.* I'd have expected a sword, being long, to have swiped all the fingers off. It's almost . . . I don't know. . . . It's almost as if he'd proffered the three middle fingers to be cut off, keeping the thumb and little one bent away from the blow."

She thought some more. "Keep talking." It was vital to maintain the pretense that Mansur was in charge. He impressed these men; she did not. Besides, *should* the two of them manage to leave alive, she didn't want the spreading of a rumor that a witch was at work in Glastonbury.

"Can you tell what happened to this man?" Mansur asked, "because if you cannot . . . They have told us too much."

"I know." She reverted to English. "My lord doctor wishes to see Eustace's knife."

The men fell over themselves in the rush

to retrieve it for him. "Right sharp, this is," said one of them. "Always kept it honed, did our Useless."

They gave it to Mansur, who, still talking, held it so that Adelia could see it as well. The blade was certainly sharp, but there was a nick in the center of it.

"When did that happen?" she asked.

Alf opened his mouth but received another hit from the baker — obviously, Eustace's knife had been damaged in another nefarious activity. "Year since," the baker told her, "and never you mind how."

Squinting, putting her head close to the damaged stumps of the hand, making sure that Mansur also made a show of examining them, Adelia saw a v-shaped splinter at the end of the third finger's middle phalange where some of the bone hadn't been cut through entirely, as if, instead, it had been ripped free of whatever had caught it. God, how terrible. The pain . . .

"I think he did this himself," she said in Arabic. "I think Eustace used this knife to cut his own fingers off."

"Why?"

She shut her eyes to bring up a mental picture of a hand outstretched, then opened them again to look carefully at the still-extant bone of the little finger. Yes, there was a scrape down one side of it.

Mansur kept talking.

"The lord doctor wishes to know how Eustace got over the abbey wall when he went thieving," Adelia said in English. "Presumably it was high. Did he climb it?"

The baker blustered. "Who says he went thieving?"

But Alf, the terminally truthful Alf, now enslaved by the Arab's reading powers, said, "With *his* leg? Couldn't climb pussy, could Useless. Burrowed under, he did, like a bloody rabbit."

The testicle scratcher chimed in. "Gor, di'n't old Brother Christopher hate them rabbits. Got at his lettuces. *Ooh,* he hated them coneys, old Brother Chris, well, hated everything, really. Set noose traps for bloody everything — foxes, badgers, birds. . . . Useless always complained about them noose traps. Got in his way. He knew where they were, though. They never caught our Useless."

Adelia nodded. Rabbits were comparatively new to England, having been introduced by Norman lords for their fur and meat, but, thanks to the escapees from the warrens in which they were kept, they were rapidly becoming a pest to gardeners everywhere.

And she'd learned something else. These men around her were well acquainted with the routine of the abbey *and* with the movements of its brethren who, before the fire, had tended and tried to guard it — presumably, if they poached its deer and, like Eustace, stole from it, they had to be.

But their knowledge could have come from only one source — the lay brother, Peter. Rhys could be absolved for chattering. Peter and the baker were closely related, had to be; their likeness was too strong for it to be otherwise. From Peter they'd heard of Mansur's supposed skill with the dead and, without reckoning the consequences, had kidnapped him. When they couldn't understand him, they'd returned to kidnap her because she could.

"Show us," she said. "My lord Mansur wishes to see where Master Eustace got into the abbey grounds."

"What bloody good'll that do?" the baker wanted to know.

"A lot." Adelia indicated Mansur. "This great reader of bones" — *Keep stressing his powers* — "thinks that he may, only *may,* be able to prove that your friend did not set the fire. But now he demands two things. First, that you will then let the two of us" — she remembered Rhys, who was still sing-

235

ing sadly to himself — "the *three* of us, go unharmed. Second, you shall then tell us what you know of our friend, Lady Emma."

An older man who hadn't spoken before said, "Here, we can't let 'em go, Will, they'll squawk on us."

So the baker was called Will. Adelia kept her eyes on him. Because he was the most intelligent of the tithing, he was also the most frightened and, therefore, dangerous. But *because* he was the more intelligent, he must know that she had a weapon in her armory belittling anything in his — if she and Mansur could prove Eustace's innocence, they had to be kept alive *in order* to prove it to the authorities.

"Who would believe *you?*" she said.

The answer was nobody. Lay proof before a court? Inarticulate men with dubious reputations, a difficult case to put, and no expert witnesses to call? An impatient judge — and all assize judges were impatient; they had too many cases to hear in too short a time — wouldn't even bother to listen.

Adelia knew it. Will the baker knew it.

She waited.

He said, and for the first time he was placatory, "An' you won't squawk on us . . . you know, 'bout the venison and such, 'bout how we, er, invited you here?"

"No," she said. And she meant it. So far they had done no real harm to Mansur or her or Rhys, and she was sorry for men so poor in education and goods. As it was, they would be punished for Eustace's predations on the abbey — but that was nothing compared to the sin of setting fire to it.

"Swear?" Will asked.

"What on?"

And that, too, was touching. There was no Bible, no prayer book — these men had only seen such things in a church. But for them, this secret spring was as inexplicable and magical as any of those made famous by the abbey.

"Arthur's spring, this is," Alf told her. "It was Eustace's dad found it, but he's passed on and nobody don't know it but us. Useless told us, di'n't he, lads? Saw Arthur drinkin' from it one night, kneelin' he was, and a light shining from his kingly crown."

"Useless saw a lot of things," Will growled. "Purple snakes among 'em."

So Mansur and Adelia and Rhys knelt, cupping their hands under the shining spiral of water and drinking from it, swearing by good King Arthur that if they could prove Eustace innocent of arson, they would not inform on anything else they had learned during their sojourn with the tithing.

Then, one by one, the tithing itself swore that if the good doctor and his assistant could prove Eustace innocent of arson, they would not cut the throats of said doctor and assistant.

"Nor mine, neither," Rhys insisted.

Nor that of the bard, either.

"And you give me back my harp?"

And the tithing would give him back his bloody harp.

All very charming with the sun hot on the backs of their heads and the chirp of grasshoppers joining a winged chorus . . .

But what, thought Adelia, *if I can't prove anything?*

The tithing's prisoners had been brought to the cave by a circuitous route; the abbey was actually within walking distance, and there was a discussion about whether the donkeys should be left where they were and the descent of the hill made on foot.

The clear sound of a horn in the distance decided the matter. "Bastards," said Will. "They've come looking for you."

Rowley. He'd brought a hunt to scour the countryside for her.

Suddenly, she didn't want to be found. Not yet. She had work to do, a puzzle to solve. She was mistress to the dead; a corpse had cried out to her.

Will addressed the testicle scratcher. "How many, Toki? Where?"

The tithing became still so that Toki could look and listen. Adelia listened with them, hearing only a blackbird and the rush of the spring.

Slowly, scratching madly, turning 180 degrees from east to west, Toki said, "Fifteen horse, I reckon. No dogs. Don't know how many foot. They're quarterin' Wearyall."

"How long afore they get to us?"

Toki shrugged. "Depends where they go next. Could be here. Could be Saint Edmund's, could be Chalice."

These, with Wearyall, were the hills of Glastonbury; therefore, by a process of elimination, Adelia knew herself to be on the Tor, that strange cone, most sacred of all the hills rising out of the flatness around the abbey.

Damn. She didn't want to spend all day skulking in a cave until the hunt had gone away, especially not with Eustace in it.

But she hadn't reckoned on the tithing's experience. It was used to pursuit; ignorant of most things, it had skills she hadn't dreamed of.

"Quick, then," Will said. He turned to her. "Keep your bloody head down. Yell and you're dead. Tell the darky that." He wheeled round on Rhys. "One peep out of you and I'll break your neck *and* your fucking harp."

The donkeys were shoved into the cave and the screen hidden with branches. It was decided that cover was thicker at the hill's lower end, and that they should make for it.

The descent began. Adelia was to look back on it as among the luminous times of her life.

Few girls had a childhood; the imperative was to grow into womanhood with a woman's skills as quickly as possible. In Adelia's case, it had been to learn how to be a doctor and then an anatomist. Training hadn't been imposed on her — her foster parents had tried to make her take up some amusement, but she had resisted them; study was the thing.

Now here, on a journey down a sacred tor, for the first time, she was granted a gift, the childhood of a common country boy who had climbed trees and stolen birds' eggs, who had scrumped apples from other people's orchards and hidden from angry gamekeepers. Or perhaps because the danger was more than a clout on the ear, she became a soldier in enemy territory, using a landscape to escape discovery and get home.

Whatever it was, she loved it.

At the beginning they went fast, dodging from tree to tree in case someone in the hunt had sight and hearing as long as Toki's. The blare of horns was louder now. Adelia could hear her name being shouted, the calls coming closer through the hot air.

Having exhausted the search of Wearyall Hill, Rowley was leading his men straight to the Tor.

"On your bellies, lads," Will said quietly. To Adelia, he said, "You goin' to give us away?"

"No."

Just in case, he kept close to her, knife in hand. Two of the other men were paired with Mansur and Rhys, ready to silence them if they cried out.

Wisely, the hunt had gone to the top of the hill and begun circling downward in spirals.

The tithing and prisoners made for cover, crawling, feeling the reverberation of the hunt's hoofbeats through their hands and knees.

It was wonderful; it was a game, it was *the* game; it was life at primitive level; it was how a species survived by craft and fear. For Adelia absorbed some of the terror of the tithing as they crawled, her back prickling with exposure, as if her life as well as theirs depended on concealment, all the while being filled with the joy of a wild thing using its habitat. She was a weasel undulating through the fragrancy of grass; she was a snake with sweet earth beneath her belly; a clump of tall, purple loosestrife was a hiding place, a patch of inhospitable gorse to be despised.

As the hunt grew closer, she became an outlaw among outlaws, her teeth exposed in a snarl, as if they had a knife between them. She'd never played hide-and-seek, but deep inside the dark, crumbling interior of a hollowed oak, she watched Rowley ride by within ten feet of her, crying her name — and she would no more have called out to him than a boar in its lair would have snorted to attract the hounds.

When he'd passed, she looked up to where Will was lying across a branch above her. Their eyes met with mutual respect, and she knew that whatever happened, he would not kill her now, just as he knew she was not going to betray him. They were feral creatures; together they had outwitted the hunt.

On a promontory with a view of the abbey and marshes, the tithing — for they were all frankpledged now — watched its pursuers set off for Chalice Hill.

"Rest a bit," Will said, and nodded toward the abbey, from which came a faint plainchant. "They'll be finishing terce any moment."

So it was the third hour of daylight, one hundred and eighty minutes since Adelia had been introduced to Eustace's cave, and not one of them she wouldn't look back on without a ferocious joy.

As she waited, lying flat, Will on one side, Alf on the other, the primeval drained out of her and, with a pang of regret, she resumed the mind and shape of Vesuvia Adelia Rachel Ortese Aguilar, Medica of the Salerno School, mistress of the art of death and agent to King Henry II of England, anxious friend to a missing woman, lover of a man who loved God and his king more than he did her. . . .

"Here they come, look," Will said as four black beetle-like figures emerged from the ruin of the church. "Bugger, I forgot as it's third Friday of the month."

For the beetles were not returning to the Abbot's kitchen; one of them was walking toward the abbey pier, where the unmistakable shape of Godwyn awaited him at the oars of a rowing boat. "Off to Lazarus," Will said. "Old abbot's a-taking communion to them lepers."

"Well, *they're* not worrying about me," Adelia said, slightly miffed at the abbey's placid reaction to her and Mansur's disappearance.

"Reg'lar as Christmas. Every three weeks, off he do go to keep them lepers' souls in trim, nothin' to come in the way of it."

"Saint he is," Alf said. "Buggered if I'd go."

"Leprosy isn't all that contagious," Adelia murmured.

"What's that mean?"

"You don't catch the sickness quickly."

"I ain't bloody riskin' it, I tell you that."

"I'm sorry for the poor sods," Toki said. "Fancy rottin' away on a lump o' mud as you can't get off of."

"But can't they walk off it?" Adelia wanted to know. From up here the mosaic of sedge, reed, and fen woodland with their differing greens that surrounded the islands' low humps looked firm enough, while surely those streams and lakes reflecting the enamel blue of the sky could be swum or waded.

"Not allowed," Toki told her. "The law. An' they ain't got no boat."

Abbot Sigward and Godwyn, apparently, when they visited that poor congregation, had to secure their punt to Lazarus's landing stage by a lock to which only they had the key.

"As for walkin'," Will said, "you don't walk the Avalon marshes less'n you been born on 'em. Not then, neither. There's quog devils out there as'll grab your feet and suck you down, an' you ain't never sure where they are 'cos they're shifting buggers, pop up anywhere them quog devils will."

"Yet I've seen people on stilts. . . ."

But stilt walkers, Adelia was told, never went that far out, being aware of the risk. Anyway, Lazarus inhabitants had learned by tragic experience not to try and escape.

"There's more'n one leper as tried to get off ain't never been seen again."

The beetles that were brothers Aelwyn, James, and Titus moved about the grounds, carrying out odd jobs, netting trout from the pool for the fish stew — for it was Friday and only fish was on the menu.

On its promontory, the tithing waited with animal patience until the monks should withdraw into the Abbot's kitchen and, while it waited, passed comment on the men it watched.

"Old Titus'll be wanting his dinner soon, greedy bugger."

"An' his ale. Old abbot sent poor Useless off for getting drunk, but he don't know the

245

half of what Titus topes when he ain't looking. Could drink Useless under the table any day, Titus could."

"Look at old James potterin' about. Bet he's talking to hisself. Mad as a weasel, James is, an' nasty with it when he's roused."

Will nudged Adelia. "Bet you don't know as why Brother Aelwyn di'n't want you and the darky messin' about in the graveyard."

"No. Why?"

" 'Cos he's got two babies buried in it."

"Babies?"

Will smirked. "Babies. Oh, there was carryin's-on with women in the old days, so they say, for all them monks was supposed to be virgins, an one of 'em had twins an' old Aelwyn give 'em to her. Left 'em on the abbey's doorstep, she did. There was a right to-do about it. Had to bury 'em in the monks' own graveyard."

"Dear God, how did the babies die?"

Will, with some reluctance, admitted that as far as was known, the twins had met a natural death.

Listening to them, Adelia began to see the fire's great scar spread over the abbey as a stain representing human frailty and misery.

There was, however, nothing but good words for Abbot Sigward. "Wasn't no carryin's-on after he were elected," Will told her. "Not a bad old boy, for a monk."

"Fancy leavin' a rich living so's you got to say prayers all day," Toki said incredulously.

"Did it for to remember his son as died fighting the bloody Saracens," Alf said. "Right upset about that, Sigward was. 'S a wonder he never sent to have the body brought back. Sir Gervase over at Street, he was brought back and put in Street Church with his legs crossed and his sword an' all."

"Cut up too bad by them black bastards p'raps, nothin' left to bring back. Or maybe he never had no friends to carry him home. Might've died a hero but didn't live like one. Weedy little bugger he was. Hilda never reckoned him much, said he was a milksop, always blubberin' an' saying he was cold."

"Crusades suited him, then," Will said. "Hot out them parts, ain' it?"

"About as hot as here," Adelia told him. She picked a dock leaf to protect her bare head from sunstroke and another to brush the flies away from the sweat on her face. "Aren't those blasted men *ever* going to go in to dinner?"

"S'pose the darky proves Useless di'n't do it, an' we can bury the poor bugger," Toki said to Will. "Where we going to throw his knife?"

"In the river, acourse."

"Which one?"

Will shrugged. "The Brue, I reckon. Liked fishin' in the Brue, Useless did. 'F you ask me, that's where King Arthur threw Excalibur like as not. Useless'd want his old knife to go the same."

"You're throwing his knife into the river?" Adelia inquired.

"Got to," Will said, shortly.

"Why?"

" 'Cos it's got to go back."

She was interested. In her beloved fens, fishermen were often getting their lines caught in rusting weapons, then, carefully and with a prayer, throwing them once again into the waters, obeying a time-fogged legend, almost an instinct, that held that a great warrior's sword or shield, however valuable, must be returned to the mystery that had given it its power. Her foster father, on his travels, had found the custom everywhere in the east. "A very ancient ritual," he'd told her, "an offering to the gods on behalf of the soul of the dead owner."

Of course — now she remembered — she'd heard Rhys singing of Excalibur being returned to the lake from which a lady's arm had once proffered it.

So the custom persisted. Pagan but, still,

beautiful.

At last the abbey grounds emptied. The tithing moved down the hill, still keeping to cover, and approached what remained of the abbey wall.

Will pointed to an area of blackened rubble. "Tha's where Useless'd go under the wall, look, only you can't see the hole now acause the fire brought the stones down on it."

"Then remove them," Adelia told him. "The lord doctor wishes to see the actual burrow."

And Adelia realized that for once she need not command through Mansur; these men belonged to a level of society so low that its women had to work at jobs other than that of a wife in order for their families to survive, holding a place of their own as fellow laborers in the fields, as ale brewers, laundresses, market sellers, maybe even as thieves, bringing in money that earned them a position of their own. Only the upper classes, where ladies were dependent on their lords, could afford to regard women as inferior. Now that she, Adelia, was accepted by the tithing as trustworthy, it was not unnatural for its members to have decisions made by a female.

Still, it was better to stick to the pretense;

one of them might give her away.

With some effort, the stones were cleared to reveal a curve in the ground that once had allowed the late Eustace to creep under the wall. "Like this, see." Alf fell flat, prepared to give demonstration in case the lord Mansur and his interpreter didn't understand the burrowing procedure.

Adelia stopped him. "Don't. The doctor believes there's a trap on the other side."

"Gor, old Useless didn't have no trouble with traps."

"I think he had trouble with this one," Adelia said. She pushed Alf aside and took his place. "Get me a stick."

A stick was brought and Adelia, crouching in the depression, extended it gingerly so that she could use it to sift through the cinders and newly grown weeds on the abbey side of the wall.

Something clinked.

And there it was. Not a noose such as tightened around the neck or leg of vermin but a spring trap, now buckled by heat yet still recognizable as the terrible thing it was, and still with the chain that had been riveted to one of the stones in the wall.

Brother Christopher had become exasperated by the night-time human rabbit that kept nibbling away at the abbey's stores, and, ignoring the command that the Church must not shed blood, he'd made sure he caught it this time.

The tithing was shocked. "I'll kill that there monkish bastard when he gets back," Will said.

"What he want to do that for?" Alf wanted to know. "Useless din't do no harm, just a sip o'wine to keep him happy, odd turnip or lettuce here or there. Bugger it, richest abbey in the world could afford a bit o'charity, cou'n't it?"

But Brother Christopher had not thought so; he'd laid in the grass outside Eustace's burrow a mechanism consisting of a pair of steel jaws triggered by a spring and welded it into place, so that Eustace, pulling himself out of the burrow, had put a hand on the base, causing the trap's teeth to jump together in a wicked bite on his fingers.

It wasn't a mantrap such as the one Adelia had once seen — and still tried not to remember — holding someone else in its jaws; this was smaller but, in its way, had proved just as fatal.

In her mind, she heard the snap as it closed, saw Eustace struggling without effect to dislodge it from its fastening . . .

"But that don't prove nothing," Will said, having given it thought. "They'll say as how

251

he got *in* some other way, set the fire, an' was trapped comin' *out.*"

"The doctor doesn't think so," Adelia said, nodding at Mansur, who nodded back. "Eustace used his own knife to cut off his own fingers; he wouldn't have done that unless his life depended on it, would he?"

The tithing shook its head. A man didn't deliberately lose the use of his right hand unless he was in extremis. Eustace would have waited until somebody released him and taken his punishment, which, under a compassionate abbot, might not have been too severe.

"No," Adelia went on, "Eustace *had* to free himself. He was coming in through the burrow ready to do his thieving. Look . . ." She used the stick again to stir through the weeds and found the proof she knew had to be there, and nearly collapsed with relief that it was. "Look." She exposed three knobbles of charred bone. "Those are his fingers."

They still didn't understand.

She said, "The fingers are on the abbey side, pointing toward it. If . . . Don't touch them, Alf; they're our proof where they are. . . . Don't you see, if Eustace had been returning from the crypt they'd have been on the *other* side of the trap. It caught him as he was going *in.* I think, *the doctor thinks,* the fire had already started and was spreading toward this wall. If he hadn't sliced off his fingers, he'd have been burned alive."

Again, she saw Eustace, helpless, flames licking through the grass toward his face, desperately sawing with his knife through his own gristle and bone to get free, tearing the flesh of his little finger away from the tooth of the trap that had nicked the edge of its proximal phalanx.

She watched him wrap the dreadful injury in moss and grass and blunder his way up the hill to die of blood loss or poisoning, praying to God or perhaps to Arthur for a relief that never came.

"Poor old Useless," Alf said quietly.

"An' you'll clear him for us?" Will asked.

"Yes," Adelia told him, "I shall tell the bishop of Saint Albans, and he will tell the sheriff."

She bent over the trap, mentally going over its evidence once more, clearing away the weeds in order that the position of the burned finger bones could be seen more clearly.

Mansur shouted.

She turned round, alarmed.

The tithing had gone. Where the men had been seconds ago, there were merely burned stones and the rise of a hillside. It was as if the sun had melted them away.

"Come back, come *back,*" Adelia yelled. "You haven't told me about Emma." But her scream raised nothing but a flight of warblers from the undergrowth.

The only thing to show that the tithing had ever been present was the harp nestling in Rhys's arms.

TEN

Rowley was so angry he could barely talk to her.

And Adelia was so tired that despite a nap after having been put to bed by a solicitous and relieved Gyltha on her return to the Pilgrim, she resented his attitude. Would he have preferred it if she'd been raped and murdered?

But no, her crime, it seemed, was in ignoring the hunting calls of his search and not throwing herself in front of his horse in gratitude at being rescued.

"I didn't *need* rescuing," she protested. "I was in no danger."

"Kidnapped by a load of cutthroats to view a skeleton is your idea of an outing, is it?"

"They were not cutthroats, they were Eustace's frankpledge. We happened to meet in the road last night, they asked if I would accompany them to the cave where they had found him — and I went."

"As one does," Rowley said.

"I hoped they might have news of Emma."

"Ah, yes, your disappearing friend. Then, of course, you had to go."

She ignored his sarcasm. "Did you inquire for her?"

"Thank you, yes, I wasted more time yesterday questioning the sheriff's reeve on your behalf. I had him called to the Bishop's Palace." Momentarily, Rowley's irritation was diverted to something else. "By God, there's incompetence here; robbery on that road is frequent, apparently. 'Wait until Henry hears of it,' I told the little bastard. 'The king will have your sheriff's bollocks. He doesn't like travelers being assaulted on his highways. . . .' "

"Emma?" Adelia reminded him.

"There has been no report of such a cavalcade as hers being attacked, nor any likelihood that it could have vanished without trace — the scum that inhabit that forest only batten on parties of two or three. I told you, she's gone elsewhere, no need to worry about her."

Certainly, *he* didn't. He turned on Mansur, speaking in Arabic. "And *your* disappearance? I suppose these rogues asked *you* equally politely to go with them?"

Mansur nodded. His eyes were half shut from fatigue — he'd had less sleep than Adelia.

It was the answer they had agreed on between them as, without bothering to talk to the monks, the two of them had helped each other back from the abbey wall to the inn.

The temptation to inform on Will the baker and the others because they hadn't honored their agreement to give what information they held about Emma was great — *very* great — but Adelia and Mansur had sworn not to betray them, and oaths must be kept.

Reluctant to accompany him back to the abbey, Adelia told Rowley of the proofs of Eustace's innocence awaiting him by the wall. While he was gone, she went upstairs to wash, put on clean clothes, and be lectured all over again by Gyltha, who punished her for a night of anxiety by brushing her hair with force. "We was worried. Well, Allie wasn't — I told her you'd been called out to physic somebody."

Adelia smiled down at her daughter. "Where did she get that?" The child was sitting on the floor regarding with intense concentration a birdcage in which fluttered a chaffinch.

"Millie. It come flying in when she was cleanin'. She found the cage from some'eres and gave it to the little 'un. That girl ain't as daft as she looks."

"No." The deaf and dumb were universally regarded as half-witted — and treated as such. But, Adelia thought, there's perception there; Millie notices things.

"Next time as you go off without saying, you leave me a message saying as you're well," Gyltha said, still brushing hard.

"Oh, I'm sorry, *ow*, I didn't have my slate-book and chalk with me."

"Couldn't have 'ciphered it even if as you had." Gyltha regarded reading and writing as exercises reserved for the effete. "A twig or summat'll do. Just so's I know it's you."

"I told you, they abducted me. There wasn't *time*. . . ." There still wasn't; Rowley's voice was echoing up the stairs, demanding her immediate presence in the parlor. "Lord, I'm not dressed yet."

"Put this on." Gyltha had been spending her evenings cutting out and stitching a swath of green silk acquired on the journey from Wales.

Adelia regarded the resultant pretty tunic. "You just want me to look nice for *him*. The old brown one will do."

"Wear it." When Gyltha was implacable,

Adelia gave in.

The two women plus Allie and her bird-cage — Adelia was damned if she was going to be without her daughter's company again — descended the stairs.

Abbot Sigward, it appeared, had returned from Lazarus Island, and Rowley had brought him and brothers Aelwyn, James, and Titus back to the inn for a conference.

Now the four monks sat silently together along one side of the Pilgrim's dining table, their black robes and hooded heads making a matte contrast to everybody else's brighter reflection in the board's high polish — Adelia's green, particularly.

Hilda, ready to give her opinion, leaned across the hatch, which, like those in a monastery refectory, gave on to the kitchen. Behind her, the clatter of pans and an appetizing smell suggested that Godwyn was preparing food.

Only two of the inn's people were missing. Rhys was upstairs asleep, still clutching his harp. Millie had been sent by her mistress to sweep the courtyard.

Allie was put on the floor, studying the bird in the cage, talking to it, tempting it with various tidbits to see which it liked best, her soft, inviting chirruping providing a background to the harsh tone of the man who was her father.

Rowley, still in hunting clothes yet very much a bishop, was in command. "We're agreed, then. The sheriff shall be told that the man, Eustace, is to be exonerated." When there was no reply, he pressed the point. "My lord abbot?"

There was a sigh from beneath Abbot Sigward's cowl. "Yes, yes. That must be done. The fire was an accident."

"I suspect it always was," Rowley said. "But caused by whom?"

Abbot Sigward made to get up. "That is a matter for discussion in the privacy of our chapter."

"No, it isn't." The bishop of Saint Albans hadn't finished. "A man was wrongly suspected, his frankpledge falsely arraigned, and only the efforts of my lord Mansur here proved their innocence. A monk died in the flames. A town burned as well as an abbey. Therefore, this is also a civil matter, and those of us here who have been closely concerned have a right to hear it."

He knows, Adelia thought. *He knows who it was.* He's been talking to the lay brother, listening to Hilda. *God help us, I think I know now.*

From over the hatch Hilda said defiantly, "An old trap don't prove nothing. That was

Useless Eustace caused the fire. Di'n't Brother Aloysius tell us when he was killed trying to put out the flames, poor soul?"

"So you say."

Hilda bridled. "Heard him with my own ears, I did, for wasn't I putting salve on his poor burns? 'Eustace, Eustace,' he was saying. His last words, the dear."

"Brother Peter was there, too, and he informs me that the words were not so distinct." The bishop's voice was quiet.

"Well, 'Eu . . . Eu,' then," Hilda said. "But Useless was who he meant."

"Are you sure it wasn't 'You . . . You . . .'? *And who was he looking at when he said it?*"

In the silence, there was only the murmurings from the child on the floor: "Pretty bird, white stripe, pretty dickie."

The last rays of the evening sun coming through the window shone on the long-fingered, blue-veined hands of the abbot clasped tightly on the table — the hands of a tense old man. His face, like those of the other monks, was invisible under his cowl.

At a glance from Adelia, Gyltha leaned down to pick up Allie and her birdcage. "That pretty dickie do need some air," she said, and carried them both outside.

In the room the silence went on, inflating

like a bubble to the point where it must burst.

Brother Titus broke it with a scream. "Stop it. *Stop it.* It was me. He was looking at me. Sweet Mary, Mother of God, *it was me.* I'd been at the wine in the crypt, I was drunk." He began banging his head on the table.

The other monks didn't move.

"And you left a candle burning?" Rowley was remorseless.

"It fell over. It caught the screen. I didn't notice. . . ." He turned to the abbot. He had blood on his forehead where it had hit the wood. "Dear God . . . how to be forgiven . . . All this time . . . I've been in hell with the devil. . . . I have scourged myself til the blood ran. I wanted . . . but it was too massive, everything gone . . . Aloysius . . . I couldn't believe . . . I couldn't . . . Father, forgive me."

He buried his head into the abbot's shoulder, blubbering like an enormous naughty toddler seeking its mother.

And Sigward cradled him like a mother. "I know, my son, I know."

Yes, thought Adelia suddenly. *You did, didn't you?*

She got up and left the room. Mansur followed her out; this was business for the

Christian Church.

They went into the courtyard, where Allie was dithering over her birdcage. "Shall I, Gyltha, shall I?"

"Up to you," Gyltha told her.

Allie took a deep breath. "I think I will, then." She untied the cage's wicker door and opened it. The chaffinch fluttered out, perched on the wellhead for a moment, and then flew off.

"That's better, isn't it?" Allie asked, the tears falling.

Adelia grabbed her and kissed her. "I love you, Almeisan. So much."

After a while, they heard the inn's front door open and the shuffle of Titus's feet as his brother monks helped him home.

Rowley came stamping out into the courtyard. "Well, that's that."

"Is it? What will you do about it?"

He shrugged. "I don't know. Nothing, probably. It was an accident, what's done is done. *Quieta non movere.*"

So sleeping dogs are to be left to lie, are they? Adelia thought. She said, "The abbot knew."

"Suspected, perhaps."

"And said nothing."

He flared up. "In the name of God, Adelia, what would you have me do? You've just seen a man destroyed. Isn't that enough?"

Yes, she had, and was sorry for it, but other men were being allowed to carry a blame of which they were guiltless.

Kindly old Abbot Sigward . . . she would never feel the same for him again.

"Mother Church is all that stands between us and the devil," the bishop of Saint Albans said. "If she loses respect, we are all damned."

He turned to look at his daughter. "And what are you crying for?" The residue of his anger at other people gave the question irritability rather than the concern he probably felt.

Adelia rose immediately to stand between them. "She's crying because she let her bird go."

"Why? I thought she favored the thing."

"She did, but she couldn't bear to see it caged. She wanted it to be free."

"Oh, God, she's going to grow up like you." He untied his horse's reins from the rail, mounted, and rode off.

And that, thought Adelia, *is the crux of everything wrong between us.*

Indoors, she was met by Hilda. The landlady's face was vicious. "See what you done to my dear abbot? You and that darky happy now?"

Adelia'd had enough. From the very first, the protestations by this woman that Eustace was responsible for the fire had been because, in her heart of hearts, she'd known he wasn't. "Your dear abbot deserved it," she hissed back and, ushering Gyltha and Allie before her, went upstairs to bed . . . and dreamed.

This time the queen was being walled up in a cave by unseen hands so that the layers of stones rose one upon the other, as if by themselves, while the woman behind them pleaded with Adelia to stop them until the last stone went into place and her voice was silenced.

Adelia woke up saying, "All right, all right, I'm coming to you."

She took Mansur, Gyltha, and Allie with her. Making sure that nobody watched them, they toiled up the Tor from the burrow under the abbey wall and followed the trail of bruised grass and snapped twigs left by the descent down it the day before. Gyltha carried provisions, Mansur an iron bar and a lantern, Adelia a knife stolen from the inn's kitchen, and Allie a frog and various beetles she picked up on the way.

Despite the trail, it would have been easy to miss the cave with its curtaining of branches if it hadn't been for a pile of mule manure hardening in the sun outside it.

The removal of the withy screen caused Gyltha to hold her nose and protest at the stink. "Me and you'll stay outside, miss," she told Allie, but Adelia felt this was too hard; what child could resist a secret cave? Besides, Eustace's bones had been reunited and covered with a patched cloak belonging to Ollie, the most silent member of the tithing.

Allie was enchanted by the place. She knelt with her mother to send up a prayer for Eustace's soul, listening to and asking questions about the circumstances of his death, but then, since there was more wildlife outside the cave than in it, eventually joined Gyltha in order to explore the hillside while Adelia and Mansur got to work on dismantling the wall.

It wasn't easy. It curved slightly outward, and whoever had built it in the first place had shaped the stones so that they would fit against one another almost with the tightness of tongue and groove, while Eustace's father, however frightened he'd been of the demon, had put it up again in exactly the same way.

It took a quarter of an hour to lever out the first stone and, though removal became easier after that, it was an hour before there was a hole big enough to squeeze through.

In none of that time did Mansur or Adelia look inside; the lantern's beam had been only enough to play on their work — and there was a stillness in the interior that made the idea of peeking somehow disrespectful.

The air coming from the hole they made was surprisingly fresh — no corruption here, nor was it completely black inside; they were aware merely of dimness.

"A saint's tomb?" asked Mansur.

Adelia shrugged, refusing to be seduced by the undoubted air of sanctity here — the Arab had felt the same about the abbey. She picked up the lantern, and Mansur helped her climb through the hole.

She was in what was, or had been, a cell — a large, hollow cairn built within the hill. The earthquake of twenty years ago had caused it to shift, bringing damage. Where the beautifully packed stones of the wall and roof should have begun descending to complete the shape of a circular beehive, they had fallen down to reveal rough rock behind them.

Cracks had opened not only in the ceiling but in the hillside above it so that thin beams of sun, green from infiltrating ferns and moss, pierced the dimness here and there like spears of sunlight through tiny arrow slits.

In the center was a pool so still that it might have been a mirror. Mansur's struggle to get his long body through the gap sent a shiver over its surface.

Beyond it, from the fallen stones of the opposite wall, dangled a skull.

Oh, God, please, Adelia thought, *not another murder.*

Here was Eustace's father's demon.

The skull had been cleaved nearly down to the forehead and was held together only by a circlet of metal like a woman's headband, though this had been dislodged slightly so that it was worn at a rakish angle, as if Death was trying to be jolly. It stared, grinning, down at the pool where its perfect reflection grinned back up at it, making two demons.

A drop of water from the roof plinked into the pool like a note from Rhys's harp. Again, the water shivered so that the demon in it rippled outward before resuming the shape of its twin.

After a long while, Mansur strode round the pool. Gently, his mouth moving silently in an Arabic prayer, he lifted the skull with two hands to put it on the ground, then began poking among the mess of stones. He crooked a finger at Adelia.

She'd been transfixed and had to blink and shake her head before she could join him.

There were other things among the stones: rotting shards of wood, bones, a battered helmet — also sliced in two at the top and corresponding to the wound on the skull where a blow from an ax or a sword had cleaved both the metal and the head that wore it.

Adelia put her hand into the pool to test its depth and found sand at the bottom. Sand? Had the sea once come up as high as this and then retreated?

She took the Arab by the arm and indicated that the two of them should leave.

When they were in the outer cave, Mansur said, "The wood in there was a bier. He was lain on it, I think. He has been treated with respect."

"Possibly."

Hearing their voices, Gyltha called from outside to ask what they'd found. They went to join her in the open air.

"A warrior, we believe," Mansur told her.

"Possibly," said the cautious Adelia again. "Certainly, he was killed by that huge dint on his head. He could be a saint — weren't some of those killed in battle when the

Danes came?"

Neither Mansur nor Gyltha had enough historical knowledge to answer her. But Mansur said, "Why, then, do the monks not know of him?"

It was a good point, and, certainly, the cell did not look like a saint's inhumation.

"We're talking about him as if he were very old," Adelia said, realizing it for the first time.

"He was in there before the earthquake," Mansur pointed out.

"But how long before the earthquake? Is he a victim only just previous to Arthur and Guinevere down there? Damn, I wish we could put a date to him."

"Blow that," Gyltha told her. "You ain't got responsibility for every bugger found dead round here. Anyway, I'm a-going to take a squint at un."

They let her go inside and waited for her, watching Allie take off her boots to splash her bare feet in the spring, letting the frog go from her hands into the water.

When, eventually, Gyltha rejoined them, she was subdued.

"What do you think?" Adelia asked her.

"I think as we should put the poor soul together and wall un in again. Leave un in his peace. Don't seem right else."

She was right; she usually was. So that is what they did.

Rebuilding the whole cell was out of the question; it was going to be time-consuming enough to close up the entrance hole. It was equally impossible to reassemble the bier, so they made a platform from branches to keep the skeleton from the bare ground. Sorting through the rubble, they discovered most of his scattered bones.

They found other things: shin guards not unlike the greaves worn by present-day knights, a brooch of lovely workmanship that had once pinned a cloak to the shoulder of a tunic and, Mansur said, might turn out to be gold if it were cleaned, the brass neck of a bottle, of which the leather had long rotted.

There was also a barbaric twisted torque, again probably of gold, from which hung a wheeled cross. He hadn't been robbed, then, but on the other hand, there were no precious grave goods among the stuff they'd found, such as would have been buried with a great chieftain. Apart from the torque, everything was battered and utilitarian.

Yet somebody had built this secret chamber and hidden him.

Allie came clambering through the hole. "Look, look, I've found a toad."

It was the first time anybody had spoken inside the cell; the adults had worked in silence. Automatically, they hushed her.

With the others' help, Adelia began to reassemble the skeleton on the platform while Allie splashed water from the pool over the toad's warty skin to cool it. It hopped away from her and buried itself in the sand of the pool's bottom. Plunging after it, she said, "Ow, there's a stone in here." She began grubbing for what she'd stepped on and came up with a dripping sword.

"Let me see," Adelia said.

It wasn't an impressive weapon, almost black, with a nick in its blade, and surprisingly light so that it swung easily in her hand.

"What they bury that in the pool for?" Gyltha wanted to know.

"It's the custom, I believe," Adelia told her, remembering that the tithing intended to throw Eustace's knife into the Brue.

At last, they had done what they could. The skeleton lay neatly on the platform, greaves in place, the torque round its neck. They put the brooch on its chest, covered it with the helmet, and folded the hands on top. The remains of the bottle were put at its side.

Gyltha looked at him. "Warrior he may have been, but he weren't very big."

He was decidedly short. Even Adelia was taller.

"But bless un anyway," Gyltha said.

Mansur had become proprietorial about the body, and objected when Adelia proposed to take the sword back to the inn with her. "He was a fighter, he should keep it with him."

But Adelia was still concerned that somebody had found it necessary to hide this man's corpse from sight; she would be happier to be sure of when he had died. Knowing nothing about swords, she wondered if they had fashions, like women's clothing, which could put a date to this one. There must be somebody who could tell her.

She and Gyltha and Allie left Mansur to block in the hole. When he'd finished, they sat silently outside the cave to eat their provisions and drink from the spring's pure water.

That night Adelia dreamed again. A lovely, elegiac dream. At first.

She stood with armored knights on the shore of the Brue, just beyond Glastonbury's marketplace. Somewhere, women's voices sang a lament. One of the knights raised his arm, holding a sword aloft for a moment so that the moon shone on its long blade and the jewels in its hilt.

The lament rose to a scream: *"Arturus, Arturus. Rex quondam, rexque futurus."*

The knight sent the sword spinning high into the air, where it made a long arc, flashing black and silver as it turned. There was a plume of water, and Excalibur swirled out of sight.

Now the voices sank to a rhythmic moan that kept time with the dip of oars from a boat shaped like a swan.

The rowers were hooded in black, but the woman in the prow, her back to the shore so that Adelia couldn't see her face, was in white. As the boat reached the bank, one of the knights stepped forward — he had an ax in his hand. . . .

"No." With a grunt of effort, Adelia woke herself up before she had to see Guinevere's body severed once more.

For a while she lay, sweltering and resentful. *I'm not a dreamer; I don't believe in dreams. What are you telling me?*

She got up, still chuntering with discontent. *Lord, how I hate Avalon. Too beautiful, too terrible. Once and future kings — you can keep them.*

She snatched her green tunic off its hanger because it was the nearest and coolest clothing to hand, put it on, stepped into her shoes, checked to see that Allie was still asleep, and tiptoed out.

Millie lay on a bed of rags under the landing's barred window, tossing and turning in her sleep. She'd thrown off her coverlet so that the moonlight shone on her naked back. Which was striped.

Oh, God, they whip her.

Adelia blundered down the stairs, rammed back the bolts of the door to the courtyard, and went out, gulping in air little fresher than that inside.

A white figure was sitting on the wellhead parapet, and for a moment she thought Guinevere had come to haunt her.

It was Mansur. He had the sword from the cave in his hand and was musing over it.

She went and sat beside him. "Can't you sleep, either?" His dreams must be as awful as hers — he was the one who'd nearly been buried alive.

He shook his head.

"Mansur, that child Millie has been whipped."

He sighed. "They are not good people here, I think."

She sighed with him. "Do you still believe Glastonbury to be the omphalos?"

"Yes," he said, "I fear that it is."

Patting his hand, she said, "Go to bed, old friend. Go to Gyltha; she's the world's only true navel."

He rose and bowed to her. "Are you coming up?"

"I'll stay here awhile. It's too hot indoors."

Full of love for him, she watched his dignified figure stalk indoors.

She got up, sent the bucket down the well — she always liked that echoing, faraway splash — and cranked it up again. The water was chilled, and she drank some, pouring the rest down her front.

Shutters were flung back and, looking up, she saw Hilda's face staring bad-temperedly down at her. The well chain's rattle had woken the landlady.

Deliberately, Adelia took up the sword, holding it by its blackened pommel, and stared back.

The shutters slammed closed.

Good, Adelia thought.

There was a quick movement behind her, and she was enveloped in a familiar smell of sweat and stale clothing as somebody seized her from behind and began carrying her away.

She lashed out with the flat of the sword and felt it connect with a shin. *"Will you stop*

276

doing this."

Will dropped her in order to rub his leg. "Where'd you get that bloody thing?"

"I found it."

"Bring it, you might be needin' it."

"I'm not going anywhere." She was shaken and angry.

"Thought you wanted to know 'bout your friend."

Adelia's eyes went wide. "Truly? Tell me now. What's happened to Emma?"

"Keep your bloody voice down, will you?" He pulled her across to the entrance. As they went, Adelia heard the shutters open again.

She tried to get her arm free. "I must tell my people where I'm going."

He wouldn't stop. "You just told 'em. Told the whole bloody county. Come on. We ain't got time for messages."

Out in the road the tithing were mounted on their donkeys, holding the reins of another, ready to ride, edgy. "Hurry up, can't you?"

There were only three of them this time: Will, Toki, and Ollie, the one who rarely spoke. "Where's Alf?" she asked.

"Waitin' for us. Get on that bloody moke." Still clutching the sword, she was hoisted up behind Toki; Will got onto his own donkey and led the way up the high road.

"Where are we going?"

"You listen to me now," Will called over his shoulder, his voice rough with the importance of what he was telling her. "You want to know what happened to your friend? Well, you're a-goin' to, but one cheep and this time we all gets our throats cut. You hear me? Never mind Glastonbury nor Wells, it's his forest an' his road. He's king of 'em both. He's doing us a favor, and he don't do many."

"Who? Who's doing us a favor?"

"He's given us three hours, but he's chancy — sweet Jesus, he's chancy. Iffen he changes his mind, we're bleeding meat."

"Who?"

"Never you mind. We calls him Wolf."

"And he'll tell me what happened?"

"He told us. He's a-lettin' us show you."

At the top of the hill, they took the Wells road.

Clinging on to Toki's back, Adelia said quietly into his ear, "Did Wolf kill them?"

Toki murmured back, "He's told us he'll be raidin' over Pennard way tonight, but you can't trust him, he's chancy, terrible chancy, is Wolf."

"Are my friends still alive?"

But they had turned onto a track leading

into the forest and Will had slowed to look back. "You startin' to listen', Toki?"

"I'm listenin', Will."

The donkeys were reined in to a walk so that their hooves trod the ground's leaf mold almost without sound. An enormous yellow moon shining through branches in dapples obviated the need for a lantern, but Adelia guessed Will wouldn't have allowed one to be lit in any case; holding on to Toki's back, she could feel a vibration in his body.

He was afraid, all the men were afraid; they exhaled fear.

There was a clearing ahead with a charcoal burner's hut in the middle of it — Adelia could smell ashes. She was lifted down. The donkeys were led into the hut and shut in.

"Now we walk," Will whispered.

They walked. If the men were silent, the forest was not. It rustled with unseen life: A nightjar gave its long churring call; somewhere an animal screamed. A badger lumbered onto the path ahead and disappeared.

At one point, Toki was hoisted to the lower branches of a tree and climbed to its top. Those at the bottom stood completely still until, after several minutes, he came down.

"Sounds like there's a to-do over to Pennard, Will. I heard screamin'. Reckon as he's kept his word and we'm clear."

"Fucking hope so." Will crossed himself. He was still afraid.

Adelia was afraid with him. She knew little of these men except that they weren't frightened easily. She didn't know where they came from; she'd begun to think that probably they'd been dispossessed of their employment by the Glastonbury fire and were surviving however they could, nibbling at the edges of criminality while trying, for the most part, to aspire to normal, law-respecting life — hadn't they gone to extraordinary lengths to prove Eustace, and therefore themselves, innocent of arson?

But here, in the forest, they were in the kingdom of Wolf, somebody who terrified them, someone who had broken away from society and recognized no law, a wolf's head, a creature — *Emma, oh, Emma* — who pounced on travelers on the Wells road, taking their goods and lives.

The tithing knew him well enough to be granted this favor, knew him well enough, too, to be scared to death of him.

Chancy, she thought, *the description of an unstable mind.*

The wonder was that in order to keep the bargain they'd made with her, they had actually approached Wolf and were risking this foray into his lair. Thieves they might be, but there was honor here — more honor than in a Christian abbey.

Moonlight took color from foxgloves, bell-flowers, and yellow archangel that in day-light would have patched the June forest. The branches of a dying tree threw shadows across the track that resembled stripes on a girl's back.

Toki stopped again; this time all of them heard a distant howling. Real wolves? Hounds? Maniacs? Whatever it was, Will urged them to a stream and they waded down it so that their scent would be un-trackable. The water was cool to Adelia's tired feet, but she felt none of the joy of avoiding the hunt that she'd experienced on the Tor; that wouldn't have killed her. Besides, its end had been to prove these men innocent. This time, she knew, she was being taken to see dead bodies.

Little Pippy. How could she bear to look on that small corpse? On Emma's?

I can't uncover terrible things. My ears are filled with the cries of the dead.

But she was what she was; she must travel on to face what she had to.

It was in a clearing. Alf's voice greeted them, shaking with nerves. "You took your bloody time."

There was a mound of earth beside him, and he stood on the edge of a long and shallow grave. "He threw 'em in the pit all higgledy-piggledy," he said. "I been straightenin' 'em out a bit."

Will lit a lantern. Then, in a move that both touched her and added to her grief, he and the others swept off their caps.

All of them dead weeks ago. Attacked on the road as they went, having been turned away from Wolvercote Manor. Armed, two-legged animals springing at them from the surrounding trees, tearing, bludgeoning. A screaming end for those dear lives.

Will was holding the lantern out to her.

"I can't," she said. "I can't."

"Better you do," he told her.

As she took the lantern from him, she realized she was still holding the dead warrior's sword. She was reluctant to let it go; it provided some comfort in this death-stricken place.

With the lantern in one hand and the sword dragging in the other, she began to walk along a grave that seemed to stretch forever. Alf had laid the bodies side by side, all facing upward, with their hands crossed on their breasts. The earthy mold of the pit into which Wolf had thrown them had preserved some flesh, but insects and mammals had taken their portions, turning the faces into unrecognizable distortions that clamored to her, echoing the shrieks and cries of the skirmish with Wolf and his robbers on the road that had been their last experience.

Father Septimus, his gnawed hands laid on the wooden cross that hung from his neck.

Emma's two grooms, so kind to Allie — it seemed terrible to Adelia that at this moment she couldn't remember their names — both had been stripped down to their hose, their leather jerkins too valuable to be left to rot. Impossible now to tell which was which.

Master Roetger's squire, Alberic, far from his native Swabia, another whose jerkin had been taken, leaving his bones to display the hacking to his rib cage.

Adelia stopped for a moment; it was unbearable to go on. Will gave her a small push. "We ain't got all night, missus."

She was approaching the women — oh, God, the women. The one with fair hair would be Alys, Emma's maid. She was naked.

The thought of what might have been done to the girl before she died made Adelia shut her eyes tight.

"Get on, missus."

Next to Alys was Mary, young Pippy's elderly nurse, the half-chewed face showing none of the patience and kindness it had borne in life. Her corpse, too, was naked.

"Did he rape them?" Adelia kept her voice low and steady.

Nobody answered her — an answer in itself.

She took another reluctant pace. Her lantern shone on an edge in the earth that rose like a step and led to a continuance of the twigs and weeds that made up the forest floor. She'd come to the end of the grave.

She turned on Will. "Is this all of them?"

He nodded.

"There are only six here." Her voice yelled shockingly through the silence, and she lowered it. "There were nine. Where's Emma? Where's her child? Where's her knight?" She let the lantern and sword drop so that she could grab the man's tunic and shake him. "You devil, what's he done with them?"

There was an exhalation of relief from the men around her. "We did wonder," Alf said.

She wheeled round to face him. "Wonder what?"

"As maybe it was your friend got away. She might've been one of these deaders, for all we knew."

"Got away? Emma got away?"

"It was like this, see." Will sat her down on a fallen tree trunk, picked up her sword, and gave it back to her like a mother restoring a toy to a baby to calm it. He squatted beside her while Alf started shoveling earth back over the bodies. "What Wolf says was there was a big fella with 'em as had his foot in a sort of basket."

"A basket," echoed Alf, pausing in his spadework.

"Roetger." Adelia was having trouble moving her lips.

"Foreign, was he?" Will asked, interested.

She managed to say, "A champion swordsman. German."

"What's a German?" Alf asked.

"You get on and cover them poor buggers up, Alf," Will told him. "We wants to get away afore we join 'em." He turned back to Adelia. "Champion, was he? Fought like one, seemingly. Held Wolf's lads off from the back of the cart, got one of 'em in the eye, sliced another's bloody hand off, stuck one more."

"Lost four of his lads that night, Wolf did," Alf said, pausing again. "Wasn't best pleased, Wolf wasn't."

"But Emma, what happened to Lady

285

Emma and her little boy?"

"Youngster, was there?" Will asked. "Wolf says as how he thought he heard a kid crying. That'd explain it, then, 'cos she fought an' all. That's one lady as Wolf didn't get to. . . . She had a dagger on her and stuck it in one of Wolf's lad's throat when he was clamberin' up on the front of the cart — the which is another as Wolf had to bury."

Adelia nodded. Emma would have fought. Her servants dying around her, Pippy behind her in the cart — she'd have fought to kill.

"Well, Wolf was surprised like. An' while he was surprised, the lady whips up the horses an' has that cart gallopin' off down the road. Wolf, he chases after it, but that big German bugger's in the back and he's still flailin' his sword about so's Wolf can't get near. He had to let it go, see."

"Let the cart go?"

Will nodded. "Lady, German, cart, and what-all as was in it. Oh, an' a pack mule as went canterin' after it — Wolf lost that an' all."

They got away.

Then she had Will by the shoulders and was shaking him again. "Where did they go?"

"I don't bloody know, do I?" Will brushed

her hands off and settled his tunic.

"What do you mean you don't know? What happened to them?"

Will shrugged.

Alf said, "How'd we know?" Toki and Ollie chimed their ignorance. There was an air of disappointment. They'd taken all this trouble, put their lives within the grasp of the chancy Wolf, gained her information — and still she wasn't satisfied.

"But . . . they've disappeared," she said. "There's been no sign of them since. If my friend was alive, she'd have contacted me. I know she would." She was near crying.

"Ain't our fault." The tithing had told her as much as it knew. It had done its bit.

"Dear heaven." It was bitter; it was cruel. All this and she was no nearer to finding Emma than she had been.

"Last seen gallopin' toward Glastonbury, wasn't they, Will?" Alf said helpfully.

"So Wolf said." Will stood up. Adelia's ingratitude had rendered him churlish once more. "Could've made Street the rate they was going, or fallen in the fucking Brue for all I care. Finished with them bodies, Alf?"

"Nearly, Will."

"Let's get off, then. We only got til dawn, and I got my bloody baking to do."

His bloody baking could wait; Adelia

wasn't leaving the dead like this.

She went to the neat strip of turned earth that now covered them, knelt down, and prayed. "Eternal rest grant unto these dear men and women, O Lord, and let perpetual Light shine upon them. May their souls rest in peace. Amen."

Silently, she promised the corpses that they would not be left forgotten in this forest. Whoever Wolf was, he was an outrage. England prided itself on being a civilized country — well, it wasn't civilized here. If the warring churchmen of Glastonbury and Wells couldn't keep safe the road and forest that stretched between them, there was one man who could. King Henry would see to it; she'd demand that he did.

When she looked up she saw that the men around her had taken off their caps again. She had been unkind to them, so she added, "And bless these friends who did not count the cost in bringing me to this place. I am grateful to them."

There was some embarrassed shuffling. Alf began patting the earth down with his spade. Then stopped.

The tithing jerked to attention. She heard the hiss of Will's breath.

A breeze had rustled the trees where there was no breeze.

Wearily, she looked toward the spot on the edge of the glade that was commanding the men's horrified attention.

A distorted bush, a green thing, which spoke. "Greetings, lads."

"We thought . . . we thought as you was over . . . over Pennard way tonight, Wolf." Will was panting.

"Some of me is, Will. The rest of me's here."

The voice had the crackle of dry leaves, as if a tree were talking.

Whether it was naked or not — and perhaps some of it was — the whorls pricked into its body and the wreath round its head — or it might have been bushy hair — made it more vegetation than animal, a thing that had lurched through primeval forest before humanity began. Even the weapon it carried was of wood — a stake ending in a pale, newly sharpened point.

Will was backing away from it. "You said . . . three hours, Wolf . . . as we could bring her . . ."

"Course I did. Course I did, Will. You was offering me a tidbit." Teeth gleamed among the foliage. "We likes tidbits, don't us, Scarry?"

The tithing gave a soft, concerted moan; another creature had come, dancing, to join the first.

It gave a shriek of joy. *"Puellae."*

"Only one this time, Scarry, only one. But she'll do for us. First me, then you, eh?"

"You and me, Wolf, you and me." More greenery decorated this taller, slimmer, swaying figure.

Will was arguing. "No need for this, Wolf . . . no need . . ." Yet as he spoke, he was walking backward. Adelia became aware that the others were melting away from her. Alf was protesting. "You promised, Wolf, you said . . ." But his shaking hands had dropped the spade, and he, too, was retreating like a cowering dog.

It was a dream. This was no longer the present; she'd been transported to a darkness where there were only trees and predators.

"Time you was going, lads," Wolf said softly to men who were already going. "Leave the lady. Me first, Scarry next. Eh, Scarry?"

There was a response of joy. *"Mirabile visu.* Let 'em stay, oh, Wolf, Lupus of mine. You first, then me. Let 'em watch."

They were half goats. They would perform a rite on her, here in their glade; she would be torn to pieces to satisfy a pagan god. They had no need for weapons; they were terror itself, the mere stink of it scattering normal men like panicked birds. She was so frightened she couldn't move, as if the ground had sprouted roots into her body.

The one called Wolf padded daintily forward until he stood opposite her with only the grave between them. Bright eyes held hers through the mask of leaves. "I'm owed," he said. "The one as got away, she robbed me of me entertainment. I likes me entertainment, and I were promised her, weren't I, Scarry?"

"You were, Wolf. The dame promised. *Filia pulchrior.*"

"But I done the ones she left behind, didn't I, Scarry? They was entertainment, wasn't they?"

"Bleated, they did, Wolf. Lambs under the slaughter. *Is agnus, ea caedes est.* Oh, rapture."

"An' I'm a-going to do you," Wolf said. "I can do anything."

His eyes never leaving hers, he began fumbling at his crotch. There was a splashing sound. He was urinating, waving his penis back and forth so that it sprayed the grave of those he'd butchered.

The other creature neighed with pleasure.

At that, a great fury was released in Adelia. She stood up, not knowing that she

291

could, nor why she did, except that she was the last remnant of civilization in this terrible place. Here were men without souls, for whom there were no limits, no restraints, who'd relinquished every decency humanity had forged in order to set itself apart from brute beasts. Chaos had come again. It had overtaken the dead, who were being dishonored, it would overwhelm her, but for their sake, however alone, she had to be on her feet to face it.

Wolf smiled.

She wasn't alone. Somebody's mumbling was coming nearer. "But you said . . . You promised us . . . Ain't right, Wolf, it ain't, it ain't." It was Alf. He was coming back, fighting against terror as against a high wind but pushing against it so that he could stand in front of her.

Wolf smiled again, fondly, twirled the stake in his hands like a baton, and struck Alf with it across the neck. He fell at Adelia's feet, still whispering protest as if he couldn't stop. "You said . . . you said . . . you said . . . ain't *right*."

"Shut the fucker up, Wolf," the thing called Scarry said casually.

Wolf twirled the stake again, catching it above his head in mid-air so that it faced downward, the moon shining wickedly white on its sharpened point.

He held it high, stepped nearer, enjoying it, a priest about to sacrifice. Adelia smelled earth. Coming forward.

Later, she was to tell herself that she killed him of her own volition. At the time, it seemed that the sword, which she'd forgotten was in her hand, leaped up by itself and lunged.

All at once, in front of her, was a bare human chest from which a pommel and part of a blade were sticking out and vibrating.

For a moment, a long, silent age, woman and creature were connected by a piece of iron; she saw the eyes flicker in surprise. This wasn't how it should be.

Wolf coughed.

There was a sucking noise as his body released itself and fell back.

Then there was just a sword point that dripped. Adelia stared at it. "Good gracious," she said.

"What've you done, you bitch?" The thing called Scarry came leaping across the glade and threw itself down to take the body of its leader in its arms. *"Aaaaah."*

Wolf's eyes, still astonished, stared up at his friend. He tried to say something. His chest heaved with dry coughs.

Scarry looked up, staring round the glade

as if for help from the gods he'd worshipped here. "He's hurt. Do something, in the name of God. Somebody do something."

It's his lung, Adelia thought. *The sword went into his lung.* The grotesque creature of which she'd been so afraid had been transformed into a patient. He was suffering. She went down on her knees and listened to the chest. Air was making a flopping sound as it flowed through the lung's puncture hole.

Scarry screamed at her like a man at the ending of his world. "Do something."

Adelia heard her foster father's voice as he'd bent over a man stabbed in a Salerno brawl whose chest was making the same sucking noise. *"If we could open the thorax and sew up the ripped lung . . . but we cannot . . . He will die in minutes."*

Already Wolf's eyes were glazing over. Beneath the mask of leaves, his face was changing color.

"I'm sorry," she said, "I'm so sorry. There's nothing to be done."

"Bloody is," a voice above her head said earnestly. Will was trying to get her to her feet. "We run."

Scarry was kissing the dying face, begging. "*Te amo.* Don't leave me, my Lupus. *Te amo, te amo.*"

"Run," Will said again. He'd taken the

sword from her, pointing it at the sobbing Scarry. "And quick. He ain't going to take this kindly."

She was pulled up. Toki and Ollie had a stumbling Alf by the arms. "Run," Will was shouting now. "He'll fuckin' kill us."

What had happened, what *was* happening, the horror of this place . . . She let herself be dragged into a run.

Out of the glade, through trees.

Behind them rose a screamed lament that ruffled the leaves. "Come back, my Lupus! *Te amo! Te amo!*"

She was leaping over fallen branches, along a stream, breath coming short; whether woodland hurtled by her or she was hurtled past it was impossible to know.

The charcoal burner's hut. They stopped, panting.

Will found his voice. "Is he after us, Toki?"

Adelia could hear nothing except the pounding in her own ears.

"He's after us," Toki said.

She was put up on a donkey; they were all on donkeys and galloping. When they reached the road, knowledge came to her. "Dear God, I killed him."

The tithing took no notice. It just galloped faster.

■ ■ ■ ■

They took her to the cave on the Tor and sat her down by the spring. It was quiet there.

The night was still dark, though. Being so near to the summer solstice, the sky had never been completely black and, even with the sun still below the horizon, was lightening as if filters were being removed from it one by one. Bats flittered against it.

"Toki?" asked Will.

A blackbird emitted its first song of the day, an isolated sound.

Toki nodded his head and puffed out his cheeks in relief. "We lost him."

"Then you get back down the hill an' wipe out our tracks. He can sniff a footprint in the dark, can Scarry."

Adelia looked up at them. "I killed him," she said.

"Pity you di'n't do Scarry while you was about it," Will told her. "He ain't a-going to like losing Wolf."

Ollie spoke for the first time. "But he don't know where she lives, Will, does he?"

"No, he don't," Will said with satisfaction. "I told Wolf as she come from Wells."

"I killed him." She, whose oath was to

296

preserve life, had *taken* life. Didn't they realize it?

"You saved Alf," Will pointed out. "He was a-goin' to do Alf."

Alf.

Here, at least, was somebody she *could* help. They'd laid him down on the grass. The skin of his throat was raw and swollen where the stake had been struck against it. She tore a strip off the hem of her green tunic, soaked it in the cold water of the spring, and applied it to the bruising. She tried to get him to drink some water, but swallowing was too painful for more than a few sips.

"Can you talk, Alf?" she asked with tenderness.

He huffed a response.

"Is he going to be all right?" Will asked her.

"I think so. His voice should come back when the swelling goes down."

"Pity," Will said savagely. "He talks us into more fuckin' trouble than he's worth. . . . Him an' his bloody truth. Everyone got to keep their word. . . . Pain in the arse, Alf is."

Adelia looked up, angry. Then she saw that Will was ashamed of his and the others' cowardice in the glade, humiliated that it had been Alf, not him, who'd come to her aid.

"He can't help it, Will," Ollie said.

That's the extraordinary thing, she thought. *He can't.*

Smoothing the greasy hair back from Alf's young, pockmarked face, she thought what a jewel was here. The Lord only knew how, petty thief that he was, the truth flamed bright in Alf's soul — not honesty, not regard for other people's deer, but the truth. It had dragged him, unwilling, moaning with fear, back to her side in the glade from outrage that Wolf had broken his oath to the tithing. He'd tried to save her life and, if she had then saved his, it was something to set against the fact that she'd had to kill to do it.

By the time Toki came back, dawn had broken. They gave Adelia some dried meat that she chewed on without identifying it, and she accepted a harsh but invigorating drink out of a filthy bottle. But when, having cleaned it, Will threw the sword down beside her, she saw only the image of Wolf's lung and the rupture this blade's tip had made in it so that air had escaped into the pleural cavity.

"I don't want it," she said.

"You bloody keep it," Will told her. "And

pray God as you won't need it."

This was such unusual piety for Will that she asked, "Who *is* Scarry?"

Will shrugged. "Don't rightly know. Wolf, now, he come from the Quantocks, always mad, he was. Strangled his mother when he were still a lad, so the story goes, and lived wild in the forest ever after. Chancy, Wolf was, and no loss, so don't you go frettin'. World's a better place with that bastard gone."

Perhaps it was, but remembering that it was she who'd sent him out of it put a weight on her that would never be lifted. She shivered. "And Scarry? He could speak Latin."

Will nodded, and Adelia noticed that he, too, had a momentary coldness and drew his cloak around him. "Educated, Scarry is. Nobody don't know for sure where he come from, up north as like as not. I heard his name was Scarlett or Scathelock, summat like that. Some say he was a priest and done wicked things so's the Church chucked him out. Or he was a noble and done wicked things so's he was outlawed. Joined up with Wolf, what, three, four year ago. Fish divin' into water that was for Scarry. Loved it, liked the killing. Don't know which of 'em was chancier, him or Wolf."

"He cried for love of Wolf." That dreadful scream: *Te amo, te amo.*

"Yeah, well." Will shifted uncomfortably. "The pair of 'em was funny like that. *What?*" Alf was tugging at his elbow and croaking.

"He wants as you should tell her the rest of it, Will," Toki explained.

Will spat. "Gor bugger, Alf, you want me to lose me best customer?"

It appeared from an indistinct whisper that Alf did.

Again, Toki translated. "Alf says as you'm a prize baker and don't need to work for that old bitch." He paused. "Maybe as we owe it to the missus, Will. She ought to know."

"What old bitch?" asked Adelia.

"All right, *all right.*" Will sat down beside her, pulled up a piece of grass, and chewed savagely on it. " 'S like this. See, Wolf knew as your lady'd be on that road. He was a-waiting for her, like."

"*How* did he know?" God, it was becoming hot; the air was accumulating weight and making her gasp for breath.

Will sucked on his grass. "See, the big manors round here, they used to suffer something terrible from Wolf. He raided their beeves, sheep, barns, nothing safe from Wolf. And that weedy old sheriff not doin'

300

anything proper to stop un, nor Glastonbury, nor Wells."

"So?"

"Well, so the lords and ladies as was suffering, they came to an arrangement, like.
With Wolf. Payin' him to stay off their land,
see?"

Danegeld. The manors had paid Wolf to
procure their peace and safety. At this moment, a disgraceful history seemed irrelevant, but Alf, in whom truth spouted
like clear water from a fountain, thought it
necessary that she should know it. "I see,"
she said.

"So that night, the night as your friend
was turned away from Wolvercote . . ." Will
paused.

The air became heavier, suffocating.

"Well, that night Wolf got a message from
there a-saying as there'd be a rich lady and
party a-leavin' of Wolvercote. Nice pickings
for him, it said. They'd be taking his road, it
said."

"A message?" Adelia said stupidly. Alf was
nodding. Then it came to her. "She sold
them? *She sold them?*"

"Don't know about that," Will said, getting up. "I'm just saying as what happened."

She'd sold them. The mistress of Wolvercote Manor had looked on Emma and the

child, seeing only a threat to her position. And wanted them dead. And set the wolves on them.

"No need to worry about Eustace," Will said, looking down at her. "He's a-laying in Street Church and, when we're off the hook for the fire, we'll bury the poor bastard, *with his fingers*, the which is still by the abbey bloody wall."

But Adelia wasn't worrying for Eustace. It was the betrayal of Emma that had wiped everything else from her mind. And the bodies in their shallow grave in a lawless forest, killed twice — once by a woman who'd turned them from her door with murderous intent, and once by an animal. And who was the guiltier? The animal? Or the lady in her velvet manor?

Adelia's mouth moved. "She sold them."

Emma, Roetger, and Pippy. The souls of the dowager's victims called out to her. Where were they?

She looked out toward the blue-and-green pattern of the marshes to clear her mind — an anatomist's mind so clinical that it could not bear untidiness, whatever jumble of monstrosity had been fed into it.

Surely they are dead, she thought. They sustained wounds in the battle with Wolf and died of them. But Lord in heaven, did all bodies vanish in this godforsaken country? Was there some hole that sucked people into it without a trace?

Clear as clear, over and over, she watched Emma on the cart lash its horses into a gallop, saw Roetger flailing at their pursuers, heard Little Pippy screaming . . . a pack mule cantering behind them.

And then nothing. They vanished. She couldn't see them anymore.

She raised her head. "Glastonbury, Alf? You said they were last seen galloping in the direction of Glastonbury. My friend and the cart."

Alf huffed his assent.

"They didn't get there."

Will said, "Horses veered, maybe. Crashed 'em somewhere 'mongst the trees. Killed 'em."

Yes, that might be the explanation: three more corpses rotting in that hellish forest, noticed only by the wildlife feeding on them.

Gently, because it was unbearable to envisage otherwise, Adelia's mind gathered the bodies up and laid them in the trench that held their companions, folding their poor hands, pleading for rest to their souls. . . .

She couldn't see their faces, just their

shapes — one large, one shorter and slim, one very little.

Shapes.

"You all right, missus?" Toki asked anxiously, offering the disgusting bottle. "Have another swig, you're a-breathin' horrible strong."

"No."

Dimensions. Shapes. One large, one shorter, one tiny. A foreigner, a woman, and her baby. Messages, *messages.* Shapes.

"Oh my God," she said aloud.

"What's up now?"

"I've got to get back to the Pilgrim." She was on her feet.

"Better wait. Toki, you get down there. Make sure all's quiet."

She couldn't wait; she began to run down the hill, the tithing following her. All she could see was the door of the inn and three shapes standing in front of it, one big, one middle-sized, one very small, urging it to open for them.

Now she knew why the landlord of the Pilgrim had fainted.

ELEVEN

As she reached the shadow of the abbey wall, Adelia slowed down. The agitation that gripped her had to be controlled; she must plan.

When the tithing caught up with her, she was rubbing her forehead with one finger, thinking hard.

She looked from one face to another. "I'm in sore need of one more favor from you," she said.

"What now?" Will snapped. He was tired; they were all tired.

She spoke slowly and clearly. "I want you to get my people out of the Pilgrim and take them to Wells. All of them, the lord Mansur, my daughter, my companion, and the Welshman. I want you to take them to the Bishop's Palace and put them in the care of the bishop of Saint Albans, who is staying there."

"What for?"

Ollie, youngest and most taciturn of the tithing, was surprised into asking, "Gordang, old Godwyn's cookin' ain't that bad, be it?"

Adelia smiled at him. "No, but it's time we moved on." She turned to Will. "Is it safe to take them along the road?"

Will looked at Toki. "What do your ears tell ee, Toki?"

"Nothin'. 'S all quiet."

Will considered. "Reckon as now they're all upsy-downy over Wolf bein' dead, getting theyselves a new leader. Might be all right then." He looked at Adelia with suspicion. "You and the darky doin' a moonlight flit? Leavin' poor old Godwyn without his dues?"

"Something like that," Adelia told him, "but I'll pay you when I can get to my purse."

"Come on, Will," Toki said. " 'Tain't as if that old Hilda ever did you a good turn."

"That's for sure," Will said. "All right, then, the palace it is, but the mokes'll need a bit of a rest and waterin' afore we set off."

"One more thing," Adelia said. "I shan't be coming with you. I want you to tell my people that I'm already at the Bishop's Palace, waiting for them."

Running away without paying they understood; this they did not.

"You staying, then?"

"Yes. If they know that, they won't come with you." Gyltha wouldn't allow herself, and certainly would not allow Allie, to accompany a collection of men as disreputable-looking as these on just their say-so — at least not without a fight.

A singed apple tree leaning over the wall still had a living branch on it. She went to it and came back with a twig. She handed it to Will. "Give this to my companion; her name's Gyltha. It's a token that she and the lord Mansur are to do what you tell them. And when you get to the palace, you must inform the bishop of Saint Albans that he's to make sure he keeps my people there and that I want him to come to the Pilgrim. I'll be waiting for him."

"Oh, yes." Will raised his eyes to the heavens. "Bishops allus do what we tell 'em. Hobnob with bishops every bloody day, don't we, lads?"

It was a good point; another token would be necessary. "Tell him . . ." She tried to think of what would convince Rowley that she was well but in need. "Tell him . . . tell him Ariadne waits for him." It had been his name for her when they'd been lovers.

She made Will repeat it several times until

he'd got his tongue round the unfamiliar syllables.

The tithing didn't want to leave her alone, Alf especially. "He's scared as Scarry'll come after you," Toki explained.

Adelia was impatient with them. She had things to do. Out here, in the early sunlight, with the abbey and its monks just over the road, was another world from the forest of last night that was already assuming the unreality of nightmare. It was the Pilgrim that was now the focus of a more pressing danger. "Will, you said yourself the man has no idea where I am."

"So he ain't, but Alf's maybe right. Scarry set a lot of store by Wolf; he'll want his revenge on us all, 'specially you, missus. You was the one who done for Wolf."

Had she? It still seemed something she'd watched rather than experienced. Well, she'd face that later, pay whatever she had to pay *later;* now was not the time. "He has to find me first."

"Maybe." Will thought it over. "He's got Wolf to bury. An' he'll be busy for a bit, seein' as if all those other bastards'll follow him now as Wolf's dead." He glared at her. "You sure the bishop'll come if so be we ask him?"

"I know he will."

There was a huff from Alf.

Toki said, "Alf says as he's going to stay."

"No." She took in a breath and tried again. "I want my people safe in Wells. It'll need all of you to get them there." Allie, Gyltha, Rhys, and Mansur would need as large an escort as possible to travel the forest road; as it was, even four men were too few.

"Maybe she's right." Infuriatingly painstakingly, Will ticked over the reasoning on his fingers. "One, Scarry thinks as she lives over Wells way, 'cos that's what I told Wolf. Two, he'll be busy for a bit, a-buryin' of Wolf and seein' as if all the other bastards'll follow him now as Wolf's dead. Three, if we gets the bishop here today, he'll keep her safer'n what we can." Head on one side, he studied his splayed hand. "Yep, reckon as she'll be safe enough for a bit."

Quietly, they all crossed the road. The courtyard was deserted and silent, the overlooking shutters barred; it was still too early even for Millie to be up.

Adelia slipped into the stables as Will began hammering on the back door.

It took time for him to be answered, and it was Gyltha who appeared at a window.

The exchange between the two was lengthy and, on Gyltha's part, bad-tempered with anxiety, but Will, waving the twig, played his part surprisingly well, eventually convincing her that Adelia was at Wells and wanted her family to join her.

The door was unbolted, again by Gyltha. "What's she doin' sending messages by the likes of you? Well, you bloody got to wait while I pack our traps. What for's she gone to the palace? Suppose you'd better come in — you can help carry. And wipe your boots."

Adelia couldn't hear the rest because the tithing, meekly stamping their feet and brushing the dust off their clothes, went inside.

After a while, Toki came out. He'd been deputed to fetch the donkeys and was sipping a tankard of ale. "Your Gyltha drew it," he told her, entering the stables. "Godwyn and Hilda, they ain't there."

"Not there? Where've they gone?" The whole point of staying here was to keep an eye on them while she hid in the stables.

Toki didn't know. "An' your Gyltha, she don't know, either. They was there last night, but they ain't now. Looks like they flitted theyselves."

"Mmm."

It took time and much arrangement, but eventually Adelia, peeping through a crack in the stable door, watched as Mansur and

310

Gyltha, carrying Allie, were helped onto two of the donkeys, their packs loaded onto another. Rhys was having to share a mount with Toki, both being light in weight.

When Will, on pretense of fetching a hay bag, came into the stables, she said, "They'll be safe on the road?"

"You better hope so," he said. He cocked his head. "You reckon your folks is in danger here, do you?"

"Yes."

"Want to tell me?"

"Later. Just get them away."

A look of disgust came over his face, which signaled he was about to say something fond. "Don't like leavin' you alone."

Dear, dear, how she did like this truculent man. To please him, she said, "I can look after myself, you saw that."

He grunted.

"And Will . . ." Adelia put her hand on his. "In the glade . . . they were demons and you weren't armed. You couldn't have done anything but what you did."

He scowled at her. "You keep that bloody sword close, that's all."

Watching the party set out, she prayed for its safety. It had been a matter of balancing one danger against another; it had seemed that getting Allie and the others out of Glas-

311

tonbury was the lesser evil, but if she were wrong, if Wolf's men should be on the rampage . . .

She tried reassuring herself; it was morning, and there would be other people on the road. . . .

Lord God, have them in your keeping.

She found it strange that the landlord and his wife had abandoned the inn. Perhaps Hilda had heard her conversation with Will when he came to collect her last night. *Damn.*

Still, she might as well take advantage of the situation. The door to the courtyard had been left open, so she went inside, sword in hand.

Rats scampered away from a dirty pot as she entered the kitchen. Flies were everywhere. A well-built fire still threw out heat. The place smelled of stale food and a bowl of milk that had turned sour. Usually, Godwyn kept his domain neat and clean — this disorder suggested that he'd left the inn in a hurry.

She threw open the shutters to let in some air and light. There was a ham hanging from its hook in the ceiling. She cut off a slice, threw it away, and cut another that the flies hadn't got at, broke a portion of stale crust from a loaf in the mesh-protected food safe, and drew herself a potful of ale — all the time listening for any sound of the innkeepers' return.

She looked for string, found a piece, and tied it round her waist to make a sword belt. The image of Wolf coming at her across the glade flashed into her mind with the memento mori: *"You have killed a man."*

Lord, she was tired; she'd think about that another time.

Taking her booty back to the stable, she carried it up to the hayloft and made herself comfortable on some straw behind a bale that hid her from the entrance.

Rowley, she thought, when he came, would be pleased with her caution; though there was a job to be done, she was not exposing herself to risk by doing it on her own.

Yawning, she wondered if he would guess her purpose and bring men with him. Useful but probably unnecessary . . .

How very hot it was. . . .

It was a sleep of exhaustion, energy-reviving and dreamless for the most part. Only at the end of it did Guinevere walk out of a mist with writhing greenery around her. Again, the queen was in white, though this time she was veiled — in none of Adelia's nightmares had she shown her face.

She was alone; there was nobody to cut her in half. Birds accompanied her, fluttering like an extra cloak in a breeze. One of them landed on her shoulder, an owl, a barn owl, its big eyes and widow-peaked head directed toward Adelia. It turned and took a corner of Guinevere's veil in its beak. Suddenly, Adelia knew that this wraith wasn't Guinevere, it was Emma.

"No," Adelia told it, "I don't want to see."

But the bird spread its wings and began to rise so that the veil in its beak rose with it. . . .

Adelia woke herself up with her own shouts, frantically brushing flies off her skin where they'd been attracted by sweat. The bolstering straw was making the loft into a hothouse. And it was dark.

Dark? Had she slept through seventeen hours of daylight?

There was a hoist at the back of the loft, and she crawled toward it to push open its door and look out.

To the west, a monstrous cloud like a horizon-wide black, sagging blanket had obliterated the sun, if sun there still was. What it was bringing would be terrible; darts of lightning were coming out of it, stabbing the distant marshland.

Without the sun, it was impossible to

know how long she'd been asleep. It might be evening by now — and Rowley had not come. Or had she missed him and, not finding her, had he gone away again?

A torn spider's web hanging from the hoist's door carried the image of what had been under Guinevere/Emma's veil. Thunder midges dancing in the half-light outside formed the same shape, and she knew she was being haunted, *hunted.*

She backed away, scrambling down the ladder and into the courtyard.

And that was stupid. Hilda and Godwyn might have come back; they'd see her.

The inn was quiet, however. Nothing moved in the oppressive air. Weeds drooped, dying among the cobbles. Birds had deserted the sky, as if afraid of what was on its way. From the west came a long grumble of thunder.

She would have liked to draw a bucket of water so that she could drink and swill herself down with it, but the noise the chain would make daunted her and, instead, she crossed to the inn's door and cautiously pushed it open, grimacing at the protest its hinges made.

Nobody came.

It was dark inside. All the heat in the world seemed to have concentrated here, like a pustule.

Why hadn't Rowley come? Allie and Gyltha and Mansur hadn't reached him, that was why. They were lying dead in the forest, Allie's little hands crossed on her breast; she could see them.

Pull yourself together. Most likely the bishop was out when they got there, at some convocation or blessing other people's babies, attending to God's business, never hers, never hers. Or had just decided not to bother.

Be damned, then, she thought. *I'll begin the search without you.*

It was unlikely that the kitchen would provide the evidence she looked for, so she left its rats undisturbed and went along the corridor that led to the parlor.

Some light from the kitchen hatch cast shadows on the room's table. There was someone sitting in the great chair at the far end, with a bow on his head.

Adelia took in a sob of breath and looked again. It wasn't a bow, it wasn't a head; it was Allie's birdcage, which someone had left balanced on the chair's back. Going the length of the table, she took it up and cradled it for a moment before putting it down to begin a search of the room's aumbries. Platters in one, pewter tankards in another, candlesticks and candles, a box of sharp eating knives. Nothing there, though it was difficult to see.

Back in the kitchen, stamping to scatter the rats, she blew on the embers of the fire and lit a candle. The flame intensified the shadows outside its range so that, going upstairs, she had to fight the impression that she was accompanied.

Godwyn and Hilda's room was meaner than those of the guests. Wherever they'd gone, it was in the clothes they stood up in, because a small press contained neatly folded tunics, skirts, bodices, trousers, and several clean aprons, all dusted with pennyroyal against the moth.

Adelia started back from a human shape behind the door. It turned out to be two cloaks hanging on a hook. There was a ewer and bowl, both empty, with a saucer of soapwort by their side. A shelf held a razor, combs, and various jars, all of which Adelia opened without finding anything but medicaments. A bottle contained a bitter-smelling tincture of burdock, suggesting one or the other of its owners had digestive problems. Probably Godwyn, Adelia thought, remembering the landlord's perpetual look of discomfort.

She got down on her knees to peer under

the bed, finding only a pisspot. She tipped over a straw mattress and examined the struts on which it lay. She tapped every floorboard to see if one was hollow.

Nothing. An innocent room.

The communal chamber in which poorer guests were put to sleep side by side was swept and empty except for an enormous platform of a bed, now stripped of covering, and a giant chest containing the inn's linens, which expelled a pleasant smell of the dried rosemary and sage scattered among the sheets.

The room she'd shared with Allie was next door, and Adelia went in, hoping against hope that Gyltha, in packing, had overlooked something that she could change into — what she was wearing had suffered in the forest.

Of course, there was nothing; Gyltha hadn't left so much as a pin behind. However, the ewer still held water for washing. . . .

A door along the landing bumped against its frame as if someone had put it to. It was the door to Mansur and Gyltha's room.

She went out to see. It couldn't have been the wind; there was no wind.

Yes, there was; the storm was sending a slight breeze ahead of itself, soughing a draft of air through the corridor outside.

Adelia bolted back into her room and barred the door. Whatever was out there, *if* there was anything out there, she could face it better clean — or, happier still, cower in here and not face it at all.

Shaking, she stripped, scrubbing and sluicing herself with manic energy, saving some of the water for her hair, which she plaited — her head veil being too torn by forest branches to be worth putting on again.

There. She'd be a fresher sacrifice if she were killed. But then, as she re-dressed, she thought, *Fool, you still hope that Rowley will come.*

She drew back bolts and, candle in one hand, the other gripping the sword hanging from her string girdle, approached the door she'd heard closing. It wasn't on the latch and trembled in a draft that had become stronger. Raindrops began hitting the inn's roof like pellets; somewhere an unsecured shutter startled to rattle.

"I warn you, I'm armed," she shouted, and kicked the door open. At the same moment a rush of air along the passage from one window to another blew her candle out.

No. No, I'm not brave enough.

As she rushed for the stairs, the storm

broke. Thunder cracked the sky in half. The inn's front door was open, letting in rain. Lightning outlined the hooded figure advancing toward the bottom of the stairs, sleek and gleaming, its arms held wide like a scarecrow's.

"I was trying to catch you," Rowley said. "I thought you were going to fall down."

"I nearly did," Adelia told him. She was still sitting on the stairs, her legs too weak from shock to stand. "Did Allie arrive all right?"

"And Gyltha. And Mansur. All apparently under the impression that you'd be waiting for them. I told them to stay and I'd come to see to it. Perhaps you'd be good enough to tell me what it is I have to see to."

Both were having to shout over the noise of the storm; outside the still-open door, rain was hitting the courtyard cobbles as if a giant overhead was sluicing them with titanic buckets of water.

Rowley produced a flask and handed it to Adelia before taking off his leather cloak and hood to shake them outside, then shut the door.

"Bolt it," Adelia told him.

He raised an eyebrow but did as she said. She took a swig of his brandy. It caused her to cough, but it made her feel better; she could cope with anything now that he was here.

He picked up a lantern and they went into the parlor, each carefully choosing a seat on either side of the table. He became benign. "Well, my child?"

Don't call me that, she thought. But she was too glad of him to start the old confrontation. She told him of her excursion into the forest and what lay buried there, of what had happened. "You see . . . oh, Rowley, I've killed a man."

"Good."

She shook her head in misery. "Don't admire me for it."

"Why not? What else could you do? He was about to spear this Alf of yours before raping you. . . ." He reverted to being bishop-like again. "Do you wish me to hear your confession, my child?"

"No, I don't," she snarled at him. "I'm telling you as a friend." She showed him the sword. "It seemed to act by itself."

"Where did you find that old thing, in the name of God?"

"Never mind." There were other things to get to. She told him what she knew of Wolf's attack on the road, of the dowager Wolvercote's part in it, and what she suspected

321

had happened to Emma, Pippy, and Roetger after their escape.

She had to speak loudly to overcome the lash of rain outside, wincing as lightning lit up cracks in the shutters, stopping altogether during rolls of thunder.

"It's a matter of shapes, you see," she said. "Representation. Last seen, those three in the cart were galloping for their lives in this direction. I believe they saw the inn here, the only building on the road, and made for its shelter."

"They could have, I suppose," the bishop said doubtfully.

Again, she suppressed irritation. Damn it, didn't he believe her? Couldn't he see, as she did, that poor trio hammering on the Pilgrim's door, begging to be let in?

Going doggedly on, she said, "Hilda and Godwyn had been told by the king's messenger to receive three guests: a foreign gentleman who would be investigating the skeletons in the abbey churchyard, a lady, and her child. And there they were, on the doorstep, Master Roetger, a foreigner; Emma; and Pippy. Fitting the expected shapes exactly."

"So?"

"So . . ." Adelia drew a deep breath. "I think they murdered them."

"What?"

"Murdered them. The circumstances were perfect; the three arrived without protection, nobody knowing they *had* arrived . . ."

"No protection, woman? Emma had a master swordsman with her."

"She also had a child. I'm not saying they were killed where they stood. Probably they were invited in, made welcome, comforted. But you only need a child to make you vulnerable." Angrily, she wiped tears from her eyes. It had happened to her during an investigation when Allie was still a baby; she'd gone quietly to what had nearly been her death because a killer had threatened to kill her daughter if she did not.

She said, "At some point Godwyn merely had to grab hold of Pippy and wave a knife. Emma and Roetger would have had to do what they were told. It was why I wanted Allie away from here. It only takes someone with a weapon."

"Why on earth should anybody do that?"

"It's something to do with the abbey skeletons. If they're disproved as Arthur's and Guinevere's, the economy of the abbey will suffer. So will the Pilgrim's."

"So three people had their throats cut? You're fantasizing, my girl. Godwyn's a common landlord, for God's sake. A weedy little man. Innkeepers don't go round murdering their guests. Not deliberately, anyway, though I've eaten some meals . . ."

Adelia gritted her teeth. "A weedy little man who fainted when Mansur, Allie, and I arrived at his inn; he knew he'd killed the wrong people." She leaned forward. "Rowley, I *know* he did. What's Emma's mule doing up in the abbey pasture? Hilda, Godwyn, they sold her goods once she was dead — horses, cart, clothes, jewels. That's what I was about when you arrived, searching for something, anything, that still belongs to her."

He teetered his chair back. The lantern on the table between the two of them threw an upward light on his face, emphasizing its bones, leaving the sockets of his eyes dark. He'd always been a big, well-fleshed man — his first years as bishop had rendered him almost plump; too many clerical feasts and dinners — but he was thinner now than she'd ever seen him. It suited him. But, blast him, he was complacent, a know-it-all. Power did that, she supposed. Too much "Yes, my lord bishop," "No, my lord bishop."

"And have you found it?" he asked, sure of the answer.

"No."

"There you are, then."

Adelia stood up. They could sit here all night while she kept advancing her theory and he kept refuting it. Well, *she* at least wasn't going to. "Come on, you can help me look." She took up the lantern.

Sighing heavily, he followed her.

It was only as they went up the stairs that she remembered the door to Mansur and Gyltha's room. "Somebody might be in there," she said, pointing. She could be brave now.

"A murderous landlord?" Dramatically, he drew his sword. "Let me at him. I'll run the varlet through."

She held the lantern so that they could both see as she went in behind him. An almost simultaneous crack of lightning and thunder made them crouch — and sent a figure scuttling under the bed. They heard it moan.

Adelia drooped with relief. "Millie, it's me. Don't be frightened, it's me. This gentleman's a friend." Then she remembered. What use of verbal reassurance to a girl who couldn't hear it?

Signing to Rowley to sheathe his sword, she went forward, letting the lantern shine on Millie's terrified face.

They took the girl downstairs to the

parlor. Rowley administered brandy. "She can't hear the thunder, you say?"

"I don't think so. But she's frightened of something, poor child. She knows. . . ." Gently, Adelia cupped the girl's face in her hands, mouthing words. "Millie, what . . . happened . . . to the lady . . . who came here . . . with her little boy? Oh, this is hopeless." She turned to the table and drew three figures in its light layer of dust with her finger — a large one with a sword in its hand, that of a woman, and, finally, that of a child.

"These three, Millie," she begged, pointing. "They came here. What happened to them?"

"She won't tell you even if she could," Rowley said. "She'll protect her employers."

"I don't think so, they beat her. Oh, look . . ."

For comprehension had come into Millie's eyes. She was nodding, her finger tracing a line under Adelia's drawing, standing up, beckoning. They followed her to the back door, where she drew the bolts, cowered for a moment at the swamping rain, and ran for the stables. Adelia and Rowley ran after her.

The storm had covered the sound of Rowley's arrival. Before he'd done anything, he'd stabled and attended to his horse, now kicking in its stall, scared by the thunder.

Rowley went to its head and soothed it. "All right, old boy, all right, it's only noise," but his eyes were on Millie, who had gone to a woodpile by the door and was throwing logs aside to reach something underneath.

Nodding emphatically, she dragged a curved, broken section of wood from others that were similar and watched Adelia as she handed it to her.

"What is it?" Rowley asked.

It was an elaborately fretted piece of oak. "A bit of the hoop from Emma's cart," Adelia said. "It held up the canvas. It's all here. They smashed it up for firewood."

Don't weep, she told herself. *You knew.*

But despite everything, she had hoped to be wrong.

"For Jesus' sake, why?" Rowley was becoming convinced. "Why would they kill them?"

"For gain. Dear Heaven, Rowley, that little boy. Emma loved him so much."

Millie was still looking up, curving her right hand over three extended fingers of the other to make sure she understood. Three people in a covered cart.

Adelia nodded and shaped the question "Where are they?"

There was ferocity in Millie's face. What had been done was wrong, *wrong;* now she could expose it. She got up, dragging Adelia back to the inn. Rowley followed, splashing through ankle-high water. If anything, the rain was intensifying; the courtyard's drain couldn't cope with it.

Millie made for the kitchen. She pointed to a large vat in one corner and then began tugging at it. It was too heavy for her.

Rowley put down the lantern and went to help. The vat moved, but its bottom hoop caught on something and they had to tip and roll it before it was free of the obstruction.

Underneath was a handle set into one of the kitchen's flagstones.

"Shit," Rowley said.

Millie held up three fingers again, her teeth bared as if in despair, then pointed. "God help them," Adelia said, quietly. "They're down there." As lightning flashed again, so did hope. "Lift it, quick, quick. They might still be alive, prisoners."

It was a heavy slab. With effort, Rowley hoisted it up and slid it to one side. A dank smell mixed with that of liquor came rushing out of the hole — but not the stink of corruption Adelia had been dreading.

Rowley knelt. "Halloo, there. Emma? *Hal-*

loo." He turned his head sideways, but there was only the beat of rain and a crack of thunder that shook the kitchen walls. "There are steps here," he said.

"Well, there would be, it's a cellar," Adelia said. "Give me the lantern."

"Reinforcement is required first, I think." Still kneeling, Rowley produced his flask, offering it to Millie, who drank and handed it on to Adelia, who, shaking her head in impatience, gave it back to him.

He took a hefty swig. He was reluctant to go into the hole, she realized — he'd never liked enclosed spaces.

She took up the lantern, ready to shove him aside, but he grabbed it off her — "I'm going, I'm going" — and began to descend the steps.

"Be careful, Rowley," she called to him, frightened, "Godwyn might be hiding down there." She turned to Millie, shaking her head and putting up a hand to keep her back in case there was violence. "Stay here."

Rowley's voice came up to her with an echo. "Nobody here, but it's not just a cellar, there's a tunnel leading out of it. Watch your step, woman, it's slimy." Carefully, she followed him down. He was right; the steps were slippery, and very steep.

She was in a cellar, a big one, part of it a

storeroom for extra tables and benches, some awaiting repair. Most of it housed ale barrels, and she wondered how they'd been carried up and down the steps before she saw a chute leading to a hatch in, presumably, the edge of the courtyard for ease of delivery by a brewer's dray.

At the far end, Rowley stood, sword in one hand, lantern in the other, peering at an opening in the wall. He came back to her, pausing to examine a rack at the foot of the steps that was filled with different sizes of wine bottles. "Glass bottles," he said, marveling and extracting one of them. "The Pilgrim does its guests well."

When it wasn't killing them. But, so far at least, there was no sign that murder had been done.

Adelia turned to look up at Millie peering anxiously down at her. She indicated to the girl that she and Rowley were going to proceed farther.

There was a crack, this time not of lightning, less loud but still vicious. Millie's eyes went blank, and her body fell over the hole. Adelia started up the steps to go to her. She saw an arm drag Millie away by her hair before the flagstone at the stairhead's entrance was slammed into place.

"*Rowley.* Oh, God, Rowley, they've killed

Millie. They're blocking us in."

There was a smash as a bottle he'd been holding hit the floor. He pushed Adelia out of the way, gave her the lantern, and clambered up the steps to try to heave the slab up.

They both heard the scrape of the barrel being put back over it.

He heaved again. "Fuck it, I can't shift the thing." He came back down. "That way. We'll get out by the chute." He began clawing his way up the slide to dislodge the courtyard hatch at its top.

Again, they heard the scrape of something heavy being pulled across. Cursing, yelling, Rowley pushed at the hatch, pushed again and again. It didn't budge.

After a while, he allowed himself to slide back. For a moment, he lay, face downward, on the chute. Then, picking himself up, he smiled at her. "Well, my love, we're going to have to investigate the tunnel — and quick, before the bastards block the other exit."

Taking the lantern, he ushered her toward the hole in the cellar's wall, talking all the time. "That's the nice thing about tunnels — they've got two ends. Not surprised to find one here. Sure as Adam and Eve it'll come out somewhere in the abbey grounds. Abbots have always liked an escape route from invaders, or their own damned monks. And I'll wager Brother Titus has nipped along this one a fair few times to sample some ale. . . ."

"It was Hilda who hit Millie," Adelia said. "I saw her sleeve."

"Nothing we can do about that yet." Pulling her behind him, he entered the tunnel.

It was a large entrance, but if Brother Titus had used its passage to go to and fro, his bulk must have been mightily squeezed, for almost immediately the walls narrowed and lowered, enclosing them in a space little more than four feet square that, as far as they could see, went on and on. They were forced to bend double — Rowley was almost crawling, and Adelia had to take the lantern, maneuvering past him into the lead. Every thirty yards or so the tunnel widened into niches, vital for allowing a strained back to gain respite. Rowley ignored them. "Get on, get *on*, woman. Go faster." He was panting. So was she.

Whoever had built the tunnel had been a craftsman; arched stones enclosed them on either side. Head bent, Adelia saw little except the mud of the floor as her boots squelched through it.

How far? Jesus, how far now? She'd lost all sense of direction and time. She was choking on her own breath. She gasped for the fresh air that was somewhere above her, the heavens impervious to the poor mice scuttling along their underground tube.

At one point, she thought she heard footsteps and imagined they were Godwyn's or Hilda's, running to block the other end of the tunnel against them. It was the thud of her own heart in her ears. *We're too far down to hear anything else,* she thought, and began to choke again. She slowed, and Rowley's head butted into her, the jolt nearly sending the lantern out of her hand so that she had to clasp it with the other to stop it from falling, burning her fingers on it. Oh, God, to be down here without light . . .

At the next niche she stopped and sat down to gain some breath, straightening her back and sucking her scorched fingers. Rowley peered at her. "Move, woman, move."

"You go on," she said. "I've got to rest."

He collapsed beside her — the tunnel's lack of height had made it harder going for him even than for her. He was looking at the lantern's candle that had burned hideously low, then shifted with discomfort. "Hello, what's this?"

He produced what he'd sat on — a plain deal box secured by a prong through a hasp.

"I think we've discovered where our inn-keeper and wife keep their treasures."

She took the box. It rattled. Something of Emma's might be hidden inside. But prong and hasp were so rusted together that she couldn't open it.

Rowley grew impatient. "Let's sit here and examine the contents, shall we? Come *on*."

Clutching the box, she followed him, like Eurydice hastening after Orpheus, remembering that, at the last, Eurydice had been condemned to stay in the Underworld, never to see daylight again.

It was taking too long; if there *was* an end to this bestial tunnel, Godwyn and Hilda had reached it first and entombed them in it as they had Emma, Pippy, and Roetger.

"What is it?" In front of her, Rowley was cursing.

"I left my bloody sword in that bloody cellar. I put it down to pick up a bottle."

"I've got mine." She'd been tempted to throw it away; the damn thing attached to the string round her waist kept bumping against her legs.

"Lot of good that bloody rusty thing is."

It killed a man, she thought. *God, don't let me think about that now.*

So far, at least, there was no sign that three prisoners had ever been down here.

Had Millie tricked them? No. Or if she had, she'd suffered for it — the girl hadn't feigned unconsciousness; there'd been no trickery there. She'd been felled by that madwoman like a sapling under the ax.

A madwoman. Up there. Shutting them in.

Adelia began to pray in time to her shuffling, splashing feet, "Almighty Lord, save us. Save us, O Almighty Lord, of Thy great mercy, save us," to a God Who, for her, automatically encompassed the Judaism and Christianity of her foster parents and something of Mansur's Allah.

It had come naturally to her as a child that the faith of three beloved worshippers must reach the same deity with the accord that they gave one another. She could do no less now as she stumbled and ached and sobbed for breath. Theology was beyond her; so, almost, was thought, only a plea for help that went lancing upward through the earth to the stars: "Save us."

All light had diminished except for the lantern that dragged along the ground in Rowley's hand ahead of her. Help was restricted to the edge of his cloak, where she clutched it. All at once, the image of his naked body in bed came to her so strongly that she was stabbed with lust and, if that was profanity at this desperate moment, she couldn't help it because here, in extremis, it was too sweet to surrender. *I have loved him, he has loved me, and that is something, dear God, it is something.*

As if the thought had power, the ceiling began to rise so that her man could stand up straight, and she with him.

Now the tunnel was sloping upward, culminating in steps that led to a ceiling. Rowley took them at a run that pulled his cloak out of her grasp.

Adelia went up more heavily, realizing for the first time that her skirts were weighing her down. In the relief of reaching the tunnel's end, the significance of the fact that, for the last few upward yards, she had been wading through ankle-deep water escaped her.

Above her, the lantern's candle guttered. For a tremulous second she watched it flutter like a moth before it went out.

The darkness then was like no other. A moonless night always held some reflection that the eye could adjust to; this was the negation of light, an absence of everything. Adelia heard the useless echo of her whimper tremble into it as if it came from somebody else.

There was a scratching and tinny sound,

followed by a blast of profanity from the bishop of Saint Albans. "What are you doing?" she screamed at him.

"There's metal up here. A hatch or whatever it is, it's metal. What do you think I'm doing? I'm trying to open the bastard."

"Try feeling for a catch."

"Oh, thank you, Doctor. I've done that. There isn't one. Either the bugger's locked in place or there's some sort of cantilever on the other side that lifts it. I'm hitting it — somebody might hear us."

Nobody would hear that. Adelia struggled to untangle the sword hanging from her waist and then held it up until it found Rowley's boot. "Try this."

She felt a fumbling hand take the weapon from her. There was a reverberating clang as metal hit against metal. That was better. But who was up there to hear? Only the couple who'd buried them — and they weren't going to lift anything.

Adelia covered her ears as clang after clang made her head rock. Between every clash, Rowley shouted halloos and curses until she thought he'd go mad — or she would. Feeling each step with her hands, she climbed up until she touched his leg. "Let me try."

He hauled her up beside him and she realized she was still clutching the box from the niche. She threw it down and raised her arms, encountering metal. She traced it with her fingertips — a shallow, inverted dome of iron. It was completely smooth, no protuberance that suggested a catch on this side of it.

"See?" Rowley gave her a push aside and resumed his assault. But that was it; she *couldn't* see. Eyes were useless; there was only touch and hearing — and terror.

After an age of noise, she couldn't bear it anymore. She reached out for his arm, found it, and held it. "Let's go back to the cellar."

The thought of a return battling through darkness . . . but there'd be space there, and comforting, normal things like barrels . . . it might be that Millie wasn't dead and could let them out . . . *something.*

She said, remembering, "The hatch on the barrel chute was made of wood, perhaps we can hack our way up through it and shift whatever was on it."

"Or at least drink ourselves to death."

That he'd stopped howling and now sounded merely disgruntled was balm to her. She could bear up if he could, but *only* if he could.

On her bottom, investigating with her feet,

she managed to hump herself down the steps. When she heard Rowley join her, she spread her arms so that she could feel the rough texture of the tunnel wall on either side and began to wade down the incline they had come up.

And she *was* wading. Water surrounded her knees. She went on. It was up to her waist.

Stupidly, she wondered if she'd started down a wrong branch of the tunnel into some massive drain. But there'd *been* no branching off. . . .

Somebody said, "There's water coming in, Rowley."

Somebody else said, "So there is, my love. We'd better go back."

She felt a hand against her face work its way down to her shoulder, guiding her backward until they reached the steps, then helping her up to the landing at the top.

She clung onto him. "Where's the water coming from? What's happening?"

"I'll tell you what's happening. . . ." And from the sound of his voice, Adelia envisaged him spitting the words from between his teeth. "Our noble landlord has opened the chute in the cellar. Taken the fucking hatch off. This is floodwater."

"Floodwater?"

"In case you didn't notice, it was raining outside. Still is, presumably. It's coming down that bloody chute. It's filled the cellar and now it's flooding the sodding tunnel."

"But . . . that would take hours."

"Sweetheart, we've been down here for hours."

In her mind's eye, Adelia saw the hills around Glastonbury. Sheeting rain, unable to soak into the drought-baked, rock-hard earth, would be funneling down their sides into the High Street like rivers in full spate. The Pilgrim's courtyard had already been an overflowing sink when she'd last seen it. With the plug hole of the barrel hatch removed, water would be pouring down the chute. . . .

"One thing," Rowley's voice said. "It'll ruin the bastard's ale."

"Will it reach us up here?"

Her answer was another ear-wounding clang. He was bashing the sword hilt against the iron hood again.

A stupid question; how could he know? It would depend on whether the rain stopped in time. And then, she thought, whether it does or not, we're dead. They were in a diminishing space formed by brick, iron, and rising water, all of them impermeable. The air would go bad. In Salerno, she'd once worked on a corpse her foster father had bought for her to practice on, that of a man who'd fallen into a large, empty wine vat, his flailing arm catching its lid and bringing it down on top of him.

"Asphyxiation," she'd said, finishing the examination.

"Correct," he'd said. "It is what happens when people are enclosed like that."

"I know," she'd said, "but why? It was an enormous vat, why couldn't he go on breathing? What causes people to asphyxiate in confined spaces?"

"Air hunger," he'd said. "Our breathing uses it up or poisons it, I don't know how."

They would die, like the man in the vat.

"Allie." Again, it was a cry of agony that seemed to come from somebody else.

The clanging stopped and was replaced by Rowley's voice: "She'll be provided for. I've made a will."

"Allie." A document couldn't pick a child up or kiss a scratch better or cure the need for a mother who wasn't there.

Another clang, the last, and she was rocked as he miscalculated where she sat and his body thumped against her before it found its place at her side. "Goddamn you, woman." Hot breath fanned her ear. "This is your fault. Why in hell didn't you marry me?"

She didn't know anymore. Why hadn't she?

"Nice little castle," the breath said. "We could have brought her up together. You stitching away at your tapestry in the solar, me on the practice ground teaching her swordplay."

It was meant to make her laugh and, oddly, it almost did, but beneath his courage she heard fury for a life missed.

My fault, she thought, *my most grievous fault. What price independence when I could have chosen happiness, his, Allie's, mine? Too high.* "I wouldn't do it again," she said.

"Bit bloody late now." Again, her skin felt his breath. "You've sent me to hell, you realize that? My soul is doomed. I've sinned at prime, at matins, at lauds; I've lifted the host to the Lord, and what I was lifting was your skinny body. I'd think, *What do I see in her?* But you were all I saw." Another sigh. "I have offended against my sweet Lord. Saint Peter's not likely to give me passage through the gate after that."

"It won't be hell for me if I'm with you," she said, feeling for him with her arms. "We'll fry on the griddle together."

Voices speaking love into the darkness. Tiny flames guttering out.

It was becoming difficult to breathe.

After a while his head fell hard against her neck, and when she spoke to him again, he didn't reply.

"No," she begged him. "Wait for me. Don't go without me."

There was a deep grinding sound, and the lid above their heads lifted, slowly, as if a cautious cook was peering into a pan.

The foulness of the death chamber rushed upward — she felt its passing, like a wind — to be replaced by damp fresh air.

"God pray we're in time," somebody said.

Dizzily, still clutching Rowley's body to her, she looked upward. The abbot of Glastonbury's face was staring down on her, Godwyn's beside it, both of them anxious.

Behind them, Hilda struggling. "Leave 'em," she was screaming, "leave 'em." Only Brother Titus's large arms were holding the woman back from hindering the resurrection of the couple she'd condemned to death.

TWELVE

Adelia made them lift Rowley out first. It took the added help of brothers James and Aelwyn to do it; Brother Titus was fully occupied in restraining the howling, kicking Hilda.

When it was Adelia's turn, she found herself rising through a wide hole and into the rubble of what had once been the house of Glastonbury's abbots, near the abbey's landing stage.

The monks wanted to take them both to the Abbot's kitchen immediately, but Adelia refused to let them move Rowley. She knelt beside him, begging him to come back from wherever he'd gone, until she saw air going easily in and out of his nostrils. He opened his eyes — they had sense in them — and said her name, at which point she sat back, allowing a prayer of such thankfulness to leave her as must have lanced upward through the ragged clouds that crossed and recrossed a pale, indifferent moon, up and up until it reached the God of mercy who had granted yet another resurrection.

Between them, Aelwyn and James supported Rowley across the charred grass to the kitchen, Titus carrying the still-shrieking Hilda after them. Adelia followed behind, leaning heavily on the abbot's arm.

"No, no," he said, as she tried to thank him. "You owe your lives to this good man." He laid his hand on the shoulder of Godwyn, walking silently beside them. "We would never have known otherwise. Indeed, I had forgotten there *was* a tunnel. Built by one of my ancient predecessors, perhaps, in the time of the Danish invasions, and its hatch rusted these many years. It was when Godwyn found he couldn't open it alone that he came running to us for help, did you not, my son?" When the landlord didn't answer, he added, "I fear there are questions to answer, but we shall leave them until you and our good bishop are recovered."

She was cold and couldn't stop trembling. Her dripping skirt was chilly against her legs. Heat had gone with the storm, leaving cool air scenting a reviving countryside, and, her mind numbed, she could do nothing but breathe it in. Being freed from the danger she and Rowley had shared hadn't lessened the intensity of its last moments; the people around her, even Hilda and her noise, were wraiths on the edges of it. Certainly there must be questions to answer, a thousand of them, but at the moment they fluttered like moths beyond her grasp.

Her body appreciated the warmth of the kitchen, but still the one solid thing in it was Rowley, who'd been seated in its only chair.

"Marsh cudweed," she said, automatically. "Get him an infusion of marsh cudweed." It stimulated the breathing system.

She heard him say, "Sod that. I'll have brandy." Such music to her ears that her wits came back and she began to be aware of other things. One of which was that their savior was the Pilgrim's landlord.

Godwyn. A good thing.

It took some adjustment of thought; for a day or more, the man had capered in her mind as the personification of evil.

They were still having trouble with Hilda. Muttering prayers to deflect the curses the woman directed at them, brothers Titus and James were having to bind her waist with rope, attaching it to a hook in the wall, to stop her from launching an attack on her husband. Her cap had come off so that her hair stood around her head like a ginger-and-gray badger's. Loops of spit hung from her bared teeth.

The abbot shook his head at her with real grief. "I fear she has gone mad, poor soul."

"An affliction of women at a certain age, so I'm told," Brother Aelwyn said, and his abbot nodded.

Godwyn stood in front of his wife, pleading. "I couldn't, sweetheart, could I? For the sake of thy soul, I couldn't let ee do it. Not to these two, and one of 'em a bishop, not to the others."

Hilda spat at him.

"Others?" the abbot asked sharply.

"No-oo." Hilda tossed herself forward and was jerked back by the rope. "Traitor, traitor, traitor."

Others? *Others?* Again, it was a revelation for Adelia to remember that she and Rowley had gone into the tunnel expecting to find corpses — and had encountered none. The long grief for Emma and her child was replaced by a desperate hope. "Are they alive? Where are they?"

"Are we talking about the lady who went missing?" The abbot was bewildered.

"See, I couldn't bear for them others to die — she'd have murder on her soul. And there was a little un with 'em," Godwyn said, "but I couldn't let 'em free or they'd have told on her. Well, I couldn't, could I? 'S only acause she wouldn't stop." He turned back to his wife. "You wouldn't stop, sweetheart. The bishop, this lady . . . it couldn't go on, could it?" There were tears on his face.

"Where are they?"

"Lazarus Island."

"Lazarus?" The abbot was sharp with him. "You've kept three people on Lazarus for over a month? Impossible — the lepers would have told me."

Godwyn hunched. "I said to 'em as I wouldn't be a-bringing you over again iffen they said anything. I'm shamed, master, but I was waiting to let things settle down like, for Hilda to get back to her right mind." He looked at his wife again. "You wouldn't, though, sweetheart, you got worse."

Abbot Sigward shook his head and sat down.

"See," Godwyn said, "them others was in a bad way, bein' down in the tunnel so long. Very bad way they was, the big fella and the little boy 'specially, and the woman, she agreed to anythin' to keep 'em alive. I had to wait til the missus were out of the inn, see, before I could let 'em up. I told 'em if they wanted to stay livin', they must do like

348

I said. So I rowed 'em across to Lazarus."
His shoulders drooped. " 'S finished now,
any old way. Couldn't let it happen again,
could I? She weren't going to stop."

Hilda spat at him again.

"Is finished, sweetheart," Godwyn said,
pleading with her once more. And then to
the abbot, "They'll let her off, won't they,
master? For being gone mad, they'll let her
off. You'll tell 'em. 'Twas all for you. All as
she's done, 'twas ever for you."

"Me?" Sigward stared at him.

"Just tell us if they're alive," Adelia
prompted sharply. There wasn't time for
side issues. *"Are they alive?"*

"Didn't know what else to do," Godwyn
said, still addressing the abbot. He jerked
his head toward his wife. "They'd a-told on
her otherwise. Been smugglin' them supplies to Lazarus when I could." His shoulders drooped. "It's finished now, any road,
God-a-mercy on both our souls."

Lepers. They'd been marooned with lepers.

Adelia clutched at the abbot's arm. "We've
got to fetch them. Now. Please, we must go
now."

Though trying to keep up with events, Sigward was firm on this. "We can go nowhere
in the dark. In the morning, my child; we'll

do what has to be done when dawn comes."

Yes, dawn. It was night now, though she had a job to remember *which* night. She supposed it must be only this morning that she'd hidden and watched Gyltha, Allie, and Mansur set off for Wells, a matter of hours since the storm had sent the rain and darkness in which Millie had . . .

Millie.

Adelia clutched at the abbot again. "The girl Millie. Hilda attacked her. . . ."

"Where did this happen?"

"At the inn. I saw her fall. . . . I must see to her. . . ."

"You will stay here." Sigward had taken authority. "Brother James? To the inn, if you please."

The monk bowed and went out into the night, taking with him the last of Adelia's immediate responsibilities and leaving her limp.

She was guided to a bench at the table, felt the smooth clay of a beaker pressed against her mouth, and tasted brandy. She swallowed a little of it, laid her head on the board, listening to Hilda rave and Abbot Sigward asking questions that Rowley was answering . . . and went to sleep.

Even during the dream, she was irritated by it. Guinevere was an irrelevance now, and the sleeping Adelia didn't want to be bothered with her, but the woman with a skull's face came walking forward out of the mist. This time she had Arthur's Excalibur in her hand; this time she spoke. "You are close now," she said. "You are close to me. Come nearer."

Crossly, Adelia woke up, not frightened — what dream could overtop the terror of reality? — merely resentful that her rest had been disturbed and left her with a nagging sense of a duty not done.

It was still dark outside, but the light of its fire showed that the kitchen was full of bodies — only the comfortable sound of snoring dispelled the impression that there'd been a massacre.

Opposite her, brothers James and Aelwyn slept, their cowled heads using the table as a pillow. Other figures, just discernible in the shadows, lay scattered around the floor on palliasses produced from somewhere. A hammock slung from two flitch hooks contained the bishop of Saint Albans. Adelia got up and hurried over to him, dislodging a cloak that someone had laid over her in the night.

Rowley's color was good; so was his breathing. Without waking him, she smoothed his hair from his face before investigating the others on the floor.

The abbot lay on his side, one elegant hand around his chin, as if he was thinking, though his eyes were tight shut. Next to him squatted Brother Titus, snoring louder than anybody, his head cradled on his knees — a sleeping guardian of Hilda, who was stretched out nearby, the rope around her waist still attached to its hook. The woman's eyelids were only half closed, and her teeth were bared, which, though she too was asleep, gave her the appearance of a chained, recumbent dog ready to snarl at any intruder.

Before Adelia had slept, Rowley, Sigward, and the other monks had been agreeing that Hilda was mad; it had settled everything for them — a neat, all-encompassing explanation that might save her from the gallows under the law that the insane, not being responsible for their actions, should escape execution. It had been male reasoning for the mysterious turbulence that they seemed to think affected women during the menopause. Last night, in the discussion that Adelia had been too tired to enter into, Rowley had been adamant that in her madness Hilda had felt impelled to protect Glastonbury from the Arthur and Guinevere skeletons being proved a fraud.

There was no cause to think otherwise; the woman was undoubtedly deranged. Equally without doubt, the Pilgrim's — and the abbey's — future depended on supplicants coming to the grave of King Arthur.

And yet, to Adelia now, it didn't answer. It could only have been Hilda who'd tried to bury Mansur and herself — the woman had a positive propensity for entombing people. Such savagery argued a deeper, more urgent reason, if reason there was.

Adelia moved on to peer at the body nearest the door. Millie, thank God. The girl was breathing steadily. There was a plaster on her head, bound in place with linen. The sallow skin of her face was no paler than it always was. Another one, then, who, with luck, had taken no harm from the desperate night.

The only person missing was Godwyn.

Adelia went out to attend to nature. Rejecting what the gentry called the *odeur de merde* emanating from the trench latrine with its neatly holed plank that the monks had dug near their kitchen garden — so enriching for the vegetables — she found some convenient bushes, then went to the pump just outside the kitchen itself for a wash.

In the east, the sky was beginning to lighten. Somewhere a thrush was attempting its first song of the day.

It would be dawn soon, and if a merciful God could again extend His munificence and allow the three souls on Lazarus Island to be found alive and well, she, Vesuvia Adelia Rachel Ortese Aguilar, would be forever in His debt.

A figure netting trout from the stew by the light of a lantern gave a hail and came stalking toward her.

Brother Peter appeared friendlier than on their previous meetings. "Here," he said, "that darky wizard's a proper marvel, in't he? Done a good job for" — he paused to wink — "you know who. Think he'd like some of me pumpkins? They've come on wonderful well with all this sun, if the storm ain't ruined 'em."

Yes, Adelia told him, sighing, the lord Mansur would be pleased to be rewarded with pumpkins for having saved Will and the tithing.

He lingered. "Heard as there was a right to-do last night. What were you and the bishop doin' down that bloody hole?"

"Not enjoying ourselves, I can tell you that," she said.

"Mad as May butter, that Hilda. Allus

was. Never could reckon as how poor old Godwyn put up with her."

Adelia had a thought. "Could you do me a favor, Brother Peter?"

They went to the site of the tunnel, its lid still lying on one side. Adelia couldn't bear to look into the hole, but, on her instructions, the lay brother clambered down happily enough and emerged with the box and sword left on its steps. They were dry; the water hadn't reached them — indeed, it had retreated. "What's these doin' down there?" he asked.

"Can I borrow your lantern?"

When he gave it to her, she merely thanked him and turned away before he could ask more questions.

The box intrigued Adelia; to have been placed so deep in the tunnel suggested that its contents were of value. Or incriminating. Or both. Emma's jewels, probably. In which case, what happiness — if Emma were still alive — to return them to someone who had been suffering all the privations of a castaway as an earnest that she was to be restored to her former life.

Then, like Pandora before her, Adelia thought, *To hell, I just want to know what's in the thing.*

There was time to open it before the rescue began, and no need to wake the people in the kitchen before then, which she undoubtedly would if she went there — a noisy business if the box's hasp continued to prove as obdurate as it had.

She took lantern, sword, and box to the only place where there was both privacy and a table.

Despite the poverty of their resting place and the drenching the storm had inflicted on the cloths that covered them, the forms of Arthur and Guinevere retained the dignity accorded to all the dead in silent immobility.

It was disturbed as Adelia, apologizing to them, shoved the covering away from Arthur's feet and placed the lantern between them before committing the same indignity on Guinevere by positioning the box between hers.

She left the door open to add what natural light there was to that of the lantern.

It *was* a noisy business. Inserting the sword tip under the hasp was difficult and caused much scratching and, on Adelia's part, much swearing under her puffing breath.

At last the hasp yielded its grip on the prong. Adelia put the sword down and lifted the box's lid.

Not jewels. Bones. Pelvic bones.

Behind her, somebody coughed.

Adelia swung round like someone guilty, hiding the box with her body.

Godwyn stood in the doorway. Godwyn the good thing, to whom she owed her life and Rowley's and, perhaps, Emma's. Godwyn the bad thing, who had permitted an uncontrollable wife to try to silence those who'd incommoded her. Godwyn, who had done nothing to stop Millie being beaten.

"What do you want?" she snapped. She was being interrupted on the brink of discovery, and she did not want him to see the box; it might be his, but its contents most certainly were not.

Anyway, there was a terrible patience to the man, which made her nerves twang. He didn't move, face impassive; only his eyes showed the resignation of an ox awaiting the fall of the poleax.

"You'll speak for her, lady, won't ee?" he said. "The bishop do think high of you; you'll tell him as she ain't in charge of what she does. Iffen she's taken to court, a word from his lordship to the judges . . . make a mort of difference that would . . ."

Adelia shook her head, not in negation

but to clear it. After all, she supposed she had a duty to listen to this man who had given back the lives that the woman he was pleading for had tried to take away.

He continued to talk, had probably been pacing half the night preparing his speech of mitigation.

"Iffen you'd a seen her when she were a girl, hair like fire, full of chatter as a cricket . . . She were a sight then, my Hilda. Come as milkmaid to the master's cows when she were eleven year old . . ."

Concentrate. There was something here, some insight into why a pretty milkmaid had turned murderous.

"The master?" Adelia asked, to get things clear. "You mean Abbot Sigward?"

"Lord Sigward as he were then, abbot as is now. Me, I started off as his stable lad, do ee see, bound to his family like my father afore me and his father afore that. Good masters to us, all of 'em, so long as we did our jobs and served them proper. I got raised to chief stabler, and Hilda, she was made housekeeper."

"Did you always love her?" The question was an impertinence. Adelia was taking advantage of someone who was her helpless supplicant, but she was impelled to ask it; in the relationship between this man and

358

his wife had to be a clue to what had gone on.

He was puzzled, offended. If he hadn't been begging for Adelia's help, he would have walked away. "Fine worker, Hilda," he said. It was the only answer he could give; love was a word restricted to the nobility and poets. He tried to smile. "Worth the wooing, she was. Took a bit of doing, mind. Her wouldn't look at me for years."

"Because she loved the master?" She was probing deep, but somewhere under her scalpel was the source of infection.

Godwyn was stung into indignation. "Never any uncleanness between 'em," he said, "never. Half the time he didn't know as she were there. Still don't."

No, he didn't; Adelia had seen that for herself. Abbot Sigward's kindness to his former housekeeper was that of a master to a pet hound. "But you went on serving him?"

Again, the man was puzzled. "He were my lord. Weren't his fault, weren't Hilda's, weren't mine. 'S how it was. Service, see. Good servant, good master, one loyal to t'other."

"I see." But Adelia knew she didn't see. She had been brought up outside the feudal system and would never fathom that bind-ing between the classes, one ruling, one serving, in mutual acceptance, a tradition that spanned centuries, holding both in place, a system capable of dreadful abuse, yet at its best — as it had been in the household of Sigward before he left it to turn to God — a form of loving.

"And his son," she asked. "Did you love him?"

Now she was causing pain. Godwyn's teeth showed in an agonized grimace, and he tapped his clenched fist against them. But he was helpless; if the woman who stood before him was to save his wife, he had to submit to the turn of the screw.

"Sorry for un," he said. "Sad little thing he was. Like his ma had been afore she died. Frit of everything. I put un on his first pony and he were afraid then. Not like his pa. Not frit of nothing, the master weren't. But the boy were" — Godwyn searched for a description — "more fond of flowers like, painting and books and such. Never squealed, though, you got to give un that. He'd puke every time the master took un hunting, but he had to go an' he went, no murmur."

"As he had to go on crusade?" *Why am I persisting with this?* she wondered. But the volition for it seemed to come not just from within her but from behind her, as if the skeletons were urging her on.

She'd gone too far. Godwyn's eyes searched for an escape.

Adelia reached for his hand. "I'll speak for her, Godwyn. So will the bishop, I promise you that." She could do no less for this imperfect, strangely wonderful man.

The landlord nodded, then took off his cap and held it to his breast in a gesture of subservience that made her want to weep. "I'll go ready the boat, then," he said.

She watched him walk away toward the landing stage, a stumpy, ordinary figure outlined against the pink and gold of a rising sun.

She turned back. There wasn't much time and she had to know *now.* Even so, she spent a second or two on her knees beside Guinevere's catafalque before, whipping off the cloth, she lifted the top half of the skeleton away from the bottom half, exposing the hideous gap where the pelvic girdle should have been. Working quickly, she began fitting the bones from the box into the space.

Some were badly splintered, but others had survived the onslaught almost untouched; the ball of the right femur, for example, went perfectly into the socket of the acetabulum.

The spine had been severed so neatly that the three fused lower vertebrae attached themselves to the rest of the sacrum without any question that they belonged together.

Adelia stood back from her work and stared at it. Undoubtedly, Guinevere had been made whole. The bones fit. This was the right pelvis in the right place at last.

Also the wrong one.

She measured, using the sword as a ruler by marking lines in the black patina of its blade; she considered the ilia, broken as they were, but still displaying unmistakable flanges. Without apology this time, she pushed Arthur's cloth away and made more measurements, comparing his pubic arch with the one she'd taken from the box.

Back to Guinevere.

Eventually, she was sure; there could be no mistake. "So that's what you've been trying to tell me," she said gently.

Guinevere was male.

She covered the skeletons and sat down on the ground, resting her head against Arthur's catafalque.

Two men. Buried together. Both killed, one viciously maimed in his sexual parts. Twenty years ago.

Nuances, sentences, dreams, clues from

362

these past days that she should have taken notice of came fluttering into her mind, settling in it to form a recognizable mosaic.

So that was the answer — love. Love could be the only connection between the living and the dead concentrated in that poor pattern of bones. Love in its many manifestations — destructive, sexual, beautiful, protective, possessive — was the link. It was love of a sort that had nearly killed Rowley and herself; in another form, it had brought the couple they called Arthur and Guinevere to their grave.

The pity of it.

Adelia went out, softly closing the door of the hut behind her.

A warm, early sun was sucking moisture from the drenched ground in the form of a mist so that the great tors rose as if out of nothing to stand against a pellucid sky, a mist into which swallows vanished as they flicked down into it to catch insects and then reappeared.

Whether or not Glastonbury was the omphalos Mansur had recognized, it was magical this morning, telling her that if Avalon was anywhere it was here, spell casting, able to raise an unquiet spirit that had haunted her, nagged her, into showing the truth about itself.

This was the place for it, so easy to have common sense undermined by breathtaking natural geographical beauty.

Adelia, practical scientist that she was, fought against its seduction. To believe that the Guinevere nightmares had come from outside rather than from unrecognized doubts that she'd had from the first, a formless guilt at assuming a skeleton was female because everybody said it was . . .

"I won't have it," she said out loud. It was almost a snarl.

But still she walked through the Glastonbury mist on invisible feet.

She made for the landing place. It was quiet there except for the yelps of seagulls and the cheeps of marsh birds attending to their young among reeds and tussock sedge. The river had been energized by last night's rainfall and flowed faster than she'd ever seen it, a dark blue ribbon winding around islands toward the sea. A little way along its right bank where the boathouse was, she could see Godwyn loading supplies into a boat, this time a large punt that was to take them to Lazarus, and the three castaways on it.

And pray God we're not too late.

Adelia took off her ruined, water-distorted, ashy shoes and sat down so that her toes could reach into the river and send up flirting, rainbow splashes.

Again, her surroundings insisted that all was right with the world, especially here — that Emma, Pippy, and Roetger *must* have survived in such a glorious landscape, that a great and ancient king could have chosen nowhere better for his last resting place.

She wished she could believe it. How nice to discount human wickedness, to be able to fall in with the nature around her, to discount evidence and allow that the mutilated bones in the hut were indeed those of Arthur and Guinevere, killed in a legendary battle in such an ancient past that its shrieks and blows had ameliorated into nothing more than the puff of a story-laden breeze.

But those shrieks, those blows, had been less than a generation ago. She had a duty to the dead; she was who she was.

She felt the little pier vibrate as somebody joined her on it. Beside her were the long, white, sandaled feet of Abbot Sigward.

"We have been searching for you, my child. Will you come and take some food before we go?"

She squinted up at him, shading her eyes. "How did your son die?" she asked.

For a moment he was as still as death. She

continued to look at him.

"So you are Nemesis," he said.

She nodded.

Then the abbot's face changed, quite beautifully, as if the sun shining on it was reflected back by an inner light. "I have been awaiting that question for twenty years." He stretched his arms sideways to embrace the view, like a cormorant holding out its wings to dry in the warmth. "See what a perfect day the Lord has chosen for it. He has even supplied a bishop for my confession." He smiled down at her. "Stay there, my child, while I fetch the others."

He strode off toward the kitchen, then stopped to turn around.

"I killed him," he said.

Later, when Adelia looked back on the journey to Lazarus, it was the incongruity of it that never failed to jolt her. It should have been made in darkness, or at least cast a shadow that withered everything they passed. Instead, as Godwyn smoothly poled the punt containing Sigward, Adelia, Rowley, and Hilda along, the sun shone on them as if on a jolly outing.

At one point, the abbot even paused in his confession and uncovered a basket that had been put up for him by Brother Titus before they left, exposing a jug of mead and cakes of oatmeal and honey, and passing them around. "Eat, drink," he urged them.

He was exalted. Sitting on the punt's middle thwart, facing the bishop of Saint Albans, he unburdened himself of his sin almost joyously, sometimes in Latin, sometimes in English, as if fearing that Adelia, his nemesis, sitting in the stern behind Rowley, would not understand him.

Hilda — he'd insisted she should accompany them — crouched in the bottom of the punt, quiet now, her head on his knee like an exhausted dog's.

His story — and it *was* as much story as confession — was of a cleaving. Of a young man hacked in two. Of an earthquake that had not only opened rifts in the ground but had separated the Sigward, lord of great estates, from the Sigward who'd become a lowly monk of Glastonbury Abbey and then its abbot.

He spoke of them as two different people. "Lord Sigward was a man assured of his righteousness," he said. "He gave to the poor, he built churches and oratories so that God should be reminded of his virtue. He ruled his little kingdom justly with a Bible in his hands, knowing he obeyed its precepts. He bathed in the admiration of his neighbors. His servants had cause to love him. . . ." Absentmindedly, Abbot Sigward patted Hilda's shoulder. "At least those he kept by him, for he was quick to punish and rid himself of the ones who did not."

Wishing she didn't have to listen, Adelia kept her eyes on the river, trailing her fingers and watching their wake in the water. A moorhen hurried her chicks away from the ripple.

"Lord Sigward chose his wife carefully, but she was a disappointment; he did not understand why she was afraid of him. She bore him a son, and she died doing it. No matter, Lord Sigward had his heir and held a great feast so that he could boast of him to Somerset's nobility. But the boy, too, was a disappointment; he was weak, like his mother. He cowered when his father spoke to him; he failed in the tiltyard, he was an inept huntsman. Like some clerk, he preferred books to pursuing the manly arts."

Adelia glanced at Rowley's rigid back; he'd averted his face from the man opposite him, as he would have done in the privacy of a confessional. There had been no moment to warn him before they set off. When the abbot, crossing himself, had spoken the formula — "Hear and bless me, Father, for I have greatly sinned" — she'd seen her lover draw away as if in protest.

He always hated hearing confessions. "Who am I to pronounce on sin?" Like Thomas à Becket before him, he'd been appointed by his king, not the Church, and had been made a priest literally overnight — ordained one day, installed into the bishop's chair the next.

The punt surged and slowed as Godwyn dug its pole effortlessly into the riverbed and lifted it again, his face without expression. The words issuing from the mouth of the man who'd been his master might have been no more than the chirp of the buntings hidden in the reeds.

"When the boy was sixteen, it seemed necessary to Lord Sigward that he should regain the admiration of the county and get credit with Almighty God by sending his son on crusade. He fitted him out lavishly with weapons, equipment, gave him a fine destrier to ride . . . which was too big for him." For the first time the abbot's voice had faltered, then, with an indrawn breath, it regained its rhythm. "A farewell feast for the county to wish the son well and praise the father who, though wallowing in his pride, also resented the boy's obvious happiness in leaving him."

A dragonfly skimmed the water and

landed on the punt's gunwale like an iridescent jewel before taking off again.

"Four years went by without a word. Other fathers received news of their offspring from those returning from the Holy Land, sometimes that they were alive and well, sometimes that they were dead. The Lord Sigward, however, heard nothing and began to think that his boy, too, had died, perhaps in the battle for the fortress of Ascalon, where so many Christian knights were slaughtered during its recapture from the Saracen. If so, it would be an excuse for him to hold another feast, this time a valedictory one — what honor to Lord Sigward that his child had given his life in the attempt to return the Holy Land to God."

Adelia watched a kingfisher that had been perching on an alder twig suddenly turn into a rainbowed arrow as it dived into the water, coming up with a frog in its beak.

It was getting hot. Abbot Sigward threw back his cowl to let the air play on his tonsured head. The exaltation was still with him, but his fingers were showing white where he clasped them in his lap — he was coming to the crux.

Adelia tried to distance the clear voice ringing over the marshes into that of just another storyteller in a market. *Twenty years ago,* she told herself. *They have been dead these twenty years. This man is not the same man who killed them.*

But he was.

It had been the evening before the Feast of Saint Stephen 1154, the abbot said, a blustery night.

Christmas festivities were over. Lord Sigward, being the kindly master he was, had already allowed his servants to set off on their annual visit to the villages they came from.

"Apart from Hilda" — the abbot patted the head of the woman crouching beside him — "who refused to leave him, and Godwyn" — he smiled up at the man poling the punt — "who refused to leave *her,* there was no one in the house."

So Lord Sigward was dining alone in his hall when Godwyn, acting as a doorkeeper, heard a loud knocking and went to answer it. Two young men were ushered in, and Lord Sigward found himself being embraced by his son, whose dripping rain cloak put wet marks on the silk of his father's robe. Laughing and exclaiming, the boy introduced his magnificently tall friend. "We have been on the road from Outremer for three months, Father, and we are very, very hungry."

Immediately, Lord Sigward felt anger; if his son had sent word ahead, he could have invited his neighbors to welcome the boy as a hero. He kept his patience, however, and called for Hilda to bring food and drink.

As he watched the young men eat, he became angrier.

"He should have been pleased," the abbot said. "His son had become the man he'd wished him to be. The years in the Holy Land had given the boy belief in himself. He looked Lord Sigward in the eye. He was no longer afraid; he was Lord Sigward's equal — and Lord Sigward resented it."

Also, there was a sweetness in the son's smile when it was directed at the friend that was missing when he addressed the father.

Both youths had pale, cruciform patches on their tunics where the crusader's cross had been stripped off. When Lord Sigward inquired why this was so, he was able to find justification for his anger with the two of them. "They denigrated the sanctity of crusade, they poured scorn on the holy purpose of driving the Saracen from the land Jesus had walked on. They had seen too much death, they said; Islam was merely being inflamed. What purpose in killing Muslim men, women, and children if each corpse added a hundred living people to the number hating Christianity? Was that following the teaching of Our Lord?"

Too furious to speak, Lord Sigward had left the hall and retired to his chamber. He couldn't sleep for thinking of the shame his son's impiety would cast on his name. In the middle of the night, he got up and went to the boy's room to argue with him.

"He found his son and the friend in bed together," the abbot said. "They were naked and performing a homosexual act."

Hubris had descended on Lord Sigward then. Quietly, he closed the door on the two lovers and went to fetch an ax.

The abbot said, "He . . . No, I must not think of myself in the third person. . . . *Me.* I was that butcher. With the ax in my hand, I burst in on those two boys and hacked them to death where they lay in each other's arms. I struck and struck and went on striking long after both were dead."

The river was beginning to straggle through reeds now, and the punt nudged aside yellow water lilies as it went. Sandpipers called from the banks, a descant to the implacable human voice.

"I considered myself justified. Had I not followed the Lord's action against Sodom and Gomorrah? Did not Leviticus say that a man who lies with a man as with a woman has committed a detestable act and should surely be put to death?"

Covered in blood, Lord Sigward went downstairs to sit at the table and stare at nothing.

Hilda had heard the shrieks and gone running to view the slaughterhouse. The dead boys were less important to her than her lord; nobody should know what the dear master had done.

She took over. Godwyn was sent to prepare a coffin while she swabbed and cleaned. The bodies were laid on a sheet; the bedding was burned.

"Not the least of my sins that night was that I involved my two good servants in it." Abbot Sigward glanced up, but Godwyn kept his eyes on the river.

The corpses were put in their coffin, ready to be buried secretly somewhere on the estate. . . .

And then the earthquake struck.

"The world tilted. The ground opened. Worst was the noise, as if God's voice had come close and was blasting destruction through the clouds." Abbot Sigward nodded to himself. "Which it was, which indeed it was. I heard Him. *Is it for you to condemn, you murderer? Was it for this that I sent My Son to preach love and forgiveness? Who are*

you to set yourself up against Him? Two moth-
ers' sons you have killed, Sigward. In your ar-
rogance and wickedness you have committed
filicide twice over and the Son of Man has
been crucified yet again."

It was the voice that Saul heard on the Road to Damascus.

As it had to Saul, it showed Lord Sigward to himself. He cowered at what he saw, a creature of hatred, a vainglorious, pitiless upholder of all law except the one that mattered most, a murderer, not least of a gentle wife who had died loveless. He saw the Pit waiting for him, and it held no flames but was barren and empty, like his soul; he would be condemned to shiver in it alone through all eternity.

"I crawled, pleading for a mercy that would not be given me because I had shown none," the abbot said. "The floor tossed beneath me in the cataclysm that was God's condemnation."

When at last the earth stopped quaking, it was another Sigward who rose to his feet, though he could barely stand upright for the horror of what he had done. He knew now that the boys he'd killed must not be buried in unsanctified ground; to placate a vengeful God, he would take their bodies to the nearest and holiest place he knew, Glastonbury Abbey.

"I was, of course, bargaining with my Lord, wicked creature that I was, leaving it to Him to say whether or not my crime should be discovered. If it were, I would take my punishment. If not, I promised Him that all my lands and possessions should go to Mother Church and I would spend the rest of my days in service of His loving Son." Sigward turned to Adelia. "I told you, my lady, that I was a gambler. It was gambling."

She nodded.

One thing he had not been able to do. "I could not let my son's body go to its rest complete. In my fury, I had hacked it into three, throwing the sexual part onto the floor. Even now . . . Sweet Mary, what twisted madness . . . I would not bury it with him, as if I might still conceal what he was. Hilda saw to its disposal separately, another sin that she bore for me."

Not Hilda, Adelia thought. *It was Godwyn;* tears were trickling down the man's face. It was him — Lord, the wonderful strangeness of human nature. She wondered what he had done with that dreadful collop of flesh until it was skeletonized and he could give the bones a more decent interment because he'd loved and pitied the boy they'd be-

376

longed to.

That night the coffin containing the two lovers was put into a boat and rowed to the abbey's landing stage. There was no one about — the monks were praying for deliverance up on the Tor.

Between them, Sigward, Hilda, and Godwyn hauled the coffin by ropes to the sanctity of the monks' graveyard. "There was a fissure there, as if God with his earthquake had readied a burial place for our burden. We lowered the coffin into it and I prayed for mercy on those two souls, and mine. For the first time in my life, I wept. . . ."

Adelia raised her head. "What was your son's name?"

Rowley jerked round; he'd forgotten that she was there. The abbot had not; he smiled at her. "Arthur," he said. "His name was Arthur."

Of course it was. "And the other boy?" It seemed imperative to her to give him an identity.

"God forgive me," Sigward said, "but if I ever knew it, I have forgotten it." He stretched out a hand toward her. "Do you damn me?"

It wasn't for her to do it. The man carried his own damnation with him. More important to Adelia was whether that one horrific sin, and its far-reaching consequences as Hilda attempted to conceal it, had damned three more people to death. How far to Lazarus? Each time they passed one of the marsh's little islands, most of them uninhabited apart from cattle and sheep, she tensed with expectation — and was disappointed.

But the landscape was changing; its air was saltier, and reeds were beginning to give way here and there to marron grass where high tides had come inland, pushing in enough sand for it to grow on.

Adelia kept her eyes on a hump of ground still some way ahead that broke the dark blue, ruler-straight line of the horizon, hardly listening to the confession that went on and on, of which she had become weary.

Once he'd taken on a monk's habit, the abbot said, he lived a life of penitence and rigid self-denial. . . . "Even then, sinful as I was, I could not admit to anyone what I had done, though I confessed to God and begged His mercy every day."

So exemplary had he been that his fellow monks had elected him as their abbot when the old one died.

He'd taken it as a sign that God was relenting to him and might relent further if he could advance Glastonbury's holiness and prosperity.

"Which, by the Lord's grace, I did," Abbot Sigward said simply. "With every improvement, I became certain that I had gained forgiveness at last." He shook his head. "But God's memory is longer than that, and so, it seems, is a Welsh bard's. When King Henry sent to tell us to dig between the pyramids, I thought, *Is this Nemesis at last? Well, I shall accept her.* But no, I was reprieved yet again; the bodies were taken to be those of King Arthur and Guinevere. The Lord has allowed me to work even harder for Him, I thought. Perhaps the fire that consumed my abbey was His final punishment, and now, in allowing my son and his friend to be misrepresented, they and I can bring the pilgrims back to Glastonbury."

Startled, Adelia took her eyes off the island ahead to glance at the abbot. He'd laughed, actually laughed.

"Our Lord has humor," he said to Rowley, "do you know that? He sent the true Nemesis in the guise of a Saracen and a woman — representatives of a race and a sex that the old Sigward despised."

Adelia turned away, grateful that the voice had stopped at last. The only sound now came from the calling of a flock of geese flying inland.

". . . *Deinde, ego te absolvo a peccatis tuis in nomine Patris, et Fili, et Spiritus Sancti.*" Rowley was pronouncing the absolution in a voice she hardly recognized.

Sigward said, "And now this poor child here, I would wish her absolved from sins which sprang from mine. Come along now, Hilda, you will feel the better for it." He might have been urging the woman at his knee to take some medicine and buck up.

Adelia heard Hilda's voice mutter something and Rowley's, forced, granting her forgiveness in the name of his God.

Lazarus was close now, and Adelia could see why it imprisoned those on it. The Brue was becoming sluggish, oozing between rises of sand that buttressed the higher ground of the island, each with a pool at its lowest point. Sphagnum moss, that wonderful bandage for septic wounds, grew in plenty like a mat.

But there was no health here. The mats quivered and stank of rotting vegetation; the quicksand beneath them slurped as if an old man was sucking his teeth.

And . . . "Oh, no, look," Adelia said.

A stag was floundering in one of the mats. Its front hooves thrashed at the moss and the sand beneath it. The antlered head turned this way and that as it tried to raise its lower body from the morass. It was bellowing in distress.

"Help it, can't we help it?"

The abbot looked to Godwyn. "*Can* we help it?"

The man shook his head. "No."

"We can pull it free," Adelia begged.

"Too heavy," Godwyn said. "The sand . . . it sucks, like. Increases weight tenfold. Be like dragging a house. That'd take us with it."

"It'll suffocate." It was unbearable to watch, to listen to.

"No," Godwyn said again gently. "He'll not go down further. He's floating, and he'll go on floating. 'Tis high tide today — we're in the estuary now, see. Then he'll drown, poor creature. 'Tis the easier death."

Adelia didn't think so. Neither did the stag. They could still hear it bellowing as they rounded the island and approached a long jetty.

Beyond was a compound no less neat than a country village, with houses of wattle and daub thatched with reed. There were gardens, and fields containing cattle and sheep, a little stone church with a bell tower. Whatever else he'd done, Abbot Sigward had made his lepers as comfortable as he could.

Somebody was ringing the church bell, and people were coming down to the landing stage, shouting a welcome to the abbot.

Rowley turned to Adelia. "They don't look like lepers."

At this distance, they probably didn't, Adelia thought. Some would still be ambulatory and able to work; others would not be lepers at all but were condemned to spend their lives here because of their contact with the disease.

Whatever they were, neither Emma nor Roetger, nor Pippy, was among them. But there were children. Oh, God, there were children. . . .

"Children?" she heard Rowley ask.

"Indeed," the abbot told him brightly. "The Church would have lepers lead lives of chastity, and I am not supposed to perform marriages, but I do. And baptisms. I have learned the value of human as well as godly love."

Like their houses, the people waiting for them on the landing stage were well accoutred though, differing from ordinary villagers, they were mostly dressed in uniform black with wide-brimmed hats not unlike a pilgrim's. As the punt drew in and Godwyn tied up, carefully locking its hawser to a bollard, they crowded forward to help Abbot Sigward out, embracing him, kissing his hands, talking, some trying to pull him toward their houses to bless the sick that lay inside.

Anxious and distressed though she was, the scientist within Adelia saw the early signs on some of them: thinness from loss of appetite, twisted hands, blotches and eruptions on their faces, but even these were energized out of leprosy's inevitable lassitude by the coming of the abbot.

If it hadn't been for Emma, she'd have liked to question and examine. What was leprosy? Was it passed down from parent to child? Why did some catch it and others did not? Which conditions encouraged it, and which didn't?

As it was . . . "Where are my friends?" she asked Godwyn sharply.

Rowley was grimacing at the sight of the people above him and scrambled ashore reluctantly to join Godwyn and Adelia on the landing stage, taking care to keep away from the crowd around Sigward.

Hilda remained kneeling on the floor of the punt, her head on the thwart the abbot had sat on, her eyes open and staring at nothing. "Back in a minute, sweetheart," her husband told her. She didn't move.

Leaving the abbot to the lepers, Rowley and Adelia followed Godwyn along the dirt track through the hamlet — except that now any resemblance to a normal village was gone. The people propped up against their doorways in the sun were not gossiping or weaving or tending to their children; they were being eaten alive, the disease chewing their flesh like a rat gnawing at a corpse. They had the dreadful similarity to one another that advanced leprosy gave to their faces, turning them lion-like.

The loss of feeling in their extremities, so that some had accidentally burned themselves or suffered cuts without knowing it, contributed to the absence of fingers and toes that necrosis had caused to drop off. One blind, bare-legged old man was unaware that a seagull was pecking at the stump of his foot.

Adelia shooed it off and, stooping, covered his legs with a flap of the blanket he sat on. Rowley pulled her away. "For God's sake, don't touch him. You can't do anything." He hurried her on.

Everything in Adelia screamed for her to do *something,* but she knew from what her foster father had told her of the disease that while opium could relieve pain in the early stages, these sufferers were beyond that; they must die slowly, inch by inch. Nothing was spared them, not even the stink from their rotting flesh.

"The firstborn of death." Rowley was quoting from the Book of Job.

Little wonder the Church maintained that these people would not go to hell when they died; they were in it while they lived. From one of the cottages came a mumbled cry for water, whether from a man or a woman it was impossible to tell. A little girl came out with a pail and went running to a pump. That would do no good, either; the thirst at the end was inextinguishable.

They were beyond the village now, with a view of the far-off sea. The tide was coming in, refreshing the marshes and the air as if it wanted to wipe their memory of what they'd seen and smelled.

Let there be one good thing in this world, Adelia thought. *Let Emma and Pippy be alive. Roetger, too.* "Where *are* they?"

Godwyn pointed ahead to where a grove of low trees sheltered a shepherd's hut. "Didn't want 'em near the lepers, did I?" he said.

Adelia broke into a run, scattering sheep as she went. Thank God, thank God, a thin filament of smoke was rising from a cooking fire.

There was a stream and a small, dirty child in rags building a dam across it with twigs. Adelia jumped the stream and scooped him up as she ran, covering him with kisses.

A scarecrow of a woman appeared at the door of the hut, shading her eyes, then dropped to her knees like a puppet whose strings were suddenly cut.

Adelia scooped her up, too, nearly squashing Pippy in the process. "It's all right now, Em, my dear, my *dear* girl. It's going to be all right."

Of the three castaways, Roetger was in the worst condition, emaciated and with a fever. "He's been so brave, 'Delia," Emma said, crying. "We would have died without him."

He had to be supported on the journey back to the landing stage, using a crutch under one shoulder and Rowley on the other side. Godwyn offered to help, but Emma spat at him. "Don't you come near, don't you come *near* us."

"Godwyn saved your lives," Adelia told her gently.

"I don't care. Keep him away."

What the landlord *was* able to do was steer them around the village so that they could approach the punt from another side and avoid the sights of the main street. They were taking a track that led past the backs of cottages when a scream came from the direction of the landing stage.

More shouts. Godwyn began running. Hampered as they were — Adelia was still carrying Pippy — they couldn't keep up with him.

The bell in the church began ringing slow, single tolls that marked a death.

Now they could see the punt. It was empty. Godwyn was on the landing stage, struggling in the arms of two men holding him back. He was howling and crying.

Bewildered, Adelia looked to where people were pointing in distress.

Rowley said, "Sweet Mary save us."

The tall figure of Abbot Sigward, reduced by distance, was striding out into the marsh. He had his arm around Hilda, who was clinging to him as he encouraged her along. Their feet sent up splashes of incoming tide.

Rowley turned on one of the men nearby. "Can we go after them?"

"Dursn't," the man said — he was crying. "Quicksand. God have mercy on 'em."

Nothing to do but watch. The bell went on tolling. The two figures were up to their knees in water, but still the abbot surged forward, almost carrying the woman flopped against him.

As if something had suddenly clamped their legs, they became still and then, slowly, began to sink until only their shoulders showed above the rising, rippling tide. The abbot hoisted the woman so that her head was level with his and for a minute or two — it seemed forever — that's how they stayed.

At the last, the abbot's arm came up to be outlined against a speedwell-blue sky, and they heard his voice echoing over the water.

"Lord Jesus, Son of God, have mercy on us."

THIRTEEN

Godwyn had to be prevented from following his wife, as if he could still drag her back. After a long, screaming struggle, he collapsed into inertia and drooped in the hands of his captors, his eyes never leaving the spot on the water where Hilda and the abbot had disappeared.

Everybody was in shock, the lepers bewildered. "But he were *happy,*" one of the men kept saying to Rowley of Abbot Sigward. "Give us Communion and blessed us. Saintly as ever, he was. Why'd he do that for?"

A woman moaned. "What we goin' to do now? What'll us do without un?"

"It was an accident," Rowley told them, making Adelia start. "An accident. He, er, took the woman for a walk; she'd been upset. He forgot there was quicksand out there."

It was a ludicrous explanation, but Rowley kept on giving it and, because it was the kindest, the lepers repeated it to themselves as they wept for their saint, preferring it to the evidence of their own eyes.

That's what he'll say when we get back, Adelia thought, *and perhaps he's right.*

She grieved for Godwyn, grieved for the two souls who had gone to such an end, grieved for the lepers, but her care had to be for the three castaways who needed it as soon as possible. Long before it was decent, she was urging them into the punt, but it was some time before the bishop of Saint Albans could be persuaded to leave the distressed people on the quay; he had a priestly duty to the bereaved, and promises to make that they would not be abandoned.

Godwyn was heaved down into the boat. He sank onto the place his wife had occupied and stayed there, silent and helpless. It was the bishop of Saint Albans who poled them all back to Glastonbury.

With Adelia's arm around her, Emma fell asleep where she sat, as if, having held up for her son's and Roetger's sake until now, she could pass the responsibility on to somebody else and rest at last. She was horribly thin; she and Roetger had seen to it that Pippy was fed as well as possible on the meager supplies Godwyn had smuggled to them on his trips. That, however, had meant going without themselves. The lepers, apparently, had been kind and offered to bring them food, but Emma had refused to accept anything from their hands and screamed at them to keep away.

Apart from being extremely dirty, young Lord Wolvercote was in comparatively good fettle; Adelia had clutched him to her so that he shouldn't see the tragedy as it occurred and, though he'd been upset by the screams, his youth kept him from dwelling on it. His only fear was that they were taking him back to the Pilgrim to be locked into its tunnel. "Don't want to go to the black place," he said. "That nasty woman frightened Mama."

"No more tunnels for you, young man. The nasty woman's gone," Rowley told him, but he glanced inquiringly at Adelia.

She grimaced in return. "It has to be the inn," she said in Latin. "They're none of them fit to travel any farther. Roetger certainly isn't."

The champion was her greatest worry; if Emma was thin, he was emaciated. Adelia hadn't yet seen him put his injured foot to the ground and suspected he couldn't. Worse, though he refused to complain, he was breathing with a difficulty that suggested he'd developed a constriction of the lungs. "Do hurry," she begged Rowley.

"I'm going as fast as I can, woman," he puffed. "I haven't poled a punt since I was a boy."

Actually, he did well. It seemed to Adelia that they had left and were returning on two different days but, when at last Glastonbury's landing place was in sight, the sun was only just leaving its zenith.

Emma put up a fight when she saw that she was being taken to the Pilgrim. "Not there. We're not going back there."

"Yes, you are," Adelia said. "Master Roetger can't go on. Look at him."

Emma looked, and her outburst dissipated into panic. "You've got to save him, 'Delia. He was our mainstay. Those brigands on the road would have killed us all if it hadn't been for him. I can't . . . oh, 'Delia, I can't do without him."

"Let's put him into a bed and you won't have to," Adelia said, hoping that it was true. Getting her patients up the slope to the inn was hard enough, and it was a relief to see Millie at its door, shading her eyes as she looked in alarm from one to the other.

There was no time to answer questions even if the maid-servant had been able to ask them, but Millie, intelligent girl that she was, realized that beds were needed and hurried upstairs to prepare them.

"And you," Adelia told Godwyn. "I'm sorry, I'm very sorry, but these people must have food. And if you've got wine, warm it. Hurry."

The man was still dazed, but being in accustomed surroundings seemed to rally him and he went off toward the kitchen, nodding.

Emma refused to take nourishment; she wanted only to sit by Roetger's bedside and weep over him. Adelia hauled her back downstairs to the dining room, where Pippy was tucking into broth.

"Eat something," she told her, "and I'll organize a bath for you."

A bath would be restorative; both Pippy and his mother needed one badly. *Come to that,* Adelia thought, *I could do with one myself.*

Hilda had boasted that the inn possessed a bath — "the nobility is set on it," she'd said — but Adelia, not able to remember seeing one, went in search of it. She found an enormous tub lined with canvas in the barn, where, during the time that the Pilgrim lacked noble guests, it had been transferred so that Hilda could do her laundry in it.

Water was boiled, and Millie set to the task of carrying buckets of it across the courtyard.

"And you," Adelia told Rowley, "will please give Roetger a bed bath. If I do it, he'll be embarrassed."

The bishop looked alarmed. "How do you do that?"

Sudden, sheer happiness filled her, making her laugh. He'd been so nearly dead, and now he wasn't. She wanted to tell him how the tunnel had changed the perspective of everything she saw, that she'd accept him on any terms as long as he'd have her — and just keep breathing in and out.

However, this bustling house and time held no moment for romance. Later, when they were alone, she would give herself up to him. She must be arranged for it, beautiful.

A clean cloth, another bucket — this time filled with cool water to help bring down the patient's fever — were carried upstairs and instructions given.

And by late afternoon, all that could be done was done. A clean mother and son were asleep in one room and a gray-faced champion was propped up on pillows next door looking no better than he had, and breathing worse.

Adelia put down the spoon of linctus she'd been trying to get him to take. "I don't know, Rowley," she said. "The crisis is coming and . . . I just don't know."

"I'd wait with you," Rowley said, "but I must go to the abbey. The brothers have to be told."

"An accident?"

"That's what I'll say. Why add to their agony, or anybody else's? The king must know, of course, but Abbot Sigward will be mourned throughout England and beyond. No point in broadcasting that the man chose to go to hell."

"Is that where he is?"

"Suicide is an offense against God," the bishop told her shortly, and went out.

Was it? Or had it been the only free choice for a man who'd tried so hard for so long to exculpate an even greater sin?

And he'd taken Hilda with him; only Godwyn mourned her. Yet what would have become of her if he had not? At best, incarceration with other madwomen. Was that why he did it? Had the woman been in a condition to know it?

Lord, judgments are too hard, I can't think about it now.

As the light began to go, Roetger broke into a sweat and his breathing became easier. Adelia sent up her gratitude for the endurance of the human body, made him comfortable, and went to fetch Millie to sit with the patient.

On the way, she took the girl into the parlor and to the table that had become their mutual slate board. "See," she mouthed, tracing stick figures in its dust. "There's the abbot, that's meant to be his hat. And that's poor Hilda." She drew a wavy line over both heads. "And that's the sea. Damn it, there must be some way of teaching you to read."

Millie, glancing from Adelia's face to the table with concern, pointed in the direction of the marshes and then toward the hatch that led to the kitchen where Godwyn sat weeping.

"Yes. She's gone, Millie. No more beatings."

The two women crossed themselves and, again, Adelia wondered whether or not Hilda had been willing to go into the quicksand with the man she worshipped and had been prepared to kill for.

God, she was sick of death; it was as if she herself generated it, infecting those she met. She wanted to be clean of it, she wanted life, she wanted Rowley, she wanted a *bath.*

Once she'd lugged more hot water to the

tub in the barn, and collected a candle, a towel, and some soapwort from the patch kept growing in the shade of the inn's outer wall, she took one, luxuriating in sweet-smelling suds, letting her overtired brain rest on matters such as where to find clean clothes and whether she could flick a bubble as far as the hay fork hanging on the opposite wall.

The barn door crashed open, making her yelp, but it was Rowley. "Well, that's done."

Damn. She'd wanted to be pretty for him, not squatted in an outsize wooden bucket with her hair tied on top of her head with string.

All at once embarrassed, she reached for a towel to cover what she could and tried to be businesslike. "How did they receive the news?"

"Badly. But I told them it was an accident."

"Did you tell them he killed Arthur and Guinevere?"

"Of course not. I just said they'd been proved to be the skeletons of two men, not how they died nor at whose hand. They're going to re-bury them quietly."

"And Hilda?"

"An accident, an accident." Then, as if in answer to a protest she hadn't made, he said, "For the Lord's sake, Adelia, they've lost enough."

She supposed they had: their abbey, their abbot. And the truth would cost the Church even more; it was the bishop of Saint Albans's job to defend it, to weigh Sigward's twenty years of penance and goodness against an appalling crime.

How she felt about that she didn't know. It was her job to uncover the truth. She couldn't control what men did with it.

Perhaps he was right; perhaps there was enough ugliness in the world without exposing people to more.

"Move over," Rowley said. He began stripping off.

"For goodness sake," she said, "this isn't big enough for both of us."

"Do you mean the tub or my manhood? In either case, the answer's yes, it is."

He was right. For a while the two of them forgot everything except each other, and the Pilgrim's courtyard was treated to the sound of splashing and delighted feminine gurgles.

Later, in her bed, he said, "I'm not letting you loose again. Rescuing you from the holes you keep falling into is becoming boring."

"I know, my love. I can't live without you, either. Not anymore. The king can go hang;

let him find some other mistress of the art of death. But what can we do?"

She'd been slaked with him, but this naked, energetic lover was also an anointed bishop, marriage forbidden to him, a man of God.

Her fault, of course. She had feared the restrictions of being a wife to an ambitious man would have sublimated her skills as a doctor and anatomist under rounds of household care and entertaining for which she was unfit and which, in the end, would have held him back, making them both un-happy.

And the thing was that ever since the day that Henry, pouncing on the opportunity to thrust a trusted man into a position of power in a hostile Church, had given him the post, he'd excelled in it. He was less judgmental, more truly Christian, than the prelates who terrified their flocks with threats of damnation while living lives just as sinful.

But by loving her, Rowley was aware of his own hypocrisy; he made light of it, but it dismayed him.

Now he was saying, "I'm going to set you and Allie up somewhere, a place where I can come and go without anybody know-ing, a secret place like Henry found for his

Rosamund." He winked and nudged her. "Don't fancy Lazarus Island, I suppose?"

She laughed, but afterward the two of them fell silent.

. . . come and go without anybody knowing, a secret place like Henry found for his Rosamund . . . secret . . . without anybody knowing.

A permanent arrangement: she a kept woman, Rowley experiencing guilt every time he opened his mouth to preach.

We're not that sort of people, Adelia thought. *Any honor either of us has will be gone. Both of us constantly aware he's betraying his God, as he's betraying Him now, snatching furtive moments together such as this like a couple of adulterers; it will tarnish us both. Could I bear it? Could he? Can we bear not to?*

Then she considered the dead of these past days, the moment in the tunnel when she thought that this man had joined them.

"Yes," she said.

Surprised, he came up on one elbow to look at her. "Really?"

"Yes. As long as Gyltha and Mansur come with us."

"I'll be away on circuit a good deal, you know that?"

"Do you want me or not?"

He kissed her hard and settled back comfortably. "If you're a good girl, I'll try and bring you a corpse or two to play with."

A home, a father for Allie, security, love . . . *I am tired of independence.*

Yet even as she dwelled restfully and with pleasure on these things, she knew that some wisp of . . . What was it? . . . Virtue? . . . No, not virtue, she didn't care about that. . . . A constituent, like sea salt, that had been in her since she'd been born would no longer be hers.

Captain Bolt and an escort came to the inn the next morning to say that the traveling courts of the assize were arriving in the town of Wells and the bishop of Saint Albans was royally commanded to attend as one of their justices.

"The king's been in Anjou, but he'll be coming to England shortly," the captain said — an announcement calculated to instill a frisson of fear in everyone who heard it, and invariably did. "And the lord Mansur's to write a report for him about what's been happenin' here in Glastonbury — the skeletons and that."

Henry wasn't going to be pleased.

Aloud, Adelia said, "Then ask my lord Mansur to return, bringing parchment and ink with him — and my daughter and Gyltha."

She would be losing Rowley but gaining those she loved as much.

Supping ale with his men in the sunny courtyard, Bolt added, "Don't you be going near the forest tomorrow; we're to clear it out. Henry ain't pleased at the trouble disturbin' the peace of the King's Highway." He scratched his head to remember the wording of his orders: "*If the dispute between Wells and Glastonbury be not resolved by them, they shall expect the Crown to intervene. Le roi le veut.* Yep, that's it. We're comin' down on them forest brigands like terriers on a rats' nest."

That would settle the tithing's fear of Scarry. She wondered how to get a message to them telling them to stay clear. *The lay brother Peter,* she thought — she'd send word to Will and the others through him.

She told Bolt about the attack on Emma's cavalcade and the resultant graves in the forest, giving directions to their position as best she could. "Lady Emma will want the bodies taken up for decent burial."

"We'll see to it," Bolt told her, and she knew he would.

She watched the soldiers ride off, taking her lover with them.

■ ■ ■ ■

Grass was growing through the abbey's cinders. Valerian and wild honeysuckle sprouted from between fallen stones. Swallows disappeared into the niches of the nave's one standing wall, fed their nesting young, and flew out again in the perpetual work of parenting.

Nature was singing of life, the monks in the ruined choir were singing of death, both of them doing it beautifully.

Kneeling beside the catafalques in the hut of withies, Adelia listened.

"In paradisum deducant te Angeli; in tuo adventu suscipiant te martyres . . ."

And when will they plead for you to be conducted into Paradise? she asked the skeletons. *Will you also be received among the martyrs? Or will you return to your grave unknown and unmourned?*

Perhaps, she thought, *it doesn't matter as long as you're together.*

In her untuneful voice, she sang to them in time to the monks' voices. "May choirs of angels receive thee; may you have eternal rest."

She got up and went out to stand in the shadow of the nave's remaining wall.

After a while Brother Peter emerged, wiping his eyes. "Can't stand no more of that; they'll be at it all day." He showed no surprise at finding her there. "What'd he do it for? What'd he *do* it for? Accident, the bishop says, but he knew them marshes. Hilda, too."

Adelia shook her head in sympathy without answering; the man's questions were rhetorical. "Brother Peter, I want you to warn Will and the others not to go poaching in the forest tomorrow."

"Poaching?" He might never have heard the word before.

She nodded. "Poaching. But not in the forest. Not tomorrow."

The lay brother stared at her, narrowing his eyes. "Here, I saw as there was soldiers at the inn. Goin' after Wolf and his gang, are they?"

"I can't say." Perhaps she'd said too much; perhaps he was well enough in with the brigands to warn them. At least his brother had not told him that Wolf was dead.

The man looked relieved. " 'Bout time that Wolf got his come-uppance. Proper terror, he's been, God rot him."

"And you'll warn Will?"

He shrugged. "Daresay I might."

She received no thanks for her trouble and

expected none. Peter was as surly as his brother; they were like the fenmen she knew in East Anglia — gratitude was shown in actions, not words.

It must be something to do with living in marshes, she thought.

"Here," he said, when she would have walked away, "Will and the lads is summoned to the assize to answer for Eustace settin' the fire — the which he didn't. So you get that darky doctor of yourn to be there and tell the judges as how he didn't do it."

"Daresay I might," she said.

Under escort, Allie, Gyltha, and Mansur made a joyful return to the Pilgrim the next morning, bringing with them Rhys the bard.

On the way, they'd glimpsed Captain Bolt and at least forty king's men, all fully armed, go galloping into the forest and heard the sound of distant clashes coming out of it. The purification had begun.

"Mansur said they were killing snakes," Allie piped, "but snakes don't scream, do they, Mama?"

Adelia hugged her. "I think those do."

Gyltha said, coldly, "An' while we're about it, what's all this Rowley's been tellin' us? Gettin' rid of us like that, I've a good mind to tan your arse for you."

"You do not do that again," Mansur told Adelia quietly in his boy's voice. "I am your protector or I am nothing."

By tricking them into going to Wells, she had humiliated them, the Arab's pride especially. Adelia tried explaining that Allie's presence at the inn had made them all vulnerable in the same way that Emma and Roetger had been forced to obey Hilda because, with Pippy in her arms, the madwoman had threatened to cut his throat. "And I knew you wouldn't go without me," she pleaded. "You wouldn't have, *would* you?"

Gyltha snorted.

She snorted again when Rhys was introduced to Emma and immediately fell in love.

"Did you hear my songs to you, lady?" he asked, sweeping off his cap. "Was they what called you back from that lonely peak of exile?"

Emma looked bewildered.

Adelia said, "It wasn't a peak. No, they didn't. And her affections are elsewhere."

It was useless. Lady Emma was the lost white bird regained. Missing, she had been the subject of his laments, and now, here in the flesh, pale, thin, beautiful, she was perfection — a being so ethereal, so far above him, that he could safely be her troubadour of a passion never to be requited. Even as he moaned, he began tuning the harp.

"Look at him," Gyltha said in disgust. "Happy as a pig in shit now he's miserable."

The well had its cover put in place so that the two reunited children wouldn't fall down it while they played in the courtyard. The adults went indoors to sit around the dining table and listen to Adelia tell the full story of the past two days and nights.

Only Roetger was absent. He wasn't making the recovery Adelia had hoped for him, too weak to leave his bed, with no interest in food nor anything else and embarrassed by the fact that either Adelia or Millie had to help him onto the pot — he refused to let Emma do it.

Here, like Mansur, was another who'd been humiliated by his inability to protect his lady. It gnawed at him. "What champion was I for her?" he asked Adelia at one point.

Emma wouldn't have it. "I keep telling him. What could he *do?* That hag, that *Hilda,* kept a knife to Pippy's throat; we had to obey her. And his bravery when we were attacked on the road . . . you should have seen him. Injured, but fighting like a tiger. Pip and I would be dead if it weren't for him. Oh, 'Delia, I don't care what people think anymore, I want to marry him. Do you think the king will let me?"

"I'm sure he will." In truth, she *wasn't* sure. Emma was valuable property, and in the king's gift to be wed how he commanded. Because Adelia's last investigation had been successful, she had been able, as a reward, to persuade Henry not to marry Emma off against her will.

But that was when she'd been successful. . . .

It grieved the German particularly that he'd lost his sword, symbol of everything he'd once been, which Hilda had made him lay down and was now nowhere to be found. "She could not sell it," he said. "It was too fine. No, she has thrown it away. Why not me, also? I am without use."

Until now, Adelia had left Emma in ignorance of her mother-in-law's attempt to have her killed, waiting for the poor girl to be stronger. Yet she had to be told, and when, round the table, that part of the tale was reached, she waited for the fury she herself felt.

Wolf and dowager, two murderers.

She was disappointed. Emma had, after all, suffered terribly: the attack on the road by Wolf and his brigands, the assumption that she had found safety when they reached the Pilgrim Inn being taken away by a mad-woman, the tunnel, forced exile on a leper island . . . Her spirit had been wrecked.

Gyltha cried out in disbelief at the news. Mansur swore horribly in Arabic.

Emma just wept for her dead servants.

"Can it be proved?" Mansur asked.

"I don't know." Adelia hadn't thought about that yet. "At the very least, the woman should be turned out of Wolvercote Manor, bag and baggage."

Emma shook her head. "There's nothing to be done. I'm not sending Roetger into another trial by combat. I'll lose Wolvercote . . . God knows I wanted it for Pippy . . . but I'll not see my man wounded again."

"Bugger trial by combat," Gyltha said. "That harpy's got to hang."

Emma continued to weep.

It wasn't the moment to tell her that Roetger would never be able to fight again; his foot was now too badly damaged.

Adelia didn't tell the champion, either, but his listlessness that evening as she tried to make him take food suggested that he guessed.

When Millie relieved her, Adelia went back to her own room and took the sword from the hill out of the chest where she kept it wrapped in a sheet. She sat on the bed to study it.

Mansur's objection to taking it had evaporated when he'd learned the sword had saved Adelia's life. "Thus Allah looked down from Paradise and saw you in need of a weapon. He gave you the warrior's."

That's one explanation for grave robbing, she thought.

What she could hardly admit to herself, and certainly not to anybody else, was that, in one desperate moment in a forest, the sword had lived. It had killed for her protection as if the function for which it was made had suddenly energized it.

The trouble was that it had enjoyed it.

Or was it me? Did I enjoy it?

She knew she had not. Wolf had been a disease, had killed, would have killed Alf, killed *her,* would have gone on killing. Arbitrarily, the occasion and means to stop him had fallen to her. She, whose job it was to preserve life, regretted it and always would, but, as Rowley'd said, there was nothing else she could have done.

The question was whether the sword now belonged to her. She felt that it did; its leap in her defense had passed ownership from the dead man in the cave to her living hand.

Loathing weapons of destruction, this thing with its encrusted pommel as warty as Allie's toad was the exception; she felt safer in its presence — not just safer, *bolder* — she could defy the world with it, challenge her enemies. *You dare not touch me now.*

She thought, *And that is how wars begin.*

Keep me, the sword said. *Though you are a woman, you shall be a warrior defending all frail women.*

Its voice was high and sweet, like Rhys's harp.

And then she knew that this was Glastonbury magic; she was being entwined by legends, holy springs, dreams, ghosts, swords that came alive . . . all of them delusion. The Salerno masters who had trained Adelia in hard truth frowned down on her, ashamed.

She came to a decision. *You are an artifact,* she told the sword. *You belonged to a warrior who has no further use for you — but I am a doctor, and I have a patient who has.*

The next morning, having told him its story, she gave the sword to Roetger.

"An ugly old thing," she said, finding the words an effort, "but until you get a better one . . ."

He was intrigued by it, brightening more than she'd seen him since the rescue from

Lazarus, as if she'd given him back his manhood. "So," he said, caressing the blade. "Old-fashioned, but ugly, no. You shall see when it is again polished. I am grateful."

Millie was sent to the kitchen for cleaning equipment, and Adelia left her patient with his new medicine to go down to the parlor and write the report that the king had demanded. She couldn't put it off any longer — the next day Captain Bolt was coming to collect it.

It was a list of disasters unlikely to put a sparkle in the royal blue eyes.

Arthur and Guinevere *not* Arthur and Guinevere but two male lovers. A favorite abbot both a killer and a suicide, taking a madwoman with him to a terrible death. The Glastonbury fire due to the carelessness of one of its own monks. A forest in which travelers on the King's Highway lay slaughtered. One of his nobility, a Somerset dowager, a would-be murderess.

And above all, as far as Henry would read it — and rage — no proof that King Arthur was dead.

Sucking the end of her quill, Adelia wondered if the king's sympathy would be evoked by her own brushes with death. It was unlikely — he was not a sympathetic man.

But this is the last time you employ me, Henry Plantagenet. Henceforth, I am to be a bishop's mistress.

A mistress, she thought, still idling, *a courtesan.* Her mind dwelt on the few houris she'd seen being carried through the streets of Salerno, painted and veiled, trailing light silks and heavy perfume.

It made her smile.

Still, she thought, Rowley will have to decently clothe his indecent woman. Since, at the moment, both she and Emma were in garments that Millie had purchased for them from a seamstress in Street's market, where, it had to be said, the standard of couture leaned more heavily on durability than style, the idea was not totally displeasing.

Again, though, she was aware of an essence that had been Vesuvia Adelia Rachel Ortese Aguilar leaching out of her. And again, she told herself it was a small price to pay for love.

From the courtyard, the mellifluous voice of Rhys was being directed toward Emma's window.

"Lay down your weapons, lady, or you kill me.
Let me not see that curling hair, those fine eyes

That spear the heart of all true men . . ."

Adelia sighed and returned to her report to the king.

Putting her two and only triumphs on the parchment showed them up as weak. What matter to Henry, lord of a great empire, that Eustace, a common drunkard, had been proved innocent of a crime? How much would he rejoice at Lady Emma and young Lord Wolvercote's rescue when he hadn't known they'd been abducted in the first place?

Oh, dear.

Gritting her teeth, Adelia dipped her quill into the inkpot and pressed on, returning to the matter that concerned her most at the moment — the dowager's perfidy.

"You, who prize justice above all things, my dear lord, will know how to right the great wrong committed by this woman according to the wish of your most devoted servant, Adelia Aguilar."

Then, in case one of the king's unknowing clerks might read the letter to him, she scratched out her signature and replaced it with that of Mansur.

She was searching for sealing wax when Allie flung the door open, ablaze with excitement. "Come and see, Mama, come and see."

Adelia followed her daughter into the courtyard, where Pippy was staring at something that had been tied to the well-head by a bit of string around its neck.

"What's that, in the name of God?"

"It's a puppy." Allie was ecstatic. "It's mine."

Whatever it was, it was the untidiest animal Adelia had ever seen; very young and wobbly on long, thin legs, with a rough coat and eyebrows that curled upward like an old man's.

"Bad," Mansur said, "a sight hound."

"A lurcher," Gyltha said. "An' it's forbidden. Verderers see that in the forest and they'll lame un, take out the ball of its foot. Bring down deer, lurchers do; bring down anything."

Allie put her arms round the animal's neck. "They're not going to lame Eustace," she said. The dog licked her face.

"Who?"

"Some men came and gave it to me. They said his name was Eustace. Look at his lovely brown eyes, Mama, he's very intelligent."

Adelia thought how typical it was of Will and the tithing to bring her a present that was illegal. But the damage was done; Allie had given her heart to the thing.

"Well," she said, weakly, "we'll just have to keep Eustace out of the forest."

Handing over the scroll to Captain Bolt the next morning, Adelia asked if the king had arrived in England.

"Not yet, mistress. Somewhere between here and Normandy, I reckon." He waved the report. "Yet he's so eager for this, we may have to send it by boat — he'll be glad to get it."

"No, captain," Adelia said sadly, "he won't."

Two days later, Roetger hitched himself down the stairs, and Adelia was asked to attend to him and Emma in the dining room.

On the table in front of them lay the dead warrior's sword in a wooden scabbard that Roetger had made for it.

He was animated, eager for Adelia to sit down. He remained standing, his back to the window, leaning on a crutch. He began explaining how he had gone about cleaning the sword.

"We take great care, do we not?" he said to Emma.

She nodded. The two of them used "we" and "us" a great deal now.

"Horsetail from the kitchen first," he said. "Millie gave it."

It was Adelia's turn to nod. The plant was an invaluable pot scourer; dairymaids polished their milk pails with it.

"No good," Roetger said, shaking his head. "So we try vinegar. No good."

"Do you know what did it in the end?" Emma asked. She couldn't wait; she was as excited as the German. "You'll never guess. Godwyn's apple-and-plum preserve."

"Preserve?"

Emma seemed to have forgiven the landlord now that he'd restored the sword. "He won't tell us what's in it apart from apples and plums, but it was miraculous."

"Apple-and-plum preserve?"

"A cleanser most excellent," Roetger said.

"Ye-es," Adelia said encouragingly. She could see little of the sword with the champion's great frame blocking the light from the window.

Roetger went on at length about how each polishing had revealed more and more of what lay beneath the thick patina. "It is old, so old."

He moved aside so that light shone on the pommel.

Adelia gasped. What had once been warts were now inset stones gleaming like the sun.

"What are those jewels?"

"Topaz," Emma said smugly.

Roetger nodded. "From my own Saxony, I think. It is the stone of strength."

"And it can make its wearer invisible if he needs to be," parroted Emma, "and it changes color in the presence of poison, doesn't it, Roetger? And it can cure anything, including piles."

Her champion frowned at her. "It has great power."

"Ye-es," Adelia said.

Still, Roetger didn't take the sword out of its scabbard. He talked of tang, fuller, weight, balance, how the hilt was attached to the blade, the "lifestone" set into the hilt, edges so perfectly formed that they might have been fashioned with a file rather than hammered in a forge.

"This weapon a god makes," he said. "Wayland the Smith himself, maybe."

"What's that little ring thing there, at the bottom of the hilt?"

"Ach now," Roetger said in the tone Adelia's foster father had used when she'd asked an intelligent question. "It is the oath ring, the ring of a great chieftain."

"You see," Emma chipped in, "Roetger says — he knows everything about the history of swords — he says that when one of

418

a chieftain's or king's men took an oath of allegiance, he knelt and kissed that ring."

Rhys the bard had sung of a sword. *"One among them finest of all, A ring on the hilt, valor in the blade, and fear on the point . . ."*

"Ye-es."

"Look, then," Roetger said. He laid aside his crutch to pick up the sword as if he must be straight to handle the thing. He asked Adelia to stand up. Flicking the sword free of its scabbard, he held it out to her.

It was a rebirth. Apart from where it had been nicked, the blade gleamed as if new from the smithy.

Rhys had sung: *"Tempered in blood of many a battle, Never in fight did it fail the hand that drew it, Daring the perils of war, the rush of the foe, Not the first time, then, its edge ventured on valiant deeds."*

"But look, look," Roetger insisted. "See the fuller."

Adelia, who knew nothing of weaponry, supposed the fuller to be the grooved bit running down the blade. She went nearer and saw a design like curling water. "What's that?" Letters had been etched into the pattern.

"Look closer," Roetger said.

Adelia squinted. "Is that an A? . . . R, T . . ."

"Arturus," the champion said.

There was silence.

A chill over her skin rose goose bumps along Adelia's arms and up her back. She couldn't speak.

Emma was bouncing in her chair, squeaking with joy like a child.

"Excalibur." In his reverence, Roetger began to sob. "What else? Where else? Are we not in Avalon?"

"But . . ." Adelia stared from face to face. "But that means . . . the body on the hill . . ."

"Yes," Roetger said simply.

Emma, too, was sobbing. "The once and future king," she said.

Roetger flung up his hand so that the weapon in it glowed amber in the light. Then he held it out to Adelia on his palms. Tears still fell, but he was smiling. "Mansur says it was passed to you. I am not worthy; it belonged to a great heart, and to a great heart it must go."

"He wants you to have it," Emma said. "You have the greatest heart we know."

FOURTEEN

Riding a sedate palfrey and with Millie up behind her, Adelia trotted along the road to Wells at the head of a cavalcade.

In one of her horse's saddlebags was a summons to appear at the Bishop's Palace before King Henry of England. Sticking out of the other bag was a long, thin woven contraption, more usually used for carrying fishing rods, containing an object for which the monarchy and abbeys of Europe would give their eyeteeth — or certainly other people's.

Captain Bolt, who'd come to the Pilgrim to fetch her and Mansur, had looked at it sideways, but she'd declined to tell him what was in it. "A surprise gift for the king," she'd said, and had been ashamed to be saying it.

When Gyltha and Mansur had been called to the inn's dining table to look on Excalibur and learn who it was that lay in the cell on the Tor, she had seen the flame in Roetger's and Emma's eyes leap into theirs like the reflection of a beacon on one hilltop sending its signal to the next.

After that, silence. Nobody had spoken of it, as if the knowledge was sufficient and would be cheapened by commentary.

Rhys, Celt that he was, had perhaps the greatest claim to know, but he'd not been told in case the wonder could not be encompassed even in song.

Adelia realized then that whoever Arthur and his sword had fought, or whatever they had fought *for,* didn't matter; their legend was enough, encapsulating an ideal around which a nation could cohere. No religion on earth, no message of universal brotherhood, could fill people's aching need for a hero who was peculiarly theirs. That Arthur had no grounding in verifiable history, as had the Franks' Charlemagne or Spain's El Cid or the Arabs' Omar bin Al-Khattab — "How can you enslave people when they were born free?" — was irrelevant; somewhere, somehow, his beacon had caught hold and its glimmer had survived centuries of otherwise impenetrable darkness.

A fairy tale, she'd thought with despair, *yet I am the keeper of it.* The oriflamme had been passed to her, whether she wanted it or not, believed in it or not.

And I am about to betray it.

For Adelia had favors to ask, and the sword in the fishing basket was to be the exchange — it was as well to have something to offer Henry Plantagenet as it was to possess a long spoon when treating with the devil — frequently the same thing.

"How did the king receive my lord Mansur's report, captain?" Adelia asked.

"They tell me he was . . . disappointed, mistress."

"Is that a euphemism for biting the carpets?"

Captain Bolt didn't know what a euphemism was, but she gathered that her translation fit the scene exactly, though, since the report had been handed over to the king in the middle of the Channel at the time, his teeth would have been grinding on planks.

Excalibur was to be not just a peace offering but a bargaining counter, and she felt dreadful about it, as if she was selling the Matter of Britain for a mess of pottage.

He'd better be worthy of it, she thought. But oh, *how* he would exploit his dead Arthur, kill the dream of the Welsh, use Arthur's bones to rebuild Glastonbury, beating a drum like any marketplace hawker to attract crowds to that quiet little hillside cell.

So Adelia, unusually indecisive, rode to Wells dreading the choice she must make when she got there.

It was partly because she was tired. When Emma and Roetger had been summoned to the assize some days before, taking Pippy with them, she had expected to spend the time restfully with Allie. So she had, but it was then, as if they had been waiting for her mind to be unguarded, that images of the past weeks had invaded it like savage dogs, spoiling the hours on the marshes with the memory of Sigward and Hilda walking into quicksand, sending her down into the tunnel at night, and making her kill Wolf over and over again.

In the middle of it, she and Mansur had been called to the abbey wall to demonstrate Eustace's innocence to the bishop of Saint Albans and the twelve men with him — the jury that was to pass judgment on the tithing when they appeared at the assize. It was easier than she'd expected it to be; the jurors were all local countrymen familiar with traps and, though at first they looked askance at Mansur, had accepted the word of the bishop that the Arab was a royal investigator, an expert, with a warrant from the king to look into the matter of the Glastonbury fire — after all, King Henry, being a foreigner himself, was expected to be peculiar in his choice of servants.

"I'd hoped that the case would be dropped now that the abbey has withdrawn its accusation of Eustace," Rowley had told Adelia, "but the fire was such a colossal event that the justices must pursue it. The tithing has been summoned to appear."

In her turn, she had hoped that Rowley would be able to spend the night with her; she needed the comfort of his body not just for its own sake but to ward off the nightmares. However, he couldn't be spared from his duties at the Wells assize and had ridden back to them with the jury in tow.

It was no help to her troubled state of mind as she rode along the forest road on this pleasant, sunny morning to find that pieces of human flesh, a leg here, a torso there, were hanging from the branches of trees lining the route.

Captain Bolt and his men had cleansed the forest thoroughly of Wolf's remaining brigands and anyone else who had no explanation or license to justify being there. "Up before the verderers' court, sentenced, and then chop-chop," the captain said graphically.

"Do they have to be so . . . displayed?" Adelia asked.

"King's orders," Bolt said. "Make any other bug . . . *brigand* think twice afore doing likewise."

And this, Adelia thought, *is the king I considered civilized.*

Well, he had been; he'd saved her life once when the Church would have condemned her; he could charm, make her laugh; he was introducing new and finer concepts into English law, but there was still an underlying savagery that marked him as a man of his time when she'd hoped for more.

He muddles me, she thought wearily. *Shall I give him his dead Arthur? Or not?*

Loggers were already cutting the trees back to the statutory bow's length from the road so that the air rang with the thud of axes and smelled nicely of raw wood — except for an occasional whiff of putrefying flesh as the cavalcade passed a piece of it.

Behind the leading horses — some way behind because the presence of a king's officer bothered them — rode the tithing on their donkeys and, in Captain Bolt's opinion, considerably lowering the tone.

Alf had got his voice back. Adelia could hear his and the others' comments as they rode — and hoped that the captain's helmet kept them from his ears. They were attempting to identify the owners of the bloodied pieces.

"Reckon as that's a bit of Scarry, Will?"

"Never. Scarry's arms had black hair on 'em. Looks more like Abel's. Abel had them sort of twisty fingers."

"So he did."

To Adelia's regret, Gyltha had remained behind at the Pilgrim. Allie had been reluctant to part from her lurcher and, since the dog was *canis non grata* among the hunting fraternity to be expected in attendance at the assize, Gyltha had said she'd stay with the child. "Anyway, I seen enough of Wells, bor, that's too noisy."

"That's not like you." Gyltha loved excitement.

"Wait til you get there. Ain't room to breathe."

A female companion had been needed for propriety's sake, so Millie's services had been called in. How much the girl understood of the drawings with which Adelia had tried to indicate both the journey and its purpose, it was difficult to tell.

Gyltha had been right about Wells; the noise of its hubbub could be heard a mile off.

The traveling assize was a visitation to be

dreaded, a new idea of King Henry II's, so everyone had been told, to introduce in the goodness of time a common law throughout the land rather than the piecemeal and frequently prejudiced judgments by the local courts of sheriff, baron, and lords of the manor, which, while the assize was in situ, were as good as overridden.

Like the mills of God it ground slowly — it had been in Wells more than two weeks with no sign of finishing yet — and it ground extremely small, listening to appeals, plaints, and pleas; inquiring into the state of the county and the business of practically everybody in it; hearing accusations of murder, rape, theft, and robbery; even making sure that the smallest bakery and alehouse were giving fair and uniform measure.

It was certainly new to Somerset, which *had* dreaded it. The justices, great and aweful lords of thousands of acres, with their own castles in both England and Normandy, had to be accommodated, not to mention their servants and the hundreds of clerks necessary for their work. Where to put them?

The choice had fallen on Wells, the biggest town in the county.

And now, God have mercy on us, the king

had come to see his terrible assize in action, even to sit on its benches. Where to put *him?*

At last the bishop of Wells had delivered up his palace to his royal master and gone to bed with a headache.

The streets were congested. Barred carts were still bringing in men and women from gaols in far-flung parts of the county to face their trials. Judges' clerks were scurrying everywhere, summonses at the ready. Official ale tasters, staggering slightly, supped at inn doorways to make sure there wasn't too much water mixed with the brew's barley and yeast. Bakers stood by their ovens while their farthing loaves were tested for the standard weight. Hucksters with licenses carefully displayed shouted their wares. Jugglers, acrobats, and storytellers were taking the opportunity to entertain the crowds. Horses were being traded; so were marriageable young women. Many people had journeyed for miles to catch a glimpse of their king.

Captain Bolt and his men cleared a way through with the flat of their swords.

In a vast field outside the Bishop's Palace, the itinerant justices — the earls, barons, and bishops whom Henry trusted to administer his laws — sat on benches in the shade of striped awnings, the accused, the witnesses, and juries in front of them. Executioners stood to their gallows beside tables holding blinding irons and axes.

Clattering over the bridge crossing the bishop's moat, Captain Bolt's cavalcade trotted through the rose-scented orderliness of the bishop's gardens to draw up outside the grandeur of the Bishop's Palace.

Mansur helped Adelia and Millie dismount and took the long basket out of the saddlebag. "Keep tight hold of it," Adelia told him.

A groom took their horses but flinched at the sight of the tithing's donkeys. "I ain't putting them mokes in my stables."

Captain Bolt produced a summons. "The bishop of Saint Albans wishes to see these men."

"What, *them?*" The groom looked from the seal to the tithing, then to Mansur. "And *him?*"

"Just get on with it," the captain said.

The exchange had to be repeated several times before they were allowed up the steps of the palace and into its entrance hall. They waited while the bishop of Saint Albans was fetched. The tithing used the time to wander around and stare at the hall's decoration and ornaments, watched by the majordomo with the air of a man whose carpets were being trampled by a flock of muddy sheep.

"Look at that, Will." Alf was staring at a particularly fine tapestry. "That's Noah building the ark, ain't it?"

"Lot of needlework gone into that, Alf. Fetch all of ten shilling, I reckon," Will said knowledgeably.

"Well, he ain't going to get the ark built that way; he's holding the adze all wrong."

Rowley came striding toward them. In full mitered regalia, he looked imposing but tired. He bowed to Mansur. "What on earth have you got there?"

"It is a basket for holding fishing rods," Mansur answered truthfully, in Arabic. Other people were listening.

Rowley raised his eyebrows but accepted it. He bowed in Adelia's direction and nodded at the tithing. "Come along."

Captain Bolt said, "My lord, I got to present Mistress Adelia here to the king soon as possible."

"The king is in conclave with the papal legate and will be for some time yet," Rowley told him. "In the meantime, the lady must translate for my lord Mansur, should it be necessary. We shan't be long."

He led the way out and along a back path going to the field of judgments. It was like threading a way through hundreds of scattered bees. Juries, that innovation demanded by the king, buzzed their accounts to the judges of what they knew of the accused and the case. A woman was up for having badly beaten her neighbor for throwing mud at her washing on a clothesline. . . .

"But we do reckon as there's always been bad blood betwixt 'em," the foreman was saying, "Alice havin' previous attacked Margaret over the matter of a milk jug. Both as bad as each other, we reckon . . ."

Adelia would have liked to linger to hear the judgment on Alice and Margaret, but Rowley was hurrying her.

Further on, a wretch was being ordered to leave the realm, the jury having declared that though he'd been acquitted of rape because his accuser couldn't prove it, to their personal knowledge he was of bad character and a pest to all women.

Adelia found herself softening toward Henry Plantagenet. How much fairer it was to employ a jury rather than throwing people into ponds to see if God made them float (guilty) or sink (innocent) — a form of trial the king hoped to get rid of eventually.

She heard the judge say, "And his goods to be confiscated to the Crown."

Well, yes, that too. Always the opportunist, Henry, when it came to money.

Adelia was followed by Millie, whose darting eyes were taking in what her ears could not. They reached their destination, an ash tree under which a judge on a dais was bad-temperedly flicking a fly whisk in front of his sweating face. Four men were being brought out of a nearby very crowded pound, which held the day's accused — Adelia assumed they were the remainder of Eustace's tithing who'd been kept in custody.

A tonsured clerk sat by the judge at a lower table, a high pile of scrolls in front of him.

Will, Alf, Toki, Ollie, and the tithing member whose name Adelia had learned was Jesse were pushed alongside their fellows by an usher with the dimensions of a Goliath.

The clerk picked up one of the scrolls. "My lord, this is a frankpledge case wherein the abbot of Glastonbury accused a certain Eustace of Glastonbury belonging to this tithing before you of having started the great fire. . . ."

The judge glared at the tithing. "I expect he did, the monster. They all look like arsonists to me."

"Yes, my lord, but . . ."

"And those rogues there kept me waiting." The judge pointed at Will's group. "That's an offense in itself."

"Yes, my lord, but the charge has been withdrawn."

"Withdrawn?" It was the bark of a vixen robbed of her whelps.

"Both the abbot of Glastonbury and Eustace being dead, my lord, and . . ."

The judge's choler abated slightly. "Good man, Abbot Sigward. Met him at Winchester one Easter. Saintly man." He gathered himself. "But because accuser and accused are dead doesn't mean Eustace didn't do it, nor that these rogues should be let off their pledges for him."

"Apparently he *didn't* do it, my lord."

"He didn't? How do we know? Did anybody see him *not* doing it? The fire was a tragedy; somebody's got to pay for it."

"Yes, my lord, but . . ."

Rowley stepped forward. "I represent the abbey in this case, my lord. Its monks are still in mourning for their abbot and cannot appear. On their behalf, the charge is withdrawn."

The judge got up and bowed. "My lord bishop."

"My lord." Rowley bowed back. "It has been proved that Eustace was innocent of the fire. . . ."

"Who by?" The judge was refusing to let go of his prey.

"It was started by one of the monks accidentally." Rowley produced a document from a pocket attached to the gold cord around his waist. "This is the deposition by a Brother Titus. . . ."

"Taking the blame out of Christian charity, no doubt. You sure this Eustace didn't have a hand in it?"

The clerk intervened, beckoning to twelve men who'd been standing by. "My lord, to make sure, a jury was summoned and has been to the abbey to see the proof of Eustace's innocence. . . ." The usher gestured to twelve men who'd been waiting nervously nearby.

In the judge's opinion, they didn't rate much higher than the tithing, being of the same class. "Summoned by good summoners, were they?"

"Excellent, my lord, and have been to view both the abbey fire and the evidence."

"There *was* evidence, then?"

The jury foreman stepped out. "My lord, that dark gentleman there showed us and explained. . . . It was all to do with fingers an' a trap, very clever it was. . . ."

The judge had turned his attention to Mansur. "A Saracen? And what's that he's holding? Some outlandish weapon?"

The foreman pressed on. "Course, the lady had to tell us what he was saying, her bein' able to jabber the same language as what he does. . . ."

"Speaks Arabic, does she?" The judge's eyes rested on Adelia. "Probably no more Christian than he is. And they're *witnesses?*"

"My lord," the bishop of Saint Albans said, "the lord Mansur is used by the king as his special investigator. . . ."

"Where *does* he find them?" the judge asked the sky. And then, "I don't care if he's used by the Angel Gabriel. It's up to the jury here. If they're satisfied . . ."

"We are, my lord. Eustace di'n't do it."

"Oh, very *well.*" But the judge was still looking for a loophole. "However, gentlemen of the jury, can you vouch for the good character of this tithing?"

There was a dreadful pause. Toki's hand went under his tunic and he began scratching like a dog sent mad by fleas.

"We ain't sure as how they've been a-livin' since their homes was burnt down," the foreman said cautiously, "but nothin's known against 'em, not really *known* like. An' Will of Glastonbury, that one there, he's a prize baker."

The judge sighed. "Then they are quit." His clerk handed him a scroll and he scribbled a signature on it. "We are obliged to the bishop of Saint Albans for his attendance. Call the next case."

The next case, a man whose feet were hobbled, was being lifted out of the pound by the usher to face the judge. A new panel of jurors shuffled into the shade of the tree.

The tithing stood where it was for a moment, bemused, before Will stepped forward and proffered a grimy hand to the judge. "Very obliged, my lord." The usher pushed him away.

Alf was running after the foreman of the departing jury, trying to kiss him.

Will doffed his cap to the bishop, grunted at Mansur and Adelia, and slouched off.

"That's all the thanks you get," Rowley said. It was the first time he'd spoken to Adelia today; he'd barely looked at her.

Affectionately, she watched the tithing disappear into the crowd. "A jury," she said. "King Henry, for these men, for all who are on trial, I thank you."

"The greatest lawgiver since Solomon," Rowley said, and then winked. "Mind you, it's lucrative. But better all the fines and confiscated goods in Henry's pocket than anyone else's."

A clerk was trying for the bishop's attention. "My lord, you are listed to sit on the Lord of Newcastle's case. If you'd follow me . . ."

With a wave of his hand, Rowley was gone.

And that's how it will be, Adelia thought, *no recognition in public, brief moments, impermanence. Still, Allie and I will be happy to opt for that.*

Captain Bolt was stamping with impatience. "The king, mistress . . ."

Adelia took the long basket from Mansur. Mentally, she apologized to the bones on the Tor: *You see, Henry is your inheritor after all; look at the justice he has brought to your island.*

At the palace, the majordomo led the captain, Adelia, Mansur, and Millie up a beautiful staircase to a long, heavily windowed gallery containing an equally long line of people. Benches had been set for them.

"Petitioners," Captain Bolt said disgustedly. "How long we going to have to wait? The king wanted to see this lady urgent."

"The lord king is with the papal legate, mistress," the majordomo said. "When he's finished . . . Oh my God, *will you stop that bloody pig shitting on the floor?*"

It was a nice floor, tiled with ceramic coats

of arms. It was a nice pig, if unstable as to its digestion. The large countrywoman holding it on a lead nodded amiably, lifted it onto her lap, and wiped its bottom with her sleeve.

"Does she have to be here?" the majordomo begged a royal clerk who stood at the door of the receiving room with a scroll in his hand and a writing desk hanging from his neck. Adelia had seen him before; she tried to remember his name.

"*All* petitioners, the king said," the clerk told him. "She's a petitioner. Maybe the pig is."

"I'll go and petition a bloody bucket and cloth, then," the majordomo said bitterly.

Most of the gallery's occupants, a motley lot, were anxious, their mouths moving as they rehearsed what they would say to the king. Only the countrywoman, with a sangfroid to shame nobility, seemed at ease.

Adelia and Millie took a seat next to her. The open windows of the receiving room where the king was in discussion allowed its occupants' exchanges to drift along the outside sunny air and through the open windows of the gallery, though only Henry's voice could be heard clearly. It rasped on the ear at the best of times — and this, obviously, was not a good time.

"I won't have it, Monseigneur. I'm not going to take out their tongues nor cut off their balls, nor any other part of their anatomy. And I'm certainly not going to execute them."

The legate's reply was lower and more controlled. Adelia caught the word "heretics."

"Heretics? Because they oppose the sale of indulgences? *I* don't like the sale of indulgences. I was taught sins were paid for in hell, not by a handful of cash to the nearest priest. Does that make *me* a heretic?"

Another murmur.

Adelia could see the clerk at the door was becoming nervous — Robert, that was his name, Master Robert.

"*You* do it, then." The king's voice again. "Let the Church punish 'em . . . oh, I forgot, you can't do it, can you? The Church can't shed blood, but it's happy to see heretics skinned alive by a civil court. Not your criminal clerks, though, oh, no, you won't do that. I've got a case in Nottingham, six-year-old boy assaulted by a priest. Try the accused in your court, I told the bishop, and if you find him guilty, *which* you will, hand him over to mine — we'll see he doesn't bugger anybody ever again. But *oh,* no, he's a priest; can't touch a priest, that's purely a Church matter — so the bastard's free to do it again."

Don't mention Becket, thought Adelia, wincing. *Don't give them cause to best you again.*

Winning the argument with his king might have cost Archbishop Becket his life, but it had gained him sainthood — *and* the continuing inviolability of the clergy from civil prosecution.

The door to the receiving room was opening. A fat, angry man in the robes and scarlet hat of a cardinal emerged from behind it. Adelia caught a whiff of scent and sweat as he lumbered past. The Plantagenet stood in the doorway, balefully watching him go.

"Um," Master Robert said unhappily.

"What," his king shouted at him.

"Well, we're on rather thin ice here, my lord. The monseigneur *does* represent the Pope. And the Pope —"

"Can put England under interdict if I won't punish its heretics, thank you, Robert, I know. How many of these bloody heretics are there?"

"Three, my lord."

Henry sighed. "All right, then. Tell the executioner to brand an H on their foreheads and let 'em go. See if that satisfies His Holiness. The iron's not to penetrate too deep, mind."

"Yes, my lord." Master Robert made a note. "I fear you will have to attend the branding; the cardinal will then at least be able to report to the Pope that you sanctioned the punishment by your presence."

The king spat. "He'll be lucky he doesn't have to report that I shoved the iron up his arse. . . . Oh, very *well,* tell me when the executioner's ready. Now then, who's next?" He caught sight of the pig. "What's that doing here?"

"I believe Mistress Hackthorn has a petition, my lord."

"No, I ain't." The countrywoman raised her bulk off the bench, still holding the pig. "I come for to say thank you, I have. This here porker's a present for you, King Henry, dear soul."

"Is it?" Henry went up to her, intrigued. "What for?"

"My lad Triffin, master. Lord Kegworth, him as owns Gurney Manor, he said as our tenement was his. He said as my Triffin weren't a freeman of it and took it away from un. The which was a lie, us holding that land since the time of King Harold. . . ."

Henry looked toward Master Robert.

"Ah, yes, my lord," the clerk said, searching his notes. "A plea by a Master Hackthorn of Westbury that he was unjustly dispossessed of his land by Lord Kegworth. He purchased a writ of Novel Dissiesin, and the matter was put two days ago to a jury of his peers, who had knowledge of the case before the justices. . . ."

"Was it?" asked Henry, suddenly delighted. He looked at Mistress Hackthorn. "How much did the writ cost you?"

"Two shilling, master. The which 'twas worth it for them . . . what's that they do call theyselves? A jury?"

"Twelve good men and true," Henry said, nodding.

"An' so they was, master. We'd a been homeless else. Saw the right of it, they did, an' give the land back to us. For which we do be grateful and hope as you'll accept this porker for our thanks, master, our sow havin' farrowed nicely this spring so's we got this un to spare."

"God, I love the English," Henry said. "Madam, I am honored."

The pig was handed over and the king carried it into the receiving room, shouting "Next" over his shoulder.

"That's you, mistress," Master Robert told Adelia.

Captain Bolt bowed and went on his way, duty done.

Followed by Millie and Mansur, Adelia went in and leaned the basket against the wall next to the door. The clerk followed her, shutting the door behind them and hurrying to close the windows.

It was a lovely room, very large and sunlit, with a molded ceiling that took Adelia's breath away. Tables, chairs, and chests were carved and polished so that they seemed to writhe with a life of their own, a jeweled astrolabe, bronzes . . . The bishop of Wells did himself well.

Henry had put his mark on it. Scrolls and parchments with hanging seals littered every surface. His favorite hawk sat on a perch, below which were its droppings; two muddy gazehounds lay stretched out before the enormous marble fireplace.

The king was richly dressed for once, but Adelia, knowing him, guessed he'd been out hunting at dawn.

He put the pig down. The two gazehounds raised their heads to look at it and then, at a word from their master, closed their eyes again.

There was a splatter as the pig made its contribution to the bishop's Persian rug. The smell of manure overpowered the scented potpourri in the bishop's rose bowls.

Henry patted it fondly. "My sentiments exactly," he told it.

"Mistress Adelia," his clerk prompted him.

"I know who it is," the king said nastily. There was the briefest of salaams to Mansur and an even briefer nod at Millie before he clicked his stubby fingers and Master Robert put the scroll that was Adelia's report into them. "I saw the bishop of Saint Albans this morning, mistress — he's looking very spry. Been giving him his oats, have you?"

Adelia compressed her lips; there would be worse to come. She'd lost the king money — the most heinous sin to be perpetrated against a man who needed to employ armies — but, Lord, he was offensive. *This is the last time I work for him,* she promised herself, *the very last time.*

He waved the scroll at her. "I've a good mind to make you eat this. What I wanted when I sent you to Glastonbury was Arthur and Guinevere. What have I got? Two sodomites."

"You asked for the truth, my lord," Adelia told him. "You have it. What you do with it is your affair. They can be resurrected as Arthur and Guinevere, I suppose." Henry wasn't the only one who could be rude.

It made him crosser. "Not by me, mistress, not by me. I also have a regard for the truth. If I hadn't, you could have stayed in the bloody fens where you belong. If they were sodomites, they'll have to remain sodomites."

He was right, of course; she shouldn't misjudge him, but it was as if the mutual respect he and she had established over these last five years had vanished. The blue eyes looking at her through their almost invisible ginger lashes might have been regarding a stranger.

"Yes, my lord. I'm sorry, my lord."

"You should be." He thought a bit. "Mind you, when I'm dead I wager the abbey'll resurrect them as Arthur and queen."

He glanced back at the letter. "What's all this about Abbot Sigward and quicksand?"

"Suicide, my lord. Out of remorse for the murder of his son — it's all there. However, the bishop of Saint Albans has informed the monks that it was an accident."

"A pity. I liked Sigward; he was on my side. God knows who they'll want to elect now. You realize this is going to cost me? Where's the money coming from to rebuild that blasted abbey now, eh?"

"I'm sorry, my lord."

The king went on reading. " *'I would wish that Godwyn, landlord of the Pilgrim, might suffer no more grief than he already has. . . .'* God's knees, woman, he was accomplice to his wife's attempted murders. . . . You'll be asking that Cain be let off for killing Abel next."

"Even so, my lord, the man was instrumental in saving the life of Emma, Lady Wolvercote, and her child. . . ."

"Ah, yes, the rich young widow." The king's face, looking at her sideways, became that of a predator. "I've had some pleasing offers for her."

Alarmed, Adelia said, "My lord, you promised me you would not sell her in marriage. She wishes to wed her champion, I beg you to allow —"

"That was before I got a sodomite instead of King Arthur." He tapped the scroll. "We'll see. In view of this, I may have to husband my resources. Now then, about the dowager Wolvercote. . . . *'You, who prize justice above all things'* . . . yes, yes . . . *'right this great wrong'* . . . What do you want me to do about the woman? Throw her out of her manor?"

"It would be only just, my lord. She sent her own daughter-in-law and the others to their death. . . ." Adelia heard her voice become shrill and tried to lower it. "Only the mercy of God and her champion's good right arm saved Emma and her child. . . ."

"Can you prove it?"

Why did he keep interrupting? *Prove it?* Adelia tried to think.

Wolf got a message from there saying as there'd be a rich lady and party a — leavin' of Wolvercote . . . Will's words. The assassin who'd received the message was dead. The person who'd taken it would have been one of the dowager's most trusted servants and was unlikely to testify against her. The tithing's knowledge was therefore hearsay. Anyway, disreputable as they were, their evidence would hardly stand up against that of a respected, well-connected, and *rich* Somerset aristocrat.

Adelia shook her head. "I doubt it."

"So do I."

"But it's not *fair.*" It was the shriek Allie used when she was crossed. "My lord, she as good as murdered six people."

Henry shrugged. "It may not be fair, but if I step in and evict her without evidence it would be something worse, it would be injustice. I must abide by the law of the land like everyone else or we revert to tyranny and from there into chaos. Law is my contract with my people."

And what of the contract with me? Adelia thought. *What of the dealings between individuals, promises, the return for loyal service, even a bloody thank-you?*

And then she saw the king look toward Master Robert and *wink.*

The room skewed and fragmented. It was Wolf's forest with the beast coming at her, it was the Pilgrim's tunnel, and she was wading through it. She was watching two figures walk into the Avalon marshes. . . .

"Goddamn you, Henry," she screamed. "You send me into hell and I get nothing . . . *nothing* . . . I've seen terrible things, terrible, *terrible* things, I work for you . . . but never again; this is the last time I'm evicted from my fens . . . never again, *never.* I'm not your subject; you're not my king. . . . I'm tired and I'm poor *and I want to go home.*" She collapsed, weeping, into a chair to drum her heels on the floor like a thwarted child.

The silence in the room was awful.

He'll kill me, Adelia thought. *I don't care.*

After a long while, reluctantly, she opened her eyes and met Mansur's, full of concern. Millie was crouching beside her, holding her hand. The room's silence was because Henry was no longer in it. Instead, a young man wearing the floppy cap of a lawyer was standing by the door.

449

The gazehounds were watching her. The pig farted in sympathy. Master Robert was pouring some wine from a silver jug into a silver cup. He crossed the room and gave it to her, supporting her hands while she drank it. He looked unperturbed, as if it were the norm for people to throw fits in the Plantagenet's presence.

"The king has left to attend the branding of the heretics, mistress."

"Has he?" she asked dully.

"It is not something he welcomes. I fear it put him into a teasing mood."

"Yes."

"But if you will follow Master Dickon here, he will take you to Lady Wolvercote. Master Dickon is the lawyer who represents her."

Master Dickon took off his cap, twirling it in an elaborate and low bow. "You come along of me, miss. Hot, ain't it? Do anybody down, this heat would."

Mansur took Adelia's arm with one hand and picked up the fishing basket with the other, and, with Millie behind them, they followed the lawyer past the petitioners and down the staircase.

"Do you really want to go home?" Mansur asked in Arabic.

While she'd been screaming, she had;

she'd wanted safety, the calm of her foster
parents' house, and the discipline of the
School of Medicine, where decisions were
based on cold fact, where there was no
moral quicksand, where the brain controlled
emotion, where she would not risk her im-
mortal soul by living in sin, where there was
a king who left her alone.

"Do you?" she asked back, tiredly.

"I have thought of it," he said, "but I have
Gyltha."

And so have I, Adelia thought. *And you,
who are my rock, and Allie, and a man I love
and who loves me even though it imperils our
chance of God's grace.*

Oh, but she was tired of *feeling,* the gift —
or curse — that England had imposed on
her. Whether it was better than no feeling at
all, at this very moment she wasn't sure.

"You did not give the king Excalibur,"
Mansur said.

"He didn't give me anything, either."

Adelia's experience of lawyers in Salerno
had been of bearded old men who talked of
digests, codices, and the Summa Azonis,
the Roman law they'd learned at the great
University of Bologna. Master Dickon was
of a kind she hadn't met before, home-
grown, young, lacking breeding but not
intelligence, and very unlawyerlike in that

he wanted to impart knowledge rather than obscure it. The son of a Thames lighterman, he had been taught a good hand in a school run by his uncle, and had begun his working life as a mere scrivener in the Chancery, where his ability had come to the notice of the Chancellor himself, and was put to the study of English law.

All this was imparted over his shoulder in a London accent as he led the way down to the entrance hall.

"See, mistress, this is my first case of the Morte d'Ancestor writ, only third in the country far as I know." He was almost bouncing with the excitement of it.

"Death of an ancestor?" asked Adelia, confused.

"You ain't heard of it? Oh, mistress, you got to know about Morte d'Ancestor; magical Morte d'Ancestor is." He looked around and saw a niche in which they could all stand while he explained the magical writ. He seemed unruffled by the presence of Mansur and included both him and Millie in his talk, using English on the presumption that they didn't speak Latin. His admiration was for Henry Plantagenet, something Adelia had noticed before among native, lower-born Englishmen, who had a greater regard for their king than the Norman nobility, having benefited from his laws and, if they were intelligent, promotion to posts formerly reserved for sons of the nobility.

"Ooh, but he's crafty is our King Henry," Dickon said. "See, he's not a lover of Roman law, and I ain't, either — too much inquisition, too stuck with them old Byzantines, too many delays. What he's doing, see, is using Anglo-Saxon law, what our great-granddads was accustomed to. He's like a baker, if you understand me, using good English dough and trimmin' it, kneadin' it, reshapin' it, and flourin' it with a touch of genius. One of these days every court in the land'll be using it."

"And Morte d'Ancestor?" Adelia asked, not seeing where all this was going, nor sure she wanted to.

"Ah, Morte d'Ancestor." In Master Dickon's mouth it was an incantation. "It's the latest of the king's writs. He's given us the writ of Right and Praecipe and Novel Dissiesin and now" — he saw Adelia's mystification — "see, they're all ways of bypassing the other courts and giving a plaintiff the right to royal justice, not in the lords' or the sheriffs' or the manors' but straight to the king's. A law available to everybody, see. You purchase a writ that suits your case."

"How much did the writ cost you?" the king had asked Mistress Hackthorn.

In her disenchantment, Adelia asked, "So you have to *buy* justice?" *How typical of Henry,* she thought.

Master Dickon frowned. "On a sliding scale, what you can afford, like. But it ain't so much a matter of buying justice as purchasing the king's aid in getting it quick. Using the old way, decisions can take years. Now, in the case of Lord Wolvercote versus the dowager Lady Wolvercote, your Lady Wolvercote's purchased Morte d'Ancestor for her lad. Well, I advised her o'course, her being a woman and Lord Wolvercote being a minor."

"She *did?*" Adelia had heard nothing from Emma and Roetger since their departure for Wells; now here they were — Emma, at any rate — with a case, a writ, and a lawyer. "Not a trial by battle?"

"Mistress." Dickon was pained. "That's Dark Ages, that is. I don't take on trials by battle, too chancy. This is a *writ.*"

A stripling with a clerk's cap flapping about his ears was tugging at Master Dickon's sleeve. "They're a-coming, master."

"Oops, oops. Better hurry. Judges are coming in."

At a smart pace, they were made to follow

454

the stripling, Adelia wondering if the boy's mother knew her child was a lawyer's clerk.

The case of Lord Philip of Wolvercote versus the dowager Lady Wolvercote, being of considerable local interest, had attracted nearly as large a crowd as a trial by battle; an usher had to clear the way through to what, in its way, was another arena. A scalloped awning sheltered the high dais of the judges at that moment taking their seats. On the grass before them, several yards apart but facing each other, had been set two ornamented chairs. Pippy, having bowed to the judges, was in one, his short legs dangling. In the other sat his grandmother.

A hand grasped Adelia's arm. "I didn't want to tell you until it was decided; it was to be a nice surprise if we won. And it's been such a rush. But I'm so glad you're here." Emma's eyes never left her son. "Look at him, he's behaving beautifully. Isn't he sweet?"

He was. But if this was a battle of sorts, the child looking happily around was outclassed by the woman opposite him; the dowager had all the dignity. With her pale, immobile face set round by its black wimple, she might have been a statue of contrasting marble. She also had more lawyers standing beside her, men who *looked* like lawyers in contrast to Master Dickon, now taking his place beside Pippy.

A voice spoke from the dais in the flat, thin timber of age that nevertheless traveled to the spectators and beyond. "Sheriff, has Philip of Wolvercote given you security for prosecuting his claim?"

"That's Richard De Luci," Emma breathed. "The Chief Justiciar himself. Oh, dear, this is so *weighty*. Should I be putting Pippy through it?"

The sheriff of Somerset, a florid, harassed-looking man in robes as scalloped as the awning over his separate bench, stood up. "He has, my lord."

"And have you summoned by good summoners twelve free and lawful men from the neighborhood of Wolvercote Manor ready to declare on oath whether Lord Ralph of Wolvercote, father of the aforesaid Philip, was seized of his fee of the aforesaid manor on the day he died?"

"I have, my lord." The sheriff waved toward a box nearby into which twelve men had been crammed like milk churns into a cart.

"Who speaks for them?"

One of the men extricated himself sufficiently to stand up. "I do, my lord. Rich-

456

ard de Mayne, knight, holding twelve virgates in the parish of Martlake. My land marches with Wolvercote's on the north."

"Have you and the others viewed the manor in this case?" The Chief Justiciar of England, like his voice, was thin. His head, which resembled a snake's, moved slowly in the direction of his questions, giving the impression that it would strike at a lie like an adder at a frog.

"We have, my lord, and of our own knowledge we can say that Lord Wolvercote was receiving the rents and services. He died elsewhere, but we are in accord that he owned the manor at the time and that after his death his mother took possession of it, having previously occupied a dower house in the parish of Shepton."

"That's *one* answered," Emma said. At Adelia's look, she explained. "Two questions. Morte d'Ancestor asks just two questions. . . . I can't stand this, I swear I'm going to faint."

Suddenly a new voice, a contralto, floated across the field, as unimpassioned as De Luci's but considerably more beautiful. "My son was unlawfully hanged for treason by the king you serve."

The Justiciar's head turned by inches toward the dowager's chair. "My understanding is that your son was hanged for murder, madam, not treason. However, that matter is not in question here. Nor, as a woman, are you permitted to speak in this court. Address your remarks through your counselor."

The intervention had caused a flurry among the lawyers surrounding the dowager's chair, the eldest among them speaking urgently into her ear. He put a warning hand on her shoulder, but, with one white finger, the dowager flicked it away.

The Chief Justiciar hadn't finished. "Master Thomas, your client has been summoned three times to attend before us, and only now has she appeared."

"I do not recognize the authority of this court." Again, the dowager's voice rang out.

This time Master Thomas's hand clamped on the woman's shoulder and would not be removed. "My lord, my client begs your mercy. The procedure is new to her, as indeed it is to us all. Her age confuses her."

There was a murmur of sympathy from the crowd; liked or not, the dowager was a woman of Somerset, a county that regarded even the adjoining Devonshire as a foreign land. "What you at?" somebody cried out, "comin' down from Lunnon to bully that poor old soul."

De Luci ignored the shout. "And now, Sir Richard . . ."

"Dear God, here it comes." Emma's grip on Adelia's arm became painful. "The second question."

". . . can you attest that the plaintiff is the heir to Lord Ralph of Wolvercote?"

There was a shifting among the jurors in the box.

The dowager's lawyer stepped forward. "My lord, my client rejects that he is. She will swear on oath that there was never a marriage between the plaintiff's mother and her son and that accordingly, the plaintiff is an impostor or a bastard or both."

The crowd turned its attention to the little boy in the chair. Impervious to what was going on, he was beginning to be bored and had taken a piece of string from his sleeve and was playing cat's cradle with it.

Emma's and Adelia's eyes met, agonized.

The dowager was right in essence; if a bride had to give consent, as according to the law she must, then Emma had never been married.

Abducted by Wolvercote, who wanted her fortune, from the Oxfordshire convent where she was being educated, her abductor's hand had been placed over her mouth as she struggled to say "No" to the priest

459

bribed to pronounce them married.

In effect, Pippy was the illegitimate child of rape.

Here was Master Dickon's turn, and he stepped forward. He was enjoying the moment, and it was noticeable to Adelia that he was also softening his London speech. "My lord, we have produced a witness before the jury *and* a sworn statement from an unimpeachable source that there was indeed a marriage and that my client was subsequently born nine months later."

"Has such a witness and such a statement been produced?" De Luci asked the jury.

Sir Richard was wriggling. "Well, they have, my lord, but we'd be glad to hear them again, to see what you think."

"It is not what I think, it is what must be proved to you. However, we will allow a repetition."

Master Dickon's stripling dashed into the crowd and came back lugging a little old man in the long tunic of a priest.

Dickon introduced him to the judges. "This is Father Simeon, my lord, a priest of Oxford who will attest that he conducted a ceremony of marriage between the late Lord Wolvercote and Emma, daughter to Master Bloat, a vintner of Abingdon."

"Mother of God, I can't bear to look at

him," Emma whispered. "He was there; he said the words." The memory made her retch.

In Wolvercote's effort to secure Emma's fortune for himself, Father Simeon had been just what he wanted, one of the Church's derelicts who, having lost any cure or parish of his own, begged his bread at the tables of the charitable, and gave his blessing to anybody who'd buy it with a pot of ale. His tunic was filthy, his tonsure almost obscured by stubble, and he shook, with nerves or old age or drink, possibly all three.

Where had Master Dickon managed to find him? Adelia wondered. And was it worthwhile? The man was hardly a credible witness.

However, Father Simeon was producing a document as tattered as himself, proving that in the distant past he had been properly ordained.

"He'll have to maintain that the marriage was legal," Adelia reassured Emma, "or he'll admit that he presided over an unlawful ceremony."

"But will they take his word? Will they want papers? I don't remember any certificate — I doubt that old pig can even write."

Since some of the jury couldn't read, the

proof of Father Simeon's priesthood had to be read out to them and then passed up to the judge.

The crowd listened with intent; nearly as good as trial by battle, this was.

At a nod from De Luci, Master Dickon began questioning his witness. On the feast of Saint Vintula in the year of Our Lord 1172 had Father Simeon solemnized a marriage between Ralph, Lord of Wolvercote, and Emma Bloat?

The priest's shakes became more pronounced, and he was ordered to speak up. "Yes, yes," he managed. "Yes, I did. Lord Wolvercote . . . yes, I remember perfectly, he asked me to marry them, and I did."

"And was the marriage solemnized according to the law of the land?"

"Yes, it was. I'm sure it was, perfectly."

Master Dickon nodded to the judge and handed over his witness to interrogation by the more formidable Master Thomas.

Was Emma Bloat's father there to give his daughter away? If not, why not? Had all the solemnities been legally performed? Had a declaration been posted on the church door? Why had Lady Wolvercote not been informed of her son's marriage?

"It was very snowy, you see," Father Simeon pleaded. "I do remember that, very snowy. People couldn't get through the drifts, I myself . . . Yes, I'm sure I put a notice on the door, but the snow, yes, I'm sure I did . . . but the snow, you see."

"Were there witnesses?" demanded Master Thomas — he used the Latin: *testes adfuerunt.*

Father Simeon was floored. "What?" he asked.

Adelia groaned.

With a graceful outstretching of his arms, Master Thomas appealed to the judge. "Is this the man we are supposed to believe?"

De Luci brought his head round to the jury. "Do you believe him?"

Sir Richard consulted with his fellows. "Well, he's a bit . . . well, my lord, his memory . . ."

Again Master Dickon stepped forward, waving a document. "My lord, if I might assist the court. I have here an affidavit from the abbess of Godstow in the county of Oxfordshire, a lady renowned for her piety and probity. She is elderly, my lord, though still keen in her wits, and could not make the journey to this court, for which she apologizes. Her affidavit has already been read to the jury, but if your lordship would care to peruse it."

His lordship did. The document was

passed up to him.

"Good God," Adelia whispered. "Mother Edyve." It was from her convent that Emma had been abducted. "How? Who?" Oxfordshire was a long way away; there hadn't been time. . . .

"The king," Emma told her. "I thought you knew. The moment he received your report, he sent messengers galloping to search out that swine of a priest along with others to secure Mother Edyve's affidavit. Apparently, Master Dickon says, Henry saw the chance of using this Morte d'Ancestor writ in my case. It's his pride and joy; he and Lord De Luci spent sleepless nights shaping it, according to Master Dickon."

So that was why Henry Plantagenet had winked at his clerk. *A teasing mood.* He'd known all along. Kept his precious writ up his sleeve . . .

"I'll kill him," Adelia said.

The Justiciar of England was reading. "Mother Edyve, abbess of Godstow, attests here that shortly after the supposed marriage, both bride and groom attended Christmas festivities at her abbey and that Lord Wolvercote in her hearing addressed the plaintiff's mother as 'wife.' "

All strictly true as far as it went, but did it go far enough?

Adelia was gripping Emma's arm as hard as Emma grasped hers.

De Luci raised his reptilian head. "I have to declare an interest in this matter. The abbess of Godstow is known to me."

"A good woman, my lord?" Sir Richard asked.

"A very good woman."

"Good enough for us, then." Sir Richard looked at the nodding heads around him. "My lord, we are prepared to declare that the late Lord Wolvercote was legally married to the plaintiff's mother and that Philip of Wolvercote is the legal issue of said marriage and, therefore, heir to the Wolvercote lands and appurtenances."

Master Dickon uttered an unlawyerlike whoop. Adelia and Emma collapsed on each other. The new Lord Wolvercote looked up from his cat's cradle, surprised by the noise. Dowager Wolvercote remained in her chair. Angrily, Master Thomas flung his cap on the ground, picked it up, put it back on, and began talking urgently to his client, who might have been deaf, a stone effigy.

"The writ's two questions having been answered to the satisfaction of this jury," De Luci went on, "this court grants immediate seisin of Wolvercote Manor to the plaintiff." He rose.

The lovely contralto belled out across the field. "I recognize neither this court nor its judgment. You, De Luci, are a Plantagenet puppet."

Over the crowd's gasp, Master Thomas began pleading for his client to be given time to remove her chattels from the disputed manor.

But the Lord Chief Justiciar of England had gone.

Master Dickon came struggling through the press to Emma and Adelia. Emma turned and kissed him on both cheeks. Roetger came hauling himself to her; she kissed him, too, before running onto the field to pick up her son and hold him high. "We've won, Pippy. Oh, you were so *good*."

Master Dickon wiped the sweat off his brow. "Nasty moment or two there," he said, "but the dowager saying she didn't recognize the court did it for us. I knew we was home; judges don't like that."

"Is that it?" Adelia asked him. "Emma's *won*? She can move into the manor?"

"Any time she likes," the young man told her. "Better take bailiffs with her, of course. But no, that *ain't* it. The dowager will appeal, for sure, contesting the marriage and the lad's legitimacy. All to be seen to later. More work for us." Master Dickon rubbed his hands in anticipation of the fees he'd earn.

"Then I don't understand."

"Don't you, mistress?" Dickon flung out an arm in the direction of the field from which people were departing and where only the dowager sat, staring over the heads of her clustering lawyers as if they were midges. "No blood on that grass, is there? Lady Em didn't have to use force to get her son's rights, nor didn't the dowager use force to defend what she thinks is hers. No battling. No wounds. Just a writ from the king. A temporary measure so's the apparent heir can be in possession of his property while the arguments over it can be sorted out legally. To keep the peace, d'you see?"

"I see."

"Barons don't like it, of course — takes authority away from their courts and makes a common law available to everybody, but they ain't prepared to go to war over it, Lord be thanked. Oooh, he's a cunning old lawmaker is Henry."

"Yes," Adelia said, and then paused. "Master Dickon, could you provide me with pen and ink? I must write a letter to the king."

On their way to view Pippy's new property,

Emma's pure soprano soared into the blue sky accompanied by birdsong, her bard's harp, her son's tremolo, Roetger's basso profundo, and the trot of their horses' hooves.

> "Come lasses and lads, take leave of your
>   dads,
> and away to the maypole hie."

Adelia swayed in her saddle to the tune while Millie, behind her, smiled at a jollity she couldn't hear.

Emma broke off to lean over and touch her lover's knee. "I didn't consent to him, dearest, ever."

Roetger took her hand and kissed it. "I know you did not, brave girl."

> "There ev'ry he has got him a she,
> and the minstrel's standing by. . . ."

Emma broke off again. "So really, we have gained by an old priest's lie."

"That worries me not at all," Roetger told her.

"God's justice to womankind," Adelia said.

> "For Willy shall dance with Jane,

and Stephen has got his Joan. . . ."

And Rowley has got his Adelia, Adelia thought happily. Except that it doesn't scan.

"To trip it, trip it, trip it, trip it,
to trip it up and down."

Coming toward them was a procession. Seeing it, Rhys laid his hand flat on the harp's strings to quiet them. Everybody fell silent and pulled to the side of the road to let it go past as if it were a funeral.

The dowager sat easily and upright on a splendid bay, her eyes on the road ahead. Behind her came draft horses pulling two great carts piled with furniture, out of which stuck the scarlet and silver battle flags of Wolvercote. Behind those were straggled servants, some on horses, some on mules, some walking, driving cows and geese before them, all burdened with belongings, like refugees.

Which, Adelia supposed, they were. And she was sorry for all of them except the murderess in front.

Emma, however, rode out to meet her mother-in-law. "You could have stayed longer," she said, quietly. "Where are you going?"

She might have been a piece of detritus dropped on the road. The dowager's eyes didn't flicker; her horse walked round the obstruction and continued on its way.

"Oh, dear," Emma said, looking after it.

Rhys struck up again. "No 'Oh, dear' about it," he said. "Sing again, lady."

"Some walked and some did run,
some loitered on the way.
And bound themselves by kisses twelve,
to meet next holiday."

Adelia imagined the voices traveling joyously through the warm air to reach the ears of the woman who had just passed, and what agony they would cause her. Not enough recompense for six bodies that had once lain in a forest grave and were now buried decently in the Wells churchyard. But some.

They saw the quiver in the sky, like a heat haze over Wolvercote Manor, long before they reached it. By the time they had urged their horses into a canter and gained the gates, the quiver had been replaced by black smoke.

The manor was in flames. Its roof had already fallen in; some men with buckets were scurrying to and from the moat in an effort to save the outbuildings. In the air, pigeons wheeled unhappily, unable to land in the bonfire that had been their cote. A hay barn had gone up like tinder and revealed the church standing behind it, so far untouched.

There was nothing to be done. Buckets of water wouldn't extinguish that inferno. The riders could only stay where they were and watch.

"The hag," Roetger said. "She set a torch to it before she went."

Adelia felt grief for a house that had been so lovely and so old. It had been like a seashell, allowing all to listen to hear the waves of its history. Now it was going and the waves would be silenced forever.

The men with buckets were standing back, giving up the battle.

"Dear, dear," said Rhys. "Oh, there's a pity, now. Such a pity."

Emma said determinedly, "No, Rhys, it is not a pity at all."

She turned to Roetger, smiling. "I would have torn it down in any case. I could never live where he'd lived. Nor her."

"We will rebuild it," Roetger said.

"Yes, new and twice as beautiful. Won't we, Pippy? Everything new."

After a while, taking Millie with her,

Adelia left them and rode on toward Glastonbury.

There was definitely newness about. No corpses polluted the air today, because the trees that had held them were gone. Instead, a wide verge of timber-strewn grass ran between road and forest edge. Women were picking up fallen branches in their aprons and carrying them to their men to be chopped up for firewood. As Adelia and Millie went by, waving, they looked up and smiled.

At the top of the turning to Glastonbury high road, Adelia and Millie dismounted. Adelia bent down to pick up a fallen leaf and pressed it into Millie's hand. "For Gyltha." She enunciated it carefully, sticking it out her tongue at the "th." It was a word Millie had learned by watching Adelia say it while patting Gyltha on the shoulder. Adelia hoped to teach her others. But how to indicate she wouldn't be long? She pointed to the sun and moved her finger a fraction to the west, then blew a kiss to an imaginary child by her knee. "My love to Allie. Tell her I'll be with her soon."

Millie nodded and started off down the hill. At its bottom, Godwyn was sweeping dust out of the Pilgrim's front door. He looked up, saw Millie coming toward him, and smiled for the first time since the marshes.

Good, Adelia thought. *That will work out very well.*

The abbey was silent, but there was life down the high street, where men were shifting the rubble that had been their houses, ready to rebuild them. Although he didn't see her, she saw Alf expertly wielding an adze on a freshly cut beam.

Better than Noah, Adelia thought, and was happy.

Yes, there was newness in the air today.

Remounting, she rode on along the lane between the abbey wall and the foot of the Tor.

Up the hill, some men on horseback, their hands shading their eyes, were straining their necks to watch a peregrine falcon circling the sky. A hound barked, causing a cluster of pigeons to go flapping up into the air out of a copse of trees. The bird above them took on the shape of a bow notched with an arrow — and dived. The pigeons separated, and one of them, perhaps realizing its danger, flew low, but the falcon coming for it was a missile; talons out, it took the pigeon in midair with an impact that sheared off its head.

By the time Adelia reached the group, the

falcon was back on its owner's wrist, only its wicked little beak, shining like steel, visible under its plumed hood.

"Good day, my lord."

With great care the falconer transferred the bird to its austringer's gauntlet, then, telling his men to wait for him — "This lady and I have private business to transact" — joined Adelia and together they rode up the hill.

"You've a very nasty temper, you know," said Henry Plantagenet. "You must learn to control it."

Adelia was wondering what would become of her reputation in the royal household. "Yes, my lord. I'm sorry, my lord."

"I hear Lady Wolvercote won her Morte d'Ancestor."

"But has lost the house." She told him of the dowager's revenge.

"Ah," the king said. He cheered up. "Well, more work for the law courts. Now then, where's this cave?"

Adelia had some trouble finding it again. With Eustace gone to his grave and with the tithing rebuilding their lives, there was no sign of its occupancy; up here, one bushy outcrop with a spring looked like another. After a couple of false casts, however, she dismounted to pull aside the fronds that hid

the entrance and the man who'd been waiting for them.

"Good day, Mansur," Henry said.

"Good day, my lord."

Inside, the elfin cave worked its magic and
nobody spoke.

Looking around, the king crossed himself
and climbed through the hole in the back
wall that Mansur had made. After a while,
Adelia joined him.

One king was kneeling in prayer by the
prone skeleton of another. Green light coming through the split in the rock above
shone on them both and the untroubled
pool at their feet.

Adelia looked at the living man with tears
in her eyes.

*Will you, too, become a legend? No, the
Church will see to that. Future generations living under the legacy you've given them will
remember you only for the murder of Becket.*

Eventually, Henry II stood up and cleared
his throat as if he, too, had been crying. The
sound echoed. "He's not very big, is he?"

"He was a Celt, I suppose," Adelia said.
"One of the short, dark ones."

"A warrior, though. Look at those wounds.
At peace now, God rest him."

"Yes." But crowding into her mind came
visions of the thousands of pilgrims, as they

would come crowding into this cave in real life, of the tawdry relic stalls that would be set up outside alongside the money changers, those descendants of rapacious men whom Jesus had once turned out of Jerusalem's Temple.

Henry sighed. *"Requiscat in pace, Arturus."* He turned and clambered back through the hole.

Outside the cave, he reached for the reins of the horses drinking at the spring, then let them drop. He looked down, toward Glastonbury. "You know," he said, reflectively, "the Welsh aren't being as obstreperous as they were, the bastards. They're finding my laws have some advantages."

"Are they?"

"Yes, they are."

He took up the reins and dropped them once more. "And that one in there" — he nodded toward the cave — "he's practically a dwarf. People'll expect a giant; they'll be disappointed."

Adelia's heart skipped a beat.

The King of England gave another sigh. "Mansur?"

"My lord?"

"Wall him up again; let him sleep on."

"Wait." Adelia went back into the cave and through the hole and retrieved the sword

from the pool to which Mansur had returned it. Coming out again into the light,
the weapon dazzled like a sunburst. She laid
it across her palms and knelt. "My lord, here
is Excalibur. It belongs to the greatest heart
of the age, which makes it yours. *You* are
the Once and Future King."

The two of them walked their horses back
down the hill, chatting.

From where he lay under the shadow of a
juniper bush, a man known as Scarry
watched them go. At least, he didn't watch
the king, because he didn't know it *was* the
king. He watched Adelia, and his eyes were
those of a stoat waiting to kill — a stoat
that spoke Latin.

AUTHOR'S NOTE

I have set the story of the "finding" of Arthur and Guinevere's grave at Glastonbury fourteen years earlier than the chroniclers who tell us it happened in 1190, but there is good reason to believe it wasn't as late as they say, because the Glastonbury monks also "found" Excalibur — it was known as Caliburn then, but I've used the now-familiar name — and the sword was undoubtedly in the possession of Henry II before his death, which was in 1189.

Eventually, Henry sent Excalibur as a present to his friend and future son-in-law, the King of Sicily. When I asked John Julius Norwich, that fine historian of Norman Sicily, if he knew what happened to it after that, he said he didn't. But, he told me, it is interesting that there is a strong tradition of the Arthurian legend in the area of Mount Etna.

Nobody knows what Excalibur looked

like, of course, and my re-creation of it is based on the wisdom and writings of an old and dear friend, the late Ewart Oakeshott, who has been acknowledged on both sides of the Atlantic as *the* great authority on medieval weaponry.

That a sword from the age attributed to Arthur (circa the mid–sixth century) and earlier could survive intact is due to the fact that thousands of them have been preserved in peat bogs or river bottoms where they have been recovered. To quote Mr. Oakeshott's *Records of the Medieval Sword* (The Boydell Press, 1991), "A sword falling into deep mud, free from stones or organic material that might trap oxygen or allow it to penetrate the close covering of mud, will initially become covered all over with a coating of rust, but as time passes the chemical interaction of this rust with the surrounding mud covers all the surface of the metal with a flint-hard coating of goethite which, once formed, prevents any further corrosion and so yields up to the archaeologist (or treasure hunter with his metal detector) a well-preserved weapon, sometimes in almost pristine condition. This coating or patina can be removed . . . by long and arduous work with abrasives."

In the book, I have Roetger bringing

definition back to Excalibur with a pickled preserve — not as mad as it sounds. Once, steering me round his private collection, Mr. Oakeshott showed me an incredibly ancient and marvelous sword dug up from a Kentish bog that he'd restored to a condition its Viking master would have recognized. He'd tried cleaning off its patina first with lemon, then with vinegar, to no avail. "Do you know what did it in the end?" he asked. "A bottle of Worcestershire sauce." Which, as far as I'm concerned, pace its manufacturers, is runny preserves.

The Arthurian legend accreted stories over the centuries, which is why I have been scrupulous not to mention the Holy Grail or Lancelot and his affair with Guinevere — all later additions to the story.

Where I *have* used artistic license is in changing the date of the great fire that destroyed Glastonbury Abbey in 1184 to the time of my story — again, eight years earlier.

After the fire, appeals for funds were sent out and the monks of Glastonbury traveled Europe in a money-raising campaign — there's nothing new under the sun, not even advertising.

Incidentally, since the pyramids between which "Arthur's grave" was found no longer exist, I've taken their description from the writings of the twelfth-century annalist William of Malmesbury, who saw them when he visited Glastonbury.

And the skeletons of two babies *were* found in the monks' graveyard. How they got there can only be speculation.

What does still exist is a tunnel leading from a cellar in Glastonbury's fourteenth-century George and Pilgrim's Hotel (I've put my twelfth-century Pilgrim's Inn on the same site on the assumption that there was always a hostelry there) to somewhere in the abbey grounds — we don't know exactly where, because it is blocked halfway through under the High Street and hasn't been excavated.

I should point out that there was no bishop of Saint Albans in the twelfth century, although there is now, so mine is a fictional predecessor. However, the dispute between the abbey of Glastonbury and the bishopric of Wells is a historical fact; the two were at daggers drawn for centuries.

Also, in those days, the title of doctor was reserved for masters of philosophy, et cetera, and not for medical men, but, again, I've used the anachronism in the interest of clarity.

The use of trial by battle to prove a

property dispute had an extraordinarily long life, though it began to die out when Henry II's judicial reforms were introduced. The last known instance of it is thought to have taken place during the monarchy of Elizabeth I. It wasn't abolished from the statute books until the eighteenth century in the reign of George III.

As to the introduction into my story of Brother Peter, there is some dispute over whether the Benedictine monks — which is what the brethren of Glastonbury were — used lay brothers to relieve them of laboring work, but I am assured that in some cases they did.

In modern times there has been speculation that leprosy, so rife in the Middle Ages, was not leprosy at all, but that other disfiguring diseases were mistaken for it. This is now mainly being disproved by the new ability to test the bones found in the graveyards of ancient lazar houses, where it has been discovered in some cases that seventy percent of the dead suffered from the leprous condition proper.

In the matter of the writ Morte d'Ancestor, the twelve men hearing the case were technically not jurors as we would understand them now; they were an "assize," men cognizant of the facts concerned.

But again, for simplification, I have called them a jury.

I am occasionally criticized for letting my characters use modern language, but in twelfth-century England the common people spoke a form of English even less comprehensible than Chaucer's in the fourteenth; the nobility spoke Norman French, and the clergy spoke Latin. Since people then sounded contemporary to one another, and since I hate the use of what I call "gadzooks" in historical novels to denote a past age, I insist on making those people sound modern to the reader.

ACKNOWLEDGMENTS

I owe knowledge of such Welsh words as I've used to Mr. Alan Jones of Datchworth, who was so kind as to instruct me in what he calls "the language of Paradise." Thank you, Alan.

As ever, I'm grateful to the wonderfully efficient team at Putnam and especially my editor, Rachel Kahan. I just wish sometimes that she and my equally marvelous agent, Helen Heller, didn't persist with their advice being right in every single instance.

The London Library, that great reservoir of knowledge, stops me from making more historical mistakes than I do.

And I don't know what I'd accomplish without the help that my daughter, Emma, gives me in coping with secretarial and financial matters, or without Barry, my husband, abandoning his own work to accompany me on research trips.

ABOUT THE AUTHOR

Ariana Franklin, is the pen name of British writer Diana Norman. A former journalist, Norman has written several critically acclaimed biographies and historical novels. She lives in Hertfordshire, England, with her husband, the film critic Barry Norman.

The employees of Thorndike Press hope you have enjoyed this Large Print book. All our Thorndike, Wheeler, and Kennebec Large Print titles are designed for easy reading, and all our books are made to last. Other Thorndike Press Large Print books are available at your library, through selected bookstores, or directly from us.

For information about titles, please call:
  (800) 223-1244

or visit our Web site at:
  http://gale.cengage.com/thorndike

To share your comments, please write:
  Publisher
  Thorndike Press
  295 Kennedy Memorial Drive
  Waterville, ME 04901